My Lady's Choosing

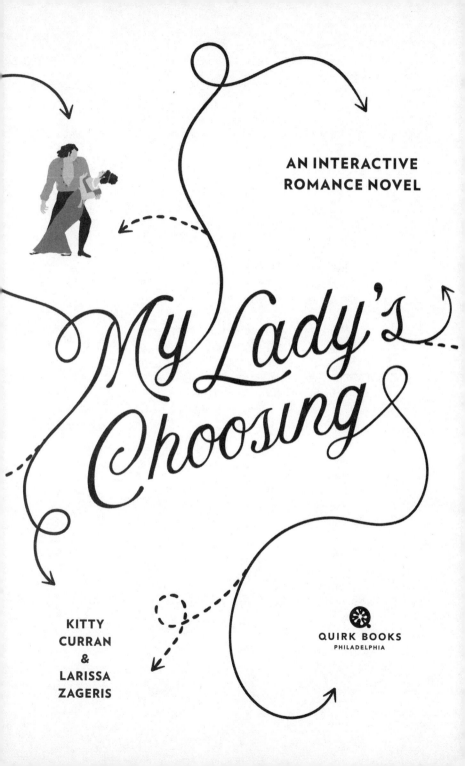

AN INTERACTIVE
ROMANCE NOVEL

My Lady's Choosing

KITTY
CURRAN
&
LARISSA
ZAGERIS

QUIRK BOOKS
PHILADELPHIA

Copyright © 2018 by Kitty Curran and Larissa Zageris

Library of Congress Cataloging in Publication Number: 2017941582

ISBN: 978-1-68369-013-9

Printed in the United States of America

Typeset in Adobe Garamond

Designed by Andie Reid
Illustrations by Kitty Curran
Cover art by Alice Mollon
Production management by John J. McGurk

Quirk Books
215 Church Street
Philadelphia, PA 19106
quirkbooks.com

10 9 8 7 6 5 4 3 2 1

To our cherished loved ones

Halt!

The course of true love never did run straight—and neither does this book. Do not submit yourself to woe and confusion by turning the pages in numerical order! Skimming to a different section or letting your eye linger too long on the entry next to your intended destination could have the same result as committing a similar act of impropriety while at a ball: SCANDAL! HEARTBREAK! UTTER RUIN!

In other words, no cheating.

Instead, begin your romantic journey on page one, and follow the instructions at the bottom of each page. These choices will guide you from the sweeping Highlands of rugged Scotland to the mysterious moors of foggy Yorkshire to the exotic plains of sand-swept Egypt. Every decision has the potential to bring you everlasting happiness or deepest despair—so select with care!

Choose wisely, and you could end up the talk of the ton, wrapped in the embrace of an exciting, eternally faithful, extremely becoming mate of superior charm and devotion. Choose poorly, and you may end up destitute and begging for scraps in the slimiest slums of London. Truly, in matters of love, anything is possible.

Now on with you—your romantic fate awaits!

Dramatis Personae

YOU are you. The plucky, penniless, Regency-era London version. As a lass of eight-and-twenty who can cover a screen just as well as she can jam out sonatas on the pianoforte, you are under the gun to find love with a suitably wealthy, good-hearted, or libidinous match—else find yourself an eternal spinster.

LADY EVANGELINE YOUNGBLOOD is a free-spirited Woman with a Past—and your very best (*ahem*, only) friend. She is a lover of intrigue, battle, and experiment; scandal attends her every move. She gives the rakes of the less-fair sex a run for their money in the roguish-behavior department, when she isn't sending her aunt, Lady Aurelia Craven, to despondence with tales of her bluestock-  ing bawdiness. She promises to save you from spinsterhood one way or another, if you insist. She has wanted to get back to Egypt for quite some time and could use a traveling companion . . .

SIR BENEDICT GRANVILLE is a well-off relation of Lady Craven. He is pretty, witty, and earns ten thousand a year. Banter is this baronet's weapon of choice in the war waged between London's marriage-hungry society mamas and eligible young bachelors. Too clever by half for most of the half-wits he interacts with, Sir Granville meets his match only when you deign to engage him in a battle of wits—and base desires.

CAPTAIN ANGUS MACTAGGART is a rugged Scotsman with a chip on his shoulder and a heart of gold. Not a man for society's frivolities, he spends his days caring for the orphans and widows of recent wars. Although a finely muscled ginger with a passion as fiery as his hair, "Mac" is more concerned with doing good works than doing others. Still, his honorable soldier's body courses with the awesome power of the Highland moors from which he hails, and the love of an honest woman could give both Mac and that lass the ride of their lives.

LORD GARRAWAY CRAVEN is so mad and bad that word round the ton is even Lord Byron finds knowing him to be dangerous. Prone to rages and prolonged unexplained absences (and no shortage of shirts worn open to reveal his rippling muscles), Lady Craven's son is master of Hopesend Manor. Could he also be master of your heart? Brutish and brooding, Lord Craven is a wild beast who cannot be tamed. But perhaps so are you . . .

ove that leg, girl!" the dowager Lady Craven hisses as she prods you with her cane. The two of you are sitting in the back of her rather shabby carriage, on the way to your first social event since you started working as her lady's companion more than a year ago. Sadly, this behavior is far from extraordinary, so you merely sigh and squeeze yourself into an even tinier part of the seat. At this point, one more prod and you would be making love to the carriage door.

"Such a miserable occasion. I can't think why Evangeline is making us attend," Lady Craven mutters.

"Well, it *is* for the widows and orphans of the war—" you venture to say politely, before being cut off with a glare that could strip paint.

"Did I sound like I wanted your opinion?" You know what's good for you and stop talking immediately. Lady Craven continues on her tirade. "Truly, you are just as woolheaded as your grandfather was. Odious man! I have no idea what your grandmother was thinking when she married him—and with no fortune to recommend him, either! I daresay your late father was just the same, seeing as he didn't see fit to provide for you after his death . . ."

Spending most of your time with Lady Craven has made you a master at biting your tongue, yet her cruel words about your beloved papa cut you to your core. Still, you depend upon the old dragon for your entire livelihood, so you have no choice but to grit your teeth and clench your fists into the worn fabric of your dress. An old castoff from Lady Craven, the frock is at least twenty years out of date, and you highly suspect that she chose it for you because the mustard-yellow color clashes horribly with your complexion.

"If it wasn't for the affection I still hold for your late mother, I should have cast you out into the street! And what would you have done then, eh?"

You brood silently yet demurely.

"Probably try to find yourself a protector, no doubt!" she continues. "Just as you have shamelessly set your cap at Sir Charles Burley-Fanshaw. Though I doubt anyone would want to have anything to do with such a silly little chit!"

Your fists grip even tighter around the fabric of your skirts. The repellent Sir Charles is old enough to be your grandpapa and has indeed been sniffing around your person, looking no doubt for a pretty, compliant, and *much* younger bride. Still, would life in a loveless marriage be any worse than the one you live now?

The carriage arrives at your destination, and you are shaken from your gloomy thoughts—if only for a moment. Perhaps tonight will be the night when everything changes?

. . . .

Do you accompany your tyrannical employer to the fundraising ball for the Society for the Protection of Widows and Orphans of the War? The company may be atrocious, but balls are fun! If so, turn to page 67.

Or do you run away from Lady Craven, only to find yourself with no other means of survival than to sell your young body into the cold, cruel night? If so, do not go to any other place in this book, for you will be utterly doomed and dead from syphilis within a year.

Sorry. This may be a choosable-path adventure, but as a penniless young unmarried woman at the start of the nineteenth century, your options are somewhat limited. They will get better, though! Turn to page 67.

"I'm sorry, Kamal, but I'm not sure it is good for me to stay here."

"I understand," he says ruefully. "I'm sorry, too."

You give him a gentle smile of companionship. You both pretend it doesn't crush him.

"Do you have a plan for what you are going to do next?" he asks with genuine concern. You stare at him calmly.

"As a matter of fact, I do."

....

What are your plans?

Do you take up that governessing job with the mysterious—and potentially dangerous—Lord Craven? If so, turn to page 14.

Or are you done with danger for good? Perhaps the dragonish Lady Craven will let you have your old job back . . . and possibly take you to a few more balls for good measure. If that sounds more up your alley, turn to page 302.

You await the cheap passage you've booked on the overnight mail coach with your belongings in your valise and your heart in your throat. Hopesend Manor, the home of your new employer, is located in deep obscurity amid the rolling moors of Yorkshire. Far from the ton, far from London, and, you hope, far from all you have already endured in your search for love. You try not to shiver in the cold, thin rain. The mysterious lord is the dark-horse son of the Dowager Dragon, a wealthy man who has made it his priority to keep his mother at arm's length and with minimal assistance. You know, too, that the man has a living son and a dead wife, and that the mourning Lord Craven never married again.

"This weather's not fit for man nor beast, miss." A friendly, handsome face appears out of the shadows—the carriage driver. "Eee, but th'art as pretty as a flower," he says breathlessly, with not a trace of guile in his broad Yorkshire tones.

"A rather wet flower at the moment, good sir." You cannot help but giggle.

He smiles back, harboring a strangely haunted look in those pure chocolate eyes, and hurries to throw himself out of the carriage and help you and your bags inside the Slaughtered Lamb, your designated meeting place. The young, handsome man's body is built with a compact, pleasing masculinity, and the rain has done both him and you a service by causing his jacket and shirt to cling to him as tightly as a lover.

"I hope tha'll be . . . comfortable." He rubs his neck nervously, as if mustering the nerve to say something out of turn . . . or out of the question. "Look, I shouldn't say . . . ," he finally ventures, ". . . but after I told me mam that I were taking a young lady to Hopesend Manor— well, she's been worrying herself sick, miss. I am, too, to be perfectly honest wi' thee. Hopesend Manor is no place for a sweet lady such as thyself."

"What the devil do you mean?" you ask, your heart racing.

"It's just that . . . folk talk foolish things round these parts, miss, and normally I take no stock in such nonsense. But still . . . it is well known that bad ends have come to young ladies at Hopesend Manor. I know I am getting above myself when I say this, but I—I just wanted thee to know I am only a walk to th' village away, should tha ever need help or shelter, miss."

"Of . . . course," you squeak, distracted as much by his warning as by his broad shoulders, which are spread in a concerned bracing stance against the carriage doorway. "Of course, Mister . . ."

"Teddy, miss. Teddy Braithwaite, at thy service, ever and always. I swear it." He kisses your hand in a rush. Improperly, he holds on a moment too long and lets his hot cocoa eyes burn you with his deep, gentle desire.

Time to embrace your gothic destiny and head on. Turn to page 188.

A life spent in Glenblair Castle might be safe, but now that you've had a taste of espionage, you know the life you truly want.

"At your service, Lord Fleming," you say with a curtsey.

"Och." A masculine voice thick with emotion rings out behind you. "I never did ken what to do with goodbyes." You turn to Mac, and he laughs to conceal the tears shining in his eyes. He looks at you, his good and glorious gaze searching yours for what might be the last time.

You kiss him tenderly. "We won't say anything, then."

"Nothing at all."

You nod at each other and then, rubbing his eyes, Mac strides away.

Ollie turns to you, bewildered. "I cannot *believe* you are being promoted from civilian to spy with absolutely no experience!"

"That is why I am choosing an experienced handler for her," Lord Fleming says tersely. "One who is well versed in the profession and has a connection with the young lady in question."

Ollie scoffs. "Good luck finding a chap that fits that bill."

Lord Fleming rolls his eyes for your benefit. "My dear Ruston, I already have. Congratulations. It appears you have a new partner."

Ollie gapes. "But . . . she's . . ."

"'Pretty as a city park, I'd love to touch her after dark'?" you offer. Ollie blushes scarlet, and even Lord Fleming lets out a patrician chuckle. "Surely you remember that verse, Ollie."

"I assure you, my dear," Ollie says, flustered, "I would write you a new poem this minute if I could think of a rhyme for 'dreadful savage upstart know-it-all.'"

You smirk. "There, there, now, partner," you say. "I promise to let you solve a few cases on your own."

Lord Fleming claps his hands. "Save it for the next mission, you two."

And with that, you and Ollie go off to become lead characters in your own series of historical thrillers.

The End

There is nothing like a carriage ride back to a country estate that is in dispute between two men—one of whom you just nearly killed and the other of whom you just passionately kissed—to further frazzle one's already frayed nerves.

You didn't know when you attended that first ball with the Dragon that the story of your life would be so full of scandal, intrigue, and deadly lamps in the shape of certain, *ahem*, body parts. You never could have dreamed that the story of you and Benedict would overflow so violently, like an upended jar of ink over a fresh sheet of creamy writing paper.

Benedict seems as tense as you are. He must take your weary silence—and aching desire—for anxiety.

"Dash it, woman, you didn't kill him. Give yourself a rest." Benedict shifts uncomfortably in his seat.

"I *nearly* killed him."

"Sorry you didn't finish the job?"

"I am sorry for the mess we made in Madam Crosby's fine rooms."

"Her fine rooms have seen much worse, I am sure," Benedict says with a sigh.

"And much better." You're content to have the last word with him, but troubled by your longing for his smart, tender mouth to once more press against yours. You wonder if he, too, is thinking of that moment back in the fray. You notice him struggle to find a comfortable position. You long to touch him and to reprimand him for not arriving at the obvious best solution to his problem.

"You do know if we simply remove this bench cover and arrange it thusly, we could both have a lie-down in this blasted carriage." You brush him aside and rearrange the seating so the carriage becomes more of a traveling bed than a torture chamber on wheels. But before thinking much of it, you have flung the man onto his back and yourself on top of him. You feel a sudden heat and pressure against your skirts and realize your newfound seating arrangement is not lost on him. Not lost at all.

You retrieve the cushion and place it under his head. He arches to receive it and, by so doing, presses his straining manhood against your beskirted sex. You cannot help moaning, slightly, with the pleasure of it.

"Is that better?" You try to keep your voice as even and rhythmic as he keeps the powerful yet restrained thrusting of his rock-hard, searching nethers.

"Much," he replies, and before the terse little word escapes his lips, they are upon you. Your mouth, ears, neck are the skin of a forbidden fruit he is desperate to taste.

"This is wrong," he whispers into your décolletage. His fingers work swiftly against the common enemy that is your bodice, and soon all of you is tumbling between his hungry hands.

"Should we?" you whisper into his knit brow before running your fingers through his thick, tumbledown curls and pulling his face into your newly freed bosom.

"Mmmmf," he answers before breaking free. "You know damn well I can't respond with your amazing breasts in my mouth."

"Did you not think that was intentional? Ohhh . . . " You lose your desire to sass as he pleasures first one nipple with his limber tongue,

then the other.

"What does it matter what I think, what does any of it matter? Whatever happens to us, we have now. We have a discreet driver and a bed-carriage and each other and—" You cut short his tragic reverie by deftly unbuttoning the panel of his pants. "We have *now*."

A bird on the wing overhead would think nothing of your carriage, a small rollicking shadow in a wide world of trees slashed with moonlight. But if that bird could hear your cries, it would know the happiness of animals who have found their mate. A joy made even sweeter by the bitter knowledge that the mate could be lost, and likely would be, in the bright light of morning.

You are a shooting star in a dark sky. Turn to page 178.

You shake your head, with your heart in your throat. Mac nods unsteadily and hugs you tightly.

"I never did ken what to do with goodbyes," he says, laughing to conceal the tears shining in his eyes.

"Especially ones you don't want to say," you agree. He looks at you, his good and glorious eyes searching yours for what you think might be the last time.

You kiss him. "We won't say anything, then."

"Nothing at all."

You nod at each other and then, rubbing his eyes, Mac strides away. You sigh as you watch his perfect, retreating form . . . but you know in your soul that this is for the best. Your time here has passed. You must make a new life.

. . . .

But where do you go?

If you want to make things a little easier on yourself and go to Lord Craven's to teach just one kid in a structure that is not falling apart, turn to page 14.

If you want to challenge yourself a little further and see the world with Lady Evangeline, turn to page 193.

Any reservations you might have had vanish when you enter Cairo market. You have never seen so many vivid colors, heard so many strange and fascinating sounds, or smelled so many delicious and enticing spices until now—not even in your years existing on the fringes of the ton.

"Oh, Kamal, this is wonderful!" you gasp. Kamal beams.

"Thank you, miss. It is my pleasure to do anything for a friend of Lady Evangeline's. She has been a great benefactor of the museum—it would not exist without her patronage."

"I did not know that!" you say in wonder. "Though I suppose I should have realized. She has shown great kindness and generosity to me as well."

"At that, I am not surprised," says Kamal. "Lady Evangeline has always surrounded herself with great beauty—" He suddenly stops himself in embarrassment.

"Oh . . . I don't think that she—that is to say—" you stammer before giving up.

You continue together down the bustling street in awkward silence before curiosity gets the better of you.

"So, this Delphine St. Croix," you begin, "is *she* a great beauty, then?"

"Oh yes!" says Kamal. "One of the loveliest women I have ever seen."

"Oh." You feel oddly crushed. "And she and Lady Evangeline were close?"

"Indeed," says Kamal. "They were a strange pair, Lady Evangeline being a respectable married Englishwoman and Delphine the neglected daughter of a French deserter. But for a long time they were always in each other's company."

"So what *happened*?" you blurt out.

"It is a mystery, though the change in their friendship coincided with Delphine suddenly disappearing from respectable society. Lady Evangeline and her late husband returned to England not long aft—" Kamal's eyes widen suddenly. The crossroads you stand in have become suddenly deserted, save four dangerous-looking ruffians. At the very head of the group stands the man you had entrusted to protect you, his green eyes coldly triumphant.

"Farouk?!" Kamal cries.

"No," says the man, ripping off the scarf to reveal a face as beautiful as it is brutal. He laughs mirthlessly. "My true name is Fabien. Fabien de Mangepoussey. You have been too preoccupied with your foolish antiques to notice that while you employ me as your guard, I have been working for another this whole time. And now my mission is almost complete."

Farouk—Fabien—takes a step toward you, his fluid movement betraying a sleek, pantherlike power.

"The young lady is coming with me."

Do you fight off the ruffians and their handsome leader tooth and nail? You'll be damned if you are going down without a struggle! Turn to page 315.

Do you run for your life, dragging Kamal with you? You haven't a hope in hell of fighting them off, and you doubt your new Egyptologist friend does either. Turn to page 270.

For some, sharing a moment such as this would erase any desire but to hold each other close and cry. But for you and Craven, the moments soon give way to each stroking the other's body and speaking fluently in the unmistakable language of carnal lust.

By the time you finish, bookshelves have toppled. The brandy bottle has broken. You both have lost a bit of hair. But you feel flushed and satisfied in the knowledge that your sexual match exists in this world and is currently slumbering peacefully: Craven, washed clean in moonlight. You dare not disturb him and rise softly to your feet.

You creep out of the room and into the hall with visions of leftovers from the sideboard in the morning room dancing in your head. You will help yourself to a brief repast and bring some back for your love. Likely, you will both need nourishment for a full night, and possibly morning, of lovemaking ahead.

You stumble blearily through the manor. When you have hit the main hall of the house, you hear the sound of a burbling brook nearby. You figure you are in that happy, half-dreaming state in which people in love operate, or so you've heard. But when the brook burbles the words "I have done all you have asked of me, my queen," you immediately sober up.

You realize you are standing just outside the morning room, and the voice you hear within belongs to none other than . . . that devil Manvers.

....

Hang on tight, sweeting. It's going to be a bumpy ride. Turn to page 64.

All hope is lost, except for that of financial gain.

"I will marry you, girl," Sir Charles Burley-Fanshaw leers at you, literally waggling his fingers in a lewd display.

"Fine," you say. Extremely begrudgingly.

On the day of your wedding, you try to restrain your tears. Oh, how you bitterly regret your choices that led to this moment! The ceremony is conducted, per Sir Charles's orders, "as swiftly as humanly possible." Afterwards, he sends you to your dressing room to disrobe for him and, in his words, "the festivities."

Your flesh crawls as you contemplate your fate. Then you hear an awful cry and a sickening thud!

You run to the bedroom and find your new husband dead on the floor.

How festive.

It is the start of the next season. You are decked out in a glamorous and expensive black ball gown that suits you perfectly. Lady Evangeline catches your eye from across the ballroom and serves you a delicious wink. All the eligible young men are whispering about you, when they aren't drinking deep the sight of you in that dress.

"The black widow!"

"They say her husband died of apoplexy on their wedding night!"

"That much of a tiger in the bedroom, don't you know!"

"Left her an enormous fortune, rich as Croesus!"

"Dash sight better looking than Croesus!"

You smile enigmatically. With your youth, looks, new title, and money, you could do anything your heart desires. But that is for another time . . . and another story.

The End

"Did some of your sense burn in the fire? I'm not going anywhere, man," you tell Mac. "I'm fully involved with . . . with the fate of the orphans. I'm sticking this out, come hell, high water, or Constantina."

Mac flinches at the name, but his clear eyes blaze with admiration. They also can't help but follow the trajectory of the parchment as you tuck it into your straining bosom for safekeeping.

You watch as the firefighters finally arrive. They do their best to put out the blaze, but the home has been demolished. Mac's spirits, too, seem to be sagging.

"Aye," he says sadly. "Before, I had a home for the orphans that was missing the comforts of such. Now I have the orphans, and nothing else."

"Not so fast, m'lad!" Abercrombie returns from whatever business he was conducting during the fire. "I just sent word to my people back home in Scotland. I own a ramshackle old place in the Highlands, and it's yours for the using. Now, a large part of the walls and roof need mending, not to mention that it is far from the only home the orphans know, but—"

"It'll do!" you and Mac respond in cheerful unison. You beam at each other, and at Abercrombie, and as a result the children respond with wild, happy confusion.

"It's settled, then!" Abercrombie roars. "I need to stay behind while I sort out a few things, but I suggest you take the orphans to the Highlands straightaway."

Abercrombie says his farewells, and you and Mac set about arranging travel. "I'm sure Madam Crosby could lend a hand," you say.

"Or a few other body parts," says a sweet, thin voice. You turn and see two ladies hovering by you who are, by the looks of them, "professionals" from the nearby Rose & the Smoke. The smaller of the two nods at you and continues speaking.

"The name's Jane, and this is Gertie." She gestures to her friend, who has a sumptuous crop of strawberry-blonde hair. "We was wondering . . . well, you see, I have been wanting to get out of London for quite some time now. But it is hard, miss, when you have been in our line of work, to move on."

"People don't like giving girls like us second chances," Gertie says, nodding in agreement. "And when I heard that you was leaving town, I thought to meself, well what if we went with you?"

"We'd help with the ankle biters, miss!" says Jane. "I'm the oldest of eighteen brothers and sisters. I know how to handle a group of screaming brats!"

"Not that we think your wards are screaming brats," Gertie says harshly, glaring at her friend. "But we could help look after them . . . Not being funny, love, but you do seem rushed off your feet."

Out of the corner of your eye, you see Timmy screaming as Dodger charges headfirst into an oyster girl, sending shellfish flying across the cobblestones and into several passersby. You and Mac exchange glances and sigh.

"That would be wonderful," says Mac.

"Oh, thank you, Captain!" exclaim Jane and Gertie.

"No, thank *you*," you say vehemently. "However, we do still have the problem of how to get twenty children from London to Scotland. You wouldn't know where I could procure a wagon or cart of some sort at a reasonable price?"

"We can do you one better than that, love," says Gertie. "Give us a couple of hours and a chance to call in a few favors, and we will find you one for free!"

A few hours later, a solid, if humble, cart lined with soft straw is ready to be filled with the children.

"You are marvels!" you say to Jane and Gertie.

"We also brought you something else," says Jane, offering a bundle of sensible but high-quality fabric. "Seeing as your dress got ruined." You look down and see the smoke- and mud-stained wreck you are wearing. They are not wrong.

You hastily go to change into the dress, made of a rich forest-green fabric. Clearly designed as simple everyday wear for the ladies of the Rose & the Smoke, it is still finer and more revealing than anything else you have previously owned. You awkwardly cross your arms over your chest, but it only seems to add to the effect.

Something, or someone, is adding to the heat of your embarrassment. You look up to catch Mac, entranced, taking in the newly revealed curves of your body. He snaps his gaze away as soon as you look, but as you load the orphans into the wagon, you are gratified to see that Mac is unable to keep his eyes from you. Your satisfaction is of course foolish—you are here to work, not expose your bosoms to handsome Scotsmen. You continue your work as primly as possible and try to concentrate.

As you do, a dark blur tugs at the edge of your vision. You turn to make out just what it is, but the figure suddenly melts into the depths of the murky shadows of the street like a soul of the damned sent to wander this earth, never finding salvation.

You dismiss it as nothing.

....

Get ye to the Great North Road! And Scotland! Turn to page 281.

The ballroom is a vast channel of well-bred, well-dressed gallimaufry, and Lady Evangeline sails through it with the earned ease of a veteran sailor.

"To me, you are a friend," Lady Evangeline says. "That is why we are drinking the good brandy."

Once you reach the other end of the ballroom, far from the prying eyes of the ton and yet farther from the still-doubled-over Cad, Lady Evangeline reveals a small flask she has secreted in her reticule. She swigs deeply and hands it to you.

"Drink," she insists. You know how to follow orders and do so gladly. After taking a sip, you open your mouth to form a question. She passes an elegant finger over her lips to hush you before you can. "Please," she says. "While I would rather you not be so intimately acquainted with the skeletons knocking about my family's closet, it appears they will stop at nothing to perform a *danse macabre* for you this very evening."

"A *danse macabre* done with two left feet, no less," you say. You both laugh conspiratorially, then right yourselves.

"Truly," Lady Evangeline continues. "But I must say, I have never enjoyed Cad's antics. I have always dismissed him as a vibrant man on the fringes of proper society with misdirected energies, but his performance tonight has me . . . concerned." Her lovely brow knits with worry.

"You, too, think there is something questionable with his claim?" you press.

"I do," she answers slowly. "But I am vexed."

"As am I," you agree. "Benedict is a vexation to me, but I see no reason he should be thrown out on the street due to the claims of a particularly theatrical half brother. Do you believe there is merit to what Cad says?"

Lady Evangeline is silent for several moments. Finally she says, "Cad and Benedict's father never spoke much on the subject of his *affaire*—or should I say marriage—with Mrs. Caddington, and all I knew for a long time was that there must be a scent of unpleasantness hanging around it. Like perfume gone stale."

"How so?" you ask, eyes widening.

"Well, Rafe is the eldest. We don't know why, but the late baronet threw Mrs. Caddington aside for a while and married Benedict's mother. A most respectable woman. But then . . ."

"But then *what*?" you ask, impatient.

"But then a few years after that, he returned to the intoxicating arms of Mrs. Caddington. He could resist her for only so long. Little Henrietta is the result of *that*."

"But why did he leave her in the first place if they were married? Was there some secret scandal . . . something in her past that made him lose his affection for a time, perhaps?" Your mind reels.

"Nothing like that, I don't think," Lady Evangeline answers. "She was already well-known as an actress when they began their liaison, but other than her profession she was by all accounts simply a respectable widow. Her first husband died long ago, after a trip to the Continent."

"Do you suspect foul play? Not to malign Mrs. Caddington, rest her soul, but could she have had her first husband . . . taken care of in order to grant her a life's pleasure with the second?" Your mind is so thoroughly in thrall with intrigue that you do not realize the candor of your own tongue until it is too late. "Oh, Lady Evangeline, I—"

Lady Evangeline looks at you with wonder and appreciation. "No. No apologies, dear. It is a thrill to watch a mind as clever as yours set itself to work. Still, I think it works in error. Mrs. Caddington was not known to be a malicious woman. She was clever and fine as well as loyal and dear. Still, she went to the Continent married and returned a widow."

Befuddled, you stare at the pattern of the brocade curtains decorating this end of the ballroom. The weave plays tricks on your eyes, and you think you see shapes that could not truly exist. Answers where there are only questions.

"It must have been a trial, bringing the body back home for the funeral," you say with empathy.

Lady Evangeline looks at you curiously. "She did not bring back a body. It was too much trouble, so he was buried there. On the Continent."

"A shame," you say, but a flutter of intrigue dances in your heart. "Do you know where?"

"She never—no one ever said," stammers Lady Evangeline, a woman unaccustomed to stammering.

"Perhaps he wasn't buried at all," you hear yourself say excitedly. "Perhaps the late Mrs. Caddington's late first husband isn't late after all. Perhaps he didn't die on the Continent. Perhaps"—your eyes flash, and Lady Evangeline's do, too—"perhaps he merely *disappeared*."

....

You are cool and sharp and a wonder to behold.

Do you take a victory turn about the room and rub your grandness in a certain deserving someone's face? Turn to page 98.

Or do you get straight to getting to the bottom of things? Time's of the essence! Turn to page 129.

Stomping through the glen, you find yourself mired in brooding jealousy—of both the mysterious Constantina and the lovely Fiona. There is no earthly reason that a man so handsome and rugged and kind and good as Mac would have lived his life as a monk prior to your meeting. Besides, he is your employer, nothing more. One torrid night in a coaching inn changes nothing of the situation.

You stamp down a tuft of heather and, you hope, your ridiculous flights of fancy. You need to right your fevered emotions before you do something stupid. Blowing off steam with a brisk walk so that you may temper your passions before you again face Mac sounds like just the remedy.

You take the scenic route that brings you alongside a magnificent loch. Sighing, you feel your blood cool. This was a marvelous idea. You continue walking, a woman reborn, until you are confronted by your inflamed emotions and desires in the form of Mac, standing among the verdant grasses. His kilt is on, his shirt is off, and the good man is working on his caber toss.

As Mac's thick, steady, clever fingers strain and stroke the larch-wood pole, you find yourself wondering how many women have ever counted themselves jealous of a tree trunk.

A haunting, alluring pennywhistle melody begins to play in the lush valley of your sex as you watch Mac's toss through from the run-up to the moment of release, following the impossibly long, perfectly thick beam as it tumbles, end over end, in glorious flight. When the wood strikes the ground, it earns a perfect score by the judge of your heart . . . and your dewy lowlands.

Sensing a presence—or perhaps hearing his own inner pennywhistle score—Mac turns to face you. His look—one that speaks of your shared longing to have continued on that night in the coaching inn—more than crosses the chasm of your desire.

What would it have been like had you continued and felt that powerful form moving between your legs, bringing you to heretofore unexplored vistas of delight?

"What are you doing here, lass?" His voice breaks you from your reverie, your face flushed as you realize you have been spotted. You raise your chin, attempt to keep your voice even, and try not to be distracted by your wish to be lifted and balanced in much the same way as the caber before you.

"I am on my way back from the village. I bought some much-needed supplies for the children . . . from your old friend."

Mac grins warmly, and you feel your heart clench. "Och, Fiona Buchanan? How is she and that great lunk she married?"

"They seem very well," you say tightly, looking away from his rippling torso lest your resolve crumbles. "She had much to reminisce about you."

"You seem almost jealous, lass," says Mac. Though he is entirely correct—perhaps *because* he is—you are outraged at his impudence.

"I am nothing of the sort!" you say. "We had a very pleasant exchange, and that was that! Now if you'll excuse me, I have work to do while you are busy throwing tree trunks about."

Cheeks blazing, you stomp back to the castle. You are too angry to notice the shadowy figure lurking near the entrance that almost stops you.

You're not jealous. Not a whit. Turn to page 162.

You hold your ground. "I will never go with you, *never*, do you hear me?" you gasp, as the wicked blade pierces your skin. A trickle of blood runs down your neck. You try not to quiver.

"You are being very stupid, *ma chère*," hisses Delphine. "Some might say . . . too stupid to live!" She throws her lovely head back and laughs. It is a strange unearthly sound, with no humor in it.

Now is your chance. You duck away as she is distracted and grab a scimitar lying abandoned next to an unconscious ruffian. You spin around and point it at her.

"Drop the knife," you command. Delphine stops cold.

"Well done!" says an admiring voice behind you. A thrill runs down your spine, for in your peripheral vision you see Lady Evangeline approaching with her small gold pistol pointed at her traitorous ex-lover. Delphine stares at her wildly.

"You—you have no loyalty!" cries the outraged woman. "I would have loved you—I *still* love you—for all time! But you prefer this boring *petite anglaise* to a woman who would do anything for you!"

Evangeline's beautiful eyes are filled with tears, but her voice holds steady.

"It's over, Delphine," she says. "You made your choice when you betrayed me. I thought I might never love again. I was wrong." She turns to you. "You showed me that, my dear. No matter what happens after this day, I must thank you."

"Lady Evangeline!" you say with a sigh.

"NO!" screeches Delphine. Although you both have weapons pointed toward her, Delphine rushes forward, knife aloft and ready to do damage. The blade sparkles ferociously in the sunlight. "You will not have this! Not while I still live—"

A gunshot rings out, and for a split second you think Lady Evangeline has fired, has killed her former love. You are startled to see a curious mixture of anguish and relief cross her face as she stares at a figure several feet from you. Following her sapphire gaze, you turn and see a familiar looming presence, silhouetted against the bright sunshine, holding a gun.

"Fabien! But why?!" you cry. He turns to you, his tormented Nile-green eyes even more tormented than usual.

"Because you stopped her from killing me," he says at last. "Consider our debt settled."

Before you can respond, he nods at you, holding your gaze for several loaded moments, and then swings himself onto his camel and rides deep into the desert, disappearing as if he were a mirage.

At the sight of their employer's demise, what remains of Delphine's hired thugs turn and flee like the mangy scum they are. Your brave battalion of Sekhmets, lionesses each and every one, whoop and cheer.

You barely notice, for Lady Evangeline has pulled you into one of Delphine's abandoned tents and kisses you fiercely yet tenderly, your bodies entwined as perhaps they had been fated to be all this time.

....

Well, *finally*, you two! Turn to page 134.

Just then, a woman runs past you in tears. Certainly, a lady fleeing a man's presence at a ball is understandable, if a bit unusual. However, the lady fleeing this certain man at this certain moment is close to you in years but prettier (alas), dressed in finer clothes than you (double alas), and you suspect that her tears have more to do with the handsome ginger man in military uniform she has just run from than any war, recent or otherwise.

"Now, lassie," the handsome ginger man—who is none other than the Captain Angus "Mac" MacTaggart to whom Lady Evangeline offered to introduce you but a moment earlier—calls after the woman while shaking his head in frustration. "I didnae come here to engage in . . . well, never mind! I came here for charity."

Mac is muscled and broad shouldered, unlike the sleek nobles of the ton that surround him. His is a body that's seen vigorous activity, and you shudder with longing to know what kind. With eyes the green-brown color of a Highland glen below a Highland moor, and a strangely sad square jaw set with a sensitive poetic mouth, he is a vision of Scottish virility. You can scarcely tear your eyes from his noble visage before Lady Evangeline kicks you sharply in the shin.

"Captain MacTaggart! I long to make your introduction to my dear friend—" Lady Evangeline gestures to you, but Mac dismisses her, not unkindly.

"I'm not one for formalities, lassie, that you know." His brogue tumbles out like stout into a pint glass. "And I am more than a mite sorry for causing a scene at the ball. I just want to raise money for the other lassies and kiddies who are without their men, as such, due to this awful war. Mother Mary forgive me, I do forget myself and can be a bit rough in my talking. I try to remember I am but speakin' to the softer sex and not the men out afield. The widows just seem to look for a strong shoulder to cry into and, well, Lady Evangeline, begging your pardon, I feel they get a bit . . . erm . . . confused."

While Mac has been brogue-ing about, he has cast what can only be described as pointedly interested looks in your direction. Several, to be precise. When, of course, he wasn't rubbing his manly temples with his manly hands and wringing those manly hands of their nervous, manly energy.

Something about his tender, helpful nature, buried in all that muscle and uniform, speaks to a place deep inside you. You slip the gold bracelet off your wrist and hand it to Mac.

"It isn't much," you say, by way of introduction, "but it was my mother's. More valuable than that to you, it is solid gold and perhaps can fetch a sum for your noble cause."

Lady Evangeline is struck temporarily dumb by your quiet act of kindness, and just as well. It gives you an opportunity to feel the heat of Mac's rough hands around your own, both of you holding each other (and the bracelet) the way one holds a promise that one intends to keep forever.

Your eyes catch Mac's for a moment, and you see they are shining with barely contained tears.

"Thank you, lassie," he manages to whisper. He squeezes your hand in such a way that suggests he would like nothing more than to pull you closer, and that he is moved by your goodness and pluck. "Thank you from the bottom of my heart."

If you haven't met Benedict yet, turn to page 232.

If you have met Benedict, turn to page 126.

Trying to steady your breath, you tiptoe nervously toward the great hall of the museum. Something hairy glances against your shoulder. You nearly scream before you realize it is just a cat who has leapt upon a ledge and is head-butting you.

"Good puss," you murmur. You rub its head.

Squaring your shoulders, you continue onward to the great hall in your mission for tea. Perhaps Kamal has made some headway in clearing the worst of the debris? Chiding yourself for foolishly fearing something as innocent as a little cat, you step through the doorway . . . and find yourself pinned down by a rock-hard arm. A heavy hand silences you before you have a chance to scream.

"Well, look at what we have here," a low voice hisses in your ear. "Madame St. Croix will be pleased."

You wildly glance up into a familiar pair of Nile-green eyes. No . . . it cannot be. Now that a scarf is no longer obscuring his face, you are shocked to find that the guard who so frightened you earlier has a countenance as beautiful and harshly unforgiving as the Sahara.

"Farouk?!" you attempt to say through the firm, calloused fingers clamping your mouth shut. It comes out sounding more like "Fmmrk?!"

Still, he seems to understand what you say. "No," he hisses under his breath. "My true name is Fabien. Fabien de Mangepoussey. And you are coming with me."

"No!" You cannot even scream as you struggle in vain against his iron strength. Another burly man you do not recognize opens the door to the outside world and nods menacingly. Farouk/Fabien nods back and swings you off your feet as though you weigh no more than a rag-doll. Despite your furious kicks and struggles, he carries you effortlessly across the great hall.

You give another stifled scream as you spot Kamal lying lifeless on the floor. Fabien shows no mercy, but only grasps you tighter.

"Ignore him. The *imbécile* was too preoccupied with his foolish antiques to notice that I have been working for another right under his nose." He smiles at you mirthlessly.

"Do not worry, he may still be alive. Perhaps." His fellow ruffian laughs under his breath.

The idea merely makes you struggle all the more. Fabien's green eyes flicker as annoyance crosses his handsomely swarthy face.

"Do not make this harder for yourself, *chérie*. You have an appointment with Madame Delphine St. Croix, and I would hate to disappoint her."

And with that he hauls you unceremoniously out the door and onto an awaiting camel. You ride away, far beyond the city, as you continue to fight desperately to free yourself . . . to no avail.

Turn to page 59.

You refuse to leave and instead offer your heart and soul to Craven. He accepts you happily and you embrace.

As the sun rises, you wait together at the sleeping Alexander's bedside. The light illuminates a painting of a sweet little girl, the very image of Alexander. It is strange, for the painting hangs in so prominent a place, but you could have sworn it wasn't there before. The girl smiles out beatifically, as if in thanks.

Little Alexander awakes and tugs your hand. "I dreamed of Helena. She said she is at peace now that the bad man is gone." A shiver runs down your spine, but not an unhappy one.

"I love you, my darling," says Craven, like a man transformed.

Blissful time passes. You see young Master Alexander off to school in the fall, a confident and changed boy. And yet . . . for all that Craven seems happy and content, he still does not ask for your hand. Rather, he pauses whenever you speak of the future. "There is something I must tell you . . . but cannot," he sometimes says. You know not how to press him on the matter, nor on his strange absences which occur once a month.

Nevertheless, a period of torrid pleasure and peaceful companionship passes . . . until you decide to take action.

On the evening that you enact your plan, the sky darkens and a full moon rises. You smile to yourself. This promises to be the night you will make Craven face the last of his demons, once and for all. But first, you make love, experiencing total ecstasy in both body and soul.

You lie entwined with your lover in a corner of the library, the moonstone of your sex still aglow with otherworldly desire for him.

He places that broken-statue hand of his on your left breast, which he has taken to calling Grecian Urn. His other hand travels to your right breast, which he has nicknamed his Sepulcher by the Sea.

His hands are as hungry as his heart, and oh! how they hunt your flesh for sustenance.

"You make me feel as if I am half woman, half beast," you moan into your lover's lush but well-groomed pelt.

Lord Craven emits a growl that could also be a knowing laugh,

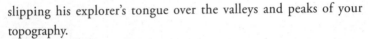

slipping his explorer's tongue over the valleys and peaks of your topography.

"Your womanly orbs undo me as much as the moon does," he whisper-growls into the soft fur of your womanhood. Your womanhood responds with some whisper-growling of its own.

The actual moon, which has heretofore been hidden by sumptuous cloud cover, breaks through the late-evening gloom with the same vigor as your pleasure breaking through your lover's embrace.

The moment a sliver of moonlight slices his ethereally pale flesh, Lord Craven screams as if stabbed by a saber.

"NO!" He flings you into a pile of watercolor silk cushions, which you can't help but wonder if he placed there much earlier to soften your landing, should he ever choose to fling you across the library floor due to an errant moonbeam.

"Run, my love! Run for your life!" The screams rip through his body, competing with the strange forms and shudders also ripping forth from him as the moonlight plays brighter across his bare, beautiful frame.

"Call Mrs. Butts!" he screams. "She knows how to chain me!"

"Chain you?" You frantically gather your silken robes around your orbs, womanhood, et cetera. "I bid the servants retire in the furthest chambers of their quarters so that we might enjoy each other in uninterrupted freedom!"

Terror colors Lord Craven's darkly handsome features, mixed with respect for your command of your desire as well as of his household staff.

"NOOOOOOO!" He screams as fur and blood tear through his desirable flesh. The transformation shows you what he truly is . . .

"A were-creature?!" You scream and duck behind a chaise lounge toppled earlier by vigorous lovemaking.

"A monster." His words are raw, his breath ragged, his teeth sharp and long. His voice is the only thing you recognize. The rest of him is a hulking mass above you, the wild night made flesh, out for blood, and out for you.

"Blanche . . . she left me for a time to be with her poet lover. When she came back, she had changed. She had become a monster."

You shake your head. "No, she was a monster long before. She merely came back a wolf."

Lord Craven stares at you, eyes drenched in sadness. "She then turned me into this—this *thing*. She wanted to change the children, too, but I wouldn't—I couldn't—let her. So she turned on them instead. She took Helena . . ." A single tear runs down his wolf face.

He could destroy you with a single swipe of his knife-sharp claws. End you with one snap of his abominable jaws. But you place your hand on the center of his chest.

"Are you not afraid?" he cries.

"Not of you." You reach out to embrace his terrifying form. He trembles at your touch.

"Not," you say as you draw his horrible maw to your delicate mouth, "of my monster."

You kiss him. He shudders in tender ecstasy. He shudders with relief.

"Make us as one," you command. "You never have to be alone. Never, as long as either of us has breath left in our bodies." You share a look between your eternal souls. You nod. He nods. The kiss turns to teeth and tongue and magic.

Together, your bodies are rewritten by the moonlight.

The legend of Hopesend Manor now speaks of two demon beasts who stalk the moors as a pair. One is never seen without the other, and when they howl at their moon-made-master, no creature has ever been said to sound happier.

The End

While Benedict unlocks secret passageways of your mind, Cad unlocks the secret passageways of your body. You know the way Benedict would love you: full of honor and wit, with repressed desire bursting out in rare moments of passion, shooting stars across a dark sky of decorum upheld, appearances kept, pants buttoned.

But what if you want a sky full of stars? What if you want to be blinded with light and passion? Why should you have to marry Benedict at all, for that matter, just because you want to love his body? Why do you need to marry well to live well, to give the color of your rose to one man alone, for all of time?

It is Benedict's world that has made you a beggar of love and station. It is Benedict's society that deems you a bad catch, in need of a savior merely to live your life. It is Benedict who has decided that you needed saving from Cad, rather than taking a moment to see what you truly wanted. As much as you feel for him, and want him, something derelict in Cad speaks to you. Something that sounds on the nature of your very own soul. You perhaps would not feel so animal if you had grown up in the cozy bosom of the ton, a gilded daughter, debuted and danced and feted as if she were destined to be a jewel in some young man's crown.

But you weren't danced and debuted. You were relegated to toil while others shone. You bathed in shadow yet, for others, created light.

"You know your mind, girl." Cad laughs, raw and sultry, his body shimmering with perspiration. He is a fool, of course, for thinking he could take down Benedict with such a hasty scheme. To raze a castle with a claw is impossible. It takes more finesse. More artistry. More watching, waiting, planning. Paperwork.

You recall his lush tongue brushing against your breasts, the shape of his kiss, the bulge in his trousers. He has a face so beautiful, your breath catches just from watching it catch moonlight.

A face like that can open doors. A mind like yours can open a world you had thought was closed to you.

"My lady." Benedict's eyes are already wounded as they search your own. He is a wit, true, but while some wits are frivolous, you know he is more savage. If only he could be as free as his foolish, fiery, fine half brother, you could see yourself living with him, taking up by his side. But you know, as he knows, that he is still far too proper to be the man you need, or the man you want.

"I came to save you, and to tell you that Henrietta had confessed the truth by the time I reached the house. I am baronet again. She has eloped with Sam. They are out for Cad's blood, of course. But all is well." Even as he speaks, his voice breaks with the knowledge of your decision.

"I am sorry, Benedict." You tenderly kiss him goodbye.

"I could make you happy, you fool," he whispers softly into your mouth.

"Perhaps," you whisper back. "But you could never make me free."

"Yes. Well." Benedict takes a deep breath, desperate to collect himself. You wish you could take him with you. Perhaps you will meet again, under different circumstances. "Run now, take the spare carriage. I will say that Cad stole it and you decided to go off to America or something. That should give you a head start. I will miss you, damnable woman."

"I will miss you, too," you say and nod in thanks. Cad, stunned, watches the exchange from his position, slumped against the high hedge of the labyrinth.

"Well, don't just stand there, man," Benedict spits at him. "She's clearly got plans for you."

You laugh, take Cad's hand, and flee down the twists and turns of the maze. You most certainly do.

By the time you and Cad reach America, you have posed as betrothed, husband and wife, brother and sister, governess and employer, heiress and manservant. He's had you in countless street corners in London, inns, riverbanks, and, one time, on horseback while crossing a riverbank. After you've swindled honest money from crooked folk (you have a predilection for conning con men of their recent takes), you point out to Cad that his error with Benedict was in trying to trick someone he knew.

"It's better this way," he agrees. "Family isn't hurt, and I get to partake of you between jobs." He spreads your legs in the back of the coach you have hired, with stolen money, to take you to some seaside American town in search of your next easy mark. "I'm famished, ma'am," he says in his best American accent.

Maybe you will never marry him. Maybe you will pose as lover, bride, sister, cousin, friend. The roles open to you are as countless as the cities that do not know your name, your station, or your scandal. For with your Cad, you live a life of freedom, a life of trickery, and a life of lovemaking out of doors.

The End

"What are you doing, lass?" Mac asks, desire sparking in the depths of his voice. You respond by sliding your dress down your shoulders, exposing your mountainous region, your foothills, and, ultimately, the lush and alluring forest of your lowlands.

"Come," you whisper into the fall of indoor rain. "The water is fine."

In mere moments, he has peeled away his clothes to reveal a pelt the color of bright flame. You hold each other and kiss with the same endless tenderness of the water washing you clean.

As Mac explores the inland ocean of your mouth, his intrepid sailor hands travel across the topography of your body, claiming new locations in the name of pleasure. As his tongue works a clear path down your neck to your breasts, you long for him to journey further. Still, there is something troubling your mind and upsetting the expedition. Something you must know first.

"Who," you gasp through waves of pleasure, "is Constantina?"

Mac freezes for a moment, shocked into silence. "She was . . . my greatest regret."

"A woman you loved and lost?" you ask. No use putting it any other way but plain.

"No," Mac says simply, darkly, sadly. "The woman I killed."

Do you flee? Because murder! The note was right! Turn to page 94.

Or do you sit it out with Mac? We've all done things we regret, and you're still a bit, ah, damp from your interlude. Turn to page 167.

Perhaps you loved Craven. Perhaps you only wanted him with the fiery desire of the forsaken and profane. In any case, your shared tale is now over, writ in a book that has been slammed shut by the hand of fate.

You make a midnight run across the moors of Craven's lands, all the way to the carriage house of Teddy Braithwaite, the handsome postman who, you will recall, carried you to the top of the hill at the beginning of this story.

He answers the door, flushed and shirtless. You want him the instant you see him, and the instant you see him, you know he wants you.

"I have been waiting for thee, miss," he says. He helps you into his humble home and frees your body from your dress as gently as one would open a stolen letter from 'neath its seal.

His hands trace the outline of your breasts with wonder and skill. Your nipples harden at the touch of his work-roughened fingers, and he licks their cherry tips with a tongue made strong from licking countless envelopes. He sets that same tongue to the task of running the length of your midsection, all the way down into the plush pocket of your sex. There, he pushes into you with the soft pressure of a first-class stamp. You both cry out, in pleasure and sweet, sweet pain, for the handsome postman is intensely endowed.

"The mail always comes on time in my district," he whispers to you. "If you know what I mean."

"It does, it does," you cry, straddling him for another round. You live happily ever after this way, simply and with much postal-innuendo-laced sex play, for the rest of your days.

Some might say the postman sends you. Oh he sends you, indeed!

The End

"**This is a fine offer, Lord Fleming,**" you say carefully. "And Ollie, seeing you come back from the dead has been one of the more . . . *thrilling* experiences of my life. But—"

Lord Fleming's shoulders droop. Ollie's heart, you suspect, breaks.

"I must say only thank you and bid you fond adieu," you conclude. "A spy's life isn't for me."

Ollie gathers your hands in his. "But what of us, my lady? I . . . I do still . . ." His eyes are so earnest and longing that it almost pains you to tell him the truth.

Almost.

"Oh, Ollie." You embrace him warmly before pulling away and chucking him playfully on the chin. "You should have thought of that before you allowed me to believe you dead for years." You now address Lord Fleming and Ollie equally. "Good day to you both, and thank you for all of your assistance."

The spies say their goodbyes, and when they have gone, there is no one but you and Mac. The mighty Scot looks at you with nothing but love (and, admittedly, a fair deal of lust) in his eyes.

"Lass," he says. "Ye'll stay wi' me?"

You have a choice.

. . . .

Do you stay with Mac for a tough but meaningful life helping the orphans while enjoying rigorous lovemaking for the rest of your days? If so, turn to page 234.

Or do you long for yet another adventure? If so, turn to page 20.

You flee to the comforting confines of the less-eldritch garden. It grows vegetables, rather than flowers planted out of jealous rage, and is the perfect place to collect your thoughts and perhaps a sprig of wild clover.

"I-I do hope I'm not intruding . . ."

You spin from your wild-clover-picking stance to face none other than the strange, handsome vicar standing in a patch of rhubarb. His eyes wear a haunted look.

"Forgive me, I shouldn't be here. But I knew . . . I knew I would never forgive myself for not saying something—" he chokes out.

"What is it, Reverend Loveday?" you implore him.

"It—it's just that . . . you wouldn't be the first beautiful young woman to disappear in Craven's care, my dear," he says, his voice soft and gentle. "If you should ever need me, my aid or my ear, I hope you know you can always come to the vicarage."

You nod and step toward him, unsure exactly why. Your movement releases something in him, and his face floods with relief. "Forgive me my boldness," he half orgasms, half whispers, before pulling you into an inappropriate embrace. "Forgive me, forgive me," he murmurs into your hair before pulling himself free and disappearing into a patch of flax.

You shake your head and watch him go. At least you have an ally in this handsome man of faith.

. . . .

This was a fun, if odd, encounter, but you didn't really gather your thoughts. Better head to the straight-up eldritch garden now. Turn to page 264.

You and Mac birth the everloving daylights out of that horse. The two of you perform the procedure with such precision, grace, and showmanship that you could have entirely revolutionized veterinary techniques of the early nineteenth century, if only someone had been there taking notes. Mac's corded arms move gently as he pats the mare, whispering tender reassurances into her ear.

After hours of exertion, the gangly, newborn foal whimpers its first nicker unto the world, and its mother nuzzles it kindly. The great beast looks at you both with gratitude, then you turn to look at each other with eyes full of pride, trust, and desperate longing. The moment is intense. You then stare at the foal, and your heart swells with the joy of birth and creation—even though you are covered in baby-horse goop.

"A miracle of life," Mac says hoarsely.

"It is," you say, also—appropriately—hoarsely.

"Nae, lass. *You* are."

You look up from the foal and into Mac's searching eyes. You never knew you could be so aroused after spending several hours with your arm inside a horse's body cavity, but here you are.

You feel thrillingly bold. "How long until it is ready to ride?" you ask.

Mac laughs. "This wee slip of a thing will have to find its legs first. It will be quite some time."

"I don't mean the horse."

Mac's eyes widen. Still sticky—mostly in the unpleasant way—you strip down and dump a bucket of water over your body. As you do, Mac's own faithful steed strains at the flap of his kilt, ready to take you on as far a journey as you wish.

"Lass," Mac says breathily, "are ye sure?"

....

What do you think?

If animal husbandry truly gets you going, turn to page 104.

If, on second thought, you feel a little less than alluring thanks to the afterbirth, and making violent love in front of two horses seems a wee bit weird, go to page 77.

Oh, how you wish you were less sensible. That you could throw caution and your underclothes to the wind and mount this magnificent, frustrating man, right here on the settee. But your lives are soon to be rent asunder. Why make it more painful for you both?

Instead you repeat yourself, sadly this time.

"Absolutely the worst idea we have ever had . . . in fact, we should stop."

Benedict nods tenderly and removes those magic fingers. You curse yourself inwardly for your good sense.

Still, you know it is for the best. As intense as your feelings are for each other, you both are now penniless and unable to support a life together. Trained for one particular life, Benedict must marry an heiress, and you know you are far from that.

"Forgive me," he whispers, as tears well in your eyes.

"No," you sigh, kissing him one last time. "I want this more than anything. But you and I both know . . . that this is impossible. That we can never be."

You stand and then run from the room, restraining your tears until well out of earshot. You need time alone to clear your head, but instead you run, blurry eyed, smack into Evangeline.

As you wipe away your tears, you see that she is comforting Henrietta, who is also crying.

"My dear, there really are other options for you," Lady Evangeline says kindly. "You can start a new life with me as my companion when I go to Egypt."

Henrietta answers with only a fresh gale of sobs. Evangeline, still kind, looks as though she is beginning to doubt the wisdom of this plan.

"Or . . . um . . . perhaps I could help you find a position more to your choosing elsewhere? "

"B-but I don't *want* a position elsewhere! I-I just want—" Henrietta stops suddenly, her eyes wide with fright.

"What Henrietta means is that she wishes only to be with her true love, a humble farmer named Sam," you explain. Henrietta gasps.

"Oh, no, please don't say anything! You don't understand! My brother says he will kill my darling Sam if our love is ever made public! That is why I have remained silent on this matter all along!"

You square your shoulders.

"This is one situation where Cad is *not* going to win. Evangeline, you say you have connections. We will need to call upon them soon—for Henrietta and Sam!"

Evangeline nods.

"You can trust me, my dear. No matter what happens, you are still my family and I will do anything to help you."

Henrietta gazes at the two of you, her eyes filled with gratitude and hope.

"She's right," you say. "Henrietta, if I cannot be happy, then I think at least *you* should be."

Off you go to page 73!

Governesses come and go. You came, and now you're going.

If you had sullied your reputation with anyone other than a mad lord who spends his time pacing the grounds of his castle in the moonlight, you could kiss all your chances at anything other than impoverished spinsterhood goodbye.

But because you chose your nights of passion and indentured childcare wisely, you get another chance at love—and *romance*.

....

But where?

Do you fancy a bit of posh and wish to zip back to London for another go-round at the crème de la crème of society? If so, turn to page 302.

Or do you feel not up to traveling quite so much and would rather take that handsome local postman and yourself to the mailbox? (By mailbox, we mean orgasm.) If so, turn to page 47.

You, Mac, and Ollie exchange looks. All this time, the traitorous Constantina was hidden in plain sight.

"We must go." Mac lays a gentle and comforting hand on Ollie's shoulder. Ollie looks up, his animosity having melted away into warm gratitude.

"Yes. Yes, you are right." Though his voice remains calm, it sounds strangely hollow. Despite everything, you cannot help but empathize. "We should leave now, in case she slips from our clutches for good!"

"Timmy," Mac says gently, "how good is Dodger as a sniffer dog?"

Timmy gulps. "Oh, he is the very best of the best!" He nods so vehemently you fear his head may fall off.

"Go to your bed now," says Mac. "Wake your friends and barricade the doors to the Great Hall. It is rough work we have to do tonight, lad, and we need you to hold the fort." Timmy responds with a shaky salute and then rushes off to raise the other orphans from their slumber.

With Dodger and a lantern, you and the men venture onto the moonlit Highlands to look for Constantina. Dodger seems instinctively to understand the gravity of the situation and practically pulls Mac's arm out of its socket as you race at full speed toward a long-deserved reckoning. You only hope you are not too late.

As you approach the loch, eerie in darkness, you find Constantina waiting for you. She has removed her false nose, heavy maquillage, and strawberry-blonde wig, revealing a mass of dark curls and a strangely foxlike beauty. You gasp. Truly a master of disguise, she looks like an entirely different person.

She also has a pistol aimed at your group.

"Constantina!" Ollie's voice is laced with pain. She raises one eyebrow.

"Ollie. How nice of you to come, and to bring your friends."

"I don't understand!" Ollie's voice cracks. "Why did you do it, Connie? How could you do it? After all the sacrifices you made! For your country . . ." He can barely choke out the last part: "For *us*?"

"Oh, my darling." Her tone remains eerily calm. "Don't you see? I had to. I had to pretend so that I would be trusted with information I could then pass on to the great Emperor Napoleon!"

"No!" Ollie cries. "You are not—you couldn't!"

"Oh, I could, and I did. But my feelings for you . . . well, they were not false. Not at all. You must believe that."

Incapable of speech, Ollie simply shakes his head. You realize you need to take over, to stall for time and distract her if you can.

"So you are a Bonapartist?" you ask. Constantina turns to you with a mocking smile.

"Of course, you foolish chit!" she spits. "I am dedicated and loyal, even to this day. Even when the great man is dead and my cause is lost!"

You lean closer to Mac, and he puts a protective arm around you. Constantina barely notices.

"Do you understand how hard it has been? After betraying Britain, faking my death with the help of dear Captain MacTaggart, and then the fall of Napoleon in France? There was nowhere safe for me to go."

"So what did you do?" you ask, unable to keep your voice from shaking. Constantina tosses back those dark curls and fixes a gimlet eye on you.

"I went into hiding. Took a job at the Rose & the Smoke to stay near to the only person who could betray me to the British. The only one who knew I was still alive."

"Abercrombie!" you gasp. Constantina smirks.

"Not quite as stupid as you seem. Yes, I needed to keep an eye on him. The old fool was consumed with guilt and was going to blab—I could tell. He did it for the money, you see, and not his beliefs. His resolve was weak. He just wanted to repair that old ruin he laughingly called a castle. Then, when the payment for his betrayal wasn't what he expected, it finally hit him that he had sold out his country."

"But why did you reveal yourself now?" you ask. "What happened?"

Constantina again throws back her head and laughs coldly. "What happened? What happened is *you* arrived."

Mac squeezes your shoulder, and you see him tighten his grip on his dirk. Ollie, meanwhile, stares at Constantina in silent horror, his eyes like those of a man who knows he is about to drown. If she notices, Constantina doesn't show it.

"I realized that when clearing out the orphanage. Anyone might come across Abercrombie's papers. I always suspected the old fool had kept something as a safeguard, in case he needed to name names in order to save his neck."

"And you couldn't allow that to happen," you say. Constantina's eyes light up with righteous fury.

"Of course not! I had to keep myself safe. I needed the evidence destroyed, and you out of the way, so I set the place on fire!"

Mac gasps and starts forward, but you place a hand on his chest. He looks at you, quizzical, and you shake your head.

"I thought that I was finally free," Constantina continues. "So I decided to use the opportunity to get out of London. But then I saw that you had that wretched paper incriminating me. And Abercrombie, that fool, had managed to save the chest with the rest in it. So, you see, I had to follow you and make sure you never found out . . ." She turns to you, her face blazing with hate. "Or make sure you were silenced if you did."

"I loved you!" Ollie cries, finally finding his voice.

"I loved you, too . . . in my way," Constantina says. "We can still be together, as one. Let us kill these two and escape!"

"Never!" Ollie hisses. Constantina starts for a second, nothing more. Then her eyes flash eerily cold, and a deadly smile twitches at the corner of her mouth.

"Then you shall die."

. . . .

Seriously, cripes.

Do you try to defeat the evil spy lady? If so, turn to page 84.

Or do you hold back? Ollie, unlike you, is a trained spy, and he can probably handle himself. If so, turn to page 119.

"Fighting is useless, chérie." Fabien regards you fiercely, yet gently, with an intensity that both shocks and arouses you.

The bustling city of Cairo is far behind and the sky darkening to night before Fabien lets go of your mouth. You scream, of course, but no one but he and his associated brigands are within earshot. One of them disembarks from his camel, carrying heavy ropes with which to bind you.

Fabien manages to swing you down from the camel with surprising ease and unstudied grace for one so powerful, while remaining seated upon his dromedary steed.

"Fighting is useless, *chérie*." He regards you fiercely, yet gently, with an intensity that both shocks and arouses you. With a rumbling chuckle, he dismounts. "We will not harm you, for we are only here to deliver you to the lady who has paid us."

"And the lady? What does she want with me?!" you pant. Fabien's Nile-green eyes flicker, if only for an instant.

"Who can say?" he says with a nonchalant shrug. You trust him not one Egyptian royal cubit.

Instead, you try to take in your surroundings and formulate a plan. Dazed and disoriented, you are unsure you know the way back to Cairo, and even less sure you would survive the journey. Still, would death be any worse than what you fear this band has planned for you?

....

If death would be no worse, and you wish to fight the brigands immediately, turn to page 173.

If in fact, now that you think on it, death would probably be worse, and you wish to focus on not being dead for the time being, turn to page 290.

You stagger through the house, drunk with moonlight, your thoughts racing. You must find Lord Craven. Feelings be damned, you must know what the hell is going on in this house. It is not long before you crash headlong into the object of your thoughts just outside his bedchamber.

You immediately fall into a rush of desperate kisses, each deeper than the last. Your entire body thrills to his touch, but that will have to wait.

"Easy, man!" you cry. "I believe I have just seen your dead wife! Do you think me mad?"

Craven drops to his knees, a sign of dramatic relief. "I have seen her, too," he answers, raking his hands through his mane of hair, wildly stoking your desire as he does. "I thought it was just me. I thought I was losing my mind."

"The specter . . ." you speak slowly. "She has haunted you before?"

"Yes," Craven chokes out, close to breaking into a sob or feeling the tender joy of sexual release. You really cannot tell with him.

"There is something very wrong in this house," you say. You allow Craven to lift your skirts with hungry hands.

"Yes," Craven murmurs into the sacred space between your thighs. Your body arches to sate his starvation. Pleasure burns straight up your spine, into your hair, sparking your eyes, roaring so loud in your ears that you almost don't hear him whisper, "Sometimes I think it will drag me down with it!"

"It won't while I'm around," you say, running your fingers through the silken waves of the dark ocean of his hair. "Tonight, we sleep together . . . to protect each other!"

He nods, his mouth worshiping at your hidden temple, and he tumbles you backward into his rooms. He lifts his head from your nethers to take a deep drink of you, his eyes running over every curve of your body. His look is so intense, you gasp. The moment you do, he kisses you so that in essence you are breathing him. He tastes of spice and blood, he smells of fire and forest, and you are so alive with desire that you forget you are a lady. You begin to tear your dress from your body in the forgetting. His limber fingers help you free yourself from any and all constriction, and he takes you there, half clothed, thrusting deeper than any fear could reach, until you are both clawing for more.

You are close to reaching a transcendent state of being, but then loud banging pierces the euphoria of your ecstasy.

. . . .

Bother. Do you stop and investigate, for there is a mystery afoot?! Go to page 326.

Or do you ignore the banging in favor of continuing some other banging? There is probably a logical explanation for the sound, plus this is seriously becoming the most euphoric encounter you've ever had. Go to page 240.

"I will travel with you anywhere!" you cry. "Wherever you go, I shall follow! I don't care about the danger, as long as I am with you!"

"Oh, my darling!" sighs Evangeline, embracing you deeply. "I don't know why, but I knew, I always knew that—" She is interrupted by a stifled but loud sob.

You look up. It takes you a moment to realize that the hard-bitten viragos surrounding you are all sniffling and sighing to a woman. Even the angry Gráinne is somewhat misty-eyed.

"Oh . . . oh, just *kiss her*, you eejit!" she mutters under her breath. You blush and look away, but Evangeline takes charge, her arm still wrapped around your waist.

"Ladies!" she says. "I have a proposition. I have much coin and am in need of some allies capable of facing the most dangerous woman I have ever met and the good-for-nothings in her employ. You, I fancy, are all more than capable of this work, and you wouldn't refuse some hefty compensation. So . . . what do you say? Will you join me in righting the terrible wrongs that have been visited upon those I care about, including this beautiful young woman?"

The entire tavern roars in approval. Evangeline turns to you and winks.

"But, my lady!" you whisper. "How will we find where she is? Even most of her henchmen don't know her whereabouts!"

Evangeline leans toward you and smiles conspiratorially.

"Well, my darling, there is one thing that those brutes don't have."

Your eyes widen.

"The contents of the canister, my dear! We've got the location of the lost Temple of Hathor!"

Turn to page 120.

"**STOP! Stop this madness!**" You aim Ollie's pistol at the two men. They stop and stare at you.

"Don't you see?!" you cry. "Constantina tried to kill Mac because she was trying to hide something! She was walking toward the French not because she was drunk, but on purpose! She was the informant!"

"But she wasn't in the chain of command for Mac's regiment!" shouts Ollie. "How could she have known the things that were handed to the French? Things that even I, in the same spy cell, didn't know about until years later?!"

"Because she was passing on information for someone else," you explain gently, fixing your eyes now on Mac. "From what you both have told me, there is only one person who could be the mole. One who is known very well to you, Mac."

Terrible comprehension breaks across the faces of the two men. You nod at them gravely.

"That is right. Constantina was the conduit, but the information was provided by Abercrombie!"

Och, man! Turn to page 137.

"I did everything you told me to, my lady. I gave the false diary you wrote to the vicar, so he in turn would give it to the next fool he saw fit to help carry out your plans. I kept your true diary to myself. Of course, I have never touched it—I know this volume must be full of your secret dreams and desires. I have been your faithful Manvers, I have, indeed."

You steal a silent step into the morning room. Oblivious to your presence, Manvers is seated before a portrait of Blanche, speaking to it as if she were a woman whose blood flowed warm and lively 'neath her flesh.

"Your hatred for Hopesend is clear as a bell," he goes on. "I hope you love what I have done with the place, my lady. The others . . . they don't love you like I love you. They don't, I swear they don't! A-ha! A-ha-ha-ha!"

Your blood chills as Manvers's cold little laugh fills the night air. You take one step farther, and the moment you do, his head turns, slow and steady, like a wicked eel. Something smells strange suddenly. Something smells wrong.

"No one loves a child as someone who should have been a father, I say!" Manvers speaks to you with blank eyes. You thrill with fear, and identify the strange scent that has vexed you—smoke.

"What have you done, Manvers?" you ask, your even voice betraying nothing of your fears. "What have you done?"

"What I should have done long ago," he answers with a simple, horrifying smile. "Burn this place to the ground."

Uh-oh. Turn to page 112.

"I see that you have something of a rapport with my bastard half brother?" Cad smirks. "It must be very disappointing, to go from having hooked a noble to having designs upon a have-not in the space of just one evening."

"I have no hooks and no designs upon your brother," you say defiantly.

"Is that so?" murmurs Cad. To your disappointment, your body is roaring at the sinewy length of him pressed against you. "Does dear Benny know that?" You look up to find Benedict staring daggers at you. You stare daggers right back and turn again to Cad.

"What he thinks is of no matter to me," you say as primly as you can manage. "For I am more interested in what is about with you . . . It must have been very gratifying to find yourself the heir to a fortune so suddenly. How did you discover the truth? Was it known to you for long, or have you just found out yourself?"

"What does that matter?" he whispers, clearly suspicious.

"Oh, nothing," you say coquettishly. "I am just interested in what you have to say."

Cad moves even closer. You realize, too late, that you might be in over your head.

"Well, what I say is that I mean to have you!" he hisses. He grabs your wrist and leans in closer still.

"I would never marry you!" You struggle to escape his grasp.

"Oh, do not mistake me, sweeting," he jeers. "I want your honor, not your hand. I have no wish to marry. Bother dear brother Benny for all that, if you have it in you to pine for a stuffed-shirt pauper!"

He raises the hand not holding your wrist in a vicelike grip and strokes your face. You recoil at his touch, but Cad continues, undeterred.

"Still, a sweet little chit like you could do worse than to be the kept woman of a man like me. Rich. Well-stationed. Legitimate. So hungry and so satisfying in all ways that matter."

Out of the corner of your eye, you see a familiar dark figure stalking purposefully toward you. Benedict's silver-gray eyes blaze with a mix of outrage and what looks oddly like concern.

"Cad . . ." Benedict's voice is a low warning.

"Not now, Benny," Cad sneers. "This lovely young lady and I are having an—AARGH!"

Suddenly, Cad is doubled over in pain, for you have taken the opportunity of his distraction to inflict deadly damage to his iron-hard manhood with your knee.

"Oops."

Benedict stares openmouthed as you gather your skirts with exaggerated modesty and step around his fallen half brother. You cannot resist turning and raising an eyebrow to that handsome face—the one that causes your foolish loins to ache.

"Shocked, Sir Benedict?" you say as confidently as possible.

"No. I'm . . . impressed."

You are startled out of your triumph. This will not do at all. Benedict seems to agree, for his expression turns uncharacteristically shaken.

Never mind that, nor the fact that you would very much like to brush the dark locks off of that beautiful, dumbfounded face. You have work to do. Squaring your shoulders, you stalk primly out of the room . . . and hear the sound of a young girl sobbing down the corridor.

. . . .

You really have no choice here, for intrigue is afoot! Follow those sobs and turn to page 206.

Lady Craven hobbles up the steps of the exquisite London manse belonging to Lady Evangeline Youngblood, her niece. An extremely rich widow, Lady Evangeline is patroness of the Society for the Protection of Widows and Orphans of the War—a position that does a great deal to quell the unkind whispers about her scandalous behavior.

You have met Lady Evangeline only a few times and were intimidated by her beauty and elegance. Still, you cannot help but like her, for she is warm, witty, and one of the few people who can get Lady Craven to behave herself (as the old witch relies on her for the occasional handout). It is for this reason that you are relieved when she swoops in almost immediately, settles Lady Craven upon a chair, and leads you by the arm around the ballroom.

"I must say, I'm impressed," whispers Lady Evangeline, her sapphire eyes flashing with humor and sympathy as you make your escape. "For you have lasted far longer than any of Aunt Aurelia's other companions. You must have nerves of steel, my dear."

You start to protest, but Lady Evangeline shushes you with a hint of a smile playing about her lush pink mouth.

"Don't worry, there is no need to be polite. Not one member of this godforsaken family is unaware of my aunt's, *ahem*, singular nature. Why, even her son barely speaks to her, and he is certainly someone who does not intimidate easily. Have you met him?"

"Lord Garraway Craven? Oh, no." You can feel the heat rising to your face. "But I have heard . . . rumors. He was an associate of Lord Byron, was he not?"

Lady Evangeline sniffs her delicate nose and tosses her elegant head. Her artfully arranged curls glimmer golden in the light of the hundreds of candles that decorate the ballroom. "Ah, yes, Garraway certainly was for a time. But that was before he managed to scare off Byron with his, *ahem*, antics."

Lady Evangeline smiles so dazzlingly, you feel you must have imagined the haunted expression that briefly crossed her face. All the same, you dare not inquire further. Instead you listen politely as she steers the subject away from her mysterious cousin.

"Still, I suppose it's all for the best. In most families, *I* would be the black sheep, but compared to the cabal of sinners I'm related to, I look positively respectable!" She winks conspiratorially. "Well, perhaps Benedict does, too. Though he has his rakish moments."

As you walk with her, you become increasingly aware of several pairs of hungry eyes turned in your direction. You can't say you blame them, for Lady Evangeline is looking even more exquisite than usual this evening, with her blue silk dress the exact shade as her eyes, cut daringly low and clinging to every curve. You look down at your shabby gown and feel even plainer and dowdier by comparison. The only fine thing you own is a simple gold bracelet, a gift from your mother before she died.

Lady Evangeline seems oblivious to the commotion she is causing among the menfolk of the ton. She turns her piercing gaze to you.

"My dear, I have a confession to make. You see, I insisted that Aunt Craven bring you to this ball for a reason—" Lady Evangeline stops suddenly as you feel someone bump into you and drench your dress. You look down and see a red river of wine spreading across your ugly yellow frock.

"Oh, dash it, I'm so terribly sorry!" says a short and nervous-looking young man. "I do hope it isn't ruined!"

He looks so frightened and is so bumbling that you take pity on him. "Oh, I assure you that with this dress, that would be quite impossible," you tell him kindly.

"Nigel Frickley, you clever dear!" exclaims Lady Evangeline. "I was looking for an excuse to disrobe this lovely young lady."

Nigel blushes even more crimson than the wine now staining your dress. "I—um—er . . ." he stammers before Lady Evangeline cuts him off.

"You see, the rags my Aunt Craven has passed off on this poor young thing are simply hideous and ought to be replaced at once. Truly, you have performed a public service."

And with that, she leads you out of the ballroom. You really have no choice but to accompany her—ruined dress aside, Lady Evangeline is not the sort of woman to whom one says no. Once you arrive in her chambers, she hands you something blue-green and silky.

"I think you will look ravishing in this," she promises before helping you out of your old gown.

She pulls you into the expensive-looking garment and helps you with the many buttons on the back as she continues her conversation. "Forgive me for being forward, but I do feel that you are unhappy in your current position."

You say nothing but turn your head toward her and nod in silent misery. She meets your gaze and continues, with genuine sympathy filling her cultured tones.

"So I must know, have you made any inquiries for other means of employment? Or received any offers?"

"I . . . I have heard that Lord Craven was looking for a governess for his young son . . . ," you venture shyly, thinking of the envelope he had recently sent the Dragon asking if she knew any prospective governesses she could soon send to him in Ravenscar. You immediately regret broaching the matter when you see the horror in Lady Evangeline's expression.

"Oh, heavens no! I would sooner throw an infant to wolves than send an innocent young woman to work for Cousin Garraway!" Lady Evangeline shudders ever so slightly. "Well, let us hope we do not become so desperate that you have to resort to *that*. Anything else?"

"Er, Sir Charles Burley-Fanshaw has been coming to call, and I think perhaps he may—"

Lady Evangeline gasps. "Oh, my dear, he is ancient! I fancy you could do much better than *him*."

"I'm afraid not, my lady," you say quietly. "You see, I have been left without a dowry nor any means of supporting myself after my dear papa was lost at sea, and—"

Lady Evangeline finishes buttoning your dress and spins you to face the mirror. "That may well be, but on the other hand, just *look*."

You look. The dress—cut demurely enough for a young unmarried lady such as yourself, yet somehow suggestive in the way it clings to your body—has utterly transformed you.

"You see, my dear, I believe you can do much better than purgatory with Aunt Aurelia or shackling yourself to an odious old toad. And it is high time we did something about that."

She leads you back downstairs and explains further. "I shall make inquiries on your behalf for a suitable position. I'm sure there will be other offers for a charming young lady such as yourself. In the meantime, I suggest you have some fun with a few eligible gentlemen."

Lady Evangeline raises an eyebrow suggestively. You only just manage to stifle the unladylike giggle that bubbles up, and she beams at you. "That's the spirit! Now, whom would you like to meet first? My cousin, Sir Benedict Granville?"

She points toward a tall, dark figure leaning casually against a pillar. "Poor Benny. He finds balls ever so tiresome. You see, half the mamas of the ton are desperately trying to get him to marry their daughters because of his fortune, but he makes the daughters so nervous with his brooding manner and good looks that they clam up entirely around him. What he really needs is someone to challenge him, I fancy. I wonder if you could liven up this sorry event for him?"

Your eyes then turn to a broad-shouldered form on the edge of the dance floor. The man's hair is the russet color of autumn leaves at sunset. Lady Evangeline grins.

"You've spotted our handsome Scotsman, Captain Angus MacTaggart! He was frightfully brave at Waterloo, but he now works for the Society for the Protection of Widows and Orphans of the War. He is a wonder at raising money—no one can say no to a war hero, especially with a face like that—but he's an even greater wonder at caring for orphans. Shall I make an introduction?"

....

You gaze at these two attractive and potentially interesting men and try to decide whom to meet first.

If you pick the handsome and nobly sardonic cousin of Lady Evangeline, turn to page 232.

If you pick the dashing and caring Scot, turn to page 35.

"I think I should stay behind," you say. "The museum needs help and Kamal must recover from his injuries."

Lady Evangeline smiles at you.

"You have a good heart, my dear. Never lose that." She rests an elegant hand on your cheek. "Just remember—you are far more capable than you realize. I think you can make a real difference here."

Over the next few weeks, you take her advice to heart. Your days are filled with industry and, in their own quiet way, excitement, as you right the fallen artifacts, match them with Kamal's meticulous cataloging, and find just the right place to display each piece. As the museum slowly comes together, you feel yourself swell with pride at the sight of each mummified cat, and each canopic jar filled with intestines fills a hole in your soul that you did not realize was there.

You also tend to Kamal as he recovers, and you find yourself looking forward to time spent with the sweet-natured Egyptologist. After the doctor pronounces him well enough to rise, you tenderly lead him to see what you have done with his life's work.

"But this is wonderful!" he gasps.

"You like it?" you venture shyly.

He gives you a lingering look from the liquid pools of his intelligent cocoa eyes, his boyishly handsome face still marked with bruises.

"I-I think I should offer you a job! You are the best curator I have ever had," he says.

"Oh, Kamal," you exclaim as you throw your arms around him. "That would be wonderful!"

Your vigorous motion upends the papers he is carrying, and a notebook falls to the floor. You are shocked to see that in it he has sketched your face lovingly in the margins, in the same delicate style in which he draws all of his beloved artifacts.

"Oh, Kamal! What is this?" you ask, blushing.

"It . . . I . . . oh, miss, I am sorry. I am too forward. It . . . it's just that . . . I . . ."

You realize that in his own shy way, this is a confession of love. You stare at him in wonder.

As you each gaze into the other's eyes for a few, deliciously loaded moments, you realize nothing more needs to be said, for you both know you have found your other half in this life. Suddenly, Kamal pulls you into his arms and kisses you with a passion you didn't know he had.

The next thing you know, you are tearing at each other's clothes and making feverish love among the mummies. It doesn't matter—they are dead. But your loins are alive!

You marry, of course, and are blissfully happy. You also feature as ongoing comedic side characters for the continued series of Lady Evangeline's adventures, always providing a safe space and a sympathetic ear when called upon. She drops in from time to time between quests to tell stories to your enthralled offspring. Little Evangeline, your eldest (and sole nonbookish) child, particularly loves these visits from her rambunctious godmother and namesake and grows up to be quite the adventurer herself.

The museum flourishes under your careful eye, and your legacy is continued in the capable hands of your many adorably studious children. The museum still stands to this day in the heart of Cairo, a wonder for all to see, with your and Kamal's names inscribed in the entranceway on its grand facade.

The End

A few weeks later, you are standing at the docks with Evangeline, seeing Henrietta off with her farmer love. Thanks to some strings expertly pulled by Evangeline, they are traveling to a new life that waits for them abroad. Now armed with assumed names to protect them from Cad, along with their blissful happiness, they wave at you from the ship.

Yet the sight of the young lovers entwined cannot help but cause you pangs. Lady Evangeline notices and tries to shake you from your gloomy reverie.

"You have truly impressed me, my dear," she says. "I have a thought."

"Yes, Lady Evangeline?" you say cautiously. She takes both your hands in hers and fixes you with a piercing sapphire gaze.

"You might have heard that I am taking a trip to Egypt soon. I was wondering, would you care to join me as my lady's companion?"

You stare at her in wonder. Egypt would be a wonderful adventure . . . but it will take you far from any chance of seeing Benedict again.

Do you take her up on the offer? Turn to page 193.

Or does your heart still beat for one impossible, infuriating, wonderful man— and for him alone? Turn to page 108.

"You . . . you are mad!" you scream at Loveday. You stagger from him, desperate to find Craven and safety.

Loveday grabs you by the neck. His elegant hands steal the breath from your throat as he lets his own fill the bowl of your ear.

"Very well, you fool. I suppose I shall have to go with my original plan. Such a shame to crush so beautiful a throat. But just think how it will play out in the press! I, the good, purehearted vicar, find your lifeless body in the eldritch garden. Then, after Lord Craven snaps and kills himself, I find out I am next in line to inherit. The headlines write themselves."

Do you fight tooth and nail to break free from the reverend's clutches? Turn to page 314.

Or do you play dead in a desperate attempt to survive? Turn to page 238.

The person who liked Mrs. Caddington least in Drury Lane turns out to be none other than assistant costumer Viola Orlando. She greets you with virtually no interest in your bona fides once you drop Mrs. Caddington's name.

"Rebecca, you mean." Viola stabs a pin into a dress form she is draping with diaphanous fabric. You have been ushered into her workshop, as well as offered tea and biscuits, despite the late hour. "Awful woman. Mediocre actress. Lovely hair. I should have been her, you know."

"Oh?" You note the faded but attractive looks of the elder costumer. The excellent diction. The fine, expressive hands.

"I was an actress first, of course." Viola's voice is flat with aged anger. "But when Rebecca came, she snapped up all the roles. She was voracious. Ambitious. Silly me, I was just *good*."

Lady Evangeline opens her mouth to speak, but you surreptitiously shake your head. Viola is only too eager to continue.

"I'm good with the fabric, of course, and I love every part of the theater, so here we are. But I'll have you know, the only good reviews her husband ever wrote about actresses here were about me. 'Luminous,' I was called. Rebecca, he had not much praise for. Not until he let her work him over, of course. And when his mind went, she chucked him in Bedlam so fast your head would spin, not that he had any family but her to mind. Lucky Rebecca, too, to have a nobleman waiting to ride in on his white steed to save her. Snatching up the men like she did the roles."

Your heart skips. "The nobleman Rebecca married, do you remember his name?" you ask.

"Granville, of course." Another pin, another stab.

"An excellent memory you have, madam," you say. "It has been some time from those days."

"I was always good with my lines. Picture-perfect memory. Yes, Granville was the name. The old nob got her in the family way, mind, hence the hasty marriage, an affront to the law and the Lord though it was."

You and Lady Evangeline share a knowing glance. The older woman plows on with her tale, each word dripping in venom.

"Rich as all get-out the second husband was. Rebecca always did land on her feet. Still, I suppose it was lucky that he was wealthy enough to support the strumpet and the babe. But I shouldn't say. I tell Mr. Caddington so, though he doesn't know what I'm saying half the time. I like to think he likes to hear the words, though. I like to think I remind him of the good old days, when he had some."

"Wait." Your voice catches. "This . . . Mr. Caddington. Who lost his sense. You are saying he is still alive . . . and in Bedlam?"

"Of course he's alive, love!" Viola laughs and gives you a queer look. "I visit the man every Sunday. Someone's got to be good to him, it might as well be me."

"Thank you, Viola," you say, thrilling at your discovery. If Mr. Caddington is still alive and not divorced by Mrs. Caddington, that would mean she married the late Sir Granville bigamously, thus making Cad an illegitimate heir and Henrietta a lovechild. You turn to leave.

"Wait." Viola stops you at the door. "What was it you wanted to ask about?"

"Whatever it was, dear lady," you say with a smile, "you have answered us already."

This seems to be a most damning situation for Cad! Hurry on to page 139.

You desperately need a proper bath, which you take, and then indulge in a moonlit stroll near the castle. Thus refreshed, you still have much to think over. But no sooner can you begin to sort things out when you stumble upon Abercrombie at one of the castle's half-ruined outbuildings. There, struck by moonlight and a fevered look, the old man sifts through papers he takes from one of the open drawers of the wooden chest he's dragged all the way from London—London, which now seems a world away.

"Good evening, Abercrombie!" you cry, suddenly heartened by the entire mess of a situation you've found yourself in by coming to the Highlands. Whatever is happening with Mac, it is certainly a thousand times more interesting than spending your life laying out the Dowager Dragon's clothes.

"Aye! Lassie!" Abercrombie responds in his hale and hearty way. "And where is your beau?"

You blush. "If you mean Mac, he is in the stable. Seems a foal decided today was fit to be his birthday."

"Sounds like Mac, aye." Abercrombie laughs, but casts a nervous glance down at the papers in his hand. He looks a bit like someone searching for something, or like a doddering old man who has misplaced his glasses.

"Looking for something?" you ask. "If one of the children has been messing about in your things, I—"

"No, no, lassie. No need to get in a twist. I'm just taking a walk down memory lane, since you and wee Angus have Lover's Lane quite marked for yourselves." Abercrombie's eyes positively twinkle with mischief.

"I don't know about that," you respond, laughing. And blushing. More than a little.

"Now, lass. You have been a blessing to us all, but more than that to Mac. Whatever ye are to each other, be forgiving of the boy's past. 'Tisn't his present, nor his future."

Doubt rises inside you like a welling cold spring. "What's gone on in Mac's past?"

"Och, you know the boy was a wild one when he was a lad. But when he was a soldier, he saw things. Did things. All soldiers do." Abercrombie's eyes still twinkle, but also search yours.

"What kind of things?" you say. Abercrombie, seemingly relieved, shakes his head.

"More will ye know in time, I am sure. Lover's Lane is that way, lass," he says with a laugh. "Take your leave and find your way back, before Mac has my head for keeping ye all to myself!"

You laugh, but the gesture feels empty. If Mac has loved many women before, you could wind up just another disposable bit o' fluff. As you contemplate, your feet somehow find their way back to the stable. Cursing your woolheadedness, you see a light burning in the window and hear the new foal's first whinny. You smile despite yourself, pleased at the good work Mac seems to do wherever he goes. Could he truly be such a rake?

You take a step toward your decided destination, but never make it there. A hand claps over your mouth, and a strange, sultry, familiar voice whispers close in your ear.

"You need to get out of here *now*!"

....

You have no choice against this powerful manly hand and its owner's voice.
Turn to page 256.

You instinctively seek out Mrs. Butts. Not only does she have the run of the house, but she must also have hold of its secrets. You try to work out how exactly you will broach the subject of vengeful ghosts and/or spiteful dead wives when your quiet march toward the servants' quarters is shattered by a sharp voice ringing in your ear.

"Dead girl! Bad man!"

You leap a mile. There, out of place and blazing with purpose, is Higgenbottom, the groundskeeper. His hoe glints in the late afternoon light. His eyes, wild and wide, express an urgency you can't quite understand.

"Who is the bad man, Higgenbottom?" you ask, searching his face for a clue.

A pained grimace contorts his features. He reaches out a gnarled hand that holds a gift: a crushed bar of chocolate.

Your throat catches when you see the label. "Swiss chocolate," you read in a hoarse whisper.

"Still here," Higgenbottom whispers. You are struck by the strained sadness of his voice.

"Who is still here, Higgenbottom?"

"It does not do well for a governess to snoop on her employer. Know your place." Ugh. There, halfway down the stairs and sneering so hard you can see up his nostrils, is Manvers.

"It does even worse for an employee to think he holds rank over his employer's lover," you spit back.

"You play with fire, girl," Manvers hisses as you stalk past him, hopefully to find Mrs. Butts.

"If I do," you toss back over your shoulder, "you, too, will be burned."

You leave the insufferable manservant in your wake, swiftly so that he can't see how badly you are shaking.

After several hours, you finally find Mrs. Butts doing some late-night dusting in the foyer, along with Betsy, the mute servant girl. The sight of Mrs. Butts, hunched over and hard at work, sends your heart out. You want nothing more than to find a happier home for you two to work in, one where you could beam with joy at jobs well done, at happy families you help raise with your expert teamwork and unflappable natures. Perhaps, in another life, such simple pleasures will be possible. In this one, you need to know . . .

"Everything, Mrs. Butts. Tell me everything!" You beg her as a coworker and, you hope, as a friend. "Please tell me everything about Helena, and Blanche, and—"

"What is all this urgency about, my dear? It's such a sad matter, my heart breaks each time I think on it. Helena were Alexander's twin. She and her mama died tragically in an accident with a fireplace."

Betsy shakes her head, her eyes wide with horror.

"Lord Craven has never spoken of this," you say, the worry saturating your voice.

"Master Craven tried to save them, love. But it were too late. It broke his heart . . . what were left of it."

Betsy turns her wide eyes at Mrs. Butts, who claps a hand over her mouth.

"I've . . . I've said too much," Mrs. Butts stammers.

"No, no, my good woman!" You are desperate. "You have not said enough! For all I know, Blanche von Badwolff was a beautiful young bride who died suddenly! You know more, you know what I need to!"

"That woman were beautiful in face and body alone, love. Not in soul. Her soul were twisted and vile. She despised those little children, the way she despised anyone she thought beneath her. But now that is me speaking ill of the dead, and I shouldn't, love." As she speaks, you watch Mrs. Butts's eyes flash with dark, unknown memories.

The situation is getting increasingly messy. You can't separate fact from feeling, and feeling from fiction. You sense all logic slipping through your grasping fingers and are wondering what to do next when the clock strikes, a crow cries, and the house's front door is flung open, all at the same time.

The handsome vicar stands in the doorway.

"Hello, Reverend," Mrs. Butts says, sliding into full-on welcome mode. "Lord Craven is occupied at the moment—"

"I did not come to call on Lord Craven, my dear Mrs. Butts. I came on urgent business . . ." He turns to face you. "With you."

Your heart drops as your temperature rises.

"Forgive my intrusion, but I will be only a moment," the vicar says in a loud, amiable way, before lowering his tone to a whisper for you, and you alone. "I need to meet with you. Tonight, in the eldritch garden."

He takes your hand and kisses it. The motion is quick but sears you to the core. He searches your eyes for a haunted moment; then, confident at what he finds there, he turns away to address Mrs. Butts and Betsy once more. "See you all at church on Sunday!"

And then he is gone.

Holy hell. Turn to page 174.

With the traitor locked up in Glenblair's dungeon, Ollie heads straight to the nearest militia, and word is sent to London. A few days later, a smartly dressed man arrives: Lord Fleming, the top spymaster in Britain. What he recounts nearly causes you to swoon.

"I don't believe it," you say, dazed. "Could this be true?"

"Believe it," Lord Fleming replies in the crisp, efficient tones of a professional turncoat. "We've ensured that Glenblair Castle belongs to the Society for the Protection of Widows and Orphans of the War. And that Ruston here has received a fair share of reward money for capturing the traitor Abercrombie, and—"

"And I want you to have it," Ollie speaks in a rush. Lord Fleming does not seem to appreciate being interrupted.

"Oh, Ollie," you say. "Thank you."

Lord Fleming takes your arm. "I hear from young Ruston that you spotted the trap laid by the blackguard Abercrombie. How the devil did you manage it?"

"Simply, my lord," you say. "After I ruled out Mac as the mole and considered what both he and Ollie told me about Constantina and the regiment, the only possible person it could be was Abercrombie. Besides the man's predilection for burning papers and the evidence hidden in his blasted wooden chest, the note he sent, which he intended to look like Ollie—Ruston—had written it, was a hopeless forgery. I have known Mr. Ruston since childhood, and he has written me many terrible poems"—Ollie's face reddens—"so I would know his handwriting anywhere. That is how I knew to bring reinforcements."

"Remarkable," Lord Fleming says. "You know, we could use a resourceful, canny, and beautiful young lady such as yourself in the secret service."

....

Well, there's a tantalizing offer!

Do you accept? Spies *are* fantastically intriguing . . . Turn to page 16.

Or do you turn down his kind offer? Turn to page 48.

You and Craven watch young Alexander as he sleeps, his sweet face now placid and smiling gently.

It is not just the boy who has been transformed. As the dawn breaks, a peace descends over the house, the likes of which you have never felt before. The rooms appear lighter, the air cleaner, and even the remaining paintings bear a more benign expression. It is as if the deadly fever that had consumed Hopesend has finally broken, and there is hope for life . . . and perhaps love.

Craven turns to you and strokes your hair.

"You have saved us all," he says. "But I know that it would be cruel to keep you here. Not when you could be free—free to love a worthy man. Free to go about your business without a care in the world." He speaks with a tremor in his voice and a mixture of sadness and hope in his eyes.

"I can find a place for you, far from here. In America, with an honorable man of my acquaintance. One who I know will be a good employer."

. . . .

Do you want to get out of here? Turn to page 183.

Or do you know that Craven is just frightened and pushing you away? He loves you! And needs you! Then turn to page 39.

You nod at Mac and lock your gaze onto his hazel eyes, sharing a moment of connection and understanding so profound that it needs no words. Which is fortunate, under the circumstances, since you hardly have time for sweet nothings.

"Death is no matter to me. It will come as a relief!" cries Ollie to his traitorous ex-lover. Constantina smirks.

"Then you are a fool. A fool who is about to learn what happens to those who cross me!"

Now is your chance. When she is busy cackling villainously and not paying a great deal of attention to her surroundings, you nod, silent as ever, and Mac takes your lead. Moving as one, you creep toward her stealthily. Mac readies his dirk, and you remove your shoes and one stocking, feeling about for a heavy rock or something similar to create a makeshift bludgeon.

"Perhaps it will be a relief," Constantina says. "But first, dear Ollie, for your foolish decision to be more loyal to your country than to me, you shall watch your friends die before you!"

She aims her pistol where you and Mac once stood . . . and gasps as she realizes that you are no longer there. Seizing the opening, you swing your stocking-rock and clock her squarely in the head. She collapses, the gun slipping from her fingers, and falls into Mac, who places his dirk at her throat.

As Ollie stares in cold rage at his former *amour*, you use your other stocking to bind Constantina's wrists.

"Let's go," you command. "To the castle."

....

Nicely rigged, you! March on to page 156.

"I choose you. I choose pleasure. I choose *now*," you whisper, releasing yourself from the trappings of the person you thought you were and the one you might become. Delphine and Evangeline are lost in each other, and for all you know you all are lost in the desert. You might as well lose yourself in the vast expanse of Fabien's pectorals and your shared desire.

"Worship me. Revel in me. Anoint me," you murmur into the soft hardness of his body, your tongue lapping his skin as if it were life-giving water.

"Yes, my queen," Fabien moans, as you slide the sword of his body first into your mouth, then into the hidden temple of your sex.

You devour each other with senseless passion as desert winds whip torrents of sand around you like so much confetti. You would be concerned about it getting in places it shouldn't, but you are too busy being overcome with a feeling of divine blessedness and crying out with ecstasy to care. You are wetter than the Nile for this man, and he navigates your depths with the skill and magic of a sailor who knows his way to and from worlds beyond the earthly plane.

Suddenly, the earthly plane beneath you shudders and bucks. At first, you think it is Fabien trying something new and a little rough, but then you realize he has been flung a small distance from you by the shifting sands. Farther away, you see that no such disruption has pulled Delphine and Evangeline from their embrace.

Fabien crawls toward you over the violently trembling sands, as what can only be the lost Temple of Hathor breaks through the desert floor like a giant hand reaching out to steal the sun.

As the temple rises impossibly high, almost blocking out the sun with its beauty and size, Fabien leans over to you.

"Do you think it is for us?" he asks incredulously.

"Perhaps," you say. "But I think not."

In fact, the more intensely Evangeline and Delphine kiss, the higher the tower seems to rise. It shimmers for a moment, and then solidifies, a mirage no longer. The temple is risen. The temple is real.

You shake your head in wonder. The sand storm quiets, and the desert is as calm as a distant sea.

As disappointed as you are to leave your friend, you cannot help but feel glad for the happy couple. Nothing will please Evangeline more than to investigate the ultimate in Egyptologist fantasy—and nothing will make Delphine happier than Evangeline's happiness. Rather than brood, you grin at Fabien and walk over to one of the camels waiting patiently on the outskirts of the camp.

"Still, maybe love's truest pleasure is shared adventure?" You mount the noble beast and gesture toward Fabien. "Shall we?" You smile wryly.

He swings himself onto another camel and nods.

You admire Fabien's fearsome, almost feline form as he effortlessly guides his beast of burden to intrigue and adventures. Who knows what will come, but you certainly will, until your next adventure. You spur your camel to follow his . . . and quickly realize the fatal flaw in your current scheme.

"Er . . . Fabien?" you call out. "How exactly does one direct one of these things?"

The End

You address None-of-Your-Business. "You there. Most ornery child." He scowls.

"What's ornery?" he asks.

"I'll tell you once you drag that blackboard into the street. We are going to make the world our schoolroom. We are going OUTSIDE!"

The children cheer. Together, you and the mass of miniature ruffians maneuver the blackboard out of the room with a minimum of sweat and tears. Just as you've passed the last bit of the board over the threshold, Abercrombie approaches.

"Aye, lass! I reckon your moxie will take Mac for quite the surprise!" While Abercrombie congratulates you, you notice his gaze search over your shoulder and alight on a fine wooden chest shoved near the back of the messy schoolroom. "I've had the stroke o' luck to round up some friends in the neighborhood. You teach your lesson, and by the time you get back, me 'n' my boys will have this place fixed up for you, good as new!"

You beam. "Thank you, Colonel Abercrombie!"

"'Tis my pleasure, miss," Abercrombie says and beams back. He starts the cleanup by moving the fine wooden chest.

You lead the children (and the blackboard) out to the gray street, then put your hands on your hips. "Ornery," you say. "Is that a word any of you know?"

The children look at their tattered shoes in shame.

"No," None-of-Your-Business says, and he scowls again.

"Well," you continue, "have you ever met a cat that creeps up close to you, but then swipes at you when you pet it?"

"YES!" the children answer in unison.

"Or a john who wants you to take it up the jacksie but don't wanna pay more for it!" shouts a passing whore.

"Or the barman who won't . . . *hic!* . . . serve you no more!" yells a drunk, passed out in a nearby doorway.

"Er, yes. Thank you." You nod and turn to None-of-Your-Business. "Or a young friend who likes to scowl more than smile?"

"YES!" All the children turn and stare at None-of-Your-Business, who grins.

"So," you say, pleased, "you all know what ornery is. And that is our first lesson: just because you don't know the name for something doesn't mean you don't know what the name means."

The children stare at you in awe. You ride the wave. "Now, we are all going to take turns with this chalk and you will all write 'ornery' on the board."

Immediately after the last child has finished, the sky breaks and deluges you in a cleansing rain. You take it as a sign of success in your new venture, and your dress takes to clinging to your figure becomingly.

"My name is Bert," squeaks None-of-Your-Business. You smile. "And I like your bristols!" he says, glancing up.

"What in the blasted devil's glen is going on here, lass?!" Mac barrels out, eyes blazing in disapproval of your alternative teaching methods.

"The children are learning," you say, barely containing a most-pleased smirk. "There is no reason they can't do so on their own street."

"The children will catch their bloody death in the rain on their own street, if they aren't carried off to the workhouse or the street corner first!" Mac's eyes flicker with anger and slowly travel down to your wet bosom before returning to your eyes. You sense that something like desire is tucked behind all his self-righteousness, but before you can take him to task for neighborhood-shaming, a smash sounds from somewhere within the home.

"Bloody hell!" Abercrombie flees out the front door, carrying the wooden chest. "The orphanage is on fire!"

"Oi, Dodger! Stop that! No!" Timmy cries as his hound bounds into the burning building. He races in after his foolish dog while the children scream at him to stop being ornery.

....

Turn to page 297.

The next day, you and Craven pick through the rubble. Though it is a shame that an obsessive madman has burned Hopesend Manor to cinders, it presents you and Lord Craven with a wonderful real estate opportunity.

With Manvers and the past gone with the original structure, and little Master Alexander finally sent off to school, you and your man are free to make furious love and rebuild your home to your heart's content.

Before you do, of course you poke around the rubble of the Forbidden Wing and find, miraculously untouched by flame, the damning small volume written in the lady's own true hand. There, in Blanche's secret tome, you learn her desire to "kill Craven, the child, and Manvers, and use Craven's moodiness to frame it all on him." You are justified in despising this wretch of a woman.

You feel happier and lighter than you ever have. You go to meet Craven in the eldritch garden for the first time since the main house burned down. You find him there, lying in handsome repose about some ruined graves, hungry for your conversation and touch.

"Do you think us wicked?" he asks, after having succumbed to climax in your mouth, sex, and crook of elbow.

"I think us lucky."

You watch his member rise as a gentleman does when a lady enters a room.

"We are lucky, indeed," he says, before filling your mouth with his tongue.

Luck, you think, as you enter into your umpteenth round of ecstasy in the eldritch garden in three or so hours, is your favorite promise kept by love.

The End

You ride as hard as you can on your camel across the desert, racing the rising sun. Unfortunately, you have already ridden Fabien as hard as you could, and the combination of hardnesses is showing your softness no mercy. Even more unfortunately, you hear a roar of outrage behind you as you gallop ineptly over the dunes. It seems you did not ply Fabien with quite enough wine.

"Er . . . faster, camel! Cha! Cha!" You urge the beast to move with the fire of a thousand suns, using your heels, your knees, and, eventually, in desperation, your elbows. It is all for naught. With a mad cry, Fabien catches up to you and grabs your waist with his powerful hands.

"You tricked me!" he snarls. His misty-green eyes narrow like an asp's when about to bite. "Love is but a trick to all women. But it is one you will never play on me again!"

Before you know it, you are bound, blindfolded, and unceremoniously thrown over the back of your camel. A cold trickle of dread runs down your spine. Despite your best efforts, you are on your way to meet the traitorous Delphine. What exactly does she have planned for you?

You have no choice but to find out. Turn to page 319.

Not long after, Lady Evangeline is shooting you the worried look friends exchange when they are stuck on late-night carriage rides to London from Derbyshire to save a family member from losing his inheritance.

"Where do you propose to go in London?" The gentle tone of her voice snaps you to attention. You have spent the better part of the long ride staring into the middle distance, reviewing your hunches.

"To Drury Lane, of course," you reply crisply. Lady Evangeline's eyes widen. You continue: "Mrs. Caddington was an actress, correct?" Lady Evangeline nods. "Who worked often at Drury Lane. In my experience, theaters are full of those who enjoy hearing themselves speak. What time will we reach London?"

"Very late, I'm afraid."

"Good. Mrs. Caddington's old place of employ will be quiet by the time we arrive, and we can hunt down someone and get them to talk while they are taking a break from treading the boards."

"You truly believe we will find answers to the question of Benedict and Cad's legitimacy at the *theater*?"

"I think we will find answers at the theater where Mrs. Caddington was once a star, yes." You readjust yourself on the carriage seat. "Theaters are always full of foolish lovers and jealous friends. I propose we head straight to the theater in which Mrs. Caddington used to perform and find the right person who would speak to us about her."

"And how on earth do you suppose we find the 'right' person?"

"Easily," you say. "We find who disliked her most and go from there."

....

You have a plan, and a good one at that! Go to page 75.

After some stalking about the house with a tightly furrowed brow, you come upon a terrified Alexander, crumpled in a heap beneath a portrait of his dead mother.

"Mama has come to hurt me again," he says. He is weeping, his eyes red with tears and horror.

"Mama is gone, Master Alexander," you say, unsure if your words are true. Unsure, to be honest, of anything anymore. "She can't hurt you."

"But I've *seen* her!" Alexander wails.

"What you've seen is the portrait," you say.

"No!" he cries. "Mama! She's here!"

The frightened child lifts a trembling finger, pointing toward a woman's skirts disappearing around the corner and into the next room.

Your heart leaps to your throat. Though you did not see the strange figure's face, you did see the locks of raven hair trailing behind her.

....

This is impossible. Do you . . .

Find Lord Craven and demand answers? Turn to page 60.

Flee to Mrs. Butts for comfort? Turn to page 312.

Or force an admission from the apparition? You are most certainly not afraid of no ghosts! Turn to page 349.

Clad in only your still-wet dress, you flee the room and the castle. You trusted this man, and perhaps were even falling in love with him. How could it be that a man so good, so kind, and so gentle could also be a murderer?

You race to the stables. You know not where you will go, but you know that you must leave this place . . . if only for a while.

Flinging open the stable door (and almost sending it off its rusty hinges), you decide to take the sturdy bay nag. As you look for a saddle, however, a strong arm wraps around you and a calloused hand clamps over your mouth.

"Be quiet. You are in more danger than you realize."

The arm releases you. You turn in a daze to see the face of your long-lost love, Ollie Ruston—whole, handsome, and very much alive!

"Ollie! But how? I thought that you were lost at sea!" you say, gaping in disbelief. You stare at his face and try to find the sweet boy you knew in the man who stands before you. He stares back, his once-innocent brown eyes now darkened with anger.

"I allowed everyone to believe that. I would have done anything to stop England from being conquered by Napoleon."

"Oh, Ollie . . ." You sigh, at a loss for words. He cups your face gently with one rough hand, but his expression is etched deep with long-held fury.

"You see, I had no choice. Not if I wanted to do right by my country . . . and those who I loved," he says, stroking your cheek with a hardened thumb. "I had to fake my own death so they wouldn't look for me when I embarked on my new life as a spy."

. . . .

If this is one of the most aggressively attractive things you have ever heard and you want to provide him with some secret services of your own (if you catch our drift), then turn to page 184.

But if you are seriously enraged—the bastard let you think he was dead for more than a decade and you want some bloody answers *right now*—then turn to page 242.

"Oh, Kamal!" You cling to his shirt ever tighter.

"Miss?" he squeaks.

You stare into each other's eyes for a few deliciously loaded moments. Nothing more needs to be said, for you both know you have found your other half in this life. Kamal pulls you into his arms and kisses you with a passion you didn't know he had.

The next thing you know, you are tearing at each other's clothes, making feverish love among the mummies. It doesn't matter. They are dead, but your loins are *alive*.

You marry, of course, and are blissfully happy. You also feature as ongoing comedic side characters for the continued series of Lady Evangeline's adventures, always providing a safe space and sympathetic ear when called upon. She drops in from time to time between quests to tell stories to your enthralled offspring. Little Evangeline, your eldest (and sole nonbookish) child, particularly loves these visits from her rambunctious godmother and namesake and grows up to be quite the adventurer herself.

The museum flourishes under your careful eye, and your legacy is continued in the capable hands of your many adorably studious children. The museum stands to this day in the heart of Cairo, a wonder for all to see. The names of you and Kamal are inscribed in the entranceway of its grand facade.

The End

"What do you mean?!" you ask.

"It had to come from the order of command in MacTaggart's regiment," Ollie says, his face a mask of pure hatred.

"That could have been anyone. You don't know that it was Mac!"

"Oh, but I do," says Ollie. "You see, apart from you there is only one woman I have ever loved . . . whom I dared ever love. Constantina. She was also a spy, and the bravest woman I have ever met. Captain MacTaggart killed her with his bare hands."

Your stomach drops as the pieces of this horrific puzzle fall into place. The fear in Mac's eyes when you said her name. His harrowing confession.

"Oh, Ollie . . . ," you whisper, with voice and hands shaking. Suddenly, the barn door bursts open again. There, like an avenging ginger angel, stands Mac.

"Unhand her, you absolute dobber!" he cries. Then he turns to you, his voice softening. "Did he hurt ye, lass?" He speaks with such gentleness that your very soul sings. But before you can answer, you hear a chilling *click*.

To your horror, Ollie has aimed his pistol squarely at Mac. "Not so fast, you bastard." The weapon glints wickedly in the early evening light.

You panic. Mac may be grumpy, he may be damaged, he may even be a murderer, but you know, somehow, that his heart is pure. You cannot stand by and watch him be killed.

Desperately, you throw yourself between the two men. Ollie glares at you.

"What is wrong with you? After all I've told you?!"

"What you've told me is not enough. I need to know everything." You walk over to Mac. Placing your hand on his ruggedly handsome face, you stare deeply into his eyes. "I need to hear it from you."

Mac sighs. "I tried to explain before ye ran off, lass. Constantina was Abercrombie's bit o' fluff when we were stationed at Salamanca."

"No!" cries Ollie. "That is a lie! It's a filthy lie!"

Mac sets his already extremely firm jaw. "No, ye bampot! It's the

God's honest truth! I saw her around him often, but what commander didn't take comfort in a sweet young woman in such dark times?"

Ollie starts to protest, but now you walk over to him. With a gentle hand, you still him and take the gun. He grits his teeth.

"What happened, Mac?" you ask gently. "How did Constantina die?"

"Och, lass." He hangs his handsome head. "I may have been a soldier, but ye must understand I dinnae hold with killing women. I have never forgiven myself for that night."

Ollie stares silently at Mac, his face twisted in pure hatred.

"I saw her late one night crossing a bridge," Mac continues. "She was walking . . . toward the French! I assumed the lass was possibly a wee bit tipsy."

"And then what happened?" you whisper.

"I went to stop her, of course! I went to warn her! But then—" Mac pauses, his hazel eyes clouded by ghosts from the past. "Then she turned on me with a knife. The fury she fought with! I could scarcely believe it of such a wee lassie, nor could I understand why. I tried to stop her but . . . we struggled. It was an accident, I swear on all that I hold dear, but in that struggle she fell off the bridge . . . to her death." He looks up, shame and fear shading his face.

"So there's the truth," he says. "Do ye hate me now, lass?"

"Oh, Mac," you sigh. "Of course not—"

"No! NO! EAAAARGH!!" Ollie screams and launches himself at Mac.

The two men begin to pummel each other.

. . . .

So, now that you have two handsome men in hand-to-hand combat before you, how do you proceed?

If you fear for their safety and want to stop this madness at once, turn to page 63.

If you are enjoying the show and want to continue watching the pair whale on each other with homoerotic vigor, turn to page 111.

The evening's festivities have finally started in earnest, though the room still throbs from the delicious gossip that has just come to pass. You bear the whispers no mind. You and Lady Evangeline take another swig of brandy and have a giggle at the expense of poor Nigel Frickley, who is asking a sobbing Henrietta to dance and only getting fiercely wept upon for his trouble.

And yet, despite your triumphant mood, you find yourself pausing for a moment when you spot a familiar dark head of hair—and handsomely brooding face underneath it—over at the card table. Remembering Benedict's harsh words earlier when you tried to offer comfort, you chide yourself for your overly tender heart. He deserves neither your comfort nor your pity.

You excuse yourself from Lady Evangeline, for the devil is in you tonight and you cannot resist strutting over to tell Benedict of your clever plan. Not that you care a jot what he thinks.

"What's trump, boys?" With all the confidence of a fellow fellow, you saunter up to the fellows playing whist in the game room. The handsome, stylish-to-the-hilt men form a rather pretty collection of well-born, possibly quite unmotivated knights errant. Benedict, their fallen King Arthur, slouches at his card table. His immoveable expression fades the moment you address the room.

"Pardon my aunt's *maid*, gentlemen," he says. Then he huffs in your direction before hissing in your ear, "What the *devil* do you think you are playing at?"

You ignore him pointedly.

"Pardon her lady's *companion*, gentlemen." You smirk. "As well as your host's fine manners. I come only to entreat you, Sir Benedict, to entertain your female guests. In fact, all of you charming gentlemen are sorely needed to fill a dance card or two. Morale is falling abysmally low among the womenfolk, I'm afraid."

A few among the crowd chuckle good-naturedly. Some men, in their cups, eye you up and down. But Benedict shifts his weight in his chair from one long, lean, well-muscled leg to the other. "These women," he drawls, "do not count you among their number, dare I say?"

"Dare as you wish, sir." You feel bold enough to seat yourself in an empty chair near the table, a bit of impudence that causes Benedict's eyes to flash with shock. "I have no desire to dance this evening. Not when there is detective work to do."

You anticipate more deliciously slow back-and-forth with old Benny, but instead he throws his hand of cards on the table, flies to his feet, and grips you firmly by the elbow. "Excuse me, gentlemen," he says with forced jollity, "but I shall help the lady find her way to the dance floor."

The jollity ceases the moment you are out of earshot.

"What do you think you're about, woman?" Benedict seethes when you have reached the chamber outside the game room. "Prattling on endlessly in your absolutely vulgar way, pretending to be one of the gentlemen when you are so clearly *not*." His eyes flicker down briefly before he rights himself. "You are barely one of the gentle*women*."

Gratified that he is so flustered (for Benedict, anyway) that he cannot even stop from drinking in a quick sight of you in your evening dress, you decide to press on.

"Well," you say sweetly, "do you wish to hear my news or not?"

"No!" he cries, disgust and exasperation coloring his strong features. "I do not wish to hear your news, nor do I wish you to discover any more that pertains to me and my family."

"But what if the information I find saves you from ruin?" You smile, all icy calm. The nerve of this man.

Benedict stares incredulously and in frustration runs a hand through his now very disheveled hair. To your annoyance, it only improves his appearance.

"Saves me from—? Listen, the only ruin that matters to me is the ruin that shall rain down if I am found strangling an impudent, gold-digging busybody of a lady's companion. Halt your line of inquiry. Let me be so-called ruined. Above all, let me be! Do you understand?" His grip is so tight, and his body so close, that you see tiny drops of perspiration appearing at his temples, sliding down the cut-crystal angles of his face, and coming to rest at the top of your cleavage.

With a quick, deep look into his eyes, you see that he has taken in the droplet's trajectory as well.

"Do I make. Myself. Clear?" he says through gritted teeth.

You stare back, aware that your breath is short and your bosom is heaving. You are not quite sure, but somehow the two of you have managed to find yourselves at the entrance of a small curtained-off alcove in a darkened corner. It is tempting. Oh, so tempting.

Do you give him what for? There's intrigue afoot and a mystery to be solved! Turn to page 125.

Or do you give in to your basest desires? Turn to page 118.

Watching Lady Evangeline at work fascinates you. Her slender hands run over the paper so delicately that you shiver to imagine such a touch. Golden curls fall from her careless coiffure and tumble down her long neck. What would those curls look like spread across a pillow? She pauses, concentrating, and bites her swollen lower lip. A lower lip that just moments ago was so close that all you needed to do was turn your head to find it touching yours. What would such a mouth be like to kiss?

This is madness. Lady Evangeline is your employer and your dear friend, nothing more. You simply need to clear your head.

"Shall I fetch us more tea?" you say. Lady Evangeline glances up, the light from a nearby window dancing across her divinely beautiful face, which she breaks with a distinctly un-goddess-like mischievous grin. Unfortunately for you, this only serves to make her even more desirable.

"That would be marvelous."

You scurry out of the room before doing something you would surely regret. You have ventured barely halfway down the corridor when you hear something close to a scuffle, followed by a sudden silence. Did you imagine it? There's not a soul in sight and it is deathly quiet. Too quiet . . .

Do you go back and alert Lady Evangeline? Yes, it's probably nothing, but many years of hardship have taught you to trust your instincts, and right now your instincts are saying "AAAARGH!" Go to page 226.

Or do you investigate by yourself? Lady Evangeline is hard at work, and an eerie silence does not an emergency make. Also, turning back would look fairly strange. Turn to page 37.

You hold your ground, as defiant as Boadicea in the face of the Roman onslaught. Craven is shocked at your boldness and bravery.

"I know this has haunted you, my love. The very weight of what happened tortures you, even now," you say to him, your voice a cool balm for his fevered soul. "But I must implore you, I must beg you, to tell me what happened. If I do fear you afterward, if I do leave you, then it will be nothing more or less than what you have assumed I would do. And if I do not, then you will know that my love for you is as unbending and unchanging as death itself!"

He stares at you warily.

"Confide in me, my love," you continue. "Let me lighten your burden. You have suffered alone for too long."

Lord Craven kisses you deeply, as though for the last time. You respond with equal urgency, your mouth ravenous. As at last you pull apart, he keeps you within his powerful arms and leans his forehead against yours, like he is seeking absolution.

"In the beginning we were happy," he says. "But as I loved her more, she loved me less. She thought it weak of me, to love her. She thought all men weak. When she bore a child, she was horrified it was a boy. She used to whisper to me, before we fell asleep, that he would be dead by morning. I would wake and run to the boy's room, place my ear to his mouth to check for breath. She would shatter me with her cruel laughter, watching me from the doorway. 'You will never know when I will strike,' she would say. And then one day, she did. She tried to stab him with a kitchen knife stolen from Cook as she slept."

You nod knowingly. "Cook does sleep a lot."

Craven nods back, his breath ragged, and continues.

"I came upon her in her chamber and screamed, begged for her to stop. She laughed at me. Her throat, her beautiful throat, thrown back in laughter as she tried to kill our son.

"'I never truly loved you,' she said to me. She was a beautiful woman, but so ugly when she laughed. She was a demon then. She—she tried to throw our boy in the fire, but I caught him. My jacket was singed, and as I went to put out the flame, she grabbed hold and tried to push me in as well. 'Nothing is according to plan,' she cried. 'Nothing but this will do, this will do! See you in hell!' And as we struggled, she must have gotten turned around. My last memory is of her falling into the fireplace, her hair aflame, her eyes red, her laughter turned to screams, her beauty consumed by the blaze."

You hold him. Your mind reels, and yet you hold him. "Surely you tried to save her?"

"Yes!" he cries in anguish. "I pulled her from the flames, but it was too late. I lay her upon the hearth, I stroked her face, and I wept. But all my weeping could not douse her. I could not save her. And perhaps"—he is fully sobbing now—"perhaps it was her wish not to be saved."

He turns to you, his eyes lost and despairing. Your heart aches for him.

"So, now you know it all," he says. "The full, ugly truth of it. What do you think? Are you repulsed?"

....

If you are not repulsed in the slightest, and hearing his confession has burned away all suspicion and distrust in the furnace of truth so that now all that remains is pure and true love between two souls, joined as one for all eternity, then turn to page 23.

If actually yes, you are repulsed—he seems like a lovely man, but he has essentially confessed to killing his wife, and this is quite a lot of baggage to deal with—*farewell!* Turn to page 54.

"Yes," you say. "I'm yours."

Mac shakes his head. "All my life, I have told myself I do not deserve the love of a good woman," he whispers. "I do not deserve to know beauty, or laughter. And you—you make gifts of your kindness and mirth, you make gifts of your soul, to all around you. To the orphans. Even to this wee foal. But to me, you make a gift of love. And I dinnae ken what to do with a gift so fine as this."

His admission leaves you breathless. Mac looks down at the foal, and you swear his stormy eyes are gilt with unspilt tears.

"You can make me a gift of your body," you say.

He pulls you into a kiss that would make other mouths ashamed of themselves, then pulls you up and onto him and slides slick fingers into your aching rainbow, searching for the gold at the end of it.

He listens to your every moan, attends every catch of your breath, and when the time is right and neither of you can resist creating the perfect union that your love, like this foal, was born to witness, he slips his dirk into your sheath.

Together, you play the most beautiful song on the bagpipes of your joined bodies. Together, you reach love's most exuberant pinnacle, screaming louder than the stable full of horses as you do.

Mac is the best, most purehearted, surprisingly nimble, and not surprisingly well-endowed man you have ever known.

And yet . . . there is something about this whole business that doesn't make sense. The name that has haunted you since you first saw it interrupts your joy again. *Constantina.* Why would a camp follower such as Constantina suddenly turn on Mac? What did he do to make her act so? Does Abercrombie have any idea of what Mac did? And why did he lie about how much he knew her? Your head is whirling.

"Excuse me," you whisper. "I've got to . . . freshen up."

Turn to page 77.

"I do understand," you say, as casually as you can muster. Fabien looks over his shoulder at you and scoffs before returning his gaze to the desert night.

"Do you, *chérie?*" he says. "You, a sheltered lady's companion, who has never known what it means to be hungry and friendless . . ."

His back is turned. Now is your moment.

Silently you reach for one of the more promising-looking rocks within reach and creep toward him. Fabien does not notice and continues monologuing into the night, his pectorals glazed by the moonlight.

". . . not knowing what the future holds, only that you are unwanted in this world and that—"

Fabien falls silent as you smack him over the head with the rock. As he slumps to the ground, you use the edge of the knife tucked in his waistband to cut through your ties.

"*Adieu*, Fabien," you whisper, and then kiss his bleeding forehead. Taking the knife, you mount a camel and head into the desert.

Unfortunately, you are not exactly skilled at camel riding and can barely make the animal move in the direction you wish. Still, it is enough to give you a head start and lose your captor.

You do not know how far you must go to reach safety, and before long it is morning. The blazing Egyptian sun beats down on you mercilessly. Your throat burns and your lips crack, but you dare not take a drink. You are running low on water, and you fear there is much more desert ahead of you.

Perhaps this was a mistake. Perhaps you may die here . . .

Suddenly you spot an object, far upon the horizon. Some large structure out here in the middle of the Sahara. Is it a mirage? No, as you draw closer you can hear, coming from within the structure, shouts, raucous laughter, wild music, and what sounds like several fights happening at once.

You fall off your camel and stagger to the door, your legs buckling and your vision blurry. As you tumble through the doorway, several curious faces turn toward you. To your unfocused gaze they all appear to be . . . women? Strange women, wearing all manner of dress . . . and undress.

Some stare at you with hardened ferocity, some gaze with sharp-eyed curiosity, and some seem not to mark you at all. The effect is unsettling, and yet . . . impossibly exhilirating. Where could you have found yourself now?

This cannot be real, you think. And then the world turns black.

Seriously, where have you got to now? Turn to page 252 to find out.

You raise an eyebrow haughtily and bore your gaze right back at him. You are damned if you will let yourself be intimidated.

"Of course, Sir Benedict," you trill as sweetly as you can manage. "I shall do as you wish. Don't mind me, I am now off to do something demure. Needlework, perhaps."

You smooth your skirts daintily and trip off to find someone to interrogate. To your misfortune, almost immediately you are waylaid by Nigel Frickley.

"Oh, it is marvelous to see you looking so well!" he exclaims.

"Thank you, Mr. Frickley, but I have to—"

Nigel summarily cuts you off with a stream of boundless enthusiasm. "I say, would—would you care to take a turn around the room with me?" he yelps, an overexcited puppy as always, and you cannot bear to reject him.

"Of course, Mr. Frickley," you say politely. "A turn about the room would be most—"

"Mind if I cut in?"

"I-I, er . . . ," splutters Nigel, as none other than Cad grabs your arm and leads you away.

"*Mr. Caddington?*" you say pointedly, trying to fight the sinking feeling that the raft of your well-being is about to be upended on the stormy seas of Cad's whims. His eyes devour every inch of you.

"That's Sir Rafe Granville now, sweeting," he says, backing you into a corner with that fallen angel's body. He leans to whisper in your ear. "You would do well to remember that."

You realize with shock that you have aroused his body. Now if only you could get him to let something slip without arousing his suspicion as well . . .

. . . .

Now that this blackguard has you cornered, it is the perfect opportunity to coax more information out of him. Turn to page 65.

"I'm sorry," you say to Lady Evangeline. "But my heart still beats for one impossible, infuriating, wonderful man, and for him alone."

Lady Evangeline smiles gently.

"I completely understand. And may I say, it is gratifying to see that my dear cousin Benny has at last found love."

"A love that cannot be," you say with a sigh.

"You might be surprised at that."

Before you can ask what she means, your heart lurches as you spot a familiar dark head coming through the crowds.

"Benedict?!" you cry. "What are you doing here?"

"I have news for you. News that I knew I had to deliver myself." He is out of breath but continues his story, his eyes afire. "You see, inspired by you I have taken upon an investigation. I have long suspected my Aunt Aurelia, your employer, of intrigue. However, my suspicions were fully aroused when I saw her receive what must have been legal documents—documents with your name on them."

"But what could they be?" you ask.

"Well, it took some pushing, and some probing, and finally some outright threats, but it seems that Aunt Aurelia has been hiding the fact that your father left you a rather large inheritance."

"But Papa died penniless!" you cry. "Bankrupted from foolish investments!"

"Not all of them," Benedict says. "It seems there was a diamond mine that was thought to have been spent, until a rather large amount more was discovered a year ago."

"So . . . I am an heiress to diamonds?" you say.

"In part, yes. But the real bulk of your fortune comes from an investment in an innovation for canning fish. You are rich beyond measure, thanks to kippers."

You stare at him in wonder. "Then . . . I have enough money to marry who I like!"

"Yes," says Benedict. "A thousand times over."

"But I don't want a thousand husbands." You gaze up at him, your eyes brimming with tears. "I want *you*."

Benedict stares at you, his silver-gray eyes filled with longing.

"I didn't do it for that," he says huskily. "I didn't do this to partake in your fortune. I only wished for you to be happy."

"You make me happy, you fool! I wouldn't care if you were a penniless beggar on the streets, I would still want you with every fiber of my being!"

"Benny's actually a long way from that," says Lady Evangeline nonchalantly. You both turn to her. She shrugs.

"Well, seeing as dear Henrietta is on that ship, sailing to a new life with her dear farmer, there didn't seem much reason to keep the truth a secret."

"'Vange . . . what did you do?" says Benedict.

"Well, I *might* have informed the papers about what happened to Mr. Caddington. Laced with scandalous testimony from several of the wardens at Bedlam, who were more than willing to talk when encouraged with some coin."

"You *didn't*," you say. You gasp in admiration.

"I did," Lady Evangeline says as she saunters off. "So I suggest that the two of you get down to the business of living happily ever after."

Neither of you answer her, for Benedict has pulled off your bonnet with exceeding tenderness. As you melt into his arms, you whisper, "Well done, you fool."

"I couldn't have done it without you, you harpy." He grins.

And with that you kiss with a white-hot ardor, there at the docks, not caring who sees.

The End

"They fight with the urgency of men who want each other dead, and the languor of men who know they are being watched by a powerful, beautiful woman."

Mac and Ollie take turns throwing each other across the barn. They fight with the urgency of men who want each other dead, and the languor of men who know they are being watched by a powerful, beautiful woman taking in every line of their bodies and becoming increasingly aroused by the thought of this ending in a lot of satisfying hair-pulling and possibly kissing.

As if Ollie can peer into the deep recesses of your mind, he tears Mac's shirt from his gleaming, heaving body. The swell of Mac's chest is so vital and hot that you almost lose your breath watching him. Then Mac follows suit, screaming, "HYAHHHH," and tearing off Ollie's shirt.

They circle each other, the red rose and the white, both armed with thorns of regret and honor. There is a wolfishness to this dance, a hungry playfulness, a deep longing.

They both shine, their bodies pearlized with sweat. You wonder what it would be like to join in the fray and have them tear into you, as well as each other, applying the same vigor of their battle to the theater of lovemaking. How they would rise and fall over you, how they would alternate between kissing your body's hills and dales and exploring the depths and chasms of each other, how the three of you could reach the happy valley—if you worked hard, and soft, and hard—together.

After you watch them wrassle a bit more, you sigh. Deeply. It is probably about time to put a stop to this madness.

Turn to page 63.

"This is the end you deserve, you stupid chit." Manvers's eyes shine with triumph. "We shall all perish for Craven's sins, and I will see my Blanche again in the afterlife."

"You will see her in hell, you mean!" Craven arrives at your side just as the smell of smoke gives way to the visible flames licking the ceiling in the hallway. He kisses you and whispers, "I've alerted the servants of trouble and they are filing out of the estate as we speak."

"But what of Master Alexander?" you whisper urgently. Just then, as if to answer, the boy appears, yelling "ARGHHHH!"

Your eyes flash to his small form just as he slams his épée onto Manvers's wrist. You see then what you hadn't noticed before: that Manvers is armed with a small golden pistol, which, you surmise, might have once belonged to Blanche. He is aiming it at your heart.

"Look, my lady! I have saved you from the monster!" Alexander cries, pleased. You scoop him into your arms and grip him tightly.

"Indeed you have, boy," you whisper. "Indeed you have!" You shiver all over, doubly so as the flames from the hallway reach ever closer to Manvers, who is seated beside the portrait of the late Lady Craven.

"Manvers!" you cry. "You must away with us or perish by this beastly fire you have set!"

"I must only wait for happiness," Manvers replies, his voice eerily calm, before he is consumed by the flames.

Turn to page 89.

"I-I'm sorry, my lady, but I feel that this is the end of my journey," you say to Evangeline. "I am just a simple woman, and certainly no adventurer. As much as I admire and respect you, I have no place here."

Evangeline nods, her eyes filled with kindness.

"I quite understand. It is a very different life that I lead, and I am aware that there are few who would wish to travel such dangerous and difficult paths."

"So you are not angry?" you ask.

"Of course not," says Evangeline. "For if there is one thing I hope you have learned in our travels together, it is to always follow your heart." She smiles bittersweetly. "You will, won't you, my dear?"

"Oh I will!" you say with a gasp, embracing her warmly.

You rush back to the museum, escorted by the enormous form of María José. No one dares hassle you on the way, for fear of having their thorax ripped to shreds. As you enter through the solid doors, you are shocked to find that Kamal has righted the museum to its former glory. Everywhere you turn there are more treasures from the time of the pharaohs, each more exquisite than the last.

"Oh, Kamal!" you cry. "This is truly breathtaking!"

"You are very kind," he says, blushing. "I am glad that you—"

He is cut off midsentence as you suddenly grab him by the shirt and cling on for dear life.

"Are you all right, miss?" he asks. You stare at him wordlessly and shake him slightly. He startles for a moment and then gives you a lingering look from the liquid pools of his intelligent, deep-brown eyes. His boyishly handsome face is still marked with bruises. "Miss?"

"I just want a normal life, Kamal," you say, your voice growing stronger with every word. "A normal, happy, boring life, working with the beautiful objects you have filled this museum with. You must give me a job! Please, Kamal, I beg you!"

Kamal's smile lights up his entire face, causing him to wince slightly because of the bruises.

"Of course! Nothing would make me happier."

Thrilled beyond words, he excitedly thrusts out his hand to shake yours, upending some of his papers as he does so. A notebook falls to the floor. You are shocked to see that he has sketched your face lovingly in the margins, in the same delicate style he uses to draw all of his beloved artifacts.

"Oh, Kamal! What is this?" you ask, blushing.

"It . . . I . . . oh, miss, I am sorry. I am too forward. It . . . it's just that . . . I . . ."

You realize that, in his own shy way, this is a confession of love. You stare at him in wonder.

Do you go for it with Kamal and his adorable bookishness? If so, turn to page 95.

Or do you turn him down gently, because bookish fellows, however adorable, are not for you? If so, turn to page 13.

You find Craven pacing the library with a snifter of brandy in hand, mumbling to himself in the soft, lurching tones of the tormented. His hair looks astoundingly (and attractively) unkempt, and he wears his shirt open to the navel. You have noticed that the more tortured he feels, the more skin he bares. This has a disorienting effect on you. You take several deep breaths before speaking.

"My lord." Your voice escapes your throat in a harsh whisper. Before the words can leave your mouth, his lips are upon it.

"I thought you would never come again." He kisses you hungrily, as though for redemption, for forgiveness, or for your body and soul. "I thought I had frightened you, had pushed you away."

Apologizing slips a little lower on your to-do list, as you allow yourself to be pushed up against the damask-covered wall. Your fingers slide down his rippling chest, and you tease him by lowering your graceful yet filthy hand into the space between his breeches and body to feel his family crest. He shudders with desire. You quake with your own, but manage to break away from kissing his vital, dangerous mouth.

"My lord, I must . . . apologize." Speaking plain, and at least at arm's length, is your best course of action. "I am sorry for disrespecting the memory of your dead wife by teaching your son to parry and joust on the very site of her demise. It must have been a shock to see me there, especially after you had expressed wishes for me not to enter that area of the house."

He stops kissing you as suddenly as he started. "Who. Told. You?"

"None but my own intellect," you say, stunned at his shift in tone and more than a little irritated by it. "I merely observed—"

"*Observed?*" Craven shakes his head and begins to circle you as a lion would its cornered prey. "So you once more returned to the room in the wing I expressly forbade you from entering. Do they not give you enough to eat in the kitchens, girl? You seem hungry for my disapproval."

"*Please.*" Now it is your turn to seethe and to circle *him*. "You could not disapprove of me if you tried."

"*You* try me now." He gathers you up in a sudden, too-tight embrace. "You have tried my patience and my strength since the day you set foot in Hopesend Manor. Do you think I wanted this? Do you think I wanted *you*? I expected a governess, not a challenge to all I knew of women in this life."

"And what should I have expected?" You snatch the brandy snifter and snift it at him for emphasis. "I came here to escape the life I knew, only to find myself living a life of never-ending happiness, of passion, of matched desire. All with a man who cannot keep his heart steady because he keeps his mouth shut!"

You place the snifter on the nearest bookshelf, your hand trembling like a leaf as you do so.

"If only," he says, his voice a hoarse whisper, his whisper the ghost of a horse that died tragically, galloping across the plains of your shared unconscious, "if only you could have been anything other than clever. If you could have been less intriguing, less beguiling, less enchanting and strange and good. If only you could have been anything other than who you are, then . . . then . . ."

"Then what, you blasted man?" you cry. It is senseless how much you feel for him. It is hopeless and obscene and true.

"Then I could have remained the monster I know I am! Without guilt. Without sorrow. Without shame." He drops to his knees. He tears at his hair. He looks up at you helplessly—so helplessly, some might call it . . . the look of love.

"Oh, Garraway, who has broken you, my love?" You caress his face.

"I have broken *myself*," he chokes out. "I have broken another. You will never kiss me again, I will never know the taste of love again, once you know the truth. Blanche hated me after the child was born— jealous, cruel, thinking I would never again find her beautiful. She called motherhood the curse of womankind and she cursed us all for it. She took lovers, that I knew from the beginning. But as long as I loved her, and thought she loved me, I didn't care . . . but then . . ."

"But then *what*?" you cry.

"But then I did something. Something terrible. Something unfor- givable." He rises to his feet. "You should leave me! You should leave here and save yourself from me and what I am!" he roars as though a wounded wild animal.

....

So do you? If you escape from him as he suggests and hie yourself to some-where safer, turn to page 54.

If you know deep in your heart of hearts that his heart is a true and gentle heart, and you wish to continue this heart-to-heart, turn to page 102.

You say nothing but hold your gaze defiantly. The very space between you crackles, like the air before an electric storm.

Benedict cups your cheek with a strong hand and checks surreptitiously for anyone observing you in this, the shadiest of corners.

"Oh, dash it!" he growls. He pulls you behind the curtain to plunder your mouth with his.

A respectable young lady should resist, should fight him, but you are tired of being respectable. Instead, your body melts into his, and you feel him smile in the darkness as his tongue parts your lips to explore the sweetness within. Your blood turns to liquid fire as you return his ardor with equal ferocity. You cling to each other, two lost souls journeying through the inferno together.

"Forgive me . . . this is wrong." He pulls away with a sudden sigh and departs, leaving you alone in the alcove to rub your tender mouth.

You are not sure how much time has passed when you finally come to your senses. You manage to stumble out from the darkness. Fortunately no one notices . . . except Lady Evangeline. She arches an inquisitive eyebrow. You walk to her with the steady calm of a soldier.

"My lady," you whisper to her urgently, "do you trust me?"

Laughter dances in Lady Evangeline's eyes. "Even if I didn't, you have me entirely intrigued!"

"Good," you say, "because I believe if I am to get to the bottom of this little *escapade*, I will need to go to London, and I will need you to go with me."

"For companionship?" The laughter has crept from her eyes to her voice.

"That," you say with a smile, "and the use of your carriage."

It seems you already have the most cunning of plans. Turn to page 92.

"Death is no matter to me. It will come as a relief!" cries Ollie to his traitorous ex-lover. Constantina smirks.

"Perhaps. But first, you shall watch your friends die before you!"

She aims the pistol at you. With heart pounding, you scream in terror, and as you cower, Ollie dives in front of you. A hideous gunshot sounds, and then silence.

Your eyes are firmly shut. But open them you must. You gasp in shock—and then relief—as Ollie staggers to his feet, a chivalrous knight reeling from his noble errand. Truly, you have always had excellent taste in men, even as a young thing.

Constantina, meanwhile, seems to have pitched backward into the loch the moment she pulled the trigger. And there, standing at attention on the banks, barking triumphantly, is—

"Dodger!" you cry.

"Och, Dodger. Good dog, good boy!" croons Mac. Dodger woofs and wags his tail.

You spring forward, not wasting a moment, and pounce on the disoriented Constantina. As Ollie stares at his former lover and current betrayer (and his former former lover and current savior), you rip off your stockings. Mac raises an eyebrow, but then smiles when you use them to bind Constantina's wrists.

"Let's go," you command. "To the castle."

. . . .

Heavens, that was a close one. Turn to page 156 before your feet get cold.

Within hours, you are sailing down the Nile toward the lost temple in Noor's swift vessel. The three sails of the sturdy little boat snap and quiver in the wind as you speed toward your destination.

You thrill with excitement. No longer the hapless waif of just a few short weeks ago, you are now armed to the teeth and assisted by an army of dangerously powerful Amazons. Lady Evangeline leads the vanguard, a modern-day Joan of Arc, filled with equal righteous determination.

"No regrets?" she asks, a smile playing about that sensuous mouth.

"Never!" You meet her gaze with enthusiasm. "But, my lady, there are still some things I want to hear from you. So that I might understand why all this is happening."

Evangeline understands you at once. "You mean how I came to be involved with such a reprobate as Delphine St. Croix?

You nod. Evangeline shrugs with a sigh and then wraps her arm around your waist once more in a familiar, yet still thrilling, gesture.

"When I was much younger, I was in a position somewhat like yours. I could not make my way in the world as I wished—not alone, anyway, as was my desire. I was expected to marry and, well, and submit to the *requirements* of marriage. But my now-late husband was an older man, and kinder than most any I had met before. He was a politician, and ambitious, but hounded by the fact that he had led a bachelor life for many scandalous years until meeting me."

"He kept many ladies, then?" you ask. The instant you do, you wish you could erase the words from the air. Evangeline laughs gently.

"Not ladies, my dear."

Understanding dawns, and you curse yourself for being so simple.

"By marrying me, he could be knighted and come into his wealth, and I thus attained that same wealth and ladyship—a classic *mariage blanc*. Years later, when he was stationed in Egypt on a diplomatic mission during the war, I met Delphine. We were two young, green women fascinated by Egyptology. We both have facility translating hieroglyphs."

Now you curse yourself for not knowing how to read hieroglyphs.

"Well, of course I loved her," she continues. "But she was French, and while I initially suspected that she was loyal to Napoleon, I learned harshly that she was more loyal to her own interests than to any country, belief, or person. She sold valuable secrets—locations and information I should never have shared with her, that my husband had shared with me. I thought I was merely processing the events of the world with a lover in bed, but Delphine thought she was making a mint. She leaked my foolishly spoken words to the French, even though her own father had turned against them. She did it for nothing but money. And since she had acquired this information behind my husband's back, it caused terrible consequences for him and his career. We were sent back to London not long after. He died with disgrace and regret on his conscience which I put there, because I trusted Delphine. Delphine, on the other hand, never forgave me for not forgiving her. And thus, she is out for revenge."

You think maybe it's fine that you don't read hieroglyphs. Now you wish you could stop reading the look on Evangeline's face, which is one of tortured, anguished love.

Turn to page 164.

You seek out a suitable room for fencing lessons. Mrs. Butts recommends the stables, which have been empty ever since the horses were poisoned by a passing vagabond a few years back. Betsy the mute maid clutches her duster in silent horror at the mention of them. This reaction does not quite convince you of the suitability of the venue.

As you leave the servants' quarters, you are cornered by Manvers. Your body stiffens at the sight of him. He bears a look you don't quite recognize. Could it be a mask of contrition?

"I want to apologize for my brusque behavior earlier, my dear," he says. "Everything has been quite high tension since the death of Lady Craven. She was so beloved, and, I humbly say, so beloved by me that I . . . I . . ." You are stunned to watch the man dab a tear from his stoic face. "I do appreciate that you are trying to right some of the wrongs of the house. And it is quite good that the child has you here, to learn from your example."

You feel a flush of shame for the hateful thoughts you have harbored toward Manvers, even if they were fleeting. "Thank you," you say, and you mean it.

"If there is anything I can do to help show you the courtesy I perhaps denied you prior to this moment, simply say the word and I will do all in my power—"

"As a matter of fact, we are looking for somewhere to fence. Any notions of a suitable place?" you ask. "Any long hallway could serve as our piste, but most of the halls and rooms I've encountered are encumbered with fine artifacts that stand too strong a chance of meeting death by épée."

Manvers considers unknown options before speaking. "Well, there is the main room in the West Wing—it is suitably large and completely unused. It would be a shame to let it go to waste. Shall I show you the way?"

"Oh, please!" you say, delighted by his suggestion.

You take Master Alexander by the hand, hoist your épée in the other, and follow Manvers through great halls and twisting passages, then up a staircase to an area of the house that seems not to have been used for some time. Yet, despite the closed-off feeling, the rooms are spotless, without a trace of dust.

You find this curious, but only for a moment. Alexander has taken to whipping his blade through the air, yelling, "HYAHHHHHHHH!"

Manvers disappears down the stairs before you can thank him. Within seconds you must dive to avoid having your eye poked out by Alexander's enthusiasm.

"I don't like this room," the boy says plainly, before slashing at the rug near the great hearth.

"So you must wish to conquer it?" You cock an eyebrow and lift your blade.

"Yes!" he squeals with delight.

"First, you must learn the basics," you say. "And the most basic elements of fencing are knowing when to keep your distance, and when to find your move—and make it!"

With some fancy footwork, you have backed the boy against the fireplace in no time. His eyes are wild with fear but he smiles, as if he

somehow knows that while in your company he need not worry.

Midway through teaching the boy how to parry effectively, in storms Lord Craven in a white-hot rage.

"GET OUT!" he roars. Alexander yelps, almost in good humor, but scampers out of the room to practice his lunging elsewhere.

"How dare you enter these rooms," Craven says menacingly. He regards you with revulsion. "These rooms are forbidden, and all in the house know this to be so. How could you bring my child to this . . . this place of *evil*."

"We took the stairs," you say simply.

"You know nothing of this house!" he yells. "Nothing of this room, nothing of me, and nothing of my son!"

You punctuate your next phrase by flicking the tip of your blade across the impudent man's vital points. "I am doing nothing more than caring for your son and giving him something to soothe his young mind. It is more than can be said for you!"

Craven grips the épée blade with his monstrous hands, tears it from your grasp, and throws it into the unlit fireplace.

"What say you now?" he spits. "Now that you are weaponless?"

"I am never weaponless," you retort, before you slide your hands through the length of his hair, then wrap it tightly around your fist and pull.

He lets out a cry of pleasure and pain. As his poet's mouth breaks, you descend to kiss it, then mercifully allow the tormented soul to come up for air.

. . . .

Well. That took a familiar turn.

Do you give in to your basest of base urges? Turn to page 198.

Do you fight your baser urges (*vincit qui se vincit* and whatnot) and get the hell out of this house of horrors? Turn to page 54.

You will not let this silver-spooned yet newly paupered brute throw his weight around with you.

"Perfectly," you respond confidently. Benedict looks uncertain but releases you from his grasp and half stalks, half staggers back into the game room. Perhaps your little encounter has had more of an effect than he thought it would. You scowl at his retreating back. You will save this fool from ruin whether he likes it or not!

Lady Evangeline, who has been watching much of the exchange from the opposite side of the room, arches an inquisitive eyebrow in your direction. You walk to her with the steady calm of a soldier.

"My lady," you whisper to her urgently, "do you trust me?"

Laughter dances in the blue depths of Lady Evangeline's eyes. "Even if I didn't, you have me entirely intrigued!"

"Good," you say, "because I believe if I am to get to the bottom of this little *escapade*, I will need to go to London, and I will need you to go with me."

"For companionship?" The laughter has crept out of Lady Evangeline's eyes and into her voice.

"That," you say with a smile, "and the use of your carriage."

Go to page 92.

"What the devil is the girl doing?" A shaky voice grates out behind you. "Flinging costume jewelry about and disgracing my name after I show her nothing but kindness!" The voice belongs to none other than Lady Craven, and from the insalubrious quality of its tone, it is clear she has had quite more than her fill of Madeira.

"Oh, my dear. You must take my wretched aunt home before she further disgraces herself," Lady Evangeline says. She tuts at the Dragon. Dejected at what could be your last turn around the ton ending so soon, you slump your shoulders and set your jaw. Your glum appearance prompts Lady Evangeline to gales of laughter. "Oh, heavens!" she cries. "You act as if you have been banished from society! If only one could be so lucky, oh. Oh!"

You adore the sound of your friend's laughter, but not so much when it is squarely at your expense.

"Have I missed something, my dear friend?" you ask as Lady Evangeline recovers from her riot.

"Of course you have, you chit!" she says with a laugh. "I have secured you an invitation to Benny's—Sir Benedict's—country-house party coming up. They're always great fun, and this way you can, *ahem*, entertain yourself with the very notion of eligible bachelors, such as my cousin."

You laugh sharply in response. This prompts Lady Evangeline to a fiercely stifled fit of giggles.

A handsome, noble ginger arrives to interrupt the laughter.

"Mac!" you cry.

"My lady," he nods a quick greeting to both you and Lady Evangeline, but his manner is all business. Yet his soulful eyes burn into yours as he speaks. "If you were sincere about helpin', lass, I may have a job for you teaching the kiddies at the Home for Orphans of the War. It is in London, so if you are ever there and wish to inquire, so will I receive ye."

With another quick nod, he is off, probably to go do good in the night.

Lady Evangeline raises a gorgeous, quizzical eyebrow.

The opportunity to mingle with the upper-crustiest of society's upper crust is supremely tempting. Indeed, with your humble background, you'd be a fool to turn down such a rare invitation to improve your standing in the company of your betters. And the presence of Sir Benedict . . . well, that certainly doesn't *lessen* your intrigue.

Yet you cannot help but be intrigued by the Scotsman's offer. You've always had a tender heart for children, and something about his rugged altruism sparks a dangerous recklessness in your chest.

What will be next?

If you wish to rub elbows with the ton—and Sir Benedict's elbows in particular—hustle your bustle to page 158.

If you think doing good for poor kiddies is infinitely better than pretending you can hang with the elites of London (and you can't help your curiosity about what Mac's got under his kilt), hop on over to page 208.

"I have just finished deciphering the parchment in the canister that dear Kamal transcribed," Lady Evangeline explains as she strides down the corridor to your rooms. You hurry to keep up with her.

You peer at the mysterious inscriptions. "What does it say?"

"Well, my dear, it seems that what we have here are directions." Lady Evangeline turns to you, her sky-blue eyes shining. "It speaks of a temple in the middle of the desert. One lost to the rages of Hathor when she was transformed into Sekhmet, goddess of war, after witnessing the weakness of humankind and their love."

"The lost Temple of Hathor!" you cry.

"Precisely. I have mapped out where this scroll says the site is. Though I must warn you, the journey is arduous. There may be sandstorms, bandits, and several varieties of poisonous snakes along the way."

"Oh," you say. You silently curse both your insatiable thirst for adventure and your burning loins.

With a roguish smile Lady Evangeline looks up from her papers. "We will need to leave right away. And pack quickly. And change our clothes into something more suitable."

Suitable for facing down would-be murderesses? You frown.

"No need to worry. You may borrow mine." She leads you to her room and throws a few garments made of sturdy material toward you before stalking behind the screen to change.

You inspect what she has given you and frown again, confused.

"But . . . my lady . . . these look like . . ."

"Breeches?" says Lady Evangeline, emerging from behind the screen clad in a scandalously tight pair of pants that cling to her every curve and a billowing man's shirt. "Quite right. The most practical thing one can wear under the circumstances."

"But surely these will cause a scandal wherever we go!" you cry.

Lady Evangeline stalks over to you and caresses your face. "Not where we are going, my dear. There, we shall fit right in."

....

Go to page 276.

"My lady," you whisper urgently, "I think I need your assistance."

Laughter dances in the blue depths of Lady Evangeline's eyes. "Anything for you, my dear, for you have me entirely intrigued!"

"Good," you say, "because I believe if I am to get to the bottom of this little, ah, escapade, I will need to investigate."

"I see . . . ," says Lady Evangeline thoughtfully. "And how may I help you in this endeavor?"

"You seem to know something of this Mrs. Caddington's associates. I was wondering if you knew any personally?"

Lady Evangeline raises an elegant eyebrow. "Well, I must confess that I do. However, as much as I admire your freewheeling, suspicion-following spirit, I'm not entirely sure that visiting the person—or their place of residence—is a good idea for a sheltered young woman."

"Oh, out with it!" you cry, cheered by the company and the good brandy. "I may be a reasonably respectable woman, but I have lived long enough to know something of the world!" Admittedly, much of this bravado is the brandy.

If she notices, Lady Evangeline does not let on. Instead, she throws her head back and laughs. "Ah, my dear, you truly are a treasure. And I certainly admire your tenacity and determination."

"So you will assist me?" you say. Lady Evangeline smiles warmly.

"Of course I will. If you wish to remain in England, I will always endeavor to assist you. Especially if it can help poor cousin Benny."

"Oh, thank you!" you exclaim, hugging her in slightly tipsy delight. As Lady Evangeline embraces you warmly, however, a thought occurs to you.

"What do you mean, if I wish to remain in England?" you ask.

"Ah. Well. You see, my dear, I plan on taking a trip to Egypt. I am somewhat of a keen Egyptologist, and I have several dear friends in the country whom I made when my late husband was stationed there during the war. It is a long journey, and possibly an arduous one. I was looking for a companion for the expedition, one with a sense of adventure and initiative, who might be able to handle the rigors of journeying to a strange land."

You stare at her, astonished at what you think she is implying.

"So, my dear, what do you say? Would you like me to assist you in your adventures in London, or would you like to assist me in my adventures in Egypt?"

Do you continue on your sleuthing journey to London? There is intrigue afoot and you must get to the bottom of it. Especially if it assists a man you feel somewhat sorry for, though you obviously don't really care for him. *Ahem.* If so, turn to page 200.

Abandon your sleuthing journey for some adventures in the land of the pharaohs with Lady Evangeline? Hell, yes. Turn to page 217.

Your encounters with the villagers so far have been limited to a brief but memorable ride with Teddy Braithwaite, the handsome postman, a dinner with the folk at the inn, and occasional visits with the handsome vicar, the Reverend Simon Loveday.

You don't know what you believe about the recent unbelievable events surrounding Lord Craven, but you do know that where there's smoke, there's usually fire. And you hope that some more distant observers than the people you share a home with have a better idea how that fire started.

You cover much moorland with brisk, long strides and soon find yourself in the village of Ravenscar. Your face bears a healthy flush of good, honest exertion. Could it be that even spending time out of Hopesend has worked you some wonders?

"It's really thee, i'n't it, miss?" A sweet, low, gorgeous Yorkshire voice breaks your concentration, and you could not be happier. You turn and see, haloed by the late-day sun, none other than Teddy. "I've been wondering if tha were well, miss."

You smile at him, but you are on a mission. "I am well as one can be, in my position," you say firmly.

"I would think tha would be well in any position," Teddy responds. And though you are sure his intentions are innocent, you find it very hard to ignore the thought of what positions you would like to try with him. "I'd hope I might see more of thee again."

You demur—for the time being—and continue on. You arrive at the vicarage, and just as you raise a fist to rap upon the door, it swings open to reveal the handsome vicar, his fair hair positively glowing white in the setting sun.

"Let's be naughty, shall we?" he says by way of greeting, offering up a plate of cold chicken. "It's leftovers from the charity picnic. If anyone asks, I didn't steal it. If God asks, let him know I already gave plenty to the poor, and his faithful servant mustn't starve. Nor must his friends in Hopesend." With a breezy laugh, he ushers you into his sweet and simple home.

Once you are settled with a picnic plate, he explains that he saw you coming down the hill some time ago. "Please forgive my little act of spying, my lady, but try as I might to be a loving shepherd to my faithful flock, there are times when a blue tit in flight proves more intriguing than the umpteenth damnation of Mr. Wilkie's bunions. 'If God exists, why must my bunions?' This is Mr. Wilkie's eternal prayer. He is quite fervent with it, and though I do not speak for God, I can only assume he is impressed. Oh, I am sorry. I only meant to say that your descent from Hopesend gave me much-needed interest and pleasure during my lovely church picnic. I did not have the slightest intention of putting you off your plate of stolen food with talk of bunions and blasphemy. Do forgive me, I am but a helpless wretch in the company of lovely young women who have done quite a bit of walking to see me."

All you can do in response to this delightfully loquacious tirade is to laugh heartily and eat a bit of chicken.

"Good. Laughter is a positive sign. Laughter is prayer. And you, now here, are an answer to my prayer," the vicar says, growing serious.

"And here I thought I would just journey down to steal some kitchen scraps," you say in jest, but you grow curious at the sudden shift in his tone.

"My lady, I . . . I do not want to speak out of turn." Unease worries the fine features of his face. "But I have been very concerned for you staying at Hopesend Manor. There has been much town gossip surrounding the death of Lady Blanche and Helena. And though I put as much stock in it as Mr. Wilkie does his bunion-meting God, some of it has me worried."

"Well, Reverend—"

"Simon, please."

"Reverend," you continue, and he smiles warmly at your impishness. "I journeyed here to speak with you on just that matter. I am concerned as well."

"I have much to tell you," he says, looking around furtively and setting down his plate of chicken. He leans close, so close you can smell his almost vivid cleanliness. His scent is that of crisp white bedsheets baked dry in the sun, in a field of freesia, touched with the barest bit of musk to make it all go heady. You almost swoon, but hold it together long enough to make out his final request.

"I can't talk here, and I can't talk now, but meet me tonight. In the eldritch garden. There is something I need to show you. It is something that you should see."

For a moment his lips are so close to your ear, without actually touching it, that you can feel each nerve sparkle and flame.

Good God, indeed.

Do you decide to meet him, for mystery and alluring vicars are afoot? If so, turn to page 174.

Or have you had enough of this gothic nonsense and wish to take up Teddy Braithwaite on his offer? If so, turn to page 47.

Evangeline's kisses are charged with a soft ferocity. All the adventure that has led to this moment seems at once vitally important and entirely inconsequential. Your life has been building to this instant and nothing else.

"Is all well, my darling?" Lady Evangeline pulls away, her mouth trembling and luscious, her hair tumbling and free.

"I am more well than I have ever been," you respond, kissing her of your own accord. It feels like riding a horse for the first time, or like taking that fiery first-ever sip of wine. Like learning a language. Like something new and strange that you want forever. It feels like blissful freedom. You dare to reach out for a lock of her perfect, silken, golden curls and twine it around your wrist.

"I am tied to you," you whisper, bringing the tendril to your nostril and breathing deeply the scent. "You smell like adventure."

Lady Evangeline pulls you in for another kiss. "You speak in verse," she laughs. "You are lucky I am as much a scholar of poetry as I am of ancient Egypt."

"I am lucky," you say. You take her hands in yours before tracing them down your sides. "You are also a scholar of love. I am inexperienced in many ways of this world. I need someone to teach me . . . *everything*." Pressing her hands under yours, you slowly inch your ragged and desert-torn skirts up and over your shapely legs. Lady Evangeline shivers at the sight of your flesh. Bare skin on bare skin tingles.

"You are already a poor pupil. The least clever student would know it is pure scandal for man or woman alike to see even a lady's bare ankles in public." Lady Evangeline's voice is low and husky with desire.

"How would you teach a wayward student intent on showing her bare thighs?" Now it is you shuddering in delight as you lift your skirts and watch as Lady Evangeline dips her lovely head to meet your spread legs with an ardent, educated, and fluent tongue.

"I have wanted this for so long," she whispers after what could be minutes or hours of silken, shivering stimulation.

"I did not know how long I have wanted this," you whisper back as you arch your back and release yourself from the lips of love. "Let me show you now, my lady, all I have learned—so far."

You ease Lady Evangeline back, over a stack of camping supplies, and burn with desert heat with her every cry of pleasure.

Afterward, as you lie breathless in each other's arms, you hear a distant rumble.

Venturing out into the bright sunshine, you are astonished to see a great tower rising from the sand, laden with exquisite carvings from every angle. The lost Temple of Hathor!

You gaze in triumph. Your love's true happiness has managed to raise a mythic temple into this, the modern age! Leaning your head on Lady Evangeline's shoulder, you sigh with happiness.

"Where to next, my darling?" she asks, a playful smile dancing about those full pink lips. Remembering where those lips were but a minute before, you cannot help but blush. "We do have a whole temple to excavate."

The magnificent structure stands proudly in the desert, beautiful and powerful as Hathor herself.

"Kamal will be happy."

Lady Evangeline kisses you gently, and the very gesture nearly makes you swoon. "He will be," she agrees. "On the other hand, Damilola did suggest that we follow her merry band on a few more adventures before we study the lost—now found—Temple of Hathor. She thinks we may turn out to be useful. And I must confess, it does sound like fun."

....

What will it be?

Do you decide to live a life of daredevilry with the fiercest of battle maidens—and the woman you love? Then turn to page 213.

Or do you take a break from life-threatening situations in favor of a less perilous—but no less exciting—existence? Do you prefer to uncover ancient treasures in the temple, and beyond, with the love of your life? If so, turn to page 325.

You race back to the castle. It is late, and the orphans are all tucked in bed in the Great Hall. However, Mrs. Ferguson, Jane, and Gertie should still be awake. You call out for them but are answered by eerie silence.

"Something is not right," Ollie says, and he pulls out his pistol again. He motions to you and Mac, and you fall in behind them. Silently, you creep into the kitchen and find Mrs. Ferguson and Jane slumped facedown on the table. A couple glasses filled with blood-red wine stand next to them.

Ollie sniffs the contents and nods to you and Mac. "Drugged." In the darkness, Mac takes your hand and squeezes it reassuringly. The gesture calms you somewhat, but a chill goes down your spine. Where is Gertie? And what has Abercrombie done with her?

As you venture upstairs, a single light shines from Abercrombie's study. Ollie readies his pistol and Mac pulls out a vicious-looking dirk from the waistband of his kilt. You grab a poker from an abandoned fireplace nearby, and the three of you rush in . . .

. . . and stop dead in your tracks. You clutch Mac. There, slumped in his chair, is Abercrombie. His eyes stare glassily at the ceiling. His throat has been slit.

"But . . . how?" Ollie asks. Mac envelops you in a comforting embrace and shakes his head.

"I dinnae ken . . . ," he whispers, tears welling in his eyes.

You hear a whimper behind you. Startled, you spin around, poker at the ready, only to see little Timmy huddled in the corner with the ever-loyal Dodger.

"Oh, miss!" he sobs, hugging Dodger close.

"Timmy!" you cry, dropping the poker and rushing to comfort the child. He throws his arms around you, sobbing hot tears into your shoulder and clinging to you tightly.

"I-I couldn't sleep, miss! So me and Dodger, we went hunting for the lost treasure!"

"Oh, Timmy," you say as you hug the boy. "Did you see . . . Did you see what happened?"

"I-it was Gertie, miss!" Timmy manages to say between sobs. "She went into the room with Colonel Abercrombie, and they was arguing for a long time!"

You hug him even tighter. "Did you hear what they were arguing about, Timmy?"

"Only th-that sh-she thought she was being followed," Timmy says, gasping through his tears. "She wanted to stage an accident, for you and Mr. Mac, and Colonel Abercrombie said no, to leave you two alone, and then . . . and then everything went quiet. But . . ."

"Oh, my darling," you whisper, "what is it?"

He looks up at you with huge, frightened eyes.

"Colonel Abercrombie called her a strange name, miss."

Your heart catches in your throat, for you already know what the child is going to say.

"He called her Constantina!"

Time to get a-movin'! Hasten to page 55.

"Give us a moment to settle some things before we set out, Hugo," Lady Evangeline calls out to the carriage driver as you two climb in, lit with an air of giddy discovery. "I dare say this is quite the dramatic turn of events," she says to you and laughs somewhat nervously.

"Indeed," you agree, "and we didn't even have to stick around for the matinee." You laugh as well, but the sound jangles your nerves. You attempt to soothe them with a nip from the flask of brandy that Lady Evangeline has brought along for the trip.

Lady Evangeline follows suit and shoots you an imploring look. "Honestly, my dear, I do not know how to proceed," she says. "What do you think?"

"Well, we have discovered that Benedict's birthright is safe, his father's first wife could be considered quite the cruel harpy or the clever girl, and I can't wait to see the look on his face when we tell him!"

"You won't have to wait long, you wretch!" You manage to drop the brandy flask with a gasp, for the insult hurled at you came from none other than Benedict, who has somehow tracked you down from London and thrown wide the door of your carriage. His handsome features are colored in anger, and, you note with amusement, he has forgotten to properly arrange his cravat in his haste to trail you.

"Your cravat is mismanaged, Sir Benedict," you say and then deftly retrieve the flask from the carriage floor.

"My cravat is as managed as a cravat need be moments before it is used to strangle an interfering fool such as you!" Benedict spouts. The slight flush of anger really brings out the animal desire in his eyes.

"Perhaps, Lady Evangeline, you could give your cousin and me a moment alone?" you say, the picture of calm composure. You offer Benedict a sip from the flask. He shakes his head, incredulous, and slaps the flask from your hand.

"Do go at once, Vange. I do not want you to witness anything you can testify to in a court of law." Benedict climbs into the carriage, hellfire blazing in his gaze. You are startled to find that the unbroken, if angry, eye contact is causing your own hellfire to blaze . . . in your loins.

"Oh, the *dramatics*, Benny," Lady Evangeline says. "You know what? Hugo will take you two back home to Kent. I will take your carriage, Benny. The seats are much nicer. Have a grand time, you two." She tosses you a wink before exiting, leaving you and a very angry, very handsome, very fancy man staring at each other in a well-appointed carriage. Alone.

"Well?" you say as the vehicle begins its rumble toward the country. Your eyes are low but expectant, missing not a single elegantly enraged angle of his frustrating, frustrated body. "Are you going to ask me what I know or sit there and huff vaguely for a while?"

"You know, woman, since we have no witnesses and a long ride before us, I will say . . . I have often wondered what it would be like to get you alone for an evening." His eyes eat up the sight of you leaning casually on the bench. Despite yourself, you flush wildly, everywhere, and Benedict smirks immediately. "Never once, though, did I think that the pretext would include you attempting to ruin my family."

"*Ruin* your family?" You are exasperated. "The delicate information I learned this night can only help you, as you know it anyway. If you'd only let me tell you—"

"Tell me what? That my father's first wife was the truly bigamous one and that her first and only legal husband is clawing at the walls of Bedlam this very instant?" He leans over to your side of the carriage, gripping you by the shoulders as he speaks. And while you do not comprehend that he has seemingly known this entire time that Rafe's claim is illegitimate, you do comprehend quite clearly that he is as aroused by your proximity as you are by his.

"What? I do not understand." You truly don't. It's hard to understand anything with his mouth, his shoulders, his entire vital, glorious mind and body just inches from your own. You reach up to pull him onto the seat with you, propriety be damned.

For a single moment you are nervous that this was the wrong move. Your worry is instantly erased when he responds to your boldness by nuzzling his gorgeous face deep in your hair. "Mmmm, of course you do not understand," he murmurs into the nape of your neck, letting his barely parted lips run down the line of your throat to the forbidden edge of the neckline of your dress. "You are a fool."

"A fool in like company, then," you say, irritated, and arrange your body so that he can press the length of his to yours more comfortably. You both silently grind against each other for a forbidden moment. You kiss softly, with the slow, secret urgency of lovers on the edge of reason. You know you have already gone too far, but to go much further would truly mean ruin for you both. "Why did you not tell me?" you say as his mouth travels the topography of your ears, your neck, your chest.

"Tell you what?" He kisses you more urgently, anxiously, as he speaks. "That the woman my father found more irresistible than his marriage vows couldn't wait to haul her first husband off to the asylum once he no longer proved of use to her? That Rafe holds me hostage by using the fate of my half sister as bait?"

You arch your body to meet Benedict's. He shudders from the contact, and you burn with the knowledge that you can create such an undignified response in such a composed man. "Henrietta may not want what fate has destined for her," you whisper.

Almost as soon as you utter the words, you feel Benedict stiffen—and not in a good way. "Henrietta is too young to know what she wants."

"She knows her heart," you hear yourself saying with more ferocity than even you thought yourself capable of.

"Our hearts all want things they shouldn't. Things that would ruin them, if given in to entirely." Benedict shifts away and sits across from you again. You cannot believe him.

"You allow your arrogance more control over your actions than your heart, I see," you say.

"You are quite observant," he retorts, his voice pure acid. "I suppose that is an excellent quality to possess, as a lady's companion."

You shake your head in disbelief. He clearly wants you, longs for you, respects you—but apparently he also thinks you are dirt.

"I may be low of station," you say, "but you are low now. Very low."

You are unable to keep your sudden anger—and a quiver of heart-break—from your voice.

Sharp tears shine in his cruel, slate-colored eyes.

"Tell that to my aunt the next time you monogram her handkerchiefs."

You suffer the rest of the ride to Derbyshire in an icy silence. When you arrive at his estate, Benedict flings himself from the carriage, and for the moment you are alone.

The nerve of the man! You have a good mind to abandon your sleuthing in favor of those who would appreciate it! And yet . . . there is something about the insufferable fool that you just cannot quite let go of.

· ·

Do you dig in your heels and keep on your track to right wrongs, uncover truths, and save this handsome fool from ruin even if it kills you? (It might, quite frankly.) If so, turn to page 241.

Or do you decide that enough is enough? If this handsome fool wants to be ruined, let him. You will find adventure, and perhaps love, somewhere else. On to page 192.

"No, Evangeline!" you scream across the desert sands.

The two most beautiful women you have ever seen—not to mention, the only two women you've seen who maybe truly love each other although one threatens to kill the other, who has set an elaborate trap for the first amid intrigue and adventure in Egypt—snap their heads in your direction.

"Delphine has done all of this to see you again," you say, working yourself up with the romance of the situation. "All of this—this *madness* to speak to you. She deserves more than to be put out to pasture like an old dog—"

"Well—" Delphine tries to interrupt.

"Or an old cow—"

"I—"

"Or a very old camel with a broken leg that cannot bear to walk unassisted!"

"*Ferme ta bouche, nom de Dieu!*" Delphine's pale features turn scarlet. You smile to yourself. Not only are you helping what could possibly be true love to bloom, you have also managed to annoy Delphine.

"I suppose she isn't entirely wrong. About you deserving your say," says Lady Evangeline, returning her gaze to Delphine.

"Then I suppose you should lower your pistol," Delphine says, arching a perfect eyebrow at Lady Evangeline.

"I will lower my pistol but not my guard. I will speak with you, Delphine, but you know why I haven't until now. You sold secrets I told you, secrets spoken in the confidence of our bed—"

As she speaks these words, you die, but you live, but you die.

"You took English secrets and sold them to the French," Evangeline continues. "To *Napoleon's* people. You made me forsake my husband, forsake my country and king, and now you look at me with your moon-cat eyes and expect *what* from me? Impunity? Trust? *Love?*" Evangeline spits in the sand. You think you might hear Fabien swoon the tiniest bit. You can't be sure over the sound of your own swooning. You definitely can't hear him over Delphine's capital-S swoon, though hers is edged in hot, long-held anger.

"I did sell secrets, yes. And I have no shame for doing so. You told me things your late husband told you, and in turn I told them to certain friends with deep pockets." Delphine seems so cool, so careless, but you know and she knows and even Fabien knows everything is riding on this one moment.

"Friends with deep pockets who were *also* friends with Napoleon." Evangeline says, her voice pure icy fire. A chill spreads across this little patch of desert.

"They could have been friends with the devil himself, and I still would have done it! The money from that commerce helped my father recover."

"That *commerce*," Evangeline spits, "imperiled my husband's reputation in his dying days."

Now it is Delphine's turn to spit. "Your husband! That was a marriage of convenience. He had no interest in you! He only had interest in other men!"

"So?" Evangeline laughs. "We were loyal to each other. We helped each other. Do you have any idea how hard it was to heal the rift your betrayal created between us? We were friends, Delphine."

"So?" Bitter tears now glitter in Delphine's eyes, like jeweled scarabs in the sand. "We were lovers. Lovers forgive each other, always. True lovers do. And if you had done the same to me, I would have forgiven you. I loved you. I love you. Love forgives."

"Love betrays!" Evangeline's golden pistol slips from her hand into the sand. Tears slip down her cheeks in hot pursuit of the gun.

"Love is sorry." Delphine drops to her knees.

"Love is foolish." Evangeline drops to her knees as well.

"Love waits. Love returns. Love grows." Delphine and Evangeline are like twinned obelisks, serving as markers to the gates of heaven. Fabien and you tremble at the sight of them.

"Love—"

But whatever Evangeline is about to say is lost in a rush of silken kisses that have been waiting an eternity to rule again.

You slump against Fabien's body, much relieved, and a little saddened. You know you should be happy to have reunited these two lovers, after so much space and time, but—

"You feel used," Fabien whispers to you. You blink a tear from your eye and shake your head.

"Not used, but—"

"The sidekick. The unchosen." Fabien's voice aches with desire for you, and you can feel it course through him—and yourself—like royal blood, or the waters of the Nile, strange, dark, and true. "I wish for you not to feel this way, my lady. I wish for you to feel the full height of your power. The full scope of my desire. I wish to choose you. I wish to choose pleasure. I wish you to choose *yourself*. Choose your joy. If even for this small speck of sand in the hourglass of all eternity, shall we choose to celebrate our bodies, and each other?"

The man drives a rock-hard bargain.

If you take Fabien up on his offer, turn to page 85.

If you're really just not in the mood, turn to page 182.

"You are a monster!" you say. The Reverend Loveday pauses and narrows his eyes. You grab his beautiful face.

"I love monsters." And with that you pull him to you to consummate your union of sin.

After some frenzied lovemaking, the two of you lie among the tombstones of the eldritch garden, your passion spent. Lazily running your fingers through his hair, which glows silvery gold in the moonlight, you coo into his ear. "It must have been hard, being the poor relation so close to inheriting a fortune, were it not for a couple of fools who do not know their good fortune."

Reverend Loveday chuckles under his breath. "Ah, my dear, there is more to it than that." He runs his fingers down your face. They are ice-cold, even after your exertions, and send a shiver of pleasure down your spine.

"You see, the real Simon Loveday Craven, third in line to inherit, died in Venice on his Grand Tour . . . I might have helped with that. And, as he was an orphan with few friends and no close family, I simply took his place."

You startle and gaze into his cool blue eyes.

"Then who are you?" you ask. He smiles, his mouth fully open for the first time. How had you never noticed before now that he had only smiled with his mouth closed? Sharp white fangs glint in the moonlight.

"I am Raven de Craven, the original Craven who came over with William the Conqueror," he says. "Hopesend was my home in the beginning, and it shall be my home once more!"

"How can this be?!" you say, shocked. He strokes your face with his hands as cold as marble.

"Don't you see? I am one who stalks in the darkness—a creature of the night!" He wraps you in his strong arms and together you float into the sky. You moan in ecstasy and cling to him for dear life.

"Let me sire you . . . let me make you my queen!" he cries as you dance among the treetops of the eldritch garden. In answer, you lift your throat to his hungry mouth and moan in pain and pleasure as his sharp teeth pierce your flesh.

As you walk back to the house, the world has changed. You feel deep in your veins that you could accomplish anything, take on anything.

Still, you feel some lingering affections for the Cravens and so you decide against killing them. Instead, you slink into the house, a sweet smile on your face, and use your lady vampire glamour to convince Craven and Alexander that the best thing would be to fake their own deaths and start a new life with new names in America. With glazed expressions, they rush out of the house intent on staging a boating accident.

You and Raven laugh at their departure and then make love so violent in every room that the servants all move out. You do not mind, for humans are always replaceable. You and your vampire love rule over Hopesend under different guises—and still do to this day!

The End

Leaving Cad in a bruised heap upon the ground, you and Benedict hurry out a side exit of the labyrinth and into the servants' quarters. The housekeeper, a fine woman, finds you a pitcher of water, some cloths and bandages, and a spare room. She then leaves you there in privacy.

"Allow me," you say as you help a wincing Benedict out of his shirt. Your eyes lock with his silver-gray ones, which smolder at your touch. Running your hand over his powerful form, you try to keep your mind on the task at hand and ease him into a seat.

You turn and soak one of the cloths, then wipe some of the dirt and blood from Benedict's firm pectorals, biting your lip at the sight of his deeply masculine chest. It is dusted with dark hair that leads down in a trail from the V of his lower torso to his . . .

Enough! You have a wounded man to tend to, not slobber over. "This might sting a little," you murmur as you apply an astringent salve to grazes that lace his firmly muscled left shoulder. Benedict's breath contracts with pain, but he remains still.

"I—I must apologize to you, I think," he says. His formerly arrogant eyes are awash with contrition.

"I think I owe you an apology as well," you admit. "I feel I went too far."

"You were trying to help. Even though you had every reason to despise me, you still tried to help," he says in wonder. "That is not a thing to apologize for. It is a thing to be admired." He chuckles under his breath. "It's funny. All my life I have tried to avoid love—after witnessing the misery that was my parents' marriage." His expression takes on an intensity that makes you giddy. "After seeing how heartbroken my mother was when my father deserted her, I never really forgave him. Or trusted love."

"I see," you say quietly, trying to hide your devastation at this confession. As you turn away slowly, he gently grabs your wrist.

"But you *don't* see!" he says in a voice so low you feel it travel down your spine. You turn back and stare at him for a few loaded moments as you watch this man, normally so composed, struggle to find words.

"I—it—it is strange."

"Strange?" you say in a whisper.

"Yes." Benedict stands and gently brushes the hair out of your eyes. "Strange that at this moment, when everything I have has been taken from me, when I should be feeling entirely lost . . . I *don't*."

You scarcely believe what you are hearing. He smiles at you, genuinely this time, his eyes darkened with desire.

"No?" you manage to say. He shakes his head.

"No. Instead, for the first time I finally feel complete." And with that he sweeps you into an ardent embrace.

Your knees buckle as you kiss him with a ferocity that is matched only by his own.

"Oh, Benedict, you fool," you sigh.

You feel his mouth smile against yours.

"Indeed. It is just my luck that when I finally feel this way, it is with a woman who drives me to distraction." You look up as laughter and desire dance in those steel-gray eyes.

"Truly, we are the unluckiest pair that has ever lived," you counter, "for the feeling is mutual."

"A tragedy, indeed," he says as he kisses you again, and you both tumble onto a nearby settee.

Benedict trails a stream of kisses from your mouth, down your neck, to your décolletage. Your back arches and you dig your fingers into his disheveled dark hair.

"We really should stop now," he murmurs, his mouth having reached the opening of your scandalously ripped bodice.

"You're probably right," you say as he rips it open even further and exposes a heaving breast. His wicked mouth opens, and his tongue traces the outline of your silken rosebud nipple as you squirm against him.

"This is a terrible idea," he whispers as his hand travels slowly up your trembling legs to the petal-soft folds of your womanhood.

"Indeed," you cry, heat pooling deep within your secret center as he strokes the glistening pearl at the apex of your thighs. "Quite the worst idea we have ever had, really."

His head rises to meet yours as he looks into your eyes with questioning intensity. You hold his face with trembling hands, knowing that despite your passion, fate may yet tear you apart.

Rafe's claim to his fortune, however false, may not be disproved. Benedict may still misguidedly refuse to do anything about it, out of love for his sister. Poverty may force him to marry an heiress . . . of the sort you are far from being. A long and dreary life of tending to the Dowager Dragon and embroidering her undergarments may await.

....

Regardless, this is hot. Do you throw caution to the wind and fornicate? Turn to page 313.

Or are you worried about your chances of happiness together in this cold and cruel world which conspires against your wishes, your desires, and your happiness? Is it, therefore, a better idea to just, ah, fool around? Turn to page 52.

"Lady Evangeline, please wait!" you cry out. She turns around, sending your heart leaping, and her beautiful, placid face lights up with sincere pleasure.

"You've changed your mind, my dear? Do you truly wish to watch an old bluestocking pore over some ancient scratchings for a few hours when you could be exploring the wonders of Cairo?"

"Oh, yes!" you cry. Lady Evangeline's mouth quirks at your sudden enthusiasm. Embarrassed, you glance at your dusty feet, if only to hide your face, which you are quite sure must be glowing scarlet.

If Lady Evangeline notices, she doesn't let on. Instead, she catches your chin with one cool pale hand and lifts it so your eyes meet. You find you can barely breathe as a smile spreads slowly across her face.

"Splendid." She links her arm with yours and starts down the narrow corridor. As you feel her velvet-soft skin touching yours, a thrill travels through you.

Still, you take a moment to look back warily at the man whom sweet Kamal calls his guard. To your surprise, he is staring at you in a manner that makes you feel as though he can see through to your very soul. Before you can ponder what this means, Lady Evangeline throws open the study door.

"Well, my dear," she says, "shall we begin?"

Go to page 101.

You clap your hands together and try to sound authoritative.

"I wanted to clean out the classroom today, but unfortunately a certain Scottish someone doesn't seem to think that possible. It's almost as if he thinks you don't have the strength to clean out a schoolroom by yourselves." The children stop punching one another for a moment and goggle at you. "'Weaker than kittens, and just as easy to scare' was the phrase, I believe is what he said." You do not feel guilty for the lie.

The children erupt into howls of outrage and darkly mutter "bloody stupid haggis-eating so-and-so" and "finks he can tell us wot to do. . ." You feel mildly bad for throwing Mac under the horse-drawn omnibus, but only just . . . and now you have more than twenty scrappy young cockneys to maneuver.

"I know!" you say, feigning outrage. "I told him that you were more than capable of cleaning out a schoolroom on your own, but he didn't believe me!"

The howls grow louder, and within minutes the classroom is filled with a horde of children rearranging furniture, sweeping, and scrubbing the walls. The room is already starting to look shockingly presentable.

Colonel Abercrombie chooses this moment to walk in, and immediately starts chuckling.

"Och, ye must have cast a spell upon the wee bairns, just like how you have bewitched young MacTaggart!"

"I-I'm not sure what you mean . . . ," you splutter, blushing furiously.

"He means Captain Mac wants to feel you up, miss," explains Sallie politely. "That is what my mum, God rest her soul, used to say about her gentleman visitors, and they liked her ever so much."

Before you can think of an answer, Colonel Abercrombie rescues you.

"Help me move these boxes, will ye, Sallie? There's a good girl." He smiles at you with fatherly tenderness. "Don't mind me. I'll just be moving a chest and a few boxes of some old papers of mine, no more, and then I'll be out of your way."

"It is no mind at all, Colonel Abercr—" The words dry up in your throat as you notice a certain strapping red-haired figure watching you in fascination from the doorway.

Mac cocks his head, grins, and walks in, nodding to the departing Abercrombie, who is lugging the heavy chest with shockingly little effort for a man of his age. Your heart flutters uncontrollably as Mac makes his way to you. What would it be like to have such a man "feel you up"? Every particle of your body aches with longing to know, and you hate yourself for it.

"What have we here?" says Mac, wincing as None-of-Your-Business deliberately knocks into him, grumbling about "bloody Scots swanning in here like they own the place." Mac doesn't notice, or chooses not to. Instead he resets the boy's course, saying, "Easy there, Bert," so kindly that it only serves to further darken the boy's mood. As the child stomps off, Mac turns to you, admiration and amusement sparkling like diamonds in those hazel eyes.

"I have nae idea how you managed this, lass, but it seems there is more to you than meets the eye." He reaches out and wipes a smudge from your cheek with a firm, calloused thumb. You tremble at his touch. "I feel I owe you an apology. Truly, you must have bewitched us all."

While you feel the very breath leaving your body as you stare into the soulful depths of his eyes, Sallie elbows another girl hard in the ribcage.

"See! I toldja, didn't I?" she hisses.

"Cor!" says her friend. "You reckon he's going to start feeling her up soon?"

You and Mac break apart instantly, but there is little time for awkwardness. The acrid smell of smoke begins to fill your nostrils, and you hear one of the children scream. Abercrombie rushes back into the room.

"We have to get out! The orphanage!" he says. "The orphanage is on fire!"

Mac immediately takes charge. "Lads! Lasses! Take one other

person's hand and follow me!" The children immediately respond and file out behind him, even angry little None-of-Your-Business.

You are relieved by how swiftly you escape, for the blaze wastes no time in consuming the crumbling building in its hot, angry flames. Mac stands in the pouring rain, his wet shirt clinging to his powerful shoulders in a highly distracting way, watching his life's work consumed by the inferno. His jaw is taut, but his eyes betray the depths of his emotions.

Instinctively, you grab his hand. He turns to you, looking as though his soul, too, has been swallowed by the conflagration. You share a moment, a sweet yet bitter moment, where it seems as though only the two of you are here, on this wet London street, the past burning away before your eyes like so much kindling. Unfortunately for you both, this is not the case.

"Oi! Dodger! No! Bad dog!"

You are broken from your reverie just in time to see Dodger racing back into the building—and little Timmy chasing after him.

Bloody Dodger. Turn to page 297.

You race Craven to young Alexander's room, and once there, you find the child crumpled in a sobbing heap on the floor.

Almost all the paintings of Blanche that hung elsewhere in the home have been gathered here, which is impressive considering their sheer number. Even more impressive, and horrifying, is that the eyes of every face have been ripped out.

You are struck by the sick poetry of it—if Blanche could see you now, trysting with her husband while her child screams for help . . .

Master Alexander turns his reddened eyes to you. "Mama's coming to get me again. Just like she got Helena!"

Helena?

"We NEVER speak that name, child!" Craven roars.

"But Papa," Alexander pleads, "she still plays with me every night!"

Something darker and more pained than any of the dark and pained looks that you've seen cross Craven's face. "Never!" he rasps. He flees the room, leaving you and Alexander alone with . . .

"Helena?" you half whisper.

"My sister!" Alexander cries. *Sister?* But you did not know of a sister . . . Your heart drops as the child grips your hands in his tiny fingers and weeps into your outstretched palms. "Helena says that she's not at peace, and neither is Mama." Hearing these words, a chill runs down your spine.

"She says to watch out for the bad man," Alexander whispers, and your blood runs cold.

. . . .

Enough of this.

If you wish to go straight to Craven and demand to know exactly WTF is going on, turn to page 337.

If you would love to get a straight answer from Craven but know that such a thing isn't possible even on a good day, let alone a day with a marathon passionate interlude just before his child brought up his dead other child's ghostly warning of danger, *maybe* you would be better off doing some sneaking around on your own first. Turn to page 310.

Constantina struggles against her captors the whole way back to the castle.

"Scum! You are all scum!" she cries.

"Of course, dear," you say, as though she is merely another recalcitrant orphan. "Now behave or you'll be sent to bed without supper."

Fortunately, the castle is old enough to have an actual dungeon, which yet more fortunately has been untouched by the ravages of time. You and Mac leave Constantina there, screaming about Napoleon.

No sooner have you stepped back into the fresh air than you run into a smartly dressed man, who can only be—

"Lord Fleming!" Ollie cries.

"The top spymaster in Britain," Mac whispers to you. "No doubt our friend's chief of command."

"We came as soon as we heard," Lord Fleming says briskly. "Well done, Ruston." Ollie whispers something in Lord Fleming's ear. The spymaster frowns, but Ollie whispers something more, and then Fleming hands him two packages, which he brings to you and Mac.

"Colonel Abercrombie's older brother died without issue several months ago," he explains. "That made Colonel Abercrombie the laird of this place. Of course, given the circumstances of this case, all his assets were seized for the crown . . ."

"So we're out, then," Mac interrupts, taking your hand in his own rough, manly paw. "Us and the orphans. Homeless."

Your heart sinks. But Ollie hands Mac the packages.

"No. You saved my life. And Lord Fleming has pulled a few strings. Since this was once property of a man who betrayed his country and caused the deaths of so many of his countrymen, it is only fitting that his lands should go to those who have suffered from such actions."

"You don't mean . . ." you say.

Ollie grins. "Captain Angus MacTaggart, it is my pleasure to inform you that this castle and all the land belonging to it is now the property of the Society for the Protection of Widows and Orphans of the War."

You and Mac exchange astonished glances. Ollie shrugs and then looks around at the crumbling structure disapprovingly.

"I may also be owed a considerable reward for finally finding the mole and uncovering rather a large amount of information that will help us find other traitors. Thanks, again, to you two," he says. "It is money I have no interest in, given the circumstances, and it seems to me you could do with some repairs around here."

"Oh, Ollie, you can't—"

But Ollie waves his hand dismissively. "I want you to have the money so you can make this hovel a suitable place to raise these children. I can think of no better purpose for it."

Mac shakes Ollie's hand vehemently. "I don't know how to thank ye." Ollie fixes his gaze on you.

"Some time alone with her would be more than enough."

You smile at Mac. You feel his gaze boring into your back as Ollie leads you to the other side of the room. "What is it, Ollie?"

He cups your face gently, and you gasp.

"I realized something tonight," he says. "That all this time, I was in love with a mirage." Suddenly, his russet hair and the hopeful expression in those rich brown eyes make him seem once more like the boy you used to love. "The only woman I have ever *truly* loved is you. And I don't want to lose you a second time."

"You mean—"

"I mean I want to keep you in my life. I have no doubt Fleming will be impressed with your pluck and quick thinking—"

"And use of stockings," you add.

"Indeed. So I have proposed that you and I work together." Ollie smiles. "Well, my darling? What do you say?"

If *yes please*, you want to be a spy and have sultry intrigues with your sultry ex-lover, turn to page 216.

If *no way*, Ollie has too wild a past, you don't know him after all these years, and you'd prefer a career that doesn't involve getting shot at, turn to page 328.

Nothing has prepared you for the spectacular yet elegant beauty of Manberley, the ancient seat of the Granvilles and home of Sir Benedict. Crossing the tastefully furnished receiving room, filled to the brim with the cream of the ton, you remind yourself that you are the longtime companion of Sir Benedict's aunt and have been personally invited to this house party by his cousin, Lady Evangeline. Truly, you have just as much right to be here as all these fine ladies and gentlemen, even if their handkerchiefs probably cost more than you make in a year. You raise your chin defiantly and search for a friendly face.

Unfortunately, Lady Evangeline is nowhere to be found. Even more unfortunately, you see the toadlike form of Sir Charles Burley-Fanshaw swiftly approaching, his face florid with excitement. And gin.

Desperate to escape, you turn sharply left and find yourself running headlong into a body that is at once familiar and disturbing. You force yourself to look up into the searing gaze of *him*, the man you detest and desire in equal measure.

"Sir Benedict," you say through gritted teeth. "What a pleasure."

"The pleasure is all mine." He kisses your hand, his eyes narrow with suspicion, and you curse your traitorous body for shivering at his touch.

"It was so kind of you to invite the Dowager Lady Craven and myself to this gathering," you continue in a honeyed tone laced with arsenic.

"Lady Evangeline would have had my head had I not."

"Of course. I forget how easily intimidated you are. I am so *very* sorry," you bite back.

"Your kindness is quite extraordinary." Benedict nods toward Sir Charles Burley-Fanshaw, who is currently hovering in your vicinity. "Especially when directed towards those who are able to give you something."

"Oh, Sir Benedict!" you trill. "Your meticulous morality, even in the face of such hardships as a baronetcy, a fine estate, and a fortune, does you credit."

Sir Benedict leans closer and whispers in your ear. A scent that is a mixture of leather, sunlight, and all man envelops you.

"By the way," he whispers, "what is it exactly that you have done with my aunt?" Your faces are so close that it would take moving but an inch for you to kiss his cruel, barb-slinging mouth.

Across the room, a glass smashes. Sudden silence descends upon the crowd.

There, at the entryway, stands a man so beautiful he looks like an angel of Botticelli's—an angel very much of the fallen variety. Behind him, a mousy young woman holds a kerchief to her mouth, fighting back tears.

"Who is that?" you whisper. But Sir Benedict is as frozen as the classical statues lining the walls of the room you are standing in, his patrician face drained of all color.

"*Cad*," he hisses. "What the devil do you think you're doing here?"

The fallen angel pointedly ignores him. "For those of you who are not aware, my name is Rafe Caddington," he says. "Or, should I say, Rafe *Granville*." The room heaves a united gasp. "You see, until recently my sister Henrietta and I believed ourselves to be mere by-blows of an *affaire* the late baronet had with our notorious mother, the famed doyenne of the stage, Mrs. Caddington. How wrong we all were." He tosses Benedict another look, at once triumphant and venomous. Another thrum of whispers travels throughout the room.

"What do you mean by that?" Benedict's silver-gray eyes are ice cold as he stares at the intruder.

"Well, brother of mine, all that has changed. You see, I have discovered a most *interesting* document." Cad thrusts a worn yet official-looking sheet of paper into the air. "What I have here is the secret marriage certificate of our late father, the baronet, and Henrietta's and my mother. You will see that it is dated two years before the nuptials of the baronet with Sir Benedict's own high and mighty mother, and six months before my birth. I believe anyone passably acquainted with mathematics has already worked out what that means . . ."

Cad stalks toward Sir Benedict like a hyena circling a lion.

"It means that Henrietta and I are the legitimate offspring of Sir

"There, at the entryway, stands a man so beautiful he looks like an angel of Botticelli's—an angel very much of the fallen variety."

Piers Granville. It means that I am the true baronet and owner of this fine estate and all its attendant privileges. What is more, seeing as my mother was alive and well until just eight years ago, it means that the marriage between Benedict's mother and father was very much illegal!" Cad steps toward Benedict until their noses almost touch. "And *that* makes dear old Benny—"

Cad pauses a moment, a golden version of his dark glowering brother, the profiles almost perfectly matched.

"—nothing but a *bastard*."

The room explodes with chatter. Several ladies faint dead away. Cad stands triumphantly, fielding questions from the hangers-on who now surround him, while behind him poor Henrietta sobs quietly— unusual behavior for a young woman who has just discovered she is a legitimate member of the aristocracy. You are at once suspicious but immediately distracted by the sight of an ashen-faced Sir Benedict, now being fully ignored by his former guests. Your heart aches for him despite yourself.

"I am so very sorry," you say gently. "Did you have any idea prior to this?"

Benedict turns to you, eyes blazing beneath his cold exterior.

"You would do very well to leave this alone."

"What?" Such a brusque dismissal is shocking, even from him. He stares at you piercingly, and you feel both your hackles rise in anger and your traitorous bosom heave with longing.

"Stay out of it," he growls. "That is *not* a request."

. . . .

The very nerve of the man, thinking he could boss you around so gruffly! If you wish to give him a piece of your mind, turn to page 260.

Or do you storm off in furious silence? The fool will only get in the way, and there is clearly a mystery to solve. If so, turn to page 107.

Fortunately, what you see when you enter the decaying entrance hall of Glenblair Castle does much to lighten your mood.

"Colonel Abercrombie!" you cry, relieved at the sight of the older man's familiar jolly face and white hair.

"Good to see you, lass, good to see you!" he says, hugging you warmly.

"How on earth did you get here so soon?!" you say. "You must have fairly raced here!"

"Och, no mind to that," he chortles. "How have you and our Captain MacTaggart been faring with the wee monsters? Any news?"

You cannot help but blush at the remembrance of exactly what you and Mac have been doing in Abercrombie's absence. The colonel raises his eyebrows but says nothing.

"We've been well," you venture at last. "And Jane and Gertie have been a great help, as has Mrs. Ferguson."

"Och, Mrs. F is a treasure, that's fer sure!" He pats your shoulder. "Though forgive me for saying, lass, but you seem a wee bit distracted."

You don't tell him exactly what has been distracting you, nor how the memory of it has been haunting your dreams these past few nights. But you *do* take the opportunity to press someone who might well know the full story of exactly what happened to Mac when he was at war.

"Colonel Abercrombie, do you remember anyone by the name of Constantina?"

Two lines appear between Abercrombie's eyebrows, as he seems to try to recall. "I reckon I do remember a lass by that name. A camp follower when we were stationed in Salamanca. A bonnie young lass, sweet as a rose in bloom."

"Do you know what happened to her?" you say, desperate to know the source of Mac's pain. Abercrombie shrugs.

"There I cannot help ye, lass. But war is a rough business, and young ladies disappear all the time, sadly. Though I hope that perhaps she simply moved on and that wherever she is, she is well."

You are glad to know more, yet something still niggles in the back of your mind. You are about to ask if he ever saw Mac with her when the man in question strolls in, shirtless and sweaty from caber-tossing practice.

"I-I must go!" you splutter to a bewildered Abercrombie and then tear out of the room.

Your mind races. What you need is something to engage it productively. Perhaps it is time to teach the children a thing or two about local Highland flora and fauna.

Alas, the orphans are busy driving Mrs. Ferguson to distraction with their attempts at sword dancing. She throws her hands in the air.

"Och, I've seen oxen move with more grace! Once again, now."

The children laugh uproariously, and you realize you do not have the heart to interrupt them.

So go find something useful to do, girl! Turn to page 306.

Lady Evangeline breaks from her sad reverie and signals for you to be silent as death. You have reached your destination—the camp of Delphine St. Croix.

Together, you sneak up to the encampment, which is presumably also the site of the lost temple. Delphine, who is exotically beautiful, with her dark hair, miraculously pale skin despite the blazing desert sun, and arresting catlike eyes, is berating a cringing Fabien. Though she is half his size, you find yourself truly fearing for his well-being.

"You are soft! You fool!" Delphine cries. "You will pay for losing her!" She pulls a pistol on Fabien. Evangeline raises her eyebrows.

"NOW!" Evangeline cries, and the gang charges into the fray. The desert quickly becomes a storm of fighting women, flying sand, and vengeful screaming, and as the epic battle rages, you lose sight of Delphine. Suddenly, you feel a sharp knife dig into your throat and a hand grasp your arm.

"Hello, little *putain*," Delphine sneers behind you. "You are coming with me."

....

Let's look at your options:

Do you fight tooth and nail, regardless of the consequences? You will not let this fiend use you as a tool against the woman you love! You will not! Turn to page 33.

Or do you prefer to stay not dead, all things considered? If so, make no sudden movements, just do what she says . . . and turn to page 236.

You rush to tend to Lord Craven, who has collapsed at the foot of your bed in a fashion both manly and vulnerable. You manage to tug down the neckline of your nightdress ever so, in order to ensure that the tops of your womanly orbs glow attractively in the moonlight.

You wrap him in your trembling arms.

"Lord Craven," you say. You know you should be scandalized, but your voice catches with desire. He places his hand against your mouth to silence you, letting his surprisingly rough fingers slip over your plush, parted lips. "You are bleeding!" you cry, your moonlit orbs heaving with every syllable.

"I have . . . *urges*." The way he emphasizes the word would bring you to your knees if you weren't already sitting. "I tried to fight them tonight. For you."

"Did you win?" you ask, not fully understanding what he's getting at—but also not minding so much because he looks so good being so bad. Any effort to solve the mystery of Lord Craven's words is abandoned the instant he wraps the width of your waist with his arm. For a moment you are both so charged with erotic electricity that you almost don't realize the painting of the lovely late wife with raven locks glaring at you.

"The painting," you whisper.

"Damn the painting! Damn her!" Lord Craven's ragged voice rips through the room as his hands rip through the portrait's canvas. "She made me this way! She made me a monster! But you!" Lord Craven tears his eyes away from the torn picture and burns his longing into your very soul. "You make me feel like a man," he growls lustily.

"Oh, Garraway!" you swoon, calling Lord Craven by his first name. A time for painting-ripping and waist-gripping is no time for formality.

"I want you," he keens, his eyes as wild as your desire for him. "I have wanted you since you arrived."

"But society dictates—" You attempt a false protest to at least appear to save your modesty.

"Society!" he spits. "What do our bodies dictate?"

He wraps you in an embrace so close you feel all the firmness of his body's dictations. You rack your mind for adequate verbiage but ascertain that the truest depth of your emotions can only be expressed by pressing the fullness of your moonlit orbs into Lord Craven's handsome, hungry mouth.

"The only society I care about," he says through mouthfuls of orb and ecstasy, "is yours."

The two of you make love with a violent passion on your bedchamber floor, atop the ruins of your purity and the painting of his dead wife's face.

Minutes, or possibly hours, later, as you lie panting in each other's arms, your reverie is broken.

"HE SAID IT WOULD BE ONLY ME! ONLY ME FOR ALL TIME!!" An eerie, feminine voice rends the air, followed by the sounds of a woman crying. Craven's face turns as pale as a corpse.

"Damnable woman!" Craven cries. He rushes from your chamber, leaving you with nothing but your tattered nightgown for company.

....

Goodness. Do you leave and never speak of this again? Turn to page 54.

Or do you investigate the voice? The source must be nearby, for it is in woman's-screaming-distance from where you are. In for a penny, in for a pound. Turn to page 93.

You are shocked, but you choose to stay. Surely he couldn't do anything in cold blood, knowing how hot he makes *your* blood run. Yet there must be more to tell. You stroke his face and look into those haunted whisky-colored eyes.

"What happened?" you ask gently. Mac explains.

"Constantina was Abercrombie's bit o' fluff back in the war, when we were stationed at Salamanca. All I knew was that she had a fine name and a fine eye for Abercrombie. One night, I was out walking, after m'guard. I had just passed a knot of Frenchmen on a bridge, thinking themselves hidden in the shadow. Here comes Constantina, headed straight for 'em, wobblin' like she was three sheets to the wind. I went to stop her, and she turned her knife on me, slashin' like a madwoman."

A shudder runs the length of Mac's glorious body. You reach out and stroke him. He moans, half in painful remembrance, half in total arousal.

"Go on," you urge.

"There was a struggle. She fell off the bridge to her death. I may have been a soldier"—he turns to you with shining eyes—"but, aye, lass, I have never held with killing women."

"Even a woman who seems to have wanted to kill you?" you say with wonder, as well as a fierce desire to untie the knots of his past.

"Ye ken," he says, deep into the valley between your breasts, "I can still hear her screaming." You are about to kiss him, to erase this tension on his brow and capitalize on the tension between the two of you, when your movements are interrupted by literal screaming: the sound of a horse about to give birth. Mac snaps to attention.

"Och, lass! A foal is needing born!" He races toward the keening sound. "We must help the mare!"

Oh, you think. Must we?

. . . .

Well . . . must you? If so, turn to page 50.

Or must you not, and instead get some air after all this drama? It's not like you've ever birthed a horse before. Turn to page 77.

A fortnight passes with no further incident with Lord Craven. In fact, the only evidence of his residing in Hopesend lies in the half-empty bottles of brandy he leaves in all areas of the house.

You wonder at the army of broken birds he has collected as his staff—to tend to them and keep them safe? Or to stalk them as easy prey? What wound does he see in *you*? Or did he lure you here to sate a different thirst?

These fantastical daydreams are interrupted only by occasional visits from the Reverend Simon Loveday, the handsome blond vicar, who comes ostensibly to check upon your well-being. Every time he leaves, he holds your hands for one delicious moment too long.

Your charge, Alexander, is a sullen child who stares into the middle distance with foreboding frequency. Perhaps his ill moods are rooted in the loss of his mother, yet you suspect something . . . darker. Still, you content him with study of the more murderous episodes of history. The child also enjoys covering screens.

By the next full moon, an unease has crept over you. The portrait of Blanche hanging in your bedchamber seems to study you whenever you undress for bed. Restless, you stroll the house in the small hours of the night, longing against your better judgment to run into Master Craven on your midnight explorations. Instead, your only company is moonlight . . . until one night, an eerie howl pierces the calm. Could it belong to the demon dog out on the moors the villagers spoke of?

Do you choose to investigate the moors like the curious wench you know you truly are? Turn to page 316.

Or do you run to your rooms and hide like the demure governess you aspire to be? Turn to page 324.

Sighing, you straighten yourself and kiss Benedict deeply, perhaps for the last time. "Goodbye, my love," you say, fighting the tears welling in your eyes at the cruelty of a world that could not allow your love to be.

Solemn and bow-legged, you walk to your rooms and change out of your dress, which is now ripped to shreds. You put on your only other frock, a drab gray affair. Most fitting, for you must ready your mind for a future so undesirable, so colorless, that to dwell on its reality would only do a disservice to the wonderful dream you just had the opportunity of living.

You resolve, at the very least, either to flee the Dragon's employ for someone less detestable or to ratchet up your kindness to her so that you may see Benedict as often as possible. You know you cannot be with him again, adding insult to his pauperhood if he decides to stay mum on the question of legitimacy for Henrietta's sake. You just can't bring yourself to decide if it is really possible to live without seeing him, even from a distance, forevermore.

As you stumble back into the great hall, you find yourself arriving the same time as your beloved Benedict. Your eyes bore into each other with knowledge of the intimacy that you once shared but now know can never be.

"Well, well, well," says a voice laced with venom, sending chills down your spine. You turn and see Cad stalking into the room, one eye blackened and his nose looking gratifyingly broken. Remembering what he came so close to doing, you shudder involuntarily. To both your joy and anguish, Benedict strides over and places a protective arm around your shoulders.

Despite it being madness to do so, you lean into him, despairing at how very right it feels to be one with him.

"So . . . I see you have made your choice," Cad hisses, his eyes narrow with rage. "It is a very stupid one and one for which you shall pay for the rest of your days."

"Don't you dare," growls Benedict as he steps protectively in front of you. You are gratified to see Cad flinch.

"I want you gone," snarls Cad. "Gone from my home, and gone

from my property. I am the rightful heir, and you have more than out-stayed your welcome."

By now, Lady Evangeline has appeared from a side door to witness the display.

"I have a dear little cottage on my grounds that you may stay in, Benny," she whispers gently before turning to you. "And you may stay with me while we resolve this whole messy issue."

Suddenly, you hear a fierce shriek. Henrietta bursts into the hall-way, her formerly meek face now lit up with righteous anger.

"You will not do this, Rafe!" she storms. Shocked that his mousy little sister seems to have grown a spine, Cad gapes helplessly for a moment, like a very surprised fish, before a chilling, icy rage crosses his face.

"You will hold your tongue," he seethes. "You know what the con-sequences are."

"I don't care anymore!" she cries. "I have stood here being a coward while you hurt the one brother who has always been good to me, even though he had every right not to be!"

Henrietta runs over to you and grabs your hand.

"And then you tried to hurt my new friend, who in the brief time I have known her has been kind, and strong, and brave enough to put herself in danger for those she loves!" Henrietta throws her shoulders back and appears to grow several inches. "So I have decided to be brave like her. I have told all the newspapers how you lied about our inheritance, the truth of what Mama did, and every single other time that you have lied, cheated, and swindled! And, as you know, there are many of those!"

You all stare at her, shocked and impressed, with the exception of Cad, who is staring at her like a man condemned.

"Y-you didn't . . ." he says incredulously, all color drained from his face.

"I did! With physical proof, too!" says Henrietta, her voice waver-ing slightly but her expression mutinous. You exchange shocked glances with Benedict and stand shoulder to shoulder with Henrietta.

She barely needs the protection.

"I don't care what you do to me anymore!" she cries. "All I care is that Benny and his true love are happy!"

"You—you little bi—" wails Cad before being cut off.

"It's over, Cad," Benedict says with frigid calm. "Get out."

Cad hesitates for a minute, looking at each of you before turning tail and fleeing, never to be seen again.

Lady Evangeline gives a round of applause and then embraces Henrietta.

"Well done, my dear," she says to the wide-eyed young woman. "You know, if it doesn't work out with your young farmer, you would be very welcome to accompany me on my travels to Egypt . . ."

As Henrietta decides her fate, you barely notice, for you have already decided yours. Benedict grins, his dark hair falling into his silver-gray eyes, now clouded with desire.

"What say you to getting the banns published today?" he says to you. "I don't particularly wish to wait any longer to be married, do you?"

You grin back.

"I think you are being exceptionally cocky, Sir Benedict, assuming that I even wish to be married to you."

"Oh, you know," Benedict says as he leans in and whispers into your ear, sending a shiver down your spine, "I can be very persuasive when I want to be."

"Then persuade me," you whisper back.

Benedict doesn't answer, but instead pulls you behind a convenient pillar.

Within seconds you find yourself extremely convinced.

The End

"*Vincit qui se vincit!*" you find yourself yelling to the small child.

"*Vincit qui se vincit!*" he yells back even louder, and then quickly breaks into fits of giggles. You both laugh and roll about the floor, which only makes him laugh harder. It warms your heart to make him happy.

"What have you taught me, miss?" he squeaks out. "It sounds like a magic spell!"

"It is a magic spell, in a way," you say. "It is Latin, an old language that hides underneath all of our new language, breathing life into it, giving it form. The words of the spell mean, 'He who conquers himself, conquers all he wishes.'"

Alexander scowls. "That sounds like it means you need to behave in order to be strong."

"In a way," you say. "It also means you must know, and conquer, what is in you that needs conquering to be able to stand strong against anything that might come your way."

"So I can be a hero?" Alexander asks, intensely skeptical.

"Of course," you answer, pleased with how motivational you are being until you notice the tears in his eyes.

"Mama said I wasn't strong." A tear slips down his face. "Mama said I was silly and bad, and that life was better before I came."

You reach out to comfort the sniffling child, only for him to flinch. "I'm sure Mama didn't mean that, darling. Mamas love their babies—"

"Not all mamas!" Alexander shrieks, his eyes now pouring tears. "Mama didn't love me! She said I ruined everything and she dreamed of killing me in my sleep! And Mama said . . . Mama said . . ." He flings himself into your arms. "Mama said I would never be a hero," he whispers. Your eyes lift to meet the taunting gaze of yet another portrait of the late Blanche Craven, née von Badwolff.

"Sometimes," you say carefully, "mamas are wrong. Come with me."

"Where are we going?" Alexander wipes the tears from his eyes.

"To be heroes, of course."

....

Time to learn some fencing, fools! Turn to page 122.

As Fabien momentarily releases your hands, you seize the opportunity as viciously as your captors have seized you. You half dismount, half tumble off the camel, punch Fabien's pretty face, then kick sand at his already streaming eyes, and flee.

Another henchman tries to tackle you. You duck, then knee him in an area that is sure to have him singing soprano for the foreseeable future. As he collapses to the ground, screaming, you grab one of the camels by the reins and attempt to swing yourself into the saddle.

Fabien's hands firmly grasp your waist and pull you off the grunting creature. Kicking and screaming, you both tumble to the ground. Fabien throws his well-muscled limbs around you and murmurs in your ear.

"Do not be stupid, *chérie*. I would hate to have to restrain you any more than is necessary. But believe me, I will do what I must bring you to my employer." He binds your wrists.

You spit in his face. He laughs.

"You have spirit. I like that." And with that he hauls you onto the camel and onward to Delphine.

. . . .

What, did you actually think you could fight off four enormous henchmen single-handed? Come on now. Think of a better plan and turn to page 290.

That evening, you wait in the eldritch garden for the handsome vicar, your bosom heaving in anticipation. Something hangs in the air tonight. Something seething . . . and unwholesome.

"I was worried you would not be here," says a gentle voice from behind. You turn and are relieved to see the smiling, golden good looks of the Reverend Loveday.

"Of course I am," you say. "What is it you wish to show me?"

The vicar steps toward you. He is close. Too close. Your body thrills, and the secret smile on his mouth colors you all over with delicious sin.

"Reverend Loveday?" you gasp. He pulls you to him and whispers in your ear.

"This was not part of the plan," the reverend says. He smooths his hand over your waist, pressing you gently against him, and you feel for a moment like a pair of lovers posing for a portrait.

"What, sir?" you cry, utterly confused and definitely turned on, despite (or because of?) the circumstances of your meeting. His once-innocent blue eyes brighten with lust.

"This," he says and leans in to kiss you.

. . . .

Do you let him?

Hell yes! Turn to page 334.

Hell no! Turn to page 258.

You are greeted at the door of the castle by a bony, frazzled older woman with a large nose and a prominent mole on her cheek. She looks like a fairy-tale witch, but her loud brogue is as cheerful and lively as a babbling brook in a glen.

"Och, it's good to see ye, good to see ye, wee Angus!" she says, warmly embracing a scowling Mac. The children nudge one another and snicker in delight.

"It's been a long time since I've been wee Angus, Mrs. F," Mac says, his voice slightly panicked. The woman throws her hands in the air.

"Don't be daft. You'll always be wee Angus to me. Good tae see you looking so well! And who are these bonnie lassies?"

Mac introduces you, Jane, and Gertie, and the woman hugs each of you warmly.

"I'm Mrs. Morag Ferguson, housekeeper and custodian of Glenblair Castle. Och, but it is a pleasure to have ye here! Though I warn ye, the castle is falling apart around us, so ye best watch where ye step!"

"I will make sure to," you say, warming to her immediately.

Mrs. Ferguson turns to the children. "And I see ye've brought a bunch of wee Sassenachs for me!"

"Is this a haunted castle?" says Sallie in excitement.

"Is it cursed?" whispers Timmy shyly.

"Was anyone murdered here?" Bert says with a grin.

"Och, indeed, indeed," says the old woman, waving her hands about. "What's left of these walls is fair stained with the blood of many! Hundreds of ghosts we have!" Timmy hugs Dodger and stares at Mrs. Ferguson in silent terror.

"Dinnae worry, wee one," she says, ruffling Timmy's hair. "Our ghosts are mostly friendly." The rest of the children moan in disappointment. Mrs. Ferguson puts her hands on her hips.

"I dinnae see why you are upset at a bunch o' boring old spooks. Not when they say there is missing treasure buried a hundred years ago within these very walls by the mad old laird!" All the orphans perk up at this news and resolve to find it immediately.

"Well, off you go then, ye wee terrors!" says Mrs. Ferguson. The children run off, intent on exploring their new home. Jane and Gertie follow in an attempt to make sure they do not break anything, or one another.

Mrs. Ferguson lowers her voice conspiratorially to you and Mac.

"Quite frankly, that buried treasure nonsense was a cover made by the Abercrombie family to hide that the old laird spent the family fortune on horses and whores. Though what I wouldn't give for a bit of that now, I tell ye."

"How bad is it, Mrs. F?" says Mac.

"Och, there is more ruin than castle these days. It will cost a fortune to restore, but even getting that roof mended is gonnae cost a pretty penny. We will all have to sleep in the Great Hall for now."

Mac looks thoughtful.

"Are the games on this year?" he asks.

"Of course they are, wee Angus!" says Mrs. Ferguson. "In fact, they are just three weeks away!"

"What's the prize money looking like?" Mac says, rubbing his ruggedly strong jawline.

"Ye thinking of entering the caber toss again?" Mrs. Ferguson says, grinning.

"Aye, that I am, Mrs. F. That I am."

Her eyes light up with delight. "Och, and I suppose I could teach the wee bairns some sword dancing! Would bring color to their cheeks, and the money from winning two events should be enough to cover the necessary repairs . . ."

Mac nods, then gathers what scant luggage you have brought and leads the horses to the collection of planks you assume must be the stable. You stare after his taciturn, manly form in annoyance—and longing.

Mrs. Ferguson puts a bony yet motherly arm around your shoulders.

"Ye should come inside and have a cup of tea, hen. Ye've already had some post arrive ahead of ye to read." And with that, she hands you two letters.

One is written in a distinctive flowing yet scrawling hand that you recognize. Once seated with a cup of hot tea, you tear open the letter, eager for news from your dear friend Lady Evangeline.

As you know, my dear, I plan on taking a short trip to Egypt soon, and I am in desperate need of a lady's companion. I understand that you may already be occupied with good works (and handsome Scotsmen) but if the shine has gone from that, please know that you would do me the greatest honor and favor should you agree to accompany this old widow to a most fascinating country.

You clutch the letter to your chest. The prospect is tempting. Still, you are loath to leave the children. And Mac, for that matter. The realization gnaws at you, and you open the other letter in a huff.

It is printed in a hand that seems strangely familiar. It is also unsigned. All this would be mysterious enough, but it is the content that truly sends a chill down your spine.

You are in grave danger. Leave this place—lest you suffer the fate of poor Constantina!

You stare at the skull-white page, reading the two sentences over and over. Is it a warning . . . or a threat?

. . . .

Well, cripes.

Do you take the letter's advice and get the hell away from the Highland mist—and potential attempts upon your life—in favor of warmer climes and Egyptian adventure? If so, turn to page 193.

Anyone could have sent that letter, and you cannot tell if that person's motives are proper. Plus, there is something about Mac that compels you to trust him and stay . . . and it isn't just his caber. Perhaps some sleuthing is in order? Turn to page 332.

You enter the great estate of Manberley solemn and bow-legged. You must ready your mind for a future so undesirable, so colorless, that to dwell on its reality would only be a disservice to the wonderful dream you have just had the opportunity of living.

You resolve, at the very least, either to flee the Dragon's employ for someone less detestable or to ratchet up your kindness toward her so that you may see Benedict as often as possible. You look over only to catch him burning a look of love into your eyes.

"Your breeches are still unbuttoned, my love," you whisper solemnly and watch his face riot with panic as he attempts to right his wrong. When he realizes you have bested him, and that his buttons are in fact entirely in order, you snicker.

"Made you look," you whisper, hoping he has not heard your voice—or heartbreak.

You take one last breath of happiness before entering the mansion, only to be greeted by an extended shriek from the Dragon, who exits the estate in an angry, agitated hurry.

"SCANDAL!" the Dragon cries. "SCANDAL AND SHAME!" Her dancing, beady eyes alight on Benedict's fine, jaggedly walking frame. "Where have you BEEN, Benedict? Henrietta! She is gone! She has run off with—with—a FARMER!" She breaks into a fit of pitiful wails.

"Now! Here! What is all this about?" Benedict asks, a man in command once more, a king returning to his kingdom.

You look about you and witness a mad scene: servants in confusion, furniture upended, and no sign of Cad or Henrietta anywhere. There, looking serene and beautiful as ever amidst the madness, is Lady Evangeline, reclining on the settee with a cordial in hand and a smile as wide as the great moors.

"How the devil did she beat us here from London?" Benedict whispers to you, his voice husky with postcoital satisfaction.

"Women have their ways," you respond, in awe of everything. Turning to Lady Evangeline, you say, "What's news with you, my lady? It seems a great happening has, erm, happened while we were away."

"It has indeed," Lady Evangeline responds calmly. "It appears someone, certainly not me, sent hard proof of the living existence of one Mr. Caddington, signed by a warden of Bedlam, to all the papers in London. Cad disappeared, as did his claims on the Granville name and fortune, as quickly as said papers were published. Oh, and Henrietta has eloped with her farmer. Do you have the time, dear cousin?"

Benedict, his beautiful face broken into a full grin, glances at the timepiece on the mantel. "It appears that it is one o'clock."

"Ah, yes." Lady Evangeline smiles. "Henrietta and Farmer Sam should be making excellent stride to Gretna Green by now."

"GRETNA GREEN! To elope?! Oh! Oh, I shall faint!" The Dragon has reappeared, if only to feign fainting dramatically.

"Please hold your faint, aunt, for a moment," Benedict says. Then, still grinning, he takes your face in his. "Cousin!"

"Yes, Benny?" Lady Evangeline says. You beam. Joy is contagious.

"Can you see about publishing the banns? I would like to make this young woman my wife as soon as possible, if she'll have me." You gaze at the man you love, the man you ferociously bedded in the carriage. There will be many carriage rides in your future.

"She will," you say, smiling. "I suppose. Certainly you need someone to keep you on your toes."

Benedict chuckles. "She supposes! It is settled then! We are to be married!" he shouts, his voice a waltz of joy you have danced before.

"No!" cries the Dragon. "Scandal! Shame! SCANDAL AND SHAME!"

"Scandal and shame, indeed, Auntie darling," you whisper, practically into Benedict's mouth.

"Scandal and shame, indeed," he says, laughing. And you drown out the rest of your laughter by kissing, kissing, kissing to the tune of the household's happy cheers—and the Dragon's pitiful cries of disgust.

The End

Two can play that game. You also storm out to the moors, in what you assume is the opposite direction Lord Craven took, judging by the trail of broken brandy bottles.

You have been storming for about half an hour before you realize you are lost. Mist swirls around you, obstructing your view so you cannot see where you have come from or where you are going. In the distance, a creature howls. The lump of fear in your throat only grows when you see a black-clad figure coming toward you. You gasp and feel about in your reticule for something that may offer some defense against the . . .

. . . handsome young vicar? Reverend Loveday smiles warmly at you.

"I am terribly sorry, I hope I didn't startle you," he says, his blue eyes full of gentle concern.

"Oh, Reverend," you cry in relief. "I fear I have lost my way here, for I do not know how to get back. Could you possibly point me in the proper direction?" You feel like a complete ninny, but the vicar smiles and allays your fears.

"Oh, I can do much better than that, I think!" He offers his arm. "Allow me to show you the way."

As you walk, you are overcome by the sensation of his warm body against the unearthly chill of the day. It is comforting, and yet somehow arousing. If the vicar notices, he gives no indication. You talk carefully of neutral topics such as the weather and funeral rites . . . until your curiosity gets the better of you.

"The late Lady Craven," you say finally, "did you know her?"

"Indeed I did," he says with enthusiasm. "She was a sweet woman, adored by all."

This is not what you wanted to hear. "She didn't seem . . . troubled to you?"

The vicar's guileless blue eyes darken. "Before her death, she *did* come to me," he says quietly. "She told me she was frightened, but of what or whom she did not say. I often wonder if I didn't do enough to help her."

"I'm sure you did everything you could," you say reassuringly. The vicar looks at you and pauses for a moment.

"I must confess, I was traveling toward Hopesend with a purpose. You see, shortly after Lady Craven's death I received a diary written in her hand, with a note from her asking me to keep hold of it and pass it on to someone who could help her beloved son." He presses a small leather-bound volume into your hands. "It felt wrong to give it to Craven, but I cannot let it languish any longer. You may have noticed my regular visits to Hopesend have been more frequent than usual? I should have—that is, I meant to give this to you earlier . . . But, the coward that I am, I lost my nerve. Forgive me."

You know not what to say.

"Reverend Loveday, I . . ." Looking up, you see the familiar foreboding shape of Hopesend looming ahead. The vicar doffs his hat politely and disappears into the mist as you clutch the book to your bosom.

Well, you can't *not* read it . . . Turn to page 218.

You take Fabien's angularly handsome face into your hands. "You are no one's second choice, Fabien, and I refuse to make you mine. Goodbye to you, and to my friends. I will see you, perhaps, in another life."

"Well spoken, my lady." Fabien drops his head, and a small tear lands softly on your still-outstretched hand. For a moment, you fancy it to be a jewel of the Nile. You blink and the jewel is gone, evaporated in the desert heat.

You walk over to the camels waiting patiently in the shadow of the newly risen temple. With ease and grace, you hop astride one.

"One last thing, Fabien," you say with a grit and authority you did not quite have when you arrived in Egypt.

"Yes, my lady?" Hope flashes in his eyes.

"Will you point me in the direction of Cairo?"

Once you make the long and arduous return to the city, you must decide what you truly wish to do.

Do you want to give the ton another chance? If so, turn to page 302.

Or are you kind of over normal society? Do you think managing a single rich child in a far-off mansion sounds like a nice departure from all this nonsense? If so, turn to page 14.

You arrive in America and soon become governess to a sweet girl who often calls you Mama by accident. This causes her to blush furiously and her handsome, young, new-money, widowed fabric-merchant father, a Mr. Haven, to laugh heartily. He lost his wife to influenza but gained you by a sheer stroke of luck, and when he gives you the gift of a fine dress, you surprise him by stripping bare in front of him to try it on.

He is a tender but ferocious lover, and the two of you have many lovely, hearty, smiling children together.

His first child is, of course, the flower girl at your wedding. Sometimes at night, when Mr. Haven has laced your ample bosom with a brocade of his ecstasy, you think of Lord Craven. You silently thank him for the gift of love, the promise of freedom, and the stroke of fate that allows you now to stroke your American lover's face as it travels south to pleasure your sex in an enthusiastic, endless demonstration of your new love's work ethic and aim to please.

The End

"Oh, Ollie!" you cry. He cups your face and then kisses you with long-unfulfilled passion, as if all those years apart, all those years of pain, had never happened. He pulls you closer and gently nips your shell-like ear.

"I cannot believe you became a spy!" you say with a sigh. "That is so . . . romantic. And thrilling."

Ollie releases your ear. "No, no, NO," he says, "this really isn't as attractive as it sounds. It's dark work I've had to do. Dark work, for the sake of my country."

"But . . ." you say, starry-eyed. Ollie groans and massages his temples.

"Listen, I've only revealed myself because you have taken a job with someone very dangerous. I've been trailing him for quite some time. When you turned up in London, I couldn't believe it. But I couldn't let you just stumble into this lion's den without warning you."

His tone and words are the metaphorical bucket of water you needed. "What?"

"My entire cell was killed!" He grabs you by the shoulders, his dark eyes like those of a cornered animal. "All of them, within the space of a week, on several separate missions! Each time, the French were ready and waiting for us. They picked us off one by one like stray dogs. And I—I was the only one who made it out alive, for I had gotten so drunk mourning for the woman I loved that I missed the appointed time of my mission!"

You stare at him, eyes wide in horror.

"Don't you see?! Someone must have sold British secrets for them to have known exactly where we were. And after much investigation I realized who the mole must be!"

"No," you whisper.

"Yes," he says, shaking you slightly. "It could only be one man. Captain Angus MacTaggart."

....

Uh-oh. Turn to page 96.

You again turn on your heel to give that insolent man one last piece of your mind—but instead you crash straight into a hot, hungry, well-dressed body. You blush. Of course he would see reason. A smile spreads across your lips as you look up and into the handsome, welcoming face of—

"*Cad?*" you say, incredulous.

For there, in all his rakishly handsome glory, is Rafe Caddington. He has the good looks and cynicism of the world's finest dandy and the eyes of the world's hungriest wolf. His smirk gives you ideas, which your other ideas must threaten with a stern talking-to in order to keep them in line.

"Why, when the madam said to have a look around and choose the woman of my heart's desire, she really meant it." His voice is as painfully luscious as a bite of rich trifle, and his hands run over you with as much relish as his gaze.

"Unhand me, sir! I am not your plaything, just as the rightful Granvilles are not your playthings!" You wrest your breast from his groping, gloved fingers. "I am merely in this house of ill repute to confirm that your repute is the illest of them all."

"It most certainly is," he growls, using his rock-hard thighs to trap you against a large Grecian urn inscribed with the filthiest of odes.

You knee him. Hard. He gasps, but grips you tight about the shoulders.

"I take pleasure in pain. And I take what I want! Wealth! My name! YOU!" His cry is savage, hungry, and cut short by a yank to his fashionably unkempt mane.

"You will stop taking this instant, you leech!" It is none other than Benedict. He cuts his eyes at Cad, then throws a tenderer gaze to you. "Please forgive my cruelty," he whispers. "I have been brutish to you because I am brutish to myself. I didn't think I would ever need worry about love, or desire, and you have swept into my life like a wildfire, making me suddenly concerned for the safety of things I took for granted. The safety of my solitude. The safety of the way things are. I see now that there is nothing safe in being so miserably unhappy that I

"Cad launches a fusillade of watercress sandwiches at Benedict before
clocking him with the fine silver tray they were laid upon."

am willing to let my life be colorless and cold without . . . *you.*"

A thousand emotions and desires cross your mind at once, and you struggle to come up with a quip that could express them all.

"Oh, darling, let me save you the trouble," Benedict says, and he drops Cad long enough to draw your face to his and bury your mouth in a kiss that would be everlasting—if Cad didn't interrupt it by tackling him.

"Damn my eyes!" he yells. "The mighty son of Lord and Lady Granville, heir to everything he has never earned, kissing a common maid in a whorehouse like the bastard he truly is!" Cad's eyes and voice are charred with jealousy.

"Oh, come now!" Benedict says, deflecting Cad's next punch and throwing his own. "You've done worse in whorehouses!"

"You dare mock me!" Cad launches a fusillade of watercress sandwiches at Benedict before clocking him with the fine silver tray they were laid upon.

"Please!" Benedict sneers, breaking a candle from its elegant pewter taper to use as a death baton. "I mock everyone!"

"Your name! Your fortune! Your station, your love"—Cad manages to sneer at Benedict and spit on you at the same time—"will do you no good where you're going, man. No one's life is respected, noble or no, when it is over!" Cad raises the sandwich tray high above him, murder in his eyes, emptiness in his heart, watercress sandwiches on the floor.

"Cad, no!" you scream.

"Slattern, yes!" he screams back.

....

Can Cad be reasoned with? If so, turn to page 230.

Or is he nothing but a lecherous weasel who needs to be taken down immediately in as violent a manner as possible? If so, turn to page 309.

Before anything can be said or done, the handsome postman nods at you, shuts the carriage door, and climbs into the driver's seat. You are rumbling off to your date with destiny without another moment's hesitation.

You try to sleep, but your mind races with thoughts—thoughts that may belong to you or to the wild night, you are not sure. Just as you are wondering how a man could be so monstrous as to inspire such a repulsed, repressed curiosity throughout the ton, your carriage lurches to a stop. A beast in the distance keens into the violet, moonlit sky. Your heart thrums. When you took your meal at the Slaughtered Lamb, there was much talk about a barghest creature the locals swore haunted the moors around Hopesend Manor. Can this far-off call be the demon dog's heartless cry, as it stalks the night for prey?

No! You steel yourself and shake all qualms from your heart. You're not some silly chit who fills her head with the nonsense of gothic novels. The carriage door opens, and you take your valise—and, with it, the situation—firmly in hand.

In the weak morning light, you approach the great carved portal of Hopesend Manor clutching the letter from Lord Craven. The house sighs like a dying maiden as the door swings open, revealing a specter with the body of an old woman and a face like a stone gargoyle whose finer features have been worn away by the harsh elements of nature. This person is missing one arm, and its other boasts a clawlike hand. You lose your grip on your valise—and, with it, your composure—and scream for your life.

"There, there, love, let's get you inside." It is a more comforting tone than you have ever heard a hellbeast emit. "You must be who the master sent for." She—for she must be a she—gathers your valise and letter into her one pleasantly plump arm.

Temporarily struck dumb, you nod slowly.

"Oh, my, are you simple, love?" Her voice is warm with patience and understanding.

"No! No, I—" You shake your head, at a loss for words. The woman hangs her head in a moment of apparent bashfulness.

"I have given you a fright. I see. Well, no offense taken, love! It isn't the first time and surely won't be the last that I give someone a scare!" Her voice is as kind as her visage is frightening. You take another curious look at your greeter: a woman of advanced years, whose face, remaining arm, and hand are roped with scars from long-ago burns. Your stomach drops at your coldhearted reaction to her appearance.

"I am so very sorry," you say, desperate to make up for your horrifying faux pas.

"No mind, love. I'm Mrs. Butts, the housekeeper round here," the creature assures you in an even kindlier manner than before. Still, you see her hand brush her scarred cheek ever so briefly. You sink under the weight of your own shame as she nudges you conspiratorially with her motherly shoulder. "Ready to meet the master?"

Your heart flutters in your nicely endowed chest. After Mrs. Butts leads you to your chambers, you quickly change into your one fine black dress and hope that the handsomeness of your figure distracts Lord Craven from the fact that the garment is at least an inch too tight and a touch too frayed to be considered fine anymore.

Thus attired, you smooth your hair, raise your chin, and descend the stairs to meet—

"Master Alexander!" Mrs. Butts cries, and you are confronted by a boy no older than eight years of age with murder in his eyes and a hoop and stick in his hands.

"The lady is here to play with ME!" cries young Master Alexander, and he sets about to smacking you with the stick element of his hoop and stick set.

So begins your career as governess to the most horrible child you have ever had the poor fortune to meet.

"Call me Master Craven! I command you!" Master Alexander now strikes you with his hoop as well as his stick. *Oh no*, you think, *this will not do*. You deftly intercept both hoop and stick during the wind-up to young Master Alexander's next fusillade and use them to expertly box the boy's ears.

Master Alexander is almost too shocked to cry. Almost. And then, quite masterfully, he wails.

"When you are done crying," you say in your most character-improving governess voice, "I shall explain the folly of your actions. Then you will apologize for your impudence. And then, since you are clearly a man of action, we can learn a brief history of fencing before we take our morning constitutional."

Master Alexander suddenly quiets, studying you through a mask of his own tears. "You know about fencing?"

"Of course I do, dear boy!" You laugh delightedly, half at the sweetness of the child's inquiry, half at your own satisfaction of having read a good deal about the history of *jeu d'escrime* in your youth in order to one day use it to silence a self-satisfied gentleman. "I even know how to fence myself. I will love to teach you if—"

"SILENCE!"

Your private, self-congratulatory reverie of how grand a governess you are becoming is immediately cut short by the angry boom of a voice so deep you could drown in it.

You look up from Master Alexander's small form, past the trembling Mrs. Butts, and into the eyes of a man you could swear was cut from stone if not for the fire burning in his sin-green eyes. Suddenly, you see what the hushed tones at the tavern were about when the locals were discussing Lord Craven. He is the epitome of manly strength, drawn with a fine hand and painted with a rage-red brush. He is as handsome as he is angry, and he is *very* angry.

"I hired you to keep the peace in my household, woman. Not," the beastly man seethes through gritted teeth, "disturb it."

You know you should show deference, but the lord is being more than a touch impossible with respect to his expectations, not to mention hopelessly rude.

"Pleased to meet you, sir. You must be Lord Craven. I do hate to be insulting, but I scarcely gathered that as governess I was hired solely to be a dampener of sound. I was merely attempting to improve the child—"

"There is no improving him," Lord Craven roars. "There is no improving anyone. We are the way we are, and that is all!"

"Greeting a woman by hitting her about the body with hoops and sticks! One would think he was raised by wolves!" As soon as the words escape your mouth, you regret them. You are speaking too boldly, but being in this man's presence awakens all your senseless passions.

"Wolves," says Lord Craven, crossing the length of the chamber in two easy strides, "would likely be a better choice of governess than you."

"Yet you didn't hire a wolf, Lord Craven," you say, astounded by your audacity. "You hired me."

The man is so close that you find yourself nearly swooning at the woodsy, musky smell of him. Though you don't know where you find the strength to do so, you return his burning gaze with fiery strength. He gives you a once-over so savage that you can't repress the shudder it produces. You attempt a more tender tack.

"He is your son, my lord. Your son."

And with those words, the life falls from Lord Craven's face.

"He has his mother's eyes," he says, cold as a crypt. Then he turns on his heel and is gone.

A full minute passes before you are able to regain a sense of equilibrium. "What—" you start to ask Mrs. Butts, but she waves you off, not unkindly.

"The lord has his ways," she says. "Never you mind. Give him his distance, follow his rule, and everything will be fine. Now, miss, to meet the staff!"

. . . .

Feeling like you don't have a choice? You chose to be a governess in a mad lord's mansion flung far on the moors. Get used to it. Turn to page 248.

Damn him. Once back in Derbyshire, you storm to your quarters and pack your bags in a rage. This is most certainly goodbye . . . for now.

Do you make your escape to the East End to do good works with a certain rugged Scotsman, and maybe get pickpocketed? Turn to page 208.

Or do you make your escape to do some gothic governessing in Yorkshire? You hear the rain is quite lovely this time of year. Turn to page 14.

As you step off the barge, you pause for a moment in wonder that this is really happening. After all, just a short time ago you were but a humble lady's companion. And now . . . well, admittedly, you are still a humble lady's companion.

Still, it is a far more companionable lady you find yourself traveling with. A very beautiful and exciting lady, who has taken you to the very heart of Cairo. Your own heart wells with excitement, for all around you are sounds, sights, and feelings that you do not recognize . . . least not when such feelings are for the lovely Lady Evangeline.

The boat lurches suddenly and the gangplank pitches you forward. You are about to fall into the murky waters of the Nile when in one swift, liquid movement Lady Evangeline deftly catches you. "Careful," she says with a smile, holding you tight for one thrilling second before setting you back on your feet.

You shake your head, hoping that will clear the sudden dizziness that has overtaken you. This is madness, madness and possibly heat stroke. Rather than dwell on such confusing emotions, you hurry to keep up with the lady as you both make your way through the bustling metropolis. Still, you cannot stop yourself from starting as she turns and grins rakishly at you, out-dazzling even the blazing African sun.

"Where are we going first?" you ask nervously. Something between you has changed on the journey, and what was once easy friendship now feels like something you can't quite put your finger on. Something fraught and raw-edged and ready to explode—at least on your part. Now you are constantly finding yourself nervous and tongue-tied in her presence.

If Lady Evangeline has noticed the shift, she does not let on. Rather, she continues with the same self-assured ease that has set your foolish heart aflutter as if you were but a schoolgirl.

"The museum, my dear girl," she says. "Of course."

Not knowing what she means by "the museum," you are momentarily struck dumb, partly from shame at your ignorance and partly from her exquisite beauty. She seems to understand your confusion and rubs your shoulder. You shiver despite the intense heat.

"The Museum of Egyptian Antiquities, I mean. Run by my dear friend Kamal Abu Habib bin Hasan al-Munawi. Such a sweet man, and quite brilliant, too. He has dedicated his life to preserving the treasures of the pharaohs and making sure such wonders remain in Egypt."

"Th-that's very good of him," you volunteer shyly.

"Oh, it is." She nods. "Just wait until you see the museum. It will take your breath away."

And indeed, what greets you when you enter the museum does take your breath away, though not in the manner intended. The white marble floors of the great central room are scattered with hundreds upon hundreds of treasures from Egypt's golden age. At the center of the chaos stands a bookishly handsome, bespectacled young man. His dark hair sticks up in all directions from nervous rubbing.

"Kamal!" gasps Lady Evangeline. "What the devil happened?!"

"Oh, my lady!" the man cries. "Intruders broke in last night! They shattered a window, knocked my best guard unconscious, and—and then . . ." He gestures in despair at the destruction around him.

Lady Evangeline steps delicately over the rubble and manages to find a seat for the trembling Kamal, before gesturing to a servant to bring tea.

"Did your guard see what they looked like?" she asks gently. Kamal shakes his head.

"No! They wore masks and hoods! And this is such a large city. It will be impossible to find them."

Lady Evangeline places an elegant hand on her friend's slumped shoulders. You watch with fascination as she gently rubs the back of the surprisingly attractive young man and are shocked to find your heart clenching with something not unlike . . . envy?

No. This cannot be. Surely the unaccustomed climate is causing your face to flush and your pulse to race. Shrugging off this unnerving feeling, you hand Kamal the tea that has just been brought in and force yourself to speak.

"I am so sorry, sir. Did they take many things?"

Kamal turns his large, soulful brown eyes—now wide with

confusion—to you.

"No, and it is very strange. I have gone through my inventory all morning. We have many fine things, but it appears the thieves took only one object: the turquoise scroll canister."

Lady Evangeline stands suddenly, her jaw tight.

"*Delphine St. Croix!*" she hisses.

Kamal's jaw drops.

"How can you be so sure?" he asks, but Evangeline is now pacing the room, barely paying attention to either of you.

"Oh, this is *so* like her! Of course she would do this. Of course!"

"Who is Delphine St. Croix?" you inquire, unable to disguise your curiosity.

Evangeline swings around, her eyes flashing azure fire. Her finely made bosom heaves before she regains her composure. "Delphine was once a . . . *friend* of mine." Behind you, Kamal coughs discreetly, and Evangeline continues. "We bonded many years ago when my late husband was stationed in Egypt. Life was somewhat constrained and lonely for us women, with the war on. What is more, she and I were the only two ladies in our circle who had the same love for, ah, ancient artifacts."

Kamal coughs again, somewhat less discreetly.

"At the time, I fancied I cared for her more than anyone. But then, well, let's just say she betrayed my confidence in a manner that I will *never* forgive her for. We parted on the harshest of terms, and last I heard she was making a living raiding tombs, selling the objects to the highest bidder with no thought to their significance, nor where they are destined to go. And now she has drawn your museum into her schemes, Kamal. I am truly, truly sorry."

Something in the way Evangeline speaks of the mysterious Delphine piques your curiosity . . . and your jealousy. You ignore the emotions roiling around your heart and manage to keep your voice steady.

"But why would she take the turquoise canister and nothing else, especially in a room filled with much worthier treasures?"

Evangeline locks her lustrous eyes with yours, and again you feel the heat rising to your face.

"Because this was no simple robbery, my dear. This was a *message*."

"W-w-what do you mean?" you stammer. Lady Evangeline smiles at you, not unkindly.

"The canister was made of turquoise, you see, the sacred stone of Hathor, ancient Egyptian goddess of love. Delphine and I . . . well, we had this foolish notion that one day we would find her temple. It was lost to the sands of time many years ago, but legend has it that the temple can be raised again should two lovers enjoy love's purest joy within its grounds."

A strange look crosses Lady Evangeline's face as she tells you these words. You find yourself suddenly out of breath.

"A silly idea conjured up by two bored young women, to be sure," she says, crisply brushing off the strange moment. "Still, I must confess myself curious to know what was on the scroll in that canister. No doubt Delphine is using it to locate some other priceless treasure that she will hawk to shady sorts, and to make sure I know she is thumbing her nose at me all the while."

"I think I can help, my lady," interjects Kamal. "You see, I make a sketch of everything that comes through these doors, including the canister and its contents." He hands you and Evangeline a finely rendered illustration of the artifact and several pages of neatly copied hieroglyphs.

"Oh, Kamal, you are a national *treasure*!" Lady Evangeline exclaims. "Do you know what this means?"

You and Kamal exchange curious glances and shake your heads. Lady Evangeline turns and grabs you by the shoulders.

"It means I shall be able to translate what is written here and get to the bottom of what exactly Delphine is up to!"

"You can read hieroglyphs?!" you say, stunned.

"It is a very new practice, but yes." Evangeline nods. "I assisted Mr. Young and Mssr. Champollion when they were working on their studies of the Rosetta Stone. When they were still speaking to each other, at least." At this, she rolls her eyes.

"Lady Evangeline is too modest," says Kamal reverently. "She has published the eminent paper on translating hieroglyphs, albeit anonymously."

Evangeline throws back her head and laughs. "Ah, Kamal, you are too kind about my little treatise. And *that* is why you are my favorite Egyptologist," she says, causing Kamal to blush.

She then turns her luminous gaze back to you. "My dear, translating this scroll may take a while. If you wish to use this time to explore Cairo, then by all means be my guest. I'm sure Kamal will be more than happy to provide an escort. I certainly think he could use a respite from this morning's unpleasantness."

Kamal nods in agreement. "It would be a pleasure, miss. I will bring my strongest guard to make sure we remain quite safe."

Lady Evangeline turns her head to the side, her hair shining in the sun as richly gold as the priceless treasures of the pharaohs she so loves.

"What do you say, my dear? Would you prefer an afternoon stuck in a stuffy room with me translating hieroglyphs or out in the sunshine in one of the most beautiful cities in the world?"

Do you take the chance to explore Cairo with the sweetly bookish Kamal? Lady Evangeline may be fascinating, but translating ancient languages you don't speak sounds dull, dull, dull. Turn to page 336.

Or do you ignore the beauty of Egypt's historic capital to spend every moment you can with Lady Evangeline? Turn to page 244.

You and Craven make extremely passionate, extremely angry love. You even manage to knock one of those damn portraits of Blanche off the wall with your acrobatics. Your lovemaking is fast and furious— but not too fast or too furious.

Sharing a moment's tenderness after many moments' roughness, you stroke the red marks you have left on his massive shoulders and trace the imprint of your teeth on his skin with your tender tongue. His body trembles.

"Even spent, I shiver with desire for you," he rasps.

"We want each other as much as we love each other," you say, simple as breath. "It makes all pleasure sweeter." You nestle into the crook of his arm, hoping for another moment's rest before starting again, but his body stiffens, and not in a pleasurable way.

"Love each other?" he asks. "You think this is *love*?"

Your body stiffens, and not in a pleasurable way.

"I do not think it," you laugh joylessly. "I know it."

"You know nothing!" He flings you from him, his body visibly rioting in your presence, even though your presence now wants to slap him upside the head.

"You are behaving monstrously!" you cry. Crying aloud is so thrilling and dramatic. You wonder why people don't do it more often.

"You do not know the half of it! You do not know the half of *me*!" he roars, throwing back his head. Even the man's throat is sensual. Damn. Then he sizes you up with insatiable lust. "This can never happen again!"

He stalks out, presumably to roam the moors.

. . . .

All right. You know what? All his games are *not* working for you. Do you finally admit defeat, call the nineteenth-century equivalent of Child Services, and get the hell out of there? If so, turn to page 54.

Oh no. All his games are *totally* working for you, especially considering what he can do with his tongue. Plus, you love Master Alexander. Of course you stay, because you are fully invested now and must know the truth! Turn to page 180.

"If I say yes, do you promise to stop being so . . . vexingly attractive?" you ask. Benedict's face breaks into a wide, hopeless grin.

"Absolutely not."

"All right then," you say, smiling. "Yes, anyway."

"SHE SAID YES, ANYWAY!" he cries, elated. The portion of the ton who aren't whispering in scandalized tones cheer mightily.

The Dragon spits fire. "I shall contest it! No paper will print the banns. I know people, you chit! I will block this union, I swear it, I—"

"You will do nothing of the sort, you nasty old bat," Benedict says. He laughs and dips you into a kiss so brazen that it makes your sex drip sunlight and causes poor Nigel Frickley to mutter a stream of frantic "Oh my"s.

"Come, my love," Benedict whispers into your ear. "We are eloping to Gretna Green!"

And so you do. You live a long and happy life together and never invite the Dragon for Christmas.

You do, however, always make sure to send her a ham every year, complete with a card which you faithfully sign:

With warmest regards from your favorite chit.

The End

"Lady Evangeline, you are too kind. But there is intrigue afoot, and I must get to the bottom of it," you say. "After all, I do worry for Sir Granville—Benedict, that is."

Lady Evangeline raises an elegant brow again.

"Not that I like the man, of course!" you say, a little too heatedly. "I just feel sorry for him."

She smiles warmly.

"Of course, my dear. And I must admit, I myself am curious what is going on. I suggest that we make a journey to London tomorrow to interview one of the late Mrs. Caddington's associates. I further suggest we make it an early night, in order to start on our journey tomorrow as soon as possible."

And with that, the two of you laugh, link arms, and make a quick exit. On your way, you see that the dowager is dozing upon a settee, her head tilted back, snoring full blast.

The next day, you rise with the dawn. Lady Evangeline plans to leave a note for the dowager claiming that she is borrowing you for an urgent haberdashery mission, but you are a little concerned that you might not have a job to return to at the end of all this. Yet, if your investigations yield good news for the Dragon's darling Benny, perhaps she can be swayed. In any case, you are willing to risk her wrath.

Urgently thrusting your scant belongings into your threadbare valise, you wonder what exactly *does* one wear to a location not suitable for respectable young ladies? Everything you own seems depressingly, well, respectable.

Creeping out of the room, your heart simultaneously leaps and falls when you realize you have run into *him* again.

"Sir Benedict," you say, as politely as you can muster. You expect to see the customary curt nod you have grown used to . . . and perhaps somewhat fond of. Instead, Benedict's formerly haughty eyes are shadowed and haunted. He shakes his head ruefully.

"I believe my name is now Mr. Granville. Or perhaps De Lacey, my mother's name."

"Surely you don't believe—"

"Does it matter what I believe? What matters is what everyone else believes. What matters is that there is proof. And what matters most of all is that now Henrietta has prospects, has a *future* that has been denied to her all this time simply due to her birth."

"You are a good brother," you say, unable to conceal your surprise. He smiles at you wryly, causing your heart to skitter like a debutante's after too much champagne.

"She's the only decent one among us, and she deserves better from her family, myself included. The one thing I'm thankful for in this sorry situation is that she has been given a chance at happiness."

"I rather think she has *lost* her chance of happiness," you counter.

"What the devil do you mean by that?" As he glares at you, you square your shoulders and raise your chin.

"I mean that she loves someone who is now beneath her in station. A young farmer. One who has been torn away from her by the recent revelations."

"Don't be ridiculous—"

"It's true! She told me herself. And I think that she is only going on with this sham of Cad's because she is frightened. Perhaps he threatened her—"

Benedict grabs your shoulders and leans so close you can see the silver that edges those steel-gray eyes.

"Didn't I tell you to leave this alone?" he growls. "Haven't you listened to a damned word I've said?!"

Your heart may be racing, your flesh may be burning with desire at his touch, but you will *not* be intimidated. Instead you narrow your eyes and hold your gaze.

"She doesn't want to be a fine lady married off to some stuffy aristocrat! She wants to be with the man she loves!"

"Love only serves to ruin lives, in my experience. Look at my father. He loved Mrs. Caddington, and it broke my mother's heart when he returned to her. And now we must live with the consequences, the misery that has come about for his children as a result of his failure to regulate his emotions and his behavior."

"It doesn't have to be like that," you bite back. "My parents loved each other! They were perfectly happy and true until the end of their days!"

"And then they died, leaving their daughter penniless and without a friend in the world!" he thunders.

You gasp in outrage at his cruel words. The nerve of the man! The very nerve!

If this will not stand, and you want to have it out with him *right now*, turn to page 239.

If you have had enough and are now done with him, turn to page 318.

"He is not my husband!" you say so loudly that the innkeeper jumps a little.

"Not even slightly?" the innkeeper asks, cruel delight in his voice.

"No!" you and Mac cry in desperate unison. The innkeeper shakes his head and gives you both a look of slight puzzlement and more-than-slight disappointment.

"Fine, then. Sleep well."

As you retire guiltily to your room, and Mac to his stable, you cannot stop thinking about how badly you wish that you were sharing a room *with him*, and that he was pouring the same energy he pours into his virtuous work into the cup of your virtue.

You undress and are struck mad with desire for your cup to run over, with Mac's true mouth working your bosom free from the bindings of your gown—and your honor. As you loosen your bodice to further aid your fantasy, the strange piece of paper that Dodger brought out of the burning building back in London falls to the ground. You pick it up and read the name again.

Constantina.

Try as you might, you cannot puzzle out Captain MacTaggart. On the one hand, he is all gruff honesty and goodness in his manner. On the other hand, he seems somewhat haunted. But by what? Oh, how you wish to smooth that furrowed brow with your delicate touch and run your fingers through the messy ruff of ginger hair.

Steady on, *messy ruff of ginger hair*? You of course meant the *truth*! You wish to run your hands through the truth . . . and all other clumsy metaphors you can apply to Mac's broken, breaking, bedeviling beauty.

You collect yourself. Handsome Scotsmen aside, you must admit something unusual is going on—there was the sudden blaze, the mysterious parchment, and something else that you cannot quite put your finger on that has piqued your curiosity and your suspicion.

You look out to the dark stables, which shimmer in the moonlight and freezing cold downpour. You ought at least to bring Mac a hot drink, and maybe feel out the truth, which is the only thing you are hoping to feel out. Nothing else.

You throw on a shawl, procure a cup of cocoa from the irritatingly bemused innkeeper, and tromp out toward the stables in search of the hard, wet truth.

Of course, your firm resolve crumbles like an oatcake when a shirtless Mac greets you at the door. You stare dumbly, clutching the mug of cocoa like a shield between you and total, animal desire. He looks startled.

"Och, lass, I thought ye were the landlord! What are you doing here?"

You proffer the mug like an acolyte presenting an offering to the God of Beauty.

"*I'msorryIthoughtyoumightbecoldherehavesomecocoa*," you splutter. He takes the mug from you, his hands lingering on yours.

"That's kind of ye, lass." He lifts the drink to his lips without breaking eye contact.

You gulp. You have so much to ask. About the parchment. About Constantina. About Scotland. About why those moss-and-wood-colored eyes of his always look so lost when he thinks no one is looking.

And you probably would have asked, had you not been so distracted by the glorious muscles currently within licking distance. Mac drains the last of the cocoa, wipes his mouth with an easy, manly gesture, and hands the mug back to you. You open and close your mouth helplessly, like an extremely aroused fish.

Yet try as you might, you cannot bring yourself to mention Constantina . . . nor contain your animal desire. You toss the mug aside and grab Mac. He grabs you back, stoking a desire that burns down inhibitions as wholly as the fire consumed the orphanage.

"Och, lass." Mac's mouth closes over yours in an exhilarating, punishing kiss. You kiss back with equal fervor, your hands digging into messy ginger hair and not, alas, the truth. Mac throws you both down in the hay and trails a series of blazing hot kisses down your throat and onto your still very exposed bosom. You wail and thrash in ecstasy, arching your back to meet his wicked mouth. "Oh, Mac!" you cry. "MAC!!"

At the sound of a loud whinny, you look up, horrified to see that you have quite literally scared the horses. What are you doing here with this man you barely know, with his rough, massive hands? A man who by all odds you shouldn't trust? Too many questions remain unanswered, and you will not get them answered rolling in the hay with the man that is provoking most of them.

"Are ye all right, lass?" Mac asks, his eyes filled with concern. How could you distrust this man? At the same time, how can you trust him?

"I—I have to go!" you gasp finally. "This—this is wrong. This is all wrong!"

And with that you scamper through the pouring rain back to your room, unfulfilled desire throbbing uncomfortably within you. You toss and turn for the rest of the night, your fevered dreams filled with rippling muscles, neighing horses, and bagpipes.

Think about what you've done. Turn to page 289.

You follow the low keening sound to the orangery. There, whimpering like a much-abused kitten, you find Henrietta.

"Miss Caddington?" you say, but then quickly correct yourself. "I mean Granville! Forgive me."

The sound of her new name throws Henrietta into a flood of fresh sobs.

Sitting down beside her, you place a sisterly arm around her shoulders. If what Cad says is true, she is a lady now and occupies a station above your own. Still, you cannot help but feel a sense of responsibility toward her. Be it her youth, her general air of bruised innocence, or the fact that she is in danger of flooding the orangery with her tears, you can't help considering her a delicate and neglected flower. Such a creature needs gentle and skilled encouragement and care, but in this moment there is only you.

"Henrietta," you say calmly, "your fate has just taken a wild turn for the better, yet you weep as one does for the dead. Forgive me my impudence, but these tears do not look to be shed in joy."

"Nargh." Henrietta shakes her head, gurgling most unbecomingly. "I'm so very happy, miss. Honestly, truly. I'm so very glad." Her voice breaks, and her shoulders wilt even further.

"Tell me what is wrong, child. I matter not a whit to your family and you may consider me an ally as a woman; I am no stranger to sadness myself." Your voice positively sparkles with authority, and sweet innocent that she is, Henrietta cannot resist you.

"It's just that I don't want to be a lady." She is again wracked with sobs. "Ladies can't marry farmers, and all I want is my farmer. My sweet, kind, gentle love from Kent. My lovely, true Farmer Sam."

You suppress a sigh and search the recesses of your memory for some trace of connection between Henrietta and Kent. Evangeline said the girl was sent away for a time to be fostered, and it was perhaps in Kent that Henrietta learned of love as a pure and true thing, unfettered by society gatherings and the lashing tongue of the ton. An illegitimate daughter may well find happiness with a farmer, but a lady? An heir to Manberley? Out of the question.

Still, this whole business makes you highly suspect. Especially because it is not just the fate of the man you detest that hinges on the most recent revelations.

"Tell me, Henrietta," you say brightly, your voice shining like sunlight on the poor girl's soul. "Are you quite sure that your brother Cad's claims are true? He presses his evidence with more flash than forethought. I just wonder if perhaps this proof is a . . . mistake . . . on Cad's part, made in haste? Earnest? Or—"

Henrietta looks up, her reddened eyes now wide with fear.

"Oh, you must not go looking into this, please! I beg of you! Should my brother ask, please say I—I told you nothing!"

"Why, dear child?" you say, your already heightened suspicions climbing further. Henrietta's voice drops to a whisper.

"He—he said he would hurt me. And he said he would do worse to my darling Sam." She grabs both of your hands so tightly it causes pain. "And he would as well! You don't know what he is capable of!"

Before you can tell the poor girl that you already have a hint of the depths to which Cad can sink, she rises to her trembling feet.

"Please—please say you never saw me!" Henrietta says in hushed tones before running from the room.

You follow her at a distance so as not to draw attention and run headfirst into Lady Evangeline. You sigh in relief.

"What happened there?" she asks, nodding toward Henrietta's fleeing form. Clearly your attempts not to draw attention failed to escape Lady Evangeline's perceptive gaze. No matter, for you need her help in getting to the bottom of this murky business.

"Lady Evangeline, we need to talk. Most urgently."

She nods, her bright blue eyes searchlights piercing the foggy haze of the evening's events.

"Of course, my dear. Come with me."

. . . .

Turn to page 28.

You arrive at Seven Dials in London, near the notorious slums of St. Giles Rookery. All around you are thieves, murderers, murderous thieves, and at least eight different people exclaiming "Lawks!" You steel yourself, for you need all the courage and fortitude you possess to embark on this, your next chapter in life . . .

. . . and perhaps love? Your mind wanders to the handsome Scot you met at Lady Evangeline's ball, Captain Angus MacTaggart. You wonder if you've beaten the letter you sent him, telling him of your arrival and interest in taking up the position he mentioned off-handedly at the ball. You know it was impulsive to come without working out the details, but the opportunity unleashed in you a new lease on life that cannot be ignored. Especially not when needy children stand to benefit.

As you pick your way through a street piled high with refuse and ladies of the night, you recall Mac's manner that evening. How he operated as a guest in the high-society world of the ton, commanded respect, charmed all, but also seemed to burn with a silent desire to move on. Then there was the kindness and humor flashing in those hazel eyes, the knowing looks and hearty laughter, the rolling, harsh softness of his brogue, the way the candlelight brought out the fire in his auburn mane, the way his tight breeches clung to his—

"Looking for work, my dear?" says a strangely accented voice. You turn and see an elegant lady, incongruous for such a rough part of town, standing in her silk dress like a lotus blossom in a swamp. "A girl as pretty as yourself could be the gem of my establishment. Sweet. Innocent. And yet with an underlying wisdom and sadness. Yes, you would do very well indeed."

"Leave the lass alone, Madam Crosby," a rugged Scottish brogue interrupts. "She's here to see me about teaching, not to become one of your doxies." The woman doesn't seem fazed in the slightest and merely shrugs. Mac leans proudly and ruggedly against the down-at-heel doorway of his fledgling Home for Orphans of the War. Many of said orphans peer down at you from the structure's grimy windows.

"More's the pity. Though the offer still stands. As you can see, my girls are the best paid and the best treated in London." Madam Crosby waves an expensively gloved hand and walks into a fine building that stands out like a diamond ring in the mud. Several lovely and elegantly dressed women follow after her.

You turn to the source of the rugged Scottish brogue and find your breath momentarily taken away. Captain Angus MacTaggart is even more handsome than you remembered, the strong angles of his face now lit up by the midday sun. He strikes you the same way statues of heroes of war do, or Greek gods. Something about him seems mythic, larger than life. And very, very muscular. Judging by the giggles coming from the women you pass, you are not the only one to notice.

"Getting in trouble already, I see," Captain MacTaggart says and then grins at you. Before you can think of a suitably witty comeback, you are interrupted by a golden wolf running out of the home and pouncing on you, followed by a small boy hollering at him and a pair of children hollering for the hell of it.

"Oi! Dodger, no!" cries the boy. The wolf reveals himself to be a cheerful yellow dog with adorably active, expressive ears on an endless quest to knock things over.

"Your stupid dog almost killed our teacher, you twat!" A rough-and-tumble little girl spits at the young dogmaster.

"Good. Can't stand teachers. They fink they're all fancy and better'n us. I ain't got time for no teachers." The third youngster, a gloomy, grim child with a black eye, scowls in your general direction.

"'Cos they *is* fancy, you knobhead. Don't *make* me punch sense into you again," the little girl says and spits once more.

"What lovely children you are," you deadpan, eyebrows arched. The children scowl at you in turn. "What are your names?"

"Timmy," the forlorn little dog owner manages.

"Sallie," spits the girl.

"None of your bloody business!" shouts the teacher-hater.

"All right, all right, quiet yerselves down now!" Mac says with a hearty laugh. "I've got about twenty more o' these little delights up in the home now, raising a ruckus. But they'll be singing quite a different tune once we get your schoolroom set up."

"Sometime in the next decade, I presume." Another, even heartier Scottish brogue booms down from an open window.

"Aye!" Mac hollers up to a jolly, avuncular fellow Scotsman, who looks more than old enough to be his father. He turns back to you. "That'll be Abercrombie—"

"*Colonel* Abercrombie," the man corrects.

"Aye. And he's the general pest of the home." Mac laughs again, harder than before.

"Aide-de-camp of the home, I prefer," Abercrombie puts in.

"Aye. My former commander. And this heap"—Mac slaps the doorway—"is my most recently won donation. My charms sometimes gain favors that help out the bairns, but it is a hustle and a task to keep the gifts coming. The wee lads and lassies are nae fond o' teachers, mostly because they have a tendency to turn tail and run back to their soft beds once the going gets tough."

Mac's eyes twinkle but display a hardness that speak volumes to his past experience with young ladies struck by a desire to "help." He looks you over with these hard, twinkling eyes, and you can't help but sense, despite his outwardly jocular behavior, that he is quite concerned about your arrival—or, perhaps, the length of your stay.

"If ye decide to follow suit," he continues, "please wait till morning so I can get ye home safely. I'll not have ye getting snatched up by Madam Crosby or other villains on my account, ye hear?"

"That shan't be necessary," you respond and hear several of the children giggle and/or curse at your posh tones. "Where can I settle in?"

"Eh, I will show ye to your quarters," Mac says, distracted perhaps by the sheer amount of work to be done. "Ye can have a lie-down until we're done doing the heavy lifting. The kiddies have waited this long for a teacher, they can surely wait another day."

"Decade!" Abercrombie shouts down. "C'mon up, lass, I will nae bite ye."

"Trust not a word he says," Mac says. He laughs, claps you on the back, hoists your valise over his head, and disappears into your new home.

Your new quarters are grimmer than the tiny room the Dowager Dragon allowed you to have and feature a considerable company of bugs and rats. You wish to scream, but the dubious and expectant look on Mac's handsome face makes you straighten your spine and don your best do-gooding smile.

"How can I get started?" you ask with forced brightness.

Mac gestures across the hall, to a room with the door thrown open, revealing a beautiful chalkboard . . . and a tangled heap of filth, school supplies, and furniture desperately shoved inside to be dealt with later.

"That'll be the schoolroom," he says, and the strong features of his face color with fret. "Look, lass." He speaks with a softness he must reserve for only the most tearful orphan or haughtiest donor. "I know ye came all this way to have a look at the rough side, get a tale to tell your bosom friends at the next ball about how ye helped this one and did this deed. Are ye sure someone jest as . . . fine and delicate as ye are wants to muck about in this? No shame at all in going home, I can escort ye myself after I take care of a few things and get the children watched over."

Your body burns with embarrassment. "I believe *you* informed me of a position regarding watching over the children. I came here for a job, not for a holiday in the slums."

"Aye, lass, but all this"—he gestures at the decrepit building around you—"it isnae a story for high tea. It's quite a piece of work."

You seethe. "I am certain you will find, Captain Angus Mac-Taggart, that so. Am. I. Now, please, I beg your pardon, but I must get to work."

"Of course, lass," Mac says. "My apologies." He knows he's stepped in it but can't quite figure how to step out. You raise your eyebrows ever slightly higher in response. "I will find ye for dinner."

You hold your head high, determined not to cry or show any sign of what Mac may construe as weakness, and when he leaves you to the rats and cockroaches, you silently scream in frustrated anguish.

It makes you feel marvelous and fuels you with the double-headed desire to do good things and make Mac sorry he ever doubted you.

The self-righteous Scottish prig! You are about to let off one last silent primal scream when you are interrupted by the orphans, who crowd around the door to your room.

"Whatcha gonna teach us, then?" asks Sallie, clearly the leader of the pack. The other kids peer at you with a mix of interest, scorn, and disappointment.

"No one can teach us nuffink," None-of-Your-Business chimes in. "'Member what the last teacher said? We're a hopeless case." He scowls and kicks another child in the shin.

"Hopeless cases are like bogeymen," you say with savage primness. The children look at you quizzically. "They don't exist."

You roll up your sleeves. It is time to take matters into your own hands. But how?

....

By teaching the children out in the streets? You see no reason why the world they live in can't be their classroom! Turn to page 87.

Or by getting the little brutes to use their strength to take ownership of their fates *and* help you clear out their schoolroom? Turn to page 152.

"We have risen the temple, so now let's raise hell!" You kiss Evangeline again, and then whoop and cheer the women into a happy frenzy.

"You're one of us now, ain't ye?" Gráinne cries with unmasked joy.

"You can bet your capstone, I am!"

You are exhilarated by the wild grins on the women's faces, but especially by the one beaming at you from Evangeline's beautiful visage. You enjoy the cool, strange shade provided by the impossible temple.

"Who knows what things may come," she says in mock warning.

"We will find out together," you respond. You kiss her once more and then mount your camel. "Last one to Cairo is a rotten egg!" you cry and ride off into a life of adventuring with Evangeline and the pirate ladies.

The End

You turn to Benedict for a moment.

"My darling, I feel a greater affection for you than I have for any man. However, I think perhaps you were right. Love *can* ruin lives if we allow it."

Benedict stares at you, astonished.

"What do you mean?"

"I mean that we barely know each other. We argue all the time. I am a will o' the wisp and you are a stick in the mud. We have passion, but in time I fear we would make each other miserable."

After a moment, Benedict says, "I—I think you might be right. But what are you going to do?"

"Well, first off I am going to ensure that the truth comes out, that you are reinstated as the true baronet, and that Henrietta gets to marry her farmer love." Before Benedict can argue, you continue. "She will be much happier away from the pressure of the ton, and you know it. I would also advise that you marry a nice, sensible young woman. But one with a brain who can go toe to toe with you. Heaven knows you need that."

Benedict nods, clearly still stunned by the evening's proceedings.

"Come, Benny," says Lady Evangeline, gently leading him out.

"I'm very impressed, I must say," says Madam Crosby. "Though I will of course need compensation for the damage caused. And I doubt *this* scoundrel can cover the cost after tonight's events," she says, nodding to the cringing Cad.

"I have nothing," he says in a hollow voice. "I'm ruined. After everything that has transpired, what can I even do? Become a gigolo?"

You seize the opportunity.

"You know, I think you would be rather good at that! After all, we have gotten rather close and personal recently. I have some idea of what you are working with."

Cad laughs but sounds somewhat intrigued.

"And where would I ply my wares, sweeting? A room at the Rose & the Smoke? I feel there are few women who could afford me who would make their way to this neighborhood."

"Oh, no!" you exclaim. "I was thinking a far more salubrious part of town. A discreet establishment, where respectable ladies who find themselves bored and with money to spend might . . . *refresh* themselves without attracting attention."

Madam Crosby looks at you with a degree of interest playing across her striking features.

"You know, my dear . . . I think you might be on to something there. A pleasure palace akin to the Rose & the Smoke, but for ladies of all tastes rather than gentlemen."

"Exactly," you nod. "I was wondering, would like to be my partner in business?"

Madam Crosby laughs low.

"Well, my dear, I certainly admire your enterprising spirit," she says. "And I have been looking for new ventures to invest in."

"Marvelous!" you say.

"And I wouldn't find it such a hardship to be your first employee," adds Cad. "I fancy I may have found my life's calling. But I shall need a new name for this venture."

"How about the Duke of Slut?" purrs Madam Crosby. Cad's face lights up.

"Perfect. I'll outrank Benny."

"Then it is settled!" you cry. "We shall go into business together."

Madam Crosby smiles enigmatically.

"We shall go into a great deal many more things together, I hope."

"Of course!" you say, and the three of you get to planning immediately.

The End

You nod, with your heart in your throat and stars in your eyes, and slowly walk back to Mac. He can already tell from your expression what you are about to say.

"I never did ken what to do with goodbyes," he says, then laughs to conceal the tears shining in his eyes.

"Especially ones you don't want to say," you agree. He looks at you, his good and glorious eyes searching yours for what you think might be the last time.

You kiss him. "We won't say anything, then."

"Nothing at all."

You smile wistfully, and Mac strides away, rubbing his eyes. You sigh at his retreating, perfect back and then walk outside where Ollie now waits in a coach.

"Where to next?" you ask, grinning at him. Before he answers, he pulls you in for a tender and passionate kiss, sweet as the first one you shared as children but with an undercurrent of passion that is entirely grown up.

"Well, my darling," he says after you finally come up for air, "I'm not sure where this road will take us next. But wherever it does . . ."

You nod at him and finish his sentence.

"I had best remove my stockings first."

Ollie's eyes sparkle with mischief, and with that you make passionate love in the carriage, on your way to a new life of adventure and intrigue as spies.

The End

Benedict can fend for himself.

"I—I should very much like to see Egypt for myself," you say, your voice sounding as though it comes from a distance. Can this really be happening?

"Wonderful!" exclaims Lady Evangeline. "I say we make our move as soon as possible. We can fetch supplies on the journey."

You nod enthusiastically. The two of you laugh, link arms, and head straightaway for the main entrance of the house. On your way, you see that the dowager is dozing upon a settee, her head tilted back, snoring full blast. You smile to yourself incredulously. Finally, you are having an adventure . . . who knows what it may bring?

Turn to page 193.

That night, you retire to your chamber with the mysterious diary. Holding the journal of Craven's dead wife sends a dark thrill through you. A woman's diary may contain intimacies so private that she would wish to keep them even from herself, locked safely away in a prison of ink and page. You know whatever is contained in these pages, Blanche surely wished it never to be known by another . . . unless something untoward were to happen to her.

You arrange yourself comfortably (and attractively) in your bed-clothes. You consider, for a moment, never reading a word of the thing. Surely there will be descriptions of certain *adventures* that Blanche had with Lord Craven. While your skin instantly turns hot as you envision him standing above you and stripping down to the beastly and powerful naked state you now associate with the mere mention of his name, your blood is chilled at the idea of him being so stripped by *her*.

You glance up at the painting of Blanche and swear you see a challenging smile twisting the corner of that perfect, bitten-nipple-red mouth.

Blast! You will read it. The damn portrait knows you will, and the devil does, too. You flash a knowing glance at the canvas. A challenging smile plays in the corner of your own mouth, as you remember how just a short time ago it made Lord Craven howl with pleasure.

It may be the wine you've been sipping, that wild moonlight playing on the painting, or something else, but Blanche's portrait seems the slightest bit rebuffed. Good. You smirk, then crack the gilt-edged volume, whose cover is the color of spilled merlot.

A most splendid morning. Played hoop and stick with Alexander-my-Wonder. Picked flowers! Skipped, and rang a festive bell.

You choke a bit on the wine. This was not what you expected to find. You read on.

I used to think loving Garraway was my life's greatest joy. After that I thought, of course, my life's greatest joy is being mother to the most wonderful, sweet, thoughtful child in all of England and surely the world, Alexander! I then wondered how this joy compared to the joy of being Garraway's truest love and wondered if I was being unfair by weighing my joys. I cried a fair deal, and was sick with worry. But then I had the realization that love need not be measured, if that love is as endless and true as mine for my boys!

You glance at Blanche's portrait once more. Your cups might be thinking for you, but she looks positively smug. You continue.

I feel low for even thinking it, Diary, but Garraway has changed since Alexander has come, hasn't he! He is cruel now, and always angry, and ever so resentful of any happiness I share with the child. Sometimes he is so fearsome I worry what will become of us if we were to rile him to the brink. I do not think him an evil man, but he does not know his own strength. Sometimes, Diary . . . sometimes I fear his anger will be the end of us all!

You throw the book from your bed. The dead woman's words do not align with what you already know—or think you know—about her. Alexander regards his mother in horrified tones, but this book paints their relationship as happy and healthy. Lord Craven's eyes flash like lightning if his dead wife is so much as mentioned, yet here, in her own hand, she writes rather sickeningly of their joy together. You don't know if what you smell is a rat, or smoke from a distant fire.

This dubious text merits further investigation.

....

If you decide to confront your fears, as well as the late Lady Blanche Craven's, head directly to the forbidden room in the forbidden wing in the dead of night. Turn to page 273.

If you wish to gather your thoughts and some intelligence by interrogating—er, interviewing—the staff of Hopesend Manor, turn to page 295.

You stagger back with the wounded Kamal from the marketplace and throw open the doors to the museum.

"L-Lady Evangeline," you stammer. She looks up from her work and fixes her lustrous eyes upon you before they widen in horror.

"What happened?!"

"Oh, Lady Evangeline! It was Farouk! He has been working for another and attacked us and—"

"Delphine!" hisses Evangeline. You nod at her, eyes wide, as you cradle the unconscious Kamal's head in your lap. To your intense relief, his soulful brown eyes flicker open.

"An angel . . . am I dead?" he says dreamily. You blush.

"Oh, Kamal, I do commend you for managing to be charming even after being knocked unconscious," Evangeline quips. "But we still need to get you medical assistance immediately. Are there any other servants here who are not secretly nefarious villains?"

"My lady, I am so sorry, I had no idea Farouk was . . ." says the still-dazed Kamal. Lady Evangeline wipes his face with a handkerchief she has retrieved from her heaving bosom.

"Hush now, Kamal. You need to rest." She gestures to a distinctly not-villainous manservant who has rushed into the room to fetch help.

As the manservant hurries out, Lady Evangeline whispers to you in urgent tones.

"This is again Delphine's work. She must be stopped!" Her eyes are afire with righteous anger, so much that you half fancy her to be Sekhmet, ancient Egyptian goddess of war, in her ferocity and loveliness.

"Oh no, my lady!" gasps Kamal from your lap. "Delphine St. Croix is dangerous, and the road to her is fraught with peril!"

"Exactly. My favorite type of road." Evangeline smirks. "Still, I would have been content to leave the foolish woman in peace had she not come after my friends." With that, her spine straightens, and a beam from a nearby window, as if sent from heaven, suddenly illuminates her fierce golden beauty. Your jaw drops with desire and admiration.

She turns to you, at once serious and businesslike.

"However, my dear, Kamal is right. I don't expect you to follow me into danger, peril, and possible dismemberment. Please, feel free to rest here with him. I have adventured solo before, and it is no matter for me to do so again."

She reaches out and strokes your cheek gently. You thrill to her touch, and also the thought of danger the likes of which you have never faced before.

....

It's decision time.

Do you throw caution, decorum, and all other respectable nouns to the wind in order to follow Lady Evangeline into the unknown? If so, turn to page 128.

Or do you value your limbs still being attached to your body and decide to sit this one out? If so, turn to page 71.

The journey to London is long. Outside the carriage, the darkening sky is already filling with stars.

You, however, are grateful that the ride has gone some way toward calming your frazzled nerves. By the time you are nearly there, you almost feel like yourself again.

Lady Evangeline laughs. "I cannot believe I'm heading all the way back to London, in secret, in my own carriage, with my aunt's companion—"

"And a half-full flask of brandy," you interrupt. "Don't forget that."

"How could I? The half that's missing is half of the reason we're here. How much longer, Hugo?" Lady Evangeline calls up to her driver.

"The rest o' the evening, my lady," Hugo answers in a booming but warm voice that somehow softens the edges of this clandestine adventure.

"Where in London are we headed, Lady Evangeline?" you ask politely. "Drury Lane?"

"Not exactly," Lady Evangeline says. "Suffice to say, I do find many other houses of ill repute more welcoming than Drury Lane. And since we are far gone now, I may as well fling the rest of the skeletons out of the closet and into the *danse*, as it were."

"Oh?" You raise a limber brow.

"It is improper to say," Lady Evangeline titters, "but I do know that after her scandalous *affaire* with the late Sir Granville, Mrs. Caddington made many associates not precisely befitting a respectable woman. She was part of a fast set who knew they couldn't act as they wished in open, proper society, so they carved out their own sort of . . . secret one."

"You speak as though you were a member of this secret society yourself," you say with a smile.

"I am a member of my own society, you devil," Lady Evangeline says, smiling in turn. You note that technically she hasn't said yes or no. Fine woman.

"Anyway," she continues, "I do know that the company she kept still keeps its company. I think they are a better target for your inquiry, if you don't mind advice from the lady in the carriage."

"As it is your carriage," you reply, "I welcome it! Let us go to this haven you speak of. Wheresoever is it located? Must we wait till morning?"

"Oh, no!" Lady Evangeline falls to giggles. "Where we are going is open around the clock. In fact, should we arrive to them at half past three in the morning, we will find it livelier than that same hour of the afternoon."

"Tell me!" you beg, and for a moment you are nothing more than two young ladies on the ride of your lives. "Where are we going?"

Lady Evangeline's smile is knowing and slow. "Hugo!" she calls to the driver. "Set your course for the Rose & the Smoke."

You feel as though a devil's age has passed since you first fled the soirée at Manberley and set out for London. You are rocked gently awake by the hubbub of the carriage, pulling into whatever street the Rose & the Smoke must be located on. While you slept, you dreamed of handsome men and lovely women, snakes cutting a path through high grass, and castle walls being held by great teams of faceless defenders working together to weave a pattern of protection. You also dreamed of Benedict's gaze burning into your own.

The carriage hits its final lurch, and you wipe the dreams—and Benedict—from your eyes.

"Here we are." Lady Evangeline smiles, pats her hair into place, and exits the carriage with an expression of barely concealed glee.

You expected the Rose & the Smoke to be, perhaps, a secret dining hall by a well-known restaurant. Maybe a clandestine meeting space within a progressive dressmaker's boutique. A salon in a wineshop, even. But you never expected this. You never expected—

"Gin Lane!" you hear yourself shout. Lady Evangeline glares back at you. "Gin Lane!" you repeat, quieter this time, but no less shocked.

"You are not in Gin Lane!" Lady Evangeline shoots a hoarse whisper your way like a huntress would an arrow. "Gin Lane is one street over. You are in Harlot's Row."

Your eyes widen. To call the street down-at-the-heels would be an insult to heels everywhere. A strong breath exhorted in pleasure could knock over most of the ramshackle structures, which makes it all the more wondrous that the symphony of sin being conducted all around you in houses of ill repute (and doorways of ill repute, and street corners of ill repute, and, from what you can tell, at least one lamppost of ill repute) does not topple the whole of Harlot's Row.

But on the corner of this street of sin stands a structure as grand and handsome as any you have ever seen in the better addresses of London. It drips with gold filigree that, you are shocked to notice, has not been chipped off and traded by the lowlier denizens of the street.

"It is the prize of Harlot's Row," Lady Evangeline whispers, as if in answer to your silent thoughts. "It is sought after by the profanely refined, honored by the downtrodden and vice-working, and thoroughly reviled by the members of high society—"

"—when they aren't in attendance?" you finish for her.

Lady Evangeline smiles in reply. "Welcome to the Rose & the Smoke," she says, before turning her attention to her driver. "Hugo, do tell Madam Crosby that I am here."

"Hugo does not need to," says a voice smooth as blue silk.

Forgetting your sense of decorum, even on Harlot's Row, you take in the owner of the voice: a woman so timelessly handsome and disarmingly calm that she looks as though she is standing in front of Buckingham Palace instead of a house of wantonness. "News of your carriage travels well before you, Lady Evangeline," the silken voice continues.

"Madam Crosby!" Lady Evangeline beams.

"It has been too long, Evangeline," Madam Crosby says, smiling in kind.

You shiver. The night has a strange quality, one that you are no longer entirely certain of. Still, you like it. You think.

Lady Evangeline links her arm in yours. Together, you ascend the staircase into the den of sin.

· ·

Off you go to page 340.

You are unsure how to broach this subject without looking like a fool . . . but broach it you must.

"L-Lady Evangeline," you stammer, "I think something might be wrong. I can't exactly say why, I just have a bad feeling."

She nods sagely. "Quite right. Always trust your instincts. Doing so has saved my skin on several occasions."

With that Lady Evangeline places a foot on the desk and swings up her skirts, revealing a shapely leg with a most well-turned ankle and . . . a small gold pistol tucked in her garter. She pulls out the pistol, straightens her skirts, and beckons you to follow her out of the room. You creep behind as quietly as possible.

The eerie silence persists as you make your way down the corridor. At the doorway to the main hall, she pauses, puts a finger over her mouth, and strides into the room with pistol aimed.

"Oh, *hello*, gentlemen," you hear her say to the sound of desperate scrambling. "I do hope I haven't disturbed you. Farouk, is it?"

Your eyes widen, your heart races, yet somehow you find yourself walking through the doorway as if in a trance.

There, in the great hall, Farouk and three other heavyset men you don't recognize are backing out the main entrance, their own weapons pointed at Lady Evangeline.

"To some, yes," snarls Farouk, his scarf now pulled back to reveal a face as beautiful and harshly unforgiving as the Sahara. "But my true name is Fabien. Fabien de Mangepoussey."

Lady Evangeline scoffs. "And what exactly are you playing at, Fabien?"

He smiles mirthlessly. "The *imbécile* was too preoccupied with his foolish antiques to notice I have been working for another this whole time."

To your horror, you see Kamal slumped lifelessly on the floor.

After what feels like a time period that could have spanned the Middle Kingdom, the ruffians leave. Lady Evangeline rushes to the door as you run to aid poor Kamal.

"Please don't be dead, oh please don't be dead," you whisper under your breath as you lift his bleeding head onto your lap.

To your intense relief, Kamal's soulful brown eyes flicker open.

"An angel . . . am I dead?" he says dreamily. You blush.

"Oh Kamal, I do commend you for managing to be charming even after being knocked unconscious," Lady Evangeline quips. "But we still need to get you medical assistance immediately. Are there any servants here who are not secretly nefarious villains?"

"My lady, I am so sorry, I had no idea he was . . . ," Kamal's voice trails off.

Lady Evangeline wipes his face with a handkerchief retrieved from her heaving bosom. "This is Delphine's work again. She must be stopped!"

"Oh no, my lady!" gasps Kamal from your lap. "Delphine St. Croix is dangerous, and the road to her is fraught with peril!"

"Exactly. My favorite type of road." Evangeline smirks. "Still, I would have been content to leave the foolish woman in peace had she not come after my friends." At that her spine straightens, and a beam from a nearby window, as if sent from heaven, suddenly illuminates her fierce golden beauty. Your jaw drops in desire and admiration.

She turns to you, at once serious and businesslike.

"However, my dear, Kamal is right. I don't expect you to follow me into danger, peril, and possible dismemberment. Please, feel free to rest here with Kamal. I have adventured solo before, and it is no matter for me to do so again."

She reaches out and gently strokes your cheek. You thrill to her touch, and also to the thought of danger the likes of which you have never faced before.

. . . .

It's decision time.

Do you throw caution, decorum, and all other respectable nouns to the wind in order to follow Lady Evangeline into the unknown? If so, turn to page 128.

Or do you value your limbs still being attached to your body and decide to sit this one out? If so, turn to page 71.

"What are you doing, lass?" Mac asks, desire sparking in the depths of his voice. You ache for him, the shape of him so impossibly long and large and near you. His eyes wish to be taken. His eyes wish to be taking.

"Trying to wash myself clean," you venture breathlessly. Taking a tender, tentative step toward you, he raises his massive hand to his sublimely thick neck and, almost imperceptibly, works a few buttons loose, sending you to madness at the sight of his fine, fiery pelt being slowly revealed.

"Of what, lass?" Another step closer, more buttons undone.

"Dirt," you answer. "And desire."

Mac strips the shirt from his shoulders as if he were a mountain shedding its treeline. Moonlight sneaks in through the leaves of the trees, through the glass in the pane, to touch him as you wish to, to drip down the ripples and curves of his body, to pool in the V of his pelvic muscles. He holds your gaze, and just barely bites his bottom lip, catching you as you drop to your knees.

"Can I help you?" he rasps. You peel his breeches from him, unveiling a haggis so impressive it would keep you sated for days.

"Please," you respond and proceed to lick him. He moans, lifting you up with one hand to kiss him, full on the mouth. Then, with the other hand, he neatly pulls up your skirts and you wrap yourself around him, making sure not to slip. The steady stream of water you have rigged to fall on you serves only to enhance his already enticing body as you make rhythmic love underneath the fall of artificially induced rain.

He dips you back low as he sends you to ecstasy, and for one sublime moment you are washed clean of all sins, all worries, all fears.

But as the afterglow passes, and the water grows cold, you regard your ragged lover with your own measure of hauntedness. You must know the truth.

"Who is Constantina?" you ask.

"My greatest regret," he whispers, shaking the dream-rain from his hair. You grip his wrist with your infinitely smaller hand, a sparrow lifting an elm.

"More," you say.

"You know nothing of such things," Mac says, and he attempts to shake his wrist loose. Your grip tightens.

"I know of regret," you say, keeping your voice low. "I loved and lost before, too. My childhood love, Ollie Ruston, died at sea. I never could tell him how I truly felt. I understand heartbreak. I have wanted others, never to have them. I understand, Mac. You can tell me if she was a woman you loved and lost."

"Loved?" Mac asks, his voice as wounded as his eyes. "Constantina wasn't the woman I loved. She was the woman I killed."

. . . .

Do you flee? Because murder! The note was right! If so, turn to page 94.

Or do you sit it out with him? We've all done things we regret, and you're still a bit, ah, damp from your interlude. If so, turn to page 167.

You throw yourself between the two men. Cad hesitates, if only for a second, and you seize the opportunity to talk sense into him.

"What is it you intend to do?" Your voice could cause frostbite. "Murder your own half brother? Your own half brother who is a member of the aristocracy?"

"He's not a—" Cad attempts to blurt out, but you cut him off.

"We *know*, Cad. We know that your mother's first husband is alive in Bedlam. We know that her marriage to your father was illegal and bigamous. We know Benedict is the rightful heir."

"Oh? And who will believe a fanciful little wretch such as yourself?" Cad bites back, expecting you to cower—which you do not.

"Indeed, the ton may very well dismiss the word of such a girl." You speak without bitterness, for you are long accustomed to your station. Cad appears unnerved by your calm, and so you press on. "However, the ton will believe the respectable Lady Evangeline!"

"You're dashed right there!" Lady Evangeline rushes back in. You turn to Cad in triumph.

"They will also believe the warden of Bedlam, who will attest that poor Mr. Caddington is one of the inmates."

"You best believe I bribed that old—"

"Men can be re-bribed," Lady Evangeline says simply.

Cad looks around in horror. You raise your chin and stand firm.

"Face it, Cad. You've lost."

Cad's powerful frame sags in defeat. He turns a pair of dazzling angel-blue eyes to you.

"What are you going to do? What am *I* going to do?"

....

If this entire incident has solidified the notion that Benedict is indeed the only man you will ever love, turn to page 266.

If you are sick of having your helping hands used against you by someone you thought you could love, or at least take to bed, and now want to see just what London and the Rose & the Smoke are all about, turn to page 214.

There are few things so deeply, so strangely satisfying as perfectly recalling an intricate dream after the mist of morning has cleared. Or being able to make love as tender as it is violent while balancing on one leg and using a bust of John Donne for support.

You hope you will be able to recall the details of this particular session of physical and metaphysical congress for the rest of your earthly days. You also hope you will be able to walk straight again.

Your eyes are heavy with exhaustion, but as you watch Lord Craven's furrowed brow smooth out in the first phase of deep, post-ecstasy sleep, you know you must scope out the "ghosts" haunting him, once and for all.

Where to first?

Do you go to speak with the servants? Turn to page 79.

Or do you seek out that unspeakably handsome vicar? Turn to page 131.

"Cousin Benedict, may I introduce my young protégée?" trills Lady Evangeline. "My dear, this is my cousin, Sir Benedict Granville." You dip your head and curtsey politely. The dark-haired figure returns a curt bow.

It is a dance of politeness you have been accustomed to engaging in since childhood, and one you have performed a thousand times before. You really should not stumble, but when you look up and find yourself staring into the most intense silver-gray eyes you have ever seen, framed by heavy, dark brows, a strong nose, and a face made entirely of dramatic angles, you find yourself doing just that. Sir Benedict raises one aristocratic brow. His black evening coat molds to his body like a second skin and does little to conceal the powerful form underneath. You detest him immediately.

Lady Evangeline has spoken to you before of her fine cousin, by way of warning. He is apparently frosty to the idea of marriage and the prospect of settling down in general, though she hasn't explained why. No doubt he views women as out for his gold and their own glory. Indeed, Lady Evangeline has recounted wearily the brusque manner the man takes in rejecting the many fine ladies who pursue him for his fortune, title, wit, and good looks.

Still, as painful as it is to admit, you can hardly blame either Sir Benedict or his admirers for their stance. A man who can look as good—and superior—as he does swirling a champagne glass in a dimly lit corner of a ballroom deserves as much attention and defense as he can muster.

"Are you schooling her in the arts of heathen women, Vange?" Sir Benedict Granville punctures your observational reverie with a weary glare toward his cousin and you. He flicks his gaze over your form with cool, practiced disinterest. You notice, however, that his eyes linger a moment too long on your own, before he settles himself into a posture even more devil-may-care than his first. Lady Evangeline claps her hands.

"Correct, dear cousin!" she says. "Now why don't you be a dear and take this lovely young lady for the next quadrille?"

Neither you nor Sir Benedict can refuse the request without

seeming rude. You turn to your new dance partner. He sighs and takes your hand.

"You are my aunt's companion, are you not?" he asks as he leads you to the dance floor.

"I am, sir," you admit. The dance begins.

"Aunt Craven has been telling me how her companion has been setting her sights shamelessly on one Sir Charles Burley-Fanshaw," he says as the dance steps take him back to you. "Rather old for you, isn't he? Or do you care not so long as his purse is full?"

Every suspicion you held about Sir Benedict has been confirmed. Insufferable man! Lady Evangeline said the only thing sharper than the lines on his suit is his tongue. Still, it didn't prepare you for the sting. Or the sweetness of a returned volley.

"Sir Benedict, you are too kind to pay such interest in the life of a simple girl such as myself," you retort, a fixed smile upon your face. "But I assure you that the only thing I am looking for, should I marry, is a man who displays wit, good sense, and kindness." The dance causes you to separate and you must wait a few seconds to deliver your final verbal blow. "Alas, there has been not one man fitting that description whom I have met this entire evening." You feel dismayed at the shiver that passes through you as he again takes your hand. Still, you keep your tones dulcet. "You wouldn't know of any, would you?"

This time it is your turn to arch a brow. You let your gaze match Sir Granville's for a moment just shy of total, delicious impudence. Though his facial features remain arranged in a most pleasing play at composure, his silvery eyes dance like the sea, full to the brim with chop.

The dance has finished. You smile winningly, turn on your heel, and head back to Lady Evangeline.

If you have still to meet Mac, turn to page 35.

If you have already met Mac, proceed to page 126.

A few weeks have passed, and the day of the Highland Games has finally arrived! Repairs to the castle are well under way thanks to the reward money Ollie donated, and now you, the orphans, and the entire village are gathered to watch the ancient sport of strong men doing hot things with their bodies for prizes.

Mac, unsurprisingly, wins the caber toss, winking at you as he gives his final heave. Thanks to Mrs. F's tutelage, the orphans perform admirably at sword dancing . . . sort of. Still, they managed to make some friends with the local wee bairns (once they got over the locals calling them Sassenachs), so a mediocre show of sword dancing is not a total loss.

The sun is low in the sky when Timmy, who you only now realize had been missing the entire day, trudges up to your happy, strange family circle. He wears a weary grin and drags Dodger along with him.

"I have good news and bad news, miss," Timmy says. You and Mac share a look and a laugh.

"Well," Mac booms.

"Out with both!" you say with a cackle.

"The bad news is, Dodger broke a wall when we were looking for secret passages," Timmy explains. You shoot Mac a worried look. How much will replacing a wall cost?

"The good news is," Timmy continues, "he found the hidden treasure! Now we can all live happily ever after!"

The children cheer. You and Mac kiss. Dodger tries to pick up a fallen caber in his mouth.

Only one thing could make the occasion sweeter. You find an obliging local blacksmith and marry Mac over the anvil in traditional, inexplicable Scottish fashion. Afterward, when the villagers have tired of the day's merriment and the children are all in bed, you and Mac take a stroll about the castle grounds and survey the glory of the first day of the rest of your lives.

The sun sets, staining the sky the pale-fire color of memory, promises, and Mac's head of hair.

You turn to your love and share a look of total simpatico. If teamwork makes the dream work, you two make that dream a very wet one, indeed. You kiss as though you are discovering islands off each other's hidden coasts. Finally, breathlessly, you pull away.

"I want you to take me in the stables," you say.

"Aye, lass." Mac takes a steadying breath.

"I want you to flip your kilt up, lift my skirts, and toss your caber deep inside me."

Mac spins you around and bends you over, right there on the shores of the loch. "Yes, lass," he murmurs. "But first can you meet the monster that haunts my depths?"

"Aye, laddie," you answer, and pull his strong hands down to slip over your slick glen.

You take great pleasure in making the large, gorgeous man shudder like a rickety guest house in a gale. As you take each other everywhere you wish, you realize something wonderful.

Living happily ever after is exactly what you'll do.

The End

You say nothing and try not to make any sudden movements. Delphine tightens her grip upon your arm and pulls you roughly out of the battle. You cannot help but tremble in fear.

"What is wrong with you?!" Delphine whispers viciously. "Why are you not fighting? Has Evangeline really moved on, really found happiness with a weak, pathetic ingénue?"

She pulls the knife closer, and you gasp as the wicked blade pierces your skin. A small trickle of blood runs down your neck. You try not to quiver lest it draw more blood. You fail. Delphine crows in simultaneous triumph and despair.

"She didn't used to be like this! She used to be free! Free and wild and in love with me! What happened to her? What did you *do* to her?" Delphine hisses this last part in your ear, her breath hot and angry.

"Unhand her at once!" shouts a cut-glass voice.

A thrill runs down your spine as you see Lady Evangeline approaching, her small gold pistol pointed at her traitorous ex-lover. Delphine stares at her wildly.

"You—you have no loyalty!" cries the outraged Frenchwoman. "I would have loved you—I still love you—for all time! But you prefer this boring *petite anglaise* to a woman who would do anything for you!"

Evangeline's beautiful eyes are filled with tears, but her voice holds steady.

"It's over, Delphine," she says. "You made your choice when you betrayed me. I thought I might never love again. I was wrong."

You gasp as Lady Evangeline turns to you. "You showed me that, my dear. No matter what happens after this day, I must thank you."

"Lady Evangeline!" you sigh.

"NO!" screeches Delphine. "You will not have this! Not while I still live—"

A gunshot rings out, and for a split second you think that Lady Evangeline has done it, has killed her former love. You turn to her and are startled to see her face crossed with a curious mixture of anguish and relief as she stares at a figure several feet away.

Following her sapphire gaze, you turn and see a familiar looming presence, silhouetted against the bright sunshine and holding a gun.

"Fabien! But why?!" you gasp. He turns to you, his tormented Nile-green eyes even more tormented than usual.

"Because you stopped her from killing me," he says at last. "Consider our debt settled."

Before you have a chance to respond, he nods at you, holding your gaze for several loaded moments. Then he swings himself onto his camel and rides deep into the desert, as if he had been a mirage the whole time.

At the sight of their employer's demise, what remains of Delphine's hired thugs turn and flee like the mangy scum they are. Your brave battalion of Sekhmets, lionesses each and every one, whoop and cheer.

You barely notice, for Lady Evangeline has pulled you into one of Delphine's abandoned tents and is kissing you fiercely yet tenderly, your bodies entwined as perhaps they had been fated to be all this time.

....

Well, *finally*, you two! Turn to page 134.

Knowing that it would be useless to struggle, you pretend to be dead. The vicar laughs triumphantly and maniacally as you lie as still as a dormouse.

Once you hear him leave, you race back to the house. Craven is shielding a trembling Alexander from the Reverend Simon Loveday, who has pulled out a small gold pistol and is aiming it at them.

"This was Blanche's gun," he hisses. "I thought it poetic that it should be the one to end both of your miserable lives."

You seize a nearby urn, stalk silently up to him, and hit him over the head with it. The vicar slumps to the ground, out for the count.

After the authorities arrive and drag off a revived and howling Reverend Simon Loveday, you take an exhausted Alexander to bed.

At the child's beside, Craven strokes your hair and turns to you.

"You have saved us all," he says. "But I know that it would be cruel to keep you here. Not when you could be free . . . free to love a worthy man. Free to go about your business without a care in the world." He says the words with a tremor in his voice and saddened hope in his eyes. "I can find a place for you, far from here. In America, with an honorable man of my acquaintance. One who I know will be a good employer."

. . . .

Do you take him up on this kind offer? Because, let's face it, life here is more than a little dysfunctional. Even without the evil vicar. If so, turn to page 183.

Or is dysfunction merely the spice that makes up a well-rounded dish of life? If so, turn to page 39.

"How *dare* you!" you seethe. "My parents were the kindest, dearest souls ever to have lived, and I will *not* hear a word spoken against them, you . . . you . . . pompous, arrogant—"

"They may have been exemplary individuals, but do you deny that your life is hardly suitable for a woman of your spirit?"

"I do not go hungry, and my wants and needs are not extravagant." You square your shoulders. "And neither are Henrietta's. She cares not for finery or titles, only that she is with the man she wants!"

"Henrietta is a child! She doesn't know what she wants!"

"How can you say that?! She is one and twenty, old enough to—"

Benedict does not let you finish. Instead he looks at you the way a drowning man would a raft. It is more than desire, more than longing that crosses his handsome yet haunted face.

"Sometimes we all want something we shouldn't," he says huskily, and then he kisses you with such abandon that it takes your breath away.

To your surprise, you find yourself succumbing to his passionate embrace. Your body is liquid gold as you melt into his. Nothing exists in this moment except you and him.

He is the one to break away first. Your arms are still intertwined as you stare at each other with equal parts horror . . . and desire. You breathe heavily. He breathes heavily.

"Oh, dash it!" you both cry out and flee in opposite directions.

You meet Lady Evangeline at the carriage outside.

"Are you quite all right, my dear?" she asks as you rub your mouth.

"What? Oh . . . yes. Yes, quite all right!"

Lady Evangeline nods but clearly does not believe you. Still, you are grateful when she trills brightly, "Well, my dear! We'd best be on our way to London."

After seating yourself in Lady Evangeline's elegant carriage, you rest your fevered brow against the cool glass of the window and curse yourself and your foolish loins for getting you into such a scrape.

....

Turn to page 222.

You climax harder than you ever have before. You lay entwined with your lover, and the moonstone of your sex glows with otherworldly desire for Lord Craven.

He places that broken-statue hand of his on your left breast, which he has taken to calling Rent Promise. His other hand travels to your right breast, which he has named Raven's Wing. He senses your soul stirring betwixt your bosom.

"I sense your soul stirring betwixt your bosom," he growls.

In answer, you make love to him again, with all the rushed intensity of spirits wrongfully dispatched from the mortal coil trying to communicate with the living from the great beyond.

You climax harder than you did the first time you climaxed harder than you ever had before, but the cries of your ecstasy are pierced by something harsher and louder: the sound of Alexander screaming in terror.

....

Go see to the child, you neglectful hussy! Turn to page 155.

It takes only a moment to stumble out of the carriage and down a snowdrop-lined path deep into a high hedge labyrinth. It takes only a few moments more until you find yourself utterly lost. You are too turned around by the uniformly mysterious shrubbery and your compromised emotional state to escape. Just when you are ready to scream in frustration, you feel strong hands pull you into a leafy alcove off this living maze.

"Miss me?" A cool, deep voice drips into your very soul. *Cad*. Before you can speak, he silences you with kiss.

It feels like kissing the wind. Brief, strong, impossible, foolish. You push him away.

"I know everything about your lies, Cad. I know about your mother. I know about your father. I know that even the truth won't stop you from trying to get what you want."

"And *who* I want," Cad adds, and he attempts to kiss you again.

"Do not try me." You move to slap him, but he seizes your wrist.

"Oh, sweeting." He laughs, dark and sharp, into the night. "You do realize the only thing stopping you from ruin right now is our own good behavior."

"*Our* own?!" You shake your wrist free of his grasp.

"Don't tell me you don't want me . . ." Undeterred by your anger, he begins to unbutton his shirt, as a sort of slow, unasked-for but not entirely unwanted striptease. Although you do not hate the show, you are of two minds about what you really want from the even more arrogant member of the Granville-ish bloodline.

Do you give him a piece of your mind?! Turn to page 293.

Do you give him a piece of your body?! Turn to page 329.

You slap Ollie across the face. You remember the long month you spent weeping in your bed when news came of his death.

"You let me think you were dead!" you cry. "I mourned for you! Why—" You reach out to slap him again, but he grabs your wrist.

"Listen! I have earned your anger, I know that," Ollie says. "I wish it were otherwise, but I had to do what I had to do, including throwing away my old life and all that I cared about."

"I cried for you for years!"

"And I wish that I could have left you with a pure memory of the boy I was. But I had to come forward, for your sake. You need to know that you have taken a job with someone very dangerous." His tone and words are the metaphorical bucket of water you needed.

"What?" you say. Ollie releases your wrist and takes your face in both hands.

"I've been trailing him for quite some time. When you turned up in London, I couldn't believe it. But I couldn't let you stumble into this lion's den without warning you."

"I—I don't understand!" Tears stream down your face. His roughened thumb wipes them away.

"My entire cell was killed," Ollie whispers, his dark eyes like those of a cornered animal. "All of them. Picked off like stray dogs—each time, the French were there waiting for us. I was the only one who made it out alive, for I got so drunk mourning the woman I loved that I missed the appointed time of my mission!"

You stare at him in horror.

"Someone must have sold British secrets for them to have known exactly where we were," Ollie says. "And after much investigation I realized who the mole must be."

"No . . . ," you whisper.

"Yes. It could be only one man—Captain Angus MacTaggart."

....

Uh-oh. Turn to page 96.

"I—I think that my time in Manberley is done," you admit gingerly. "And my time with the Dowager Lady Craven. But Lady Evangeline! Whatever shall I do next?!"

"Ah, my dear. Well, my offer to take you to Egypt still stands." A strange smile plays across her lovely mouth, too full for fashion and all the more intoxicating for it.

"Thank you, my lady," you say. "You are very kind. And now that I have calmed down enough to think on it, I know that I have had two other offers of employment. One caring for the orphans of the war with brave Captain MacTaggart. And one as a governess for your other cousin—Lord Craven!"

It is now Lady Evangeline's turn to widen her eyes. "Oh, my dear, are you sure? Those are harder paths than a life of excitement in Egypt with a good friend."

. . . .

Do you choose a life of excitement in Egypt with a good friend? Because, well, it would be easier. If so, go to page 217.

Do you choose to do good works with the orphans in the West End and get to know a certain rugged Scotsman better? If so, go to page 208.

Do you choose to make your bed with the most mysterious Lord Craven and his manor upon the Yorkshire moors? If so, go to page 14.

"Are you sure, my dear?" Lady Evangeline asks. "I wouldn't want to hinder your fun on your first time abroad."

"It is no trouble at all, my lady!" you cry, a little too enthusiastically. Feeling embarrassed, you glance at your dusty feet, if only to hide your face, which you are quite sure must be glowing scarlet.

If she notices, Lady Evangeline doesn't let on. Instead, she catches your chin with her cool, pale hand and lifts it so your eyes meet. You find you can barely breathe as a smile spreads slowly across her face.

"In that case, my dear, I would be very glad for the company."

"You may have my study to work in," volunteers Kamal. "It is just down the corridor."

Lady Evangeline releases your chin so swiftly you feel you must have imagined it.

"Splendid," she says, and she links her arm with yours and starts down narrow the corridor. As you feel her velvet-soft skin touching yours, a thrill travels down your body.

"I've always found the study of artifacts fascinating," Lady Evangeline says, "even as a young girl. Which, as you can imagine, made me as much a rarity among girls as it makes me a rarity among my scholarly colleagues now. But I don't believe we of the fairer sex should be restricted from such pursuits. If nothing else, it's a waste of half the intellectual brilliance and human insight in the world, don't you agree?"

"Of course, my lady."

Before you reach the study, a large, shadowy figure swathed in loose black garments almost blocks your path. You gaze up in alarm at the impassive frame and see a face almost completely concealed save a striking pair of Nile-green eyes. Lady Evangeline is undaunted.

"Excuse me, Farouk," she says primly, and then guides you around the hulking mass of a man.

Once out of earshot, she turns and whispers into your ear, her full lips so tantalizingly close you can feel her gentle breath. "One of Kamal's guards. I can't say I've ever trusted him, but I suppose he's useful for scaring off the worst of what Cairo has to offer." She throws another glance over her shoulder at the glowering brute. "Not that it did much good last night."

Warily, you look back at the man, who is staring at you in a manner that makes you feel as though he can see through to your very soul. Before you can ponder what this means, Lady Evangeline throws open the study door.

"Well, my dear," she says. "Shall we begin?"

Turn to page 101.

You depart for the loch that night. Alone, as instructed.

The chill air makes a fine companion for your uneasy mood. You wrap your shawl tighter and reach the shores of the loch just as a shadowy figure rises you greet you. The clouds clear and you see . . .

"Abercrombie?"

The sweet old man looks uncharacteristically menacing in the moonlight. "I see ye got my letter, lass." His usual light tone is now a growl. The moonlight catches on something, and for a moment your heart stops. There, glinting in the darkness, is Abercrombie's pistol. And it is pointed at you.

"I hate to do this, lass," he continues. "I do like ye. But ye are much too fond of getting too close to the truth."

"Constantina . . . ," you breathe.

"A fine woman, aye. Always goin' on about her wee bonnie Ollie and the life they'd make together. Stuff and nonsense." Abercrombie cocks the pistol. "She didn't know that spies don't live to love. They live to die."

"She wasn't the mole, then?" you ask. Your eyes dart around in search of a weapon, a path, anything to aid in your escape. Abercrombie snickers at your frantic display.

"O' course not. I was the mole, she was merely my conduit. That's why the lass turned on Mac, who was clueless to all of it. He thought she was tipsy and needed warnin' away from the nest o' French, when really she needed to get close enough to pass them information. She went for him to save her skin but got herself killed in the process, the foolish bitch."

You cringe.

"Ye and wee Angus are two peas in a damn pod, ye ken? Each always sticking your nose in everybody's business, when ye should be minding your own. Now," he sighs, "I'm going to kill ye. How ye've been whoring yourself out to him—even the actual whores with ye haven't dared . . . " Abercrombie snickers, and cocks the pistol. "Everyone will believe when I say Mac's the one who done it."

"You're a monster!" you cry. Abercrombie narrows his eyes at you.

"This was all for the money, love," he says. "Fat lot of good it did, since ye started looking through my papers and I've had to burn them—yes, the papers I needed to get the fortune I'm owed! I inherit a crumbling estate, and not a penny with it. What was I meant to do?!"

"Not betray your country!" says a booming voice. Mac emerges from the shadows and throws his powerful arms around you.

Abercrombie laughs bitterly. "Perfect! A murder-suicide, right by a romantic loch! No doubt the villagers will start saying it is haunted!"

"By *you*!" A pistol-wielding Ollie leaps up from yet other dark shadows. "You betrayed us. Constantina betrayed us."

"All's unfair in love and war," Abercrombie retorts.

"Now I have nothing to live for," Ollie continues, his pistol trembling. "I have nothing to lose."

His wild eyes grow clear, and he levels his gun at Abercrombie's heart. Mac releases you, which causes only momentary disappointment, as he is trying to prevent a murder.

"Careful, man," he says. "Dinnae do something ye'll regret."

"Shut yer infernal take-charge mouth, laddie. I'll kill ye all!"

"No you bloody well won't!" screams a high-pitched cockney voice. Out of yet another part of the shadows come Timmy, Dodger, the rest of the kids, Mrs. Ferguson, Fiona and her husband, Rose and Gertie, and literally all the villagers.

"How?!" Abercrombie blusters.

"Allow me to explain," you say calmly. "You thought you were setting a trap for me. However, it was *I* who set a trap for *you*."

The burliest villagers grab Abercrombie's arms to lead him away, but with a quick twist of the arm, he escapes—until Dodger leaps forward with a snarl and pins him down.

"Dodger, yes!" you shout. The thwarted Abercrombie curses your name to the night sky.

Mac grins. "Good boy."

....

Turn to page 82.

You are overwhelmed by the sheer expanse of Hopesend, as well as by the fact that most of its halls and great rooms are decorated with portraits of an ethereally beautiful woman with raven locks and a devious look. You are certain these are depictions of the late Lady Craven, and despite your confidence in your own personality and good looks, you know your beauty cannot compare to her mysterious, commanding, dead-as-a-doornail brand of it.

You have never trusted ethereally beautiful women, and you wonder bitterly how Lord Craven has held onto any of his fortune, since he or his wife clearly spent a good deal of it commissioning portraits.

The eyes of each painting seem to scrutinize you as you follow Mrs. Butts down hallway after hallway, through rooms fine and rooms bare, to meet the cracking staff that Craven has assembled to care for himself and his home. *Your* home. You shudder.

To a man and woman, every member of Lord Craven's staff bears the mark of some tragedy. Mrs. White, the cook, has a problem with falling asleep suddenly and deeply for odd spans of time. "You never know when tea will be ready with Cook, but it's always worth the suspense!" Mrs. Butts insists while gently yanking the dozing woman up and off the pastries.

Then there is the mute scullery maid Betsy, a slip of a thing even younger than you, with eyes as wide as saucers and twice as expressive. "Betsy doesn't use her words, I'm afraid," Mrs. Butts explains. "But you will find she communicates just as fine as you or I might, love."

As if to demonstrate, Betsy takes your hands into hers and squeezes them tightly, shaking her head vigorously *no*. You are unsure if she means that you have made a terrible decision, or the right one.

Before you can decide, a gentle cough interrupts you. A handsome young blond man dressed in black, with the flat-brimmed hat and white collar of a country vicar, smiles warmly at you.

"I am terribly sorry, I hope I didn't startle you," he says, his innocent blue eyes full of sincere concern. You merely gape, your mouth incapable of speech for your heart has leapt into it. The young man nods and holds out a hand in greeting. "I am the Reverend Simon Loveday, vicar of Ravenscar parish. I didn't mean to intrude, but I thought I should pay a visit and welcome you to—"

"Fresh blood! Fresh blood!" A well-built middle-aged man with wild hair and wilder eyes barrels past Mrs. Butts and the Reverend Loveday, clutching a terrifyingly sharp shovel in his rough-hewn hands.

The handsome vicar maintains most of his composure. "Should you ever need my assistance, please call on me." He smiles, clutching your hands warmly. "We should very much like to see you at church on Sunday." With that he scampers away, leaving you with Mrs. Butts and the madman with the murderous gardening implement.

Mrs. Butts smiles her warmest smile yet and nods in his direction. "And that'll be Higgenbottom, the groundskeeper. He keeps a lovely lawn and has few words, but blurts things out from time to time. Who among us doesn't? He's a good soul."

"He's a fool." A voice, sharp as ice in winter, makes the hair on your neck stand on end. A man whose once-fine features have been whittled away by years to reveal a skeletal mask of pained distaste descends the stairs. He is dressed impeccably, his chin lifted defiantly, with all the pomp and self-importance of—

"Are you the butler?" you ask, knowing the moment the words escape your lips that they will give the haughty man the slap your hands cannot. His pale eyes narrow.

"I am Manvers," he says brusquely and brushes past you, evidently intent on polishing the golden frame of a particularly imposing portrait of the late Lady Craven. "You may notice I am not quite as . . . *compromised* as the rest of Lord Craven's staff. I was the late *Lady* Craven's butler in the house where she grew up, when she was still Miss Blanche von Badwolff. I followed her here after her marriage to Lord Craven."

You merely nod, at a loss for words while he sizes you up and clearly finds you wanting.

"There are many exquisite things in this house, which you will take care not to disturb," Manvers continues as if he started the conversation with you, rather than the other way around. "Evidence of theft will lead to your immediate dismissal. Is that clear?"

"As crystal," you respond through gritted teeth. You know you are required to be civil and polite to this man, but you find him irksome and in no measure attractive.

"Then good day." Manvers finishes his polish with a flourish and a curt nod to you and Mrs. Butts. Then he turns on his heel and is gone.

"Never mind Manvers, love," Mrs. Butts says, trying to keep an edge of darkness from her voice. "If you can."

You are not sure you can, but you still have a job to do! Turn to page 168.

With simmering anger and a barely concealed air of dejection, you approach Madam Crosby. She and Lady Evangeline are playing cards in what some would describe as a Sapphic paradise and others would not bother to describe at all because no words could do it justice.

"Madam Crosby, you have a soft spot for ruined women," you say in the confident way of someone from whom everything they wanted has been torn away by the gnarled claws of the Way Things Are.

"Ruined, experienced. *Comme ci, comme ça*." The madam is focused on her hand of bridge, but her eyebrows are arched impossibly high.

"May you spare this *experienced* woman before you a carriage?"

"Surely, you can take my carriage—" Lady Evangeline insists, looking concerned, but you nod at her as a means of assurance and adieu.

"Of course. Where to?" the madam responds.

"Hopesend Manor in Ravenscar, Yorkshire." Lady Evangeline gasps, but you press on. "I feel I need a new start. One far away."

Madam Crosby stares. You shift awkwardly from foot to foot until she finally breaks the silence.

"Yorkshire is a long way to go for a new start. Still, my man can take you as far as York. You'll have to take Ravenscar's mail carriage from there. Best of luck to you, girl. And remember, you are always welcome here. For friendship, work, or—"

"Thank you, Madam Crosby, but . . ." your voice trails off. No, a fresh hand of cards has been dealt. It is on you to play them. It is on you to win. "I need to get far away."

Lady Evangeline stands. "Then come with me instead, dearest. Come be my lady's companion on my trip to Egypt."

....

Do you head off to the heat of Egypt for adventures with Lady Evangeline? If so, turn to page 193.

Or do you want no reminder of Benedict, including his lovely cousin? A trip to Yorkshire to do some governessing would fit the bill nicely. If so, turn to page 14.

"Step aside, all of you!" says a low, commanding voice. "She needs air."

"You heard her, you miserable *sān bā*!" spits out another voice, this one higher in pitch but raspier. "Move aside before I make you!"

Your eyes open slowly, and you wince as bright points of light pierce your foggy vision. Trying to determine exactly where you are, and what you are doing there, you force yourself to rise and are greeted by a heavy throb between your temples.

Some cool, sweet liquid is brought to your lips. "Drink," says the low, commanding voice. You gulp it down gratefully, and to your amazement the throbbing begins to subside. You turn to the source of the voice and see a graceful, dark-skinned woman, her hair braided in delicate strands tightly to her head. She smiles at you, radiating calm.

"Better?" she asks.

"Much better," you admit. She nods.

"Welcome to the Wahhat Ranya," she says, "a simple tavern, run by our great proprietress, Ranya Abd al-Sayyid." She points to an older woman standing behind the bar; she has a shock of gray hair and wears an eye patch. The older woman nods at you. You nod back weakly and turn back to your healer.

"My name is Damilola Adebisi," she says. "And I am leading this band of vagabonds through the desert to our next, shall we say, *job*?" An audible snicker rises among the women, which Damilola silences with a look.

"I—I am very pleased to make your acquaintance." Your voice sounds as if it is traveling down a distant tunnel to your ears.

"Oh, Jaysis, she's an Englishwoman! And a posh one at that!" says another voice. You turn and see a mass of red curls framing a youthful face with a turned-up nose and a dusting of freckles. The face is currently scowling at you.

Damilola sighs. "This is Gráinne. She is an expert shot, and not too shabby with a cutlass either."

Gráinne spits and says nothing.

Damilola continues her introductions, pointing to a wiry young woman, whose slim brown arms ripple with lean muscle. Her dark hair is pulled back in a long, neat braid and her large brown eyes sparkle with amusement.

"This is Noor, our master sailor. There is not a vessel around that she cannot work."

Noor raises a dark eyebrow. "Among other things."

The rest of the women roar with laughter. You blush as Damilola then points to a pair of heavyset women who had previously been arm-wrestling in the corner. "This is María José and Amirah. They can best any man in a fight—or any woman, for that matter." You glance at their hulking forms. You don't doubt it.

"Lastly, this is my second-in-command, Ming." Damilola points to the woman who had earlier ordered everyone to give you room. Ming is tiny and yet gives you the impression of a tightly coiled spring, ready and waiting to launch into action at a moment's notice. "She is the deadliest woman alive when she has a knife. But I have seen her kill men with her bare hands, too." Ming looks at Damilola with eyes filled with pride and love. You gulp.

"We are all of us travelers here, and we have many women from all walks of life," Damilola continues. "But I think that you are new to this world. Tell me, how did you come here?"

Before you can answer, a lush, womanly figure bursts through the door. She is clad scandalously in breeches and a shirt like a man, but there is nothing masculine about the way the clothing clings to her supple curves.

"Ladies!" cries a thrillingly familiar voice. "I've come looking for reinforcements!"

You can scarcely believe it.

"Lady Evangeline?!" you say. The vision at the door turns and spots you, freezing for a second in sheer disbelief. Suddenly, her lovely face cracks open into a smile of pure joy and relief, and she comes running toward you full tilt. You are halfway to her when you realize that you are running, too.

"Oh, my dear!" she cries and throws her arms around you,

momentarily lifting you off your feet in a warm embrace. "I thought I had lost you forever!" You bury your face in her shoulder and take in her scent, delicately feminine and intoxicating.

Lady Evangeline takes your face in her long, elegant hands, concern shining from the depths of those ocean-blue eyes. For a moment the world melts away.

"They didn't hurt you?" she asks.

"Not as much as I hurt them!" you say.

Lady Evangeline throws back her head, laughing. "I'm very glad to hear it, my dear." The cerulean depths of her eyes darken further. "Still, Delphine must pay for what she has done. I have let this go on for too long, accepting what she does, whom she hurts, due to a lingering misspent . . . affection. But when she involves those I love within her schemes? Well, then I must take *action*."

"Action?" You stare into those bright sapphire orbs, which now burn with righteous fury.

"Yes, my dear," says Lady Evangeline, casually rubbing your cheek with her thumb. "It will be an extremely dangerous journey, and one that may end in death. I have resigned myself to it . . . but I do not expect you to join me in this. I ask that you leave."

"But—"

"Listen to me," Lady Evangeline interrupts. "You are still young. Your life is stretched out before you, full of possibilities. I do not expect you to sacrifice yourself for my own mess."

You have no idea what to say and can only stare mutely back at her. She turns her head ruefully.

"Well, my darling?"

. . . .

Do you insist on venturing onward to stop the dastardly Delphine once and for all? Turn to page 62.

Or do you leave the adventuring to the adventurers? You know your limits, and rushing headfirst into likely death with no weapons training goes very far beyond them. Turn to page 113.

"I know very well what I saw, Manvers, and it was no angel." You positively seethe at the vile manservant. "It could be an intruder of ghostly or earthly variety, or a shared figment of imagination between the boy and me, due to our heightened emotional states. The fact remains that something upsetting did happen, perhaps because many upsetting things have already happened, and I would like to find the root of the upset. I would also like to have my raw edges smoothed by a tender mind, such as the one belonging to Mrs. Butts. There is no shame in seeking comfort after a trying event. I am very sorry there is no one in your purview who can provide this service to you. Your attitude would be much improved by spending a moment in the company of a living person who could stand the sight of you!"

You know you are being defiant to the point of extremity, but extremity be damned! Manvers is a miserable sod and you won't stand for him sassing you about hither and thither.

Apparently, Manvers won't stand for you not standing for his antics. "Suit yourself, you guttersnipe," he sneers before stalking away.

....

Do you stick around and have tea with Mrs. Butts? You are, to be perfectly honest, still feeling mighty frazzled from all these strange encounters. If so, turn to page 268.

Or do you clear your mind of these odd detours from the job you came here to do? If you know that, above all, it is your sworn duty to be the best damned governess young Master Alexander has ever had, turn to page 172.

The hand releases you, and you turn slowly, in a daze. You already know the person you will see, but you can scarcely believe it. Are you going mad?

No, there he is. Standing before you, whole, handsome, and very much alive, is your long-lost love, Ollie Ruston!

"Ollie! But how? I thought you were lost at sea!" You stare at his face, at once completely recognizable and utterly strange, and try to find the sweet boy you knew in the man you now see. He stares back, his once-innocent brown eyes now darkened with anger and cynicism.

"I allowed everyone to believe that. It had to be done. Napoleon was a monster. I would have done anything to stop England from being invaded and conquered by such a man."

"Oh, Ollie . . ." you say with a sigh, feeling overwhelmed. He cups your face gently with one rough hand, but his expression is etched deep with long-felt fury.

"You see, I had no choice. Not if I wanted to do right by my country and those who I loved." He strokes your cheek with a hardened thumb. "I had to fake my own death so they wouldn't know to look for me when I embarked on my new life as a spy."

You stare at him, dumbfounded, as your heart races and long-forgotten memories rush back. Your first kiss. Your first . . . few other things. The long nights you spent weeping when he went to sea to avoid the brutal abuse his stepfather dealt. And the month you spent in bed after learning of his death. Which, apparently, he faked.

You slap Ollie across the face.

"You let me think you were dead! I mourned for you! You utter, utter bast—"

Ollie grabs your wrist.

"Listen to me! I have earned your anger, I know that. I wish it were otherwise, but I had a duty to my country, which included throwing away my old life and all that I cared about."

"What do you mean?" you cry, still furious.

"I am a spy. I've been tracking one target for quite some time. But when I saw that you, of all people, had found work with him, I had to warn you. You have taken a job with someone very dangerous."

"I don't believe it," you say. "And I can handle myself."

"Listen! The French killed my entire cell, all except for me. Someone must have sold British secrets for them to have known exactly where we were. It had to be a person in his battalion's chain of command. They were the only ones who knew all the information that was passed over."

"No!" you cry. "That doesn't mean it was Mac!"

"What is it? Who goes there? Are ye there, lass?" Your heart throbs at the sound of Mac's voice, but Ollie grabs you by the shoulders and stares at you with manic intensity.

"You have to listen to me! He is a murderer and a traitor!" he hisses. "You have to get out of here! There is no doubt in my mind that he will kill you, just like he did Constantina!"

"You knew her?!"

Ollie nods. "She was a fellow spy, the bravest woman I ever knew . . . and the only woman I ever loved. Apart from you."

And with that he disappears into the night. As you stumble out from the darkness, Mac catches you in a warm, deliciously masculine embrace that smells of salt and spice.

"Are ye all right, lass?" he says into your hair. "What happened?"

You stare up at him, tears in your eyes, and have no idea what to do.

. . . .

Still, you best make a choice, lassie.

Do you go snooping around by yourself? You trust Mac. Mostly. But still, you need hard evidence to disprove Ollie's accusations. Turn to page 311.

Or do you go a-pouring your heart out to him? You are with friends now, no matter what Ollie says. So turn to page 271.

You push him away apologetically.

"So you love him, do you?" the Reverend Loveday says.

You look away, blushing, and nod.

"Oh, dear . . . ," he says. "But also, how perfect."

He reaches out to tenderly caress your face . . . then savagely pins your neck in his surprisingly mighty grip so that you cannot escape. You stare at him in horror as he begins his monologue.

"My real name is Simon Loveday Craven, and I am truly next in line to inherit Hopesend. I was Blanche's lover the whole damn time she was married to Craven. No one could please her like I could, and no one was ever more devoted than she was to me. I urged her to get Craven and the children out of the picture so the house would be mine, she would be mine, and happiness would be ours! If she had managed to take out the foolish boy and Craven along with the girl, they would be under our feet right now, and you, Blanche, and I would be making filthy love on his grave!"

His cornflower-blue eyes glow with bloodlust. You wish to claw them out with your bare hands. "I wouldn't be here if you had killed Craven. Craven sent for me. So, actually, I wouldn't be able to make love, filthy or otherwise, on his grave."

He ignores your logic and continues with his monologue (and with gripping your neck very hard).

"So I had to come up with a new plan. I would kill Craven and the brat Blanche didn't get to throw in the fire and make it look like a murder-suicide by Craven's hand. To convince the villagers that Craven was crazed enough to do this, I enlisted Manvers to help me by dressing up in Blanche's garments in an attempt to haunt sense into the man. Manvers was obsessed by the idea that Craven was desecrating the memory of the late Lady Craven by screwing the help. Once Craven and the child were out of the picture, I would inherit everything, and then silly Manvers would have a terrible accident and die by falling down the stairs."

"You're a monster!" you squeak. He ignores you and continues with his speech apace.

"When you showed up, warming his bed and his soul and teaching his child confidence, I had to change my plan yet again!" His eyes light up with a murderous gleam, and he tries to choke you. "Don't you see? You make it all the more perfect. Craven will be responsible for losing a woman he loves, *again*. And then I, the good, purehearted vicar, find your lifeless body in the eldritch garden. After Lord Craven snaps and kills himself, I will discover that I am the next in line to inherit. The headlines write themselves. History writes itself!"

Loveday presses you into a filthy, disgusting, murderous kiss.

Do you fight tooth and nail to break free from his clutches? Turn to page 314.

Or do you play dead in a desperate attempt to survive? Turn to page 238.

How dare this man of high station and good breeding use his natural-born position to put you in some sort of place?

"Perhaps you mistake me for an errant servant, sir?" You let the hard tone of your address take a stab at the old boy. "While I appreciate your concern for my ladylike frailties, I insist I am made of hardy enough stuff to withstand a bit of scandal at a ball. In fact"—you muster your iciest tone in spite of the heat you feel pricking your temples and, dare you admit it, your loins—"I do hope to think I will get to the bottom of this intrigue on my own!"

Benedict's eyes burn yours with the caustic sting of a man shown up by a woman. "Is that so, miss—"

"It is." You do not give him time to insult you and attempt to wear an air of calm as you march away from this most detestable man.

With a concerted effort to give not a single damn about the whereabouts of Benedict's quietly seething, handsomely dressed body, you cast a glance about the guests in the ballroom. Those who have not recovered from the shock of the evening's events are gossiping in barely hushed tones or stuffing their faces with refreshments—shrimp and cucumber sandwiches, from the look of things.

In the corner, wringing her hands, is Henrietta. If what Cad says is true, she is a lady now and occupies a station above your own. But be it her youth, her general air of bruised innocence, or the fact that she is in danger of flooding the reception room with her tears, you can't help but consider her a wayward ship and yourself a beacon of safe light, beaming from a not-so-distant shore.

"Henrietta," you say as you approach her. "Your fate has just taken a wild turn for the better, yet you weep as one does for the dead. Forgive me my impudence, but these tears do not look to be shed in joy."

"Nargh." Henrietta shakes her head, gurgling most unbecomingly. "I'm so very happy, miss. Honestly, truly. I'm so very glad."

You feel the heat of a gaze upon you and, sure enough, glance up to find Benedict attempting to incinerate either you or his own eyebrows with a look that could sear meat. You can't help but arch a defiant brow his way as you lead Henrietta by her elbow into a private alcove off the main ballroom.

"If there is something you are frightened to say, child, say it to me. I matter not a whit to your family, and you may consider me an ally. I am no stranger to sadness myself." Your voice positively sparkles with authority, and, child that she is, Henrietta cannot resist you.

"It's just that I don't want to be a lady, miss," Henrietta says, wracked with sobs. "Ladies can't marry farmers, and all I want is my farmer. My sweet, kind, gentle love from Kent. My lovely, true Farmer Sam."

You suppress a sigh and search the recesses of your memory for some trace of connection between Henrietta and Kent. Lady Evangeline said the girl was sent away for a time to be fostered, and it was perhaps in Kent that Henrietta learned of love as a pure and true thing, unfettered by society gatherings and the lashing tongue of the ton. An illegitimate daughter may well find happiness with a sweet farmer, but a lady? And heir to Manberley? Out of the question.

"Tell me, Henrietta," your voice works quickly. "Your brother, Rafe Caddington. Cad. He presses his evidence with more flash than forethought. It makes the whole affair smell of a rat. Do you wonder if perhaps it is a . . . mistake on Cad's part, made in haste? Earnest? Or—"

"Or revenge?" Henrietta's voice is dry as a bone. It is the voice of a woman weary of the world, a survivor, not a child of one and twenty. Your eyes widen just long enough for Henrietta to realize her mistake. Her candidness is swept swiftly away, hidden under a curtain of shaking curls. "Forget I said that, miss. My brother Cad is very honorable. Both of my brothers are very . . . honorable."

"Henrietta, I—" You cast a glance around you. You have never been so casting with glances as you have been this evening. You pull the girl close and search her wide eyes for evidence. Of what, you do not know. "Does Cad . . . has he . . . ," you whisper.

"Has he what, sweeting?" a voice like poisoned honey drips down the back of your neck. You startle. Henrietta flees. *Cad.*

....

Egads! Turn to page 350.

"No, Evangeline!" you scream across the desert sands. "Do not throw away your life by ending hers!"

"Your little plaything thinks she knows that love is living. But living without your love is a living death." Delphine sneers not at you, but at Evangeline.

"This isn't love! This is madness! Pure, jealous madness!" you cry. "She has done all of this just to see you again."

"Shut your plaything's mouth!" Delphine cries, tears carving desperate tracks down her face. "Shut it or I will—forever!"

"You will do no such thing, Delphine," Evangeline spits. "She is not my plaything. She is the love of my life. The real oasis. You are now, and have always been, merely a mirage. You took English secrets and sold them to the French. To *Napoleon's* people. You made me forsake my husband, forsake my country and king, and now you look at me with your moon-cat eyes and expect what from me? Impunity? Trust? *Love?*" Evangeline laughs joylessly and spits again in the sand.

Now it is Delphine's turn to spit. "Yours was a marriage of convenience. He had no interest in you! He had interest in other men!"

"So?" Evangeline laughs. "Do you have any idea how hard it was to heal the rift your betrayal created between us? We were friends, Delphine."

"So?" Bitter tears glitter in Delphine's eyes, like jeweled scarabs in the sand. "We were lovers. I loved you. I love you. Love forgives."

"Love, to you, is a plaything. And I no longer have interest in your make of toy." Evangeline raises her golden pistol. "You have to the count of ten to mount your camel, take this man, and leave."

"Love is—" Delphine trembles.

"Something you know nothing about. One. Two. Three. Four." Evangeline holds her line. Fabien nods a pained farewell to you, mounts his camel, and is gone.

"Love—"

"Five. Six. Seven. Eight."

Whatever Delphine was about to say is lost on the wind as she beats a hasty retreat to her camel. Soon she is gone, and you can no longer care a fig about her because your mouth is lost in a rush of Evangeline's silken kisses.

"My goodness," Evangeline says when she finally pulls away. "I thought she would never leave!"

With that, you and your lady love ravish each other senseless as desert winds whip torrents of sand around you like so much confetti. You would be concerned about it getting in places it shouldn't, but you're too busy being overcome with a feeling of divine blessedness and ecstasy to care. You are wetter than the Nile for this woman, and she navigates your depths with the skill and magic of a sailor who knows her way to and from worlds beyond the earthly plane.

Suddenly, the earthly plane beneath you shudders and bucks. At first, you think it is Evangeline trying something new, and a little rough, until you realize that what can only be the lost Temple of Hathor is breaking through the desert floor like a giant hand reaching out to steal the sun.

As the temple rises impossibly high, nearly blocking out the sun with its enormous beauty and size, Evangeline leans over to you.

"Do you think it is for us?" she asks.

"Who else would it be for?" You laugh, then she laughs, and the more you laugh and kiss, the higher the tower seems to rise. It shimmers for a moment and then solidifies, a mirage no longer. The temple is risen. The temple is as real as your love.

You both marvel at it, then at each other, awed.

"Well," Evangeline asks after a moment, "what do you think?"

"I think"—you flash her a roguish grin, before rising to your feet and flashing her a good look up your skirt—"we should continue this, *inside*."

You two have many adventures ahead of you, don't you think?

The End

The eldritch garden definitely does not have vegetables in it. This garden is like your soul right now: overgrown, ripe, rotten. You are unsure how to right the wrongs you've done, if you even want to. You came to Hopesend Manor a silly little chit, and now what are you? Your blood burns with desires you have no shame for, and your heart beats with love and fear so strong, you worry that your mind will be completely drowned out by this minor-key symphony.

You are about to plant yourself on an overturned gravestone to have a good cry when none other than Lord Garraway Craven emerges from a tragically tangled curtain of wisteria.

"This is for you, my love." He hands you a small, smooth, polished-ash box.

You take it. "What is it?"

"A new beginning." A diamond dewdrop of a tear slides down his plush lashes and explodes onto the box lid.

You remove the lid to find a letter of recommendation on his finest stationery commending your governessing skills, along with full first-class passage to America. Your mind scrambles to work out what this all means when he speaks again.

"Of course, I will give you any money you need, any amount at all, for whatever it is you choose to do. A woman of your skills and drive will most likely wish to work, even if she doesn't need to. Hence the recommendation. But if you do not wish to work, and perhaps want only to travel, that is just as well. I can pay to—"

"Pay me to leave you?" you interrupt, your broken heart lodged in your throat.

"No, love, I—" he stammers like a child. "This is not payment. It is the best way I can think of for you to be free."

"What if I do not wish to be free?" You allow your tears to fall like daggers. "Do you not love me?"

"Of course I love you, woman! I love you more than life and breath and reason! I love you more than wind and air and—"

"Then why send me away?"

"Because I am terrible for you. I am a monster, and you are an angel—" This time you interrupt him by snorting and rolling your eyes. "A fallen angel, fine. But still, you are more angel than I."

"Then confess." You silence him with a kiss, and the box falls from your hands to the half-lush, half-stony ground. "Confess your sins to me, the sins you have committed, the sins that make you loathe yourself and loathe this love. Confess what would have you send me away, rather than gather me close, closer, closest. Speak now."

You throw yourself at his mercy, fast and filthy and gorgeous. He pulls your undergarments aside just enough to allow his staff entry to your hallowed hall, and you free your breasts from your dress and into his hungry mouth with the ease and desire of a champion lover.

....

How could you ever leave a man who is so eager to please all the damn time? Turn to page 307. Hot tramp.

However . . . this is a more plum offer than you're likely to ever get. If you'd rather pick up that box, forget his confession, and get thee to America, turn to page 183.

"You will have to work that out for yourself," you sniff at Cad. Taking Benedict's arm, you stalk out of the room with your head held high.

"This is not over! Not as long as I live!" cries Cad, lunging wildly at the two of you. You nod at Benedict, your eyes meeting in an almost psychic connection. Benedict grabs an erotically shaped lamp and strikes the blackguard squarely across the jaw. As Cad staggers away, you stick out your foot.

Cad, blinded by rage and the remnants of the smashed lamp, fails to notice. He trips and goes flying into an elegant glass-fronted cabinet. There is an almighty crash, and he slumps unconscious to the floor.

"Well, I think we best be going," mutters Benedict. "But first . . ." He throws the suggestive lamp to one side, turns to you with fire in his eyes, and kisses you deeply. You cling to him like a drowning man to a raft. But you cannot spend all evening kissing in a brothel when you may have accidentally killed a man.

A low groan rises from the shattered remains of the cabinet. Cad is clearly still alive, if not entirely happy.

You and Benedict reluctantly pull away from each other and gaze at the broken man, broken furniture, and crushed watercress sandwiches strewn before you.

"We did it, my darling!" you say. "We won!" Benedict turns to you, his expression that of a lost soul in the inferno.

"Have we?" he says, his voice hollow. "I am glad that you tried to intervene peaceably with Cad, and that your clever words put us at an advantage. But don't you see, my darling? It doesn't change a thing."

"What do you mean?" you cry.

"I mean that Henrietta will still be ruined if the truth comes out. I mean that I have opportunities as a man that she will not have. Don't you see? I have a better chance in this world as a penniless bastard than she does."

"And so you will allow yourself to be ruined in order to save her? Even if she doesn't want it?"

"I'll do it because she needs me to. A fortune and legitimacy will give her a chance at making a match with any number of men—it is her best shot at escaping the clutches of Cad. As much as it pains me to see him as owner of Manberley."

"But it isn't *fair*!" you sob.

Benedict only shrugs.

"Life generally isn't. But still. Whatever am I to do with you?" he murmurs into your hair as you cling to him.

"Well, whatever it is, you best do it far away from here," Lady Evangeline says gently. "Go, take my carriage. I'll follow you shortly after I've cleared up this mess." Benedict smiles at her gratefully.

"You're a lifesaver, Vange."

"Believe me, Benny, I know," she says. She winks at you as you beat a hasty retreat from the room.

....

Turn to page 17.

You and Mrs. Butts take tea. It is a balm for your soul. "You see and hear strange things at all hours in a house like this. I know, for truly I am a strange thing myself!" She laughs warmly, and you find that the sound softens the sharp edges of your fears.

"Ghosts, aye," she continues. "What be they but memories having a look around? I wouldn't worry about ghosts. I did wonder, though, if such things could be, when her ghost would come and say a piece about how she met her end. He were with her when she died, as were the child, but of course you can't get him to breathe a word of the ordeal. Too pained about it, I'd wager."

You choke on your tea. "Master Craven witnessed the death of his wife?" you ask gravely as you refill her cup.

"Of course he did, love." Mrs. Butts regards you with twinkling eyes. "Haven't you heard talk of how he might have caused it himself?" Upon hearing this you spill the tea all over your lap. You leap up and yelp, in part due to the tea and in part due to this revelation. She dabs at your lap with a napkin. "Not for sport, mind you, or for jealousy, though it were oft said she had a wandering eye. Pretty woman like her could have her pick of men, and she liked to, I suppose. No, the real problem were that she weren't much for mothering. She did not want to be tied down in the family way, and she certainly did not want to be at Master Alexander's beck and call."

"Did you . . . ," you begin to say, but then swallow hard. "Did you observe her mothering? Often?" Your words feel thick on a clumsy tongue.

"I would say . . . ," Mrs. Butts thinks a moment. "I observed her being upset about her lot in life. Some of the other servants might say harsher things, like she hit the child, or broke his spirit with words lashed like a whip, or turned him away like a beggar in a storm. And that by doing so, she broke Lord Craven's heart."

You visibly start when she mentions Lord Craven's name. She smooths your hair with her hand. "Oh, love, you mustn't worry," she says. "If he did kill her, I'm sure it were an accident. Even if it were on purpose, whatever happened that night surely has not let the man rest since. So take that as a cold comfort, whatever you do. Biscuit?"

Mrs. Butts extends a small silver tray. You take a biscuit and eat it dumbly while considering your next move.

Your next move turns out to be eating another biscuit. Then another. And another. Finally, Mrs. Butts snatches the plate, not unkindly, from your hands.

"Perhaps it's time to gather your thoughts, love?" she offers. You nod. It's time for you to gather something, all right.

....

Do you decide to gather information and confront Craven directly to find out what the devil is going on? If so, turn to page 60.

Or do you decide to gather resolve, be the Best Governess Ever, and teach Master Alexander some swordplay? If so, turn to page 122.

"Run, Kamal!" You pull his arm and flee in the opposite direction.

Though your escape is hindered by the teeming crowds, you push on, pulse racing, as Fabien and his henchmen close in.

"Miss! This way!" Kamal points to a narrow alley. You force yourself through the small gap between a market stall holder and a haggling customer, and have almost made it to freedom when a small child nods, as if on cue, and upends a barrel of apples. The bright red fruits roll underfoot, causing several bystanders to lose their balance. One older man lands upon Kamal as he falls, breaking your grasp on him.

"Run ahead, please! I will try to distract them!" Kamal pushes off the old man and staggers to his feet.

"No, Kamal!"

"You must go! It is you they want!" Kamal runs back toward your pursuers, the crowd closing around him. "Save yourself, I beg you!"

Alone, with no choices left, you continue your escape, leaping over a stall filled with dates through to a narrow entryway in a crumbling wall.

The crowds thin out and you race past the curious eyes of Cairo's citizens. After a left turn toward what you think is the museum, you spy one of the henchmen careening toward you. He viciously pushes a little girl out of the way as her parents cry out.

You turn and flee in the opposite direction but find yourself caught suddenly in a vicelike grasp. Before you can scream, a heavy hand presses over your mouth while your arms are pinned down by an arm so solid it feels like it must be made of granite.

"Where do you think you are going, *chérie*?" Fabien whispers into your ear. You attempt in vain to wrench yourself free. "You have an appointment with Madame Delphine St. Croix, and I would hate to disappoint her."

And with that he hauls you unceremoniously onto a camel, wraps his powerful hand around your mouth, and steers you both away. You continue to fight desperately to free yourself . . . to no avail.

....

Turn to page 59.

You run your hands down Mac's strong arms and search his clear eyes with your own. This is a man you trust, by look and feel and heart. He is also, not coincidentally, a man you want to spend many naked, adventurous hours with. Your trust is not informed by your desire, but your desire is heightened by your trust.

"Mac, impossible things have happened this night. A lost love of mine returned and tried to steal me away. He thinks you sold out his fellow spies by revealing their location to Bonapartists, and that you were directly responsible for the death of his love, Constantina." You take a steadying breath. "Were you ever a spy? Were you ever a mole?"

"Nae, I wasn't, lass." Mac's eyes are wide. You believe him.

"Mac," you whisper, "I trust you."

"Aye, lass. And I you." Mac kisses you full on the mouth. Oh, how you are tempted to lose yourself in this moment forever. But many other moments, and likely your safety and the safety of Mac, the children, Dodger the dog, and a great many others, depend on you quashing your desire like an errant bedbug. At least for now.

"Oooooooh!"

You jump back. There is nothing like a chorus of prying orphans to interrupt the burgeoning bagpipe serenade of two lusty bodies.

"You have ta get married now!" Sallie yells. "Also, someone left you a letter on the doorstep, miss! Prob'ly a lover out to ruin it all. I will have him in a fight if I need to, miss! I will kick his bits to smithereens!"

"A letter?" Mac says, his manly brow furrowing. "Let's see it then." Together, you read the hastily scrawled note.

You must meet me tonight, by the loch. Alone. I have new information we have to discuss. —O

You and Mac share a look. This impossible letter will no doubt lead to impossible things.

Ooh . . . turn to page 246!

"The woman was lovely, but did she need two
score mirrors and portraits to prove it?"

You stalk the halls of the great house with the stealthiness of a very intelligent, confident, uniquely beautiful cat. You creep up the stairs, around the bend, down the hall, around the other bend, and up the other stairs and down the other hall and around the other bend until you reach the Forbidden Room, where you once fenced with Master Alexander. Moonlight and terror are your only companions, and an eerie glow is cast upon your decision: to turn the knob on Blanche's bedroom door, or to run?

You are no ninny. You turn the knob.

You are surprised to be greeted by a whisper of wind, wild and cool, reaching out to loosen a few disobedient strands from your demure coiffure. Someone has recently been in this room. The source of the gust is a mysteriously open window. The room is flooded with moonlight, and the rustle of the sheer curtains resemble a sad woman dancing for her lost love.

You will have no more of this senseless poetry. As you draw the sash of the window, you cast your eye about the room, taking an inventory of potential clues. A sumptuously appointed bed, a handsome wardrobe, more portraits of Blanche. You cannot help but roll your eyes. The woman was lovely, but did she need two score mirrors and portraits to prove it? Your gaze catches on a fine writing desk, boasting many drawers and cubbies.

Drawing near, you notice that one drawer is partially obscured by a lady's handkerchief. The initials *BvB* wink at you from a delicate corner. Is this a signal? A clue? A message from Blanche from beyond the grave that this drawer, hidden by the flimsy fabric, contains the truth of her very soul and the nature of her relationship with Craven?

You yank hard on the drawer and reveal . . . nothing but laundry receipts and used hairbrushes. *Damn.*

You shut the drawer and cast another look around the room. Fireplace, hearth rug. Bed, wardrobe. You open the topmost drawer of the wardrobe and feel around for clues. Your fingers swim in a sea of silk and retrieve nothing but negligee after negligee. Some are so thin, you can see your hand through the fabric! You curse yourself for blushing and feel the heat of imagined eyes burn a hole in your neck.

Just as you are about to open the next drawer, a little voice, clear and frightening as a funeral bell, calls to you. You spin wildly on your heel to find Alexander in the doorway, staring with saucer-wide eyes and clutching a stuffed toy.

"I know what that is," he says, his odd voice dropping to an even odder whisper. "Those are Mama's struggling clothes."

"Whatever do you mean?" you ask, and suddenly realize you are clutching one of the late Lady Craven's negligees.

"Those shiny things," Alexander continues. "Mama wore them when she was struggling with a man."

"Struggling? Whatever do you mean by—oh." You realize what the child means. He must have witnessed his mother and Lord Craven . . . *enjoying* each other. "Master Alexander, struggling is something your mother and father did to—"

"No!" the boy cries. "Mama never struggled with Papa. It was another man. A dark angel, Mama said, when she was struggling." He changes tack before you can gather your thoughts. "Do you want to see something?"

Master Alexander shuffles over to the rug before the hearth and pulls it back to reveal a dark scorch mark, the size and shape, your late-night mind thinks, of a beautiful lady.

"I look at this sometimes, when I'm afraid," he says. "Then I know I can't be hurt anymore."

Your mind reels, however sluggishly. The scorch marks. The fireplace. The forbidden room.

There are so many things you don't know, or don't know for certain, but now you have stumbled onto at least one fact. You finally realize why Lord Craven didn't want you to fence with his son in here: this was the very room in which he lost his wife. Likely, you shudder to think, due to some sort of horrific, fiery accident—and possibly due to some sort of affair. Though you know Lord Craven is brooding, his brooding does not seem like that of one pining for a dead lover. Begrudgingly, you realize it is a brooding perhaps more in line with a devoted lover who has been thoughtlessly passed over for another.

Whatever the case, you realize now how Lady Craven died.

You know you must apologize for the wrong you've unknowingly done to Craven by fencing with his child on the site of his wife's death.

. . . .

You must apologize to Craven, but properly. Therefore, you need advice concerning the right words to say and the right time to say them. Turn to page 295.

You must apologize to Craven immediately. It is unspeakably bold of you, but you know you must seek him in his chambers. Hop to and turn to page 115.

Evangeline takes you on a long, twisting camel ride through secret tent towns and hidden passages. Before you know it, you are pulled through a flapping tarp into what you can only describe as a rogues' watering hole wonderland.

"Welcome to the Wahhat Ranya," says a graceful, dark-skinned woman, her hair braided in delicate strands tightly to her head. She smiles at you, radiating calm. "A simple tavern, run by our great proprietress, Ranya Abd al-Sayyid." She points to an older woman standing behind the bar; she has a shock of gray hair and wears an eye patch. The older woman nods at you.

"My name is Damilola Adebisi," she continues. "And I am leading this band of vagabonds through the desert to our next, shall we say, *job*?" An audible snicker rises among the women, which Damilola silences expertly with a quick, cool look.

"I am very pleased to make your acquaintance," you say politely.

"Oh, Jaysis, she's an Englishwoman! And a posh one at that!" The voice comes from a scowling, youthful face with a turned-up nose and a dusting of freckles, framed by a mass of red curls. Damilola sighs.

"This is Gráinne. She is an expert shot, and not too shabby with a cutlass either." Gráinne spits and says nothing.

Damilola points to a wiry young woman whose dark hair is pulled back in a long, neat braid. Her large brown eyes sparkle with amusement.

"This is Noor, our master sailor. There is not a vessel around that she cannot work . . . among other things." The rest of the women roar with laughter.

You blush as Damilola then points to a pair of heavyset women who had been arm-wrestling in the corner. "This is María José and Amirah. They can best any man in a fight, or any woman for that matter." You don't doubt it.

"Lastly, this is my second-in-command, Ming," Damilola says. Ming is tiny yet gives you the impression of a tightly coiled spring, ready to pounce. "She is the deadliest woman alive when she has a knife. But I have seen her kill men with her bare hands, too." Ming looks at Damilola with eyes full with pride and love. You gulp.

"We are all of us travelers here, and we have many women from all walks of life," Damilola continues. "But I think that you are new to this world. Tell me, how did you come to meet Lady Evangeline?"

Before you can answer, Evangeline claps her hands. "Ladies!" she says. "I'm in need of reinforcements! Delphine must pay for what she has done. I have let this go on for too long, accepting what she does, whom she hurts, due to a lingering misspent . . . affection. But when she also involves those I love within her schemes? Well, then I must take *action*."

"Action?" you say and stare into those bright sapphire orbs now burning with righteous fury.

"Yes, my dear," says Evangeline as she casually rubs your cheek with her thumb. "It will be an extremely dangerous journey, and one that may end in death. I have resigned myself to it, but I do not expect you to join me in it. I ask that you leave."

"But Lady Evangeline . . ." you say.

"Listen to me," she says. "You are still young. Your life is stretched out before you, full of possibilities. I do not expect you to sacrifice yourself for my own mess."

You have no idea what to say and stare mutely at her. She turns her head to the side ruefully.

"Well, my darling?" Evangeline asks. "Are you going to make the sensible choice and return to Cairo like I ask? Or are you going to go see that Delphine gets her just deserts with me?"

. . . .

Do you venture onward to stop the dastardly Delphine once and for all? Turn to page 62.

Or do you leave the adventuring to the adventurers? You know your limits, and rushing headfirst into likely death with no weapons training goes very far beyond them. Turn to page 113.

Your slightly blurred vision does not lie. There, bursting through silken curtains, piercing the night as a member would a sex, Benedict breaks through the entrance of Madam Crosby's chambers. His handsome face is fully flushed with anger and exertion that hasn't a lick to do with the licks and exertions happening in the sumptuous, scandalous rooms that surround you.

With his fine clothes, finer features, and tousled mop of aristocratic curls, you can't help but imagine him as a passionate patron of the Rose & the Smoke. Perhaps it is the champagne, but you can almost see him rushing into Madam Crosby's chambers to request—no, beg—the opportunity to run spendthrift with his wild passions in her very boudoir, in front of all watching, with *you*. He would tear his blouson asunder and urge your elegant, trembling hands to explore his surprisingly thick pelt, before you both teach the finest whores in London a thing or two about making love.

But the flesh-and-blood Benedict before you now speaks through gritted teeth. "Damnable woman!" he seethes, displaying what you know is Benedict's version of screaming. "Damn, damn, damn your eyes!"

"Damn me later, Benedict!" you cry. "Listen now. Your claim to the Granville name is safe. Your father's marriage to Mrs. Caddington was the bigamous one, not his marriage to your mother. Cad is no heir but a bastard, a damnable bastard! The Granville name, estate, and fortune are all yours. What we must needs do is acquire some hard proof that the bigamous husband is alive, perhaps from a warden of Bedlam, and all will be well. Here, have a snack. You look peaked." You toss him the watercress sandwich you were saving for later. He slaps it away as if it were a gnat rather than a valuable and tasty late-night delicacy.

"I would have eaten that!" you say. As you reach to retrieve the sandwich, he catches your wrist in a vicelike grip.

"You are a fool." Benedict says. He stamps upon the fallen morsel. "You have told me nothing I did not already know."

"But I do not understand—"

"Of course you do not understand! How could you understand? For ages I have known these facts that you have so expertly *detected* while you drink and carouse with London's demimonde."

"But you did not tell me!" you cry. "Why did you not tell me?"

"Tell you what? That my bastard half brother used my half sister as hostage to steal my name and fortune? That to properly maintain or stake my claim on what is rightly mine, I must subject Henrietta to her true, lowborn fate? The fate of a lovechild of a bigamous marriage, with no fortune or station to save her? To add further insult to her injuries, after having allowed her a taste of the life she will never know, her fate is ruined because a chit like you plays detective and exposes our family's secrets in some sad attempt to feel important." With each word he speaks, you feel more dejected. With each angry phrase, you feel the bars of the cage that surrounds your own life, as well as Henrietta's, should this truth come out.

"Benedict," you whisper, "I had only wanted to save you—"

"What do I need saving for? Rich or poor, I am a man. It is Henrietta I am concerned for. You know, woman?" he grinds out. Any love light that may have danced in the corners of his cruel silver-gray eyes is snuffed out with each word. "You are extraordinary," he sneers. "I have managed to keep myself out of scandal—and the Rose & the Smoke— my entire life before meeting you. Now I have managed to become mired in both, merely because someone of low station has mistaken a bit of my kindness and momentary desire as some grand form of intimacy."

"Benedict, I—" Anger—and tears—shine in your eyes.

"Save it," he hisses. "Tell it to my aunt the next time you monogram her handkerchiefs."

You feel your heart torn apart like a rejected proposal letter. There is nothing left for you and Benedict to do now but turn on your heels— in opposite directions.

At a safe distance from his angry gaze, you rest against a wall and sob. Hateful man! And yet the thought of him thinking badly of you pierces your heart in a way you didn't think possible. How could this be? What is wrong with you?!

No, this is foolish. You shake your head and force yourself to think sensibly. Even lovers who aren't exactly full-fledged lovers quarrel. You have come to Harlot's Row with the intention to help, and now all you do is hurt. Perhaps you have done enough. Perhaps Benedict's words are the harsh reprimands of a man scared of his fortune . . . and his feelings.

You cannot let things with Benedict end this way. At least not without having the last word. Turn to page 185.

If you are entirely over all of this nonsense and ready to get the brot-hell out of here, turn to page 251.

The Great North Road to Scotland is long, muddy, and interminably dreary. Fortunately, the orphans don't seem to mind and treat the cart in which they're traveling as an impromptu wrestling ring. As Sallie roundhouse-kicks Bert in the face (no doubt giving him another black eye), you sigh and remember when you, too, partook in such innocent childish pleasures.

How you wish you had their youthful exuberance, stripped as it was from you after a series of tragedies that left you forever marked. Alas, it does no good to dwell, so you huddle in your cape, water dripping from your bonnet, and watch Mac's firm hands with fascination as he expertly takes the reins of the coach. Imagining what else those hands could do helps the journey go a little faster.

"My sweet Sassenach, I wish to ken what entices ye so about these hands o' mine," Mac says. "Are ye fixing to chop 'em off and use them as ingredients in yer witch's brew?" A somewhat sad smile plays on his broad, fine lips. You burn at having been caught staring, but you hold your head high and return his smile in kind.

"Your hands would not be good for magic, dear Mac," you say as primly as you can. "They have too much work in them, and not enough playfulness. Magic is work, to be sure, but it needs lightness. Deftness."

"Wildness," Mac agrees with a nod, his voice almost a groan. You are momentarily shocked by the desire you hear in it. You share a look that says you want to share more. You imagine his hands working your wildness. Now more than your face burns for him.

You remedy the situation by resolving to stare at your shoes for the remainder of the journey. Mac clears his throat and focuses his attention entirely on the road.

It is a long and arduous day's travel before you find a suitable inn that can fully house the mob you are traveling with. As Mac sees to the cart and horses, you make sleeping arrangements with the innkeeper.

"The young 'uns can probably just about fit in the great room, miss," he says in his flat East Anglian whine. "It will be a tight squeeze for sure, but there is room for them and maybe one or both of the ladies. We also have a small room to the side that you and your husband can take."

"Husband?" Mac half chokes, half laughs as he walks in from the freezing cold. His shirt clings to him as he shakes droplets from his red hair, which has been darkened by rain.

The innkeeper raises an eyebrow. "Unless your husband prefers to sleep in the stables?"

"Och, the stables will do me fine!" Mac says quickly, and he turns on his heel as if about to run to them. "I've slept in much worse, believe me!"

You don't doubt it, but it doesn't seem right that the man who has worked so hard and so long should spend the night in a freezing stable instead of a cozy bed. It also infuriates you that he would make such a show of being virtuous, although propriety (and the fact that you don't trust your quivering loins to behave themselves) demands that you do not sleep in the same room together under any circumstances. You bite your lip as you gaze at his muscular back and consider what the devil you are going to do—when you aren't lost in thoughts of what you would *love* to do.

If you let him sleep in the stable on his freezing ownsome for propriety's sake, turn to page 203.

If you decide to give the martyr a run for his self-righteous money, turn to page 299.

"Nigel," you say, still in disbelief of how things have turned out, "I don't know how to say this, but—"

"You need to marry me so your life is not in ruin?" Nigel says hopefully.

"Ah . . . yes." The words are barely out of your mouth before he drops to one knee and slips a ring onto your finger.

"Marry me! Please! If you please! My darling!"

"Yes . . . fine. Sure. Nigel, have you just been carrying a ring around—"

"On the off chance that you might ever be inclined to marry me? Yes, my love, I have! Let us away so you may meet Mama!"

You journey to the country in a swift carriage while Nigel excitedly describes all his relations and how much you will like his country home. You cannot much focus on his talk, but when you do, you are surprised to find yourself laughing at his good-natured sense of humor. When the carriage finds itself caught behind a simple farmer's cart, stuck in a muddy track, you are impressed by how helpful and kind Nigel is in response. Instead of feeling inconvenienced, he strips off his fine shirt to reveal a pleasing, surprisingly muscular body and then proceeds to deftly free the cart from the mud, sending the happy farmer on his way to market.

Once you arrive at his country home, you are fussed over by his sweet mama, who is delighted to meet you and puts you up in their house while you plan a hasty wedding. His family is entirely delightful, and you think that being a parson's wife might not be such a terrible fate. Your heart warms as you realize that you shall help the poor and make some small difference in the world.

One fine afternoon, when Nigel, his mother, and the rest of the family have gone to town on various errands, you find yourself entirely alone in the house. You are dizzy at the prospect of things going well in a way you never anticipated.

"You look happy, my lady," says a calm voice. You start and then turn to see Nigel leaning against the doorway, smiling in that plain, happy way of his.

You return his smile. "I thought you were in town this day."

He laughs, reddens, and looks down at the floor. "Yes, I . . . I said I was going to town so I could have some time to myself so I could . . . to . . . um, I . . ."

"What, Nigel?" you ask. Your interest is piqued.

Nigel searches the ceiling for his words. "Well, I thought if I said I was going to town, you might go out walking for hours on end, as you like to do, and I could have time to myself in the house alone to . . . practice."

"Practice what?" You cock your head to the side and lock eyes with his. A flush burns across the bridge of his nose. He now searches the floor for his words.

Finally, he lifts his eyes to yours and speaks. "Our wedding night."

An inexplicable fire burns through you. Nigel takes a tentative step toward you, and you are shocked at the little race your heart runs as he does so. You take your own tentative step toward him. He emits the gentlest hush of a gasp. The sound makes the hair on the back of your neck, as well as your nipples, stand at attention. Nigel notices, and a pleased smile plays at his lips. How had you not noticed until now how fine they are? They are barely parted, but the little space between them makes you want to explore what is inside.

"Do you wish," you find yourself asking, breathlessly, as you take his hand and run it slowly, loosely, barely over your face and side, "to practice with me?"

Nigel tilts his head back as you stroke his neck and emits an unself-conscious moan of pleasure. "Yes, my lady." He takes your hands and kisses the tip of each finger, one by one. Then he flicks his tongue against each tip in such a delicate fashion that your body riots with the tease of it. Gently, he guides your hands down his throat, to the buttons clasping his shirt. You understand his meaning and begin to unbutton them.

"Please, my lady," he says, his voice straining with desire. "I always practice this part slowly, to make it last."

You nod, feeling heady, and slowly reveal his chest. When you have reached his navel, he takes your hands again. "My turn?" he asks.

You stare into each other's eyes, taking in this new side of your personalities. He seems so different, yet is still the same Nigel. Just one who is now, very tenderly, just barely, licking your ears, brushing his lips against the line of your neck, warming your very care with every moan he emits, just because he has the privilege of slowly lowering your neckline to reveal your—

"Glorious body," he says, drinking you up in wonder. "Oh, my lady, you are beautiful." Now it is your turn to moan as he flicks his tongue over your nipples, kissing each one with a fierce, rhythmic tenderness he must have studied from the moon and the ocean tides. Within moments, he has your body burning up and your sex shimmering with desire.

"Do you want your ecstasy now, my lady?" he asks, his breath catching as you pull him in for a deep kiss. He lets his lips, wet with yours, slide gently over your mouth as he pulls away slightly to speak. "Or do you want to wait, and see what else I practice?" He slides his hands around your waist, down the small of you back, and ever so gently draws you closer.

"Show me," you respond, and he brings two of his fingers to your mouth.

"Take these into your mouth, as if they were . . . my manhood," he instructs, and you do as he asks. He watches your face, and his eyebrows arch in such pleasure that you find yourself ready for anything he proposes. "Now, my lady, will you lift your skirt? Slowly, so I can watch your beauty unfurl?"

Heavens, are you happy to oblige. He delicately leans you back on the settee and watches with reverent desire as you reveal yourself to him. Once you do, he slides his fingers inside you, slow, teasing, deep. He watches your face, notes the arch of your back, the tension in your knees, the grip of your fingers. He charts your response, as well as his course, accordingly, until you see nothing but pale fire before your eyes.

"There is more, my lady," he says, his voice ragged and all the more beautiful for it. Somehow, despite the waves of complete pleasure overcoming you, you want more. "Do you want more?"

"Oh, I want more, Nigel." You arch your back again, and this time he gently slides his lush, long manhood over your wet sex.

"I love hearing you say my name," he gasps, sliding over you again, and then gently, teasingly, he gives you a taste of him. The pressure, the surprise, the desire makes you want to grip him and drive him into you, again and again. He keeps sliding over you, making you long more and more. "I love the way you smile. I love thinking about you undressing for bed. I love thinking about easing those clothes off your beautiful body and kissing every inch of you. Of making love to you, and watching your face change as I bring you pleasure."

"Make love to me." As you speak the words, he fills you with himself. And oh, does he bring you pleasure. Again, all you see are sparks and stars.

"There is more, lady," he gasps between moans of pleasure. More? Oh, this Nigel has such stamina. "If you want it—"

"I want it." You shift yourself on top of him, sliding up and down to play a sensual symphony on his magic flute for your rapt audience.

"I want you." He kisses you, deep, as deep as he is inside you. "And sometimes I practice . . . I imagine . . . you this way." He gently tips you onto your knees and slowly begins thrusting his goodness into your valley, making your flowers bloom, over and over.

"There is more, my lady," he says.

"YES."

He pauses. "Do you wish me to take you roughly now, my lady?"

"Yes," you say and grip his forearms. He releases a ragged scream of delight, and then releases his full force into you. He is so hungry for you, so lusty, and you are so closely entwined that you feel every flexing muscle, every breath, every shudder. Your bodies are silk ribbons, woven together, smooth as water undulating in a deep well of desire. Together you bend like young trees in a storm, limber and strong. He flips you and dips you and together you are acrobatic air, water, earth. You climax screaming his name, becoming stardust.

After you recover some sense of yourself, you turn to face him. He is half draped on the settee, half on the floor. His eyes are full of you.

"Where," you finally manage, "did you learn all that?"

Nigel Frickley smiles. "I . . . I had a professor at Cambridge whose, um, wife, took quite a shine to me. She and her husband had an, um, arrangement where they were free to do as they wished as long as it was . . . discreet. She was a very demanding and thorough educator. With inventive techniques."

Your eyes widen in shocked delight.

"Are you angry, my lady?" he asks, worry coloring his strangely beautiful face.

"Not at all, Nigel," you say. He breaks into a wide smile.

"Wonderful!" he cries. "Now I will have to come up with something new for our wedding night. Let us sneak some wine before Mama returns and we must be respectable!"

He bounces out of bed to fetch the carafe. You lie back in satisfaction and sigh with happiness. You resolve to send a ham to the professor's wife every Christmas from now until your end of days.

Life is good. It is very, very good.

The End

"Oh, Garraway!" you swoon, calling Lord Craven by his first name. A time for desire is no time for formality.

"I want you," he keens, his eyes as wild as your desire for him. "I have wanted you since you first arrived."

"But—" You attempt a false protest to at least appear to save your modesty. "But I am a governess, and you a lord. Society dictates—"

"Society!" he spits. "What do our bodies dictate?"

He wraps you in an embrace so close you feel all the firmness of his body's dictations. You rack your mind for adequate verbiage, but ascertain that the truest depth of your emotions can only be expressed by pressing the fullness of your moonlit orbs into Lord Craven's handsome, hungry mouth.

"The only society I care about," he moans through mouthfuls of orb, "is yours."

You make love with a violent passion there in the eldritch garden, amid the ruins of your purity and the angel statue bearing the face of his dead wife.

As you lie panting in each other's arms, your reverie is broken by the haunting wails of a woman crying.

"HE SAID IT WOULD BE ONLY ME! ONLY ME FOR ALL TIME!!"

Lord Craven's face turns as pale as a corpse. "Damnable woman!" he cries and leaves you alone among the eerie statues.

Do you decide to get the hell out of here? Turn to page 54.

Do you investigate the sound? In for a penny, in for a pound. Turn to page 93.

In the morning neither of you speaks of the previous night. You have many orphans to tend to, so the day is full of hard work and tension, but nothing more.

You spend the remainder of the journey in uncomfortable silence. Fortunately, the children are too excited seeing sheep and grass for the first time to pay much attention. Jane and Gertie, on the other hand, offer you sympathetic looks.

"All men is heathens," says Jane. "Even the good ones."

"Worse than heathens," adds Gertie darkly.

Mac scrupulously keeps his distance from you, and you from him, and the rest of the stops in a variety of coaching inns along the way are extremely uneventful. Well, except at Doncaster, when you have to physically restrain Sallie from maiming Bert after he suggests that milk comes from cows and not bottles. And except when, you swear, you see that shadowy figure again. But of course this is impossible—to see someone from London this far north. Unless you have been followed . . .

Lamentably, the uneasy silence currently hanging between you and Mac has given you much time to dwell on things, and dwell you do. You cannot stop thinking about Constantina and what she could have meant to Mac to cause him such pain. About the fire and how it could have started. And about the shadowy figure and whether it is a product of your fevered mind . . . or something much darker. What can it all mean?

The universe smiles on your gloomy soul, for you hear the orphans cry out with excitement. You look up to see that you have arrived at Abercrombie's crumbling ruin of an ancestral home, Glenblair Castle.

. . . .

Och, you're in Scotland now, lassie! Hoots, mon. Turn to page 175.

To your surprise, the rest of the henchmen take off in the opposite direction from the route you and Fabien are taking.

"What is going on?" you demand.

"Madame St. Croix reveals her whereabouts to only a select few. These men have done their part, they have no need to go any farther or see where we are going."

"And what about me?" you spit back. "Am I one of these select few?"

"No, *chérie*. You are one of the blindfolded." He quickly ties a heavy black cloth around your eyes, then whispers into your ear. "It is safer for you this way."

The motion of the camel's gallop causes your body to rub against Fabien's manly form in a way that makes you uncomfortably aware of the dangerous yet alluring brute . . . and all that he may offer. With one sense deprived, all others awaken.

"Why did you bring two camels if you were going to carry me with you?" you ask in an effort to distract yourself from the masculine length at his groin that is pushing against you.

"You were meant for the other camel, but I don't trust you not to try to escape," says Fabien's voice. "And I will need two to carry the gold she will pay me for fetching you."

"Am I worth so much to her? Me, a simple nobody?"

"The one who will come for you is worth it to Madame St. Croix. Though if you ask me, you are the true jewel to be claimed."

"I am no one's to be claimed!" you bite back. He responds only with a throaty laugh. In return you settle into a brooding but extremely charged silence.

It seems an age later when finally you stop. The animal heat of the virile body pressed close to you departs, leaving in its place only cool desert air. But there is no time to ponder your chilly situation. From a little way off come strange sounds that you can't quite place, and then a blazing light that manages to pierce even your blindfold.

A firm, meaty pair of hands pulls you down from the camel with surprising gentleness and removes the blindfold. You gasp in astonishment despite yourself.

Before you stands a beautiful white tent, a dove's wing against the void of the desert's nighttime sky. Deep within, a latticed lantern throws exotic patterns against the pale fabric, illuminating a simple dinner laid for two. In front crackles a fire, offering respite from the chill in the air. You are loath to admit it, but you are impressed.

Fabien shrugs his enormous shoulders. "You see I have done this before."

"I can see that." You take measure of this powerful specimen of a man. He moves with the sleek confidence of a jungle cat, and yet there is something in his eyes that looks strangely haunted.

"How do you think I have survived this long?" he says, leading you into the tent where you seat yourself.

"You have had a hard life?" you ask as casually as possible, wondering how such a man came to be in work such as his.

"No harder than most," he says as he eases himself down next to you with an inherent grace. He continues in that strange accent of his, almost French, almost Egyptian. "I was born the illegitimate child of the Chevalier de Mangepoussey, who came with Napoleon on his campaign to Egypt, and an Egyptian princess."

"So you were brought up with wealth, then?" This would explain his surprisingly courtly manners.

"I was brought up in disgrace!" He glowers back at you, his pale jade orbs lit with strange fire. "My very existence was a scandal and a shame. My family provided a scant education, but nowhere to go in life. It would have been better for them had I not existed at all."

"I see," you say primly. "And then you met Delphine St. Croix?"

The Nile-green eyes rise to meet yours.

"Ah, Madame St. Croix . . . she rescued me in a way," he says. "Gave me work. Gave me purpose. Gave me her body, if only for a while."

You shudder and wonder at the thought. He glances at you with a nonchalance that you wish you felt.

"Ah, but *chérie*, it does not mean anything to her, desire. She sates her appetite only for an evening. You may feed her body, but her heart . . . her heart is hungry for only one."

"Evangeline!" you gasp, as understanding dawns. He nods.

"You and I are but pawns in their game. But it matters not to me. I have lived all my life on the outskirts of society, with nothing to do except be a hired thug for those who can pay. I do not expect much out of life."

At this he stands and walks to the entrance of the tent. The desert wind tosses his dark locks around his face like waves in an ebony sea. His mostly unbuttoned shirt clings barely to the muscular body it struggles to contain.

"I have a contempt for society and all of its rules. In a strange way, it is freedom. You understand?" he says, still not looking at you.

Because he is distracted, you realize that now is the perfect time to escape from whatever Delphine has planned for you. You look around wildly to see what you have to work with. Wine, a dish of flatbread and *fuul*, a few promising-looking rocks . . . and a man so beautiful, it takes your breath away.

Time to make your plan.

Are you a lover, not a fighter? Does seducing your way out of this scrape, and getting your jollies while doing so, sound appealing? If so, turn to page 346, you hussy, you.

Are you a fighter, not a lover? Does seducing your captor sound a bit too dicey, and would you rather solve this issue using a sharp rock and violence? If so, turn to page 105.

You find yourself wondering what it would be like to be entertained by such tempting wickedness and such pleasing physicality.

"I don't know what to say, Cad," you whisper.

"You know exactly what to say!" He grips your shoulders. "If you use your body to do the talking, instead of your blasted mind. Your body knows we are meant to be. Once I knew I wanted you for a moment . . . but now I know I need you for all time!"

"Well, I don't know if I need you for all time, for one forbidden evening, or absolutely not at all!"

"I am not my brother. Your wit works less wonders on me than the wonders on display here." He presses you into a kiss, and to punctuate his desire, he literally rips your bodice.

"Get your filthy hands off her, you odious piece of bodice-ripping *trash*." Benedict's sharp, superior voice cuts through the night.

"Oh, Benny. What a spoilsport." Cad winks at you, then turns to Benedict, who is glowering at him from the shrubbery. "Didn't anyone ever teach you, brother, that it's polite to share your toys?"

An exquisite moment passes in which the men regard each other with unspeakable disgust and you with immeasurable desire. You shake your head breathlessly and watch as the two brothers—one light, one dark, yet perfectly matched—tear at each other with handsome hands, hungry for vengeance. Cad lands several slugs to Benedict's stomach, which Benedict returns with a deft punch to Cad's jaw.

"Not the face!" cries Cad. He throws Benedict against a statue of Cupid with such ferocity it makes you wince. Dazed, Benedict staggers to his feet.

"Always so easy to provoke, Benny," Cad jeers. "No wonder Father preferred me to you! Just like he preferred my mother, his true wife, over your cold, snobbish bitch of a mother!"

If Cad meant to throw Benedict off-balance with his taunts, he could not have chosen a worse way to do it. A strange light that crosses Benedict's dark silver eyes makes you shiver in both fear and desire.

"How dare you," Benedict says a little too quietly, his voice like the eerie calm before the storm.

Even Cad seems to sense his mistake. He swings a right hook that Benedict expertly dodges. A fire has been lit under Benedict now, and he comes at Cad with a series of brutal punches that send the other man collapsing to the ground.

Undeterred, Benedict launches himself onto the slumped golden form of his half brother with another volley of blows. As Cad whimpers, you realize with horror that the strange light in Benedict's eyes is in fact a death gleam. It is up to you to intervene—lest this goosecap, who has somehow managed to touch your heart, does something he regrets.

"Stop this madness at once!" you cry, throwing yourself between him and Cad. The action seems to break Benedict out of his murder daze, and he stares at you in wonder. You stare back, your jaw obstinate and your expression unflinching.

"Do you wish to hang for fratricide?" you say coolly, your voice a bucket of ice water dousing the flames of the fight. Benedict shakes his head and raises himself off the ground. He offers a bruised hand to you and helps you up.

"You are not worth it," he spits at Cad's slumped form. The blackguard sits up and has the nerve to grin with self-satisfaction.

"It seems to me the young lady in question threw herself upon me to save my life." Cad looks at you with an expression both mocking and hungry. He raises an eyebrow.

"It appears I am in your debt. And yet I think that you are perhaps having second thoughts about your allegiance to my brother. You know, sweeting, it is not too late. It's never too late to make another choice . . ."

....

He's not wrong . . . you do indeed have another choice!

Do you spit upon Cad's caddishness and tend to Benedict's wounds? Turn to page 148.

Or do you, upon reflection, want a piece of Cad's caddishness? Turn to page 43.

The best person you can question is Mrs. Butts, and you seek her out presently. You aim to find her in the kitchens, but are waylaid by a manic Manvers.

"You are too bold for your own good, you sly little chit!" he spits at you, his eyes wild with unhinged rage. "You know, if you died here at Hopesend Manor, you would be the second lovely young thing to meet her end under the care of Garraway Craven! The authorities should be quite interested in *that*, I should think! Quite interested indeed! A-ha! A-ha-ha-ha!" Manvers laughs in the unsettling way of those who are about to commit unspeakable acts of violence, and you find yourself quite eager to flee his presence.

....

But flee to where?

If you wish to flee Hopesend entirely, perhaps returning to the safety of London, turn to page 54.

If you wish to flee momentarily and gather your thoughts in the less-eldritch garden, turn to page 49.

*"Finally, Mac staggers out, with Timmy in his arms
and Dodger at his heels."*

"I must save the boy!" Mac yells, but you grab him by the collar and hold him back. He shoots you that intense, dare you say smoldering (although that's perhaps too apt given the circumstances) look, and your temperature quickly rises. The smell of smoke reminds you that, indeed, the orphanage is engulfed in flames. You drag Mac to a nearby water pump, tear his shirt from his rippling chest, and fully drench it.

"What are ye doing, lass? I wasn't wet enough to save the damn child?" he rages.

"Not as wet as we all got in this blasted rain. Now you are more protected." You toss the shirt back at him. He covers his face with it, lit with newfound respect for your practical foresight, and races into the burning building.

He is gone for five minutes, though you feel as if an age passes. Finally, Mac staggers out, with Timmy in his arms and Dodger at his heels. He collapses, choking. You give man and boy water and see to it that both revive. As they do, you notice that Dodger has a parchment in his mouth—he must have saved it from the house. The paper is covered with strange markings that you do not understand.

"Do you recognize this document, Mac?" you ask. "It seems important. There are symbols, and . . . only one word I recognize, a name: Constantina," you read aloud.

Mac's face pales. He grips your shoulders with surprising strength for someone who has just cheated death. "Listen, lass. I appreciate all that ye have done here, I truly do. But there is nae job and nae home for ye here anymore. Have ye anywhere else you can go?"

....

If you are now fully committed to Mac and his drenched abs of intrigue—er, his orphans—and there is no way you are leaving them, turn to page 25.

On the other hand, you *do* have a standing job offer with a certain Lord Craven. Sure, he sounds fairly terrifying, but you have only a single kid to teach in a structure that has not burned down. If you'd like to bid Mac adieu, turn to page 14.

"I'm sorry, Benedict," you whisper to him and then gently unweave your fingers from his. "But the ton is not the place for me. There is good work to be done, and I must strive to do it."

You give him a gentle pat-on-the-shoulder goodbye before side-stepping his heartbroken form to approach Mac.

"Mac," you say, your heart in full flutter, "I am ready to do good. May I do good with you?"

"Aye, lass!" The mountainous Scotsman beams at you with delight as a beautiful, flame-haired woman walks up and kisses him on the mouth. "My new and lovely wife Anjelica and I do most of the good work together, o'course, but the orphans never say nae to a kindly lass reading them a bedtime story here and there!"

Anjelica walks up to you and grasps your hands with genuine warmth.

"We are always so short-staffed, and the children are such brave little soldiers . . ." Her eyes swim with tears of gratitude. "Thank you so much."

Mac beams at his beautiful, perfect wife. "Isn't she the best and most wonderful creature ye've ever beheld?"

She really is, damn it. You want to be happy for them, but you feel your heart sink. You turn and see Benedict glare and roll his eyes.

So . . . you've exhausted your last good options. What are you going to do now?

....

Throw yourself on the mercy of Nigel. He hasn't much money, given that he just started a job as a country parson, but he is sweet and devoted. Turn to page 283.

Throw yourself on the mercy of Sir Charles Burley-Fanshaw. Yes, he is super gross and odious, but he is also loaded and probably too old to bother you . . . much. Turn to page 24.

"Of course my husband is joking," you laugh. You reach for Mac's incredibly taut bicep, pulling him close. He gasps audibly, causing the innkeeper to raise a bemused eyebrow. "He thinks I snore like a 'bloody dragon, lass!'" you add in your best attempt at a brogue. The innkeeper laughs, and Mac stares daggers at you. "But I promise to be quiet, sir," you tell the innkeeper conspiratorially. "He will be the only man I keep up all night." You and the innkeeper share a round of wicked laughter, and you lead a dazed Mac into the cramped quarters where you will be spending the evening—together.

"What the devil are ye up to, lass? Goin' and pretendin' we're married folk?" Mac asks once the innkeeper is well out of earshot.

You extend the privacy screen so you may undress, and as soon as you have hidden yourself from him, you begin to strip off your clothes. "After such a journey, there is no way you should take your rest in the stable. As husband and wife, you can get as good a night's rest as I. We can split up the bedding so one of us is on the floor, if you wish. In any case, I trust you."

"Aye, but what if I dinnae trust ye?" he says. "Ye are being reckless with your honor, as much as ye are being reckless with my—" He cuts himself off. "Fine. I will change here, but as soon as ye are asleep, I will head out to the stable and be proper about it."

"Suit yourself, husband," you say, smiling despite yourself at his bullheadedness and his slip of the tongue. You imagine several more ways you could enjoy his slipping tongue while you strip down to your underthings. As you do, the strange bit of paper that Dodger brought out from the fire falls from its hiding place in your bodice. You bend to pick it up and read the name again. *Constantina.* You remember Mac's strange expression when you said the name before.

Who could she be, you wonder. A lover? A sister? A friend? An enemy? Clearly, she means a lot to Mac. You wonder if you could ever mean a lot to him, or if he sees you merely as an impulsive, reckless woman with a caring streak.

You are so distracted by these confusing thoughts that you lean against the screen to contemplate, forgetting that it is a flimsy bit of screen and not a solid wall built for contemplative leaning.

You tumble, mostly naked, into Mac, who, you are thrilled to discover, is mostly naked as well.

You hold yourself over him, arms trembling, and he holds your waist with thick, limber fingers.

"You're naked," you whisper, both surprised and pleased.

"Ye said to trust you," Mac offers by way of weak explanation.

"Well," you say, and ever so gently arch your valley to meet his throbbing tor. Mac groans with rare pleasure and release at the slight movement, and your heart races at the thought of what other symphonic exultations the undulations of your bodies could bring. "Better than the stable floor?"

Mac throws his impressive caber against you in sweet release. "We can't, lass," he gasps. "It's improper." He kisses you, his tongue as true in its aim as his mind is in deed.

You kiss like moss growing, wet and lush and full of secret direction. Your kisses give the other guidance, to lick here, bite there, pull, push, ride.

"Honor my body," you whisper into the cup of his ear. He shudders, and you spasm just to witness this great lighthouse of a man shine on you. He worships your breasts, kissing them as fully and forcefully as he has your mouth, as tenderly as he strokes the wet apex of your sex. You thrum and thrill at his touch, at the final show of desire from which he does not hide. The fact that it is desire for you heats his touch all the more, until you are blazing hotter than his red hair.

Just as you both are tearing at his belt to free yourselves completely, and you imagine the sweet, pleasurable pain you will feel when he throws his impressive caber deep into the sky of your sex, he pulls away.

"We must . . . be honorable," he gasps, raggedly. "You deserve . . . honor." His massive shoulders sag, and he cannot help but kiss you once more. "I am sorry, bonnie lass. I-I will be in the stables."

He leaves you, heading off to sleep among the horses and deny both of you your desires.

But why? As you dress yourself, you again catch sight of the strange slip of paper. The word *Constantina* burns you like a brand. You stuff the damn thing back into your bodice.

Your unfulfilled desire throbs uncomfortably within you, and you toss and turn for the rest of the night.

Damn it. Turn to page 289.

Well. You've had some times, haven't you?

While you're glad to have your feet back on solid London ground, your head is still stuck in the clouds of your recent memories—as well as the London fog.

But despite your adventures away from home, you feel pulled to this city, the Big Smoke, and you know it holds something better for you than anything you have experienced so far. It is also dead expensive, and with empty pockets and a heavy heart, you swallow your pride and beg the Dowager Dragon to give you back your old job.

After Lady Craven has begrudgingly accepted you, you find yourself in another London ballroom. She takes no small delight in detailing how happy Lady Evangeline is in Egypt, still, and that she plans to be abroad for quite some time. "You're all alone now, aren't you?" she trills, before narrowing her eyes. You begin to make your rounds. "Stay close. Stay quiet. And for heaven's sake, fetch me my sherry," she seethes under her breath.

"Of course, my lady." You smile through gritted teeth. Oh, how you hate the taste of humble pie. You beeline for the refreshments.

"Truly, my lady, is there no greater thrill in this life than serving my wicked relation her happy water?" A cool, bemused voice caresses your ear. Benedict. You smile, all the way down to your bones, and turn to him, keeping your face calm but letting your eyes betray your delight. He continues, eyebrows raised. "I've tried to work it out, and I see it as the only compelling reason you would return. That surely must be it." He offers to take your hand and bends low to kiss it, with ridiculous ceremony. You stifle a laugh.

"And that alone," you reply as he rises to meet your gaze. You are standing close, face to face, just a little too close to be completely proper. Just close enough to feel the heat simmering beneath his sass . . . and waistcoat.

"If you're holding your breath for me to confess I've missed you, I am rather afraid you will die of asphyxiation, my dear. Aunt will be most displeased."

"As will you?" You arch an eyebrow. Oh, it is delicious to slip back into this banter.

"Me? Oh, I will—" But before he can finish, Benedict is interrupted by a clap on the shoulder. He spins to face a man built just as finely as he, but twice as wide across the shoulders and a full head taller, boasting a mane of fire-red hair.

"Aye! How goes the legislation to benefit the orphans and wives of the war then, laddie?" Captain Angus "Mac" MacTaggart's voice booms a hole through Benedict and lands straight in your heart.

"It . . . goes . . . slowly, as things unfortunately—" Benedict stammers, losing his cool momentarily in the presence of the large, do-gooder captain.

"Always do. Aye, aye." Mac laughs ruefully. "Just remember, as we fine folk here enjoy our sherry and reels, the folk left bereft by the war snatch what sleep they can, tossin' and turnin' on a bed of empty promises and broken dreams. Aye!" Mac slaps Benedict on the back so hard, you fancy you hear a bone break. Benedict takes his leave, and you are left alone for a moment with the fireball of rugged handsomeness and beneficence that is Mac.

"Hello, Mac," you say softly. His eyes twinkle—and perhaps peer a bit longingly—at you.

"Aye, lass," he returns, as soft as his body is hard. "If you aren't jest a sight for sore eyes. I have oft wondered what ye were getting up to out there, in the great wide world. And if, perhaps, were needin' helpin'."

"Does the lady need help? May I be of assistance? Would the lady like a glass of brandy? I have fetched you brandy, my lady, here is, oh, oh my!" The excitable voice belongs to none other than the hopelessly goofy, awkward, and adoring Nigel Frickley. He stumbles all over himself (and several others) to hand you a glass of brandy.

Unfortunately, the proffered refreshment ends up all over your dress, instead of in your mouth. "Thank you, Nigel," you demur. "But really, you shouldn't have."

"Yes, he should!" Sir Charles Burley-Fanshaw leers at you from across the room. "And he should do it again!" The old coot's eyes dance with delight at the sight of your clinging gown, and you and most of the ball's attendees shudder with deep disgust.

"Where the devil is my sherry?!" the Dragon shouts. Despising yourself for it, you scurry toward her with the drink outstretched.

"Here you are, my lady," you say, extending the glass to her. She snatches it, and in front of all of the ton, throws the drink full in your face!

"Oh . . . oh my," Nigel stammers. "I shall fetch my lady another napkin—"

"You shall fetch nothing of the sort!" the Dragon spits. Nigel freezes in his somewhat adorably goofy tracks. She turns her nigh-villainous gaze on you and narrows her already beady eyes. "I have longed for the moment you would come crawling back to my employ. I have longed for it expressly because, in turn, I longed for the moment I would teach you a valuable lesson. You do not bite the hand that feeds, my dear, and you most certainly do not caress longingly the hands that are related to the hand that feeds. You have invited scandal into my family, and for it, you shall pay. You are a terrible, ungrateful, spiteful little chit. You have disgraced yourself and my family with your life choices, and you shall pay for your actions. You, my *lady*, are fired."

Ninety percent of the ton gasps, scandalized. Eighty percent of that ninety percent do so with cruel delight.

Your heart drops to the floor. You are now penniless, jobless, beau-less, and drenched in two types of aperitif. Clearly, the Dragon took you back only to publicly humiliate you, dismiss you, and leave you with neither income, home, nor dry change of clothes.

"Get thee hence, harlot!" she cries, casting her beady eyes about for more cocktails to heave at you. Benedict locks eyes with you and takes a deep, shivering breath before stepping forward and gathering your hands in his.

"This harlot is my fiancée!" he says, loud enough for everyone, even those at the fringes of the ton, to hear.

Several members gasp so hard they need to sit down to catch their breath.

"Benedict," you say, burning partly with desire, partly with humiliation, "you do not need to marry me to save my honor."

"No," he responds, and his eyes search yours in that intense back-and-forth way that future generations will know only by watching romantic comedic narratives on a sort of moving screen. "I need to marry you to save myself. From a life of boredom, from a life of mediocre sex, from a life of grinning and bearing it when all I want is to sass around. I need to marry you to save myself from a life spent without you. Any moment I continue to live without you as my wife is one moment too many."

Your eyes widen, your blood thrums. Benedict drops to one knee.

"Marry me, my lady," he asks, breathless, and in love.

"No! No! NOOOOO!" the Dragon screams.

One hundred percent of the ton awaits your response, none with more eagerness than Benedict. You see Mac look down at his boots. Nigel's eyes shine with terror. Sir Charles Burley-Fanshaw mimes groping your chest and buttocks.

Lady's choice. What will it be?

....

Benedict, *duh!* You are totally in love and you want to find some rainy garden and kiss on him all over it. Get thee hence to page 199, you damnable woman!

Benedict is great but . . . you just can't resist throwing your tiny scrap of remaining caution to the wind and get back to orphan-helpin' with your favorite rugged Scotsman, Mac. Turn to page 298.

The children really could do with a wash, you think to yourself as you head out to the collection of junk and scrubby grass that passes for the castle's garden. But how would one be able to use that single tin bath to clean all of them effectively?

Perhaps some of these spare parts thrown haphazardly in a pile might help? Digging in, you find an old pump mechanism, a leaky watering can, a long piece of piping, and a rusty but usable spring. Together, they remind you of something . . . a device you once saw in an exhibition back in London that you attended with your dear papa when he was still alive.

You have an idea. You haul your finds into one of the rooms near the kitchens and set to work. Assembling the pieces with your nimble fingers and ingenuity, within a short time you have made a makeshift shower.

The water you put on to heat earlier is now, thankfully, hot. You haul it in, pour it in the tub, and start testing your invention. The mist on your previous walk has left you already drenched and caked in mud, so you decide to keep your dress on.

As you luxuriate in the feeling of hot water cascading down your body, making the fabric cling to every curve, Mac enters the room. You startle at the sight of every hot, sweaty magnificent inch of him. There is an equal hunger in his eyes and in your loins . . . but still a nagging doubt in your heart.

. . . .

Do you throw caution to the wind and pounce upon the handsome lug for what might be the first shower sex in the history of the world? Turn to page 228.

Or do you decide that now is the time to have it out with him regarding Constantina? You really cannot enjoy yourself while curiosity preys upon your mind. Turn to page 46.

Lord Craven kisses you deeply as if for the last time. You respond with equal urgency, your mouth ravenous for his. As you finally pull apart, you set out on the walk back to Hopesend Manor together, and he begins to speak.

"Before the child, we were happy. I did not love her just because she was beautiful, but she was, and she was well acquainted with how otherworldly her beauty was. But when she bore the child, she became obsessed with the look of herself. She saw ugliness where there was only age. She saw weakness where there was only experience. She wished she could have undone it, she said. She no longer wished to be touched. She no longer wished to touch. She wanted only to brush her hair, look upon her reflection, and remember when she was young.

"'If I could be young and beautiful forever, I could be happy,' she would whisper to me, 'I would give anything for that.' I told her she *was* young and beautiful, but she scoffed at me. 'You are a pottering old fool before your time,' she said. And she despised my attentions to the child. 'You love him more than you love me,' she would say.

"'We will all grow too old to be beautiful,' she would whisper to me before we fell asleep. 'I must save us all.' One morning, I woke and she was not next to me. I had a horrible sense of what was about to happen. I ran to her chambers. She was holding the boy before the fire, ready to throw him into the flames.

"'This way, he will be a boy forever!' she cried. I stole him away, and, in so doing, my jacket caught fire and was singed. She grabbed hold of it and tried to push me in as well. 'Nothing is according to plan,' she cried. 'Nothing but this will do. See you in hell!' We struggled, and as we did so, she must have got turned around. My last memory is of her falling into the fireplace, her hair aflame, her eyes red, her laughter turned to screams, her beauty consumed by the blaze."

Your mind reels. Hopesend Manor looms in the near distance. "Surely," you whisper, "you tried to save her?"

"Yes!" he cries in anguish. "I pulled her from the flames, but it was too late. I lay her upon the hearth, I stroked her face, and I wept. But all my weeping could not douse her. I could not save her. And perhaps"—Lord Craven is now fully sobbing—"perhaps it was her wish not to be saved."

He turns to you, his eyes lost and despairing. You kiss him and together enter the house and near the morning room. Your heart aches for him. You are about to open your mouth and offer some form of redemption, or at least a tongue kiss, when you hear voices arguing within.

Quick, turn to page 343.

That does it. You grab the nearest erotically shaped lamp and smash Cad over his hot, handsome head with it. Down he goes, like and unlike so many before him, in the Rose & the Smoke.

"And don't you ever, *ever* lay a hand upon him again!" you spit at his inert frame. Turning, you see Benedict staring at you with eyes aflame.

"Benedict?" you gasp.

"You . . . you damnable . . ." He stands shakily.

". . . maddening . . ." He takes your face in his hands and stares deeply into your eyes.

". . . *wonderful* woman." And with that he kisses you so intensely it takes your breath away. You melt into his arms. The world could end at this moment and neither of you would notice.

Until, that is, you feel a gentle tap on your shoulder.

"*Ahem*," Lady Evangeline says gently. "Think it might be best if you make a quiet exit. We really don't want to draw attention to ourselves."

As one, your eyes travel from the broken furniture, to the broken man, to the dozens of crushed watercress sandwiches that litter the room.

"You—you might be right, Vange," Benedict admits.

"Of course I am, Benny," she says briskly. "I suggest the two of you journey back in your coach as soon as possible before anyone notices you are missing."

"And what will you do?" you ask.

"I . . . am going to clean up this mess," says Lady Evangeline. "Don't worry, I've done this before."

"I wish I could say I was surprised," says Benedict as he ushers you out the door.

Turn to page 17.

You give a last lingering look at the empty doorway, then turn your attention back to the boy. "How did you lose your sister, Master Alexander?" you ask as tenderly as you can manage.

"I think the wolf ate her," Master Alexander says, wiping at his steady stream of tears.

"The barghest? The wolf from the tales in the village?"

"Not that one. That one is just a village wolf. The one that got my sister was a bad wolf. A very bad wolf. Mama said wolves are always hungry for naughty children and that Helena was very naughty. But she wasn't naughty! She just knew about Mama and . . . the man."

"What man?"

"A man who did rhymes in Switzerland. He was always writing Mama poems, like 'She walks in beauty like the night' and other nonsense! And Papa found them and it made him upset. Mama always said *Papa's* poems were best used to line the rubbish bin!"

"This, ah, man . . . ," you say. You know you must tread carefully. "Was he a special friend of Mama's?"

"Yes, and Helena saw them struggling. She was going to tell Papa, but then Helena was gone! Do you want to know what I think?" The little soul quakes in your arms. You can scarcely believe it, but you think you think what he thinks.

"What, my darling?"

"I think—I think Mama was the bad wolf! And she got Helena, and she's going to get Papa, and me, and you, too!"

Your heart breaks for the poor child. You vow to get to the bottom of this mystery for his sake, and the sake of his tortured father.

. . . .

But how?

If you go to speak with the servants, turn to page 79.

Or if you seek out that unspeakably handsome vicar, turn to page 131.

The next day, you leave the children with Mrs. Ferguson as she heroically struggles once more to teach them sword dancing. As you retreat, you can hear her yelling, "Sallie! Punching your partner is not part of this dance!"

You feel mildly guilty, but also relieved. Now is your chance to search the castle for clues. You poke your head into one chamber and see the infernal wooden chest that Abercrombie has dragged over hill and dale. You shake your head—he lugs it around like a child totes a favorite toy. Seeing no one nearby, you enter the room and open the chest. Maps and papers spill out in disarray. But what do they all mean?

"Searching for something, lass?" Abercrombie's voice sends your heart to your throat.

"Just some linens," you lie. "Dodger has soiled yet another set."

Abercombie laughs, but the twinkle in his eye is dimmer than usual. "Aye, ye will not find linens in there, or at all. We are short of staff, and short of resources, so there is very little to be done about Dodger's keen desire to mess them other than wash the filthy things clean."

"I will get to that, then." You bid Abercrombie good day, and stride with forced confidence out onto the castle's decayed gardens—and straight into Mac's burly, beckoning chest.

"Aye, lass. I missed ye, too." He laughs, and you feel relieved at the sight of him. You drown each other in a kiss that tunes your bagpipes.

"You have ta get married now!" screeches a joyful Sallie. You and Mac break apart to see that the orphans have arrived. Sallie hands you an envelope.

"This was left on the bloody castle doorstep, miss," she says. "Is it your marriage certificate?" You ignore her question and tear a parchment from the envelope, revealing a hastily scrawled note:

You must meet me tonight by the loch. Alone. I have new information we must discuss.—O

. . . .

Ooh . . . turn to page 246!

Mrs. Butts has the true run of this home. Why would you waste your time talking to anyone else?

You are sure you will find her in the kitchens at this time of night, and so you make a beeline there. But as you break into a run, you stumble, suddenly thrown back against the wall of the gallery by a forceful, unseen hand.

"What in heaven's name are you doing, girl?" The savagely prim voice of Manvers slashes at you in the darkness. Your eyes adjust to the dim lighting, allowing you to make out the manservant's face in all its seething glory. "You look like a lunatic on the run from Bedlam. It is unbecoming. It is beneath us all."

"I have urgent news for Mrs. Butts," you spit back at the little troll of a man. You despise the way he sneers at you. As if he knows you. As if he *owns* you.

"You have hysteria, is what you have. You are too weak-minded to care for a high-spirited boy like Master Alexander. You know you were only brought here as a plaything for a sick man. The boy ought not be punished for the sins of the father. The boy ought not be exposed to such a shrill harpy. Not when his mother was an angel! Not when his father struck her down!"

Shrill harpy! Oh, how you quiver with hatred for this detestable little man.

Do you tell him where he can stick his loathsome misogyny? Turn to page 255.

Or, if you feel that you have overreacted to the events of the evening and wish to request that Craven explain himself, turn to page 60.

Nothing else matters as long as there is fire in your loins!

"Quite the worst idea we have ever had . . ." you repeat. "But don't stop."

Benedict gazes at you in wonder before plundering your mouth with an intensity that takes your breath away. His clever fingers work dark magic, until you see fireworks and are soaring, metaphorically, as high as one.

It is your turn to rip his clothing, pulling at his breeches to expose his tumescent member.

"Let us have this moment of happiness," you say as you wrap your hand around his rigid maleness. "Just once. So that whatever happens next, we will at least have this memory. Of us. Together."

The heat smoldering in Benedict's silver-gray eyes becomes an inferno, and you wrap your legs around him as his swollen shaft is embraced by the glistening portal of your womanhood. You move your bodies together in an ancient rhythm, reaching an apex of ecstasy until both of you collapse in a golden haze of stars.

· ·

Well, now you've gone and done it! Turn to page 169, you wanton orgasmic harlot.

You reach for a broken statue with which to bash Loveday's head in. But it is too far away, and so you claw at the vicar's traitorous blue eyes—to no avail. The world starts to go black . . . and then brightens again as you awaken to find Craven breathing new life into your mouth.

"I heard your whole sorry tale," he says to Loveday. "I would have gotten here sooner, but I had to scale the locked gates of the garden."

"This is my house," Loveday spits.

"This is my *home*," Craven spits back.

The two men fight.

To your horror, Loveday, though smaller and more finely made, turns out to be stronger than you realized. Craven might actually lose. You watch with dizzying hopelessness, but then you hear a tiny voice in your ear: "Find your move."

It is young Alexander, who has followed you all, unseen, into the eldritch garden. He manages to throw Loveday off his father with far more strength than a child should have, and he speaks in a strange, high-pitched voice.

"You got Mama to kill me. It was a big knife. Then she pushed me in the fire. I fought so hard, but it wasn't enough. Papa tried to save me, but I was already gone. Mama didn't expect to trip and fall in the fire. I watched her burn. She deserved it. You deserve it, too."

Loveday's face contorts with disbelief. "NO! NO! I will kill you all! And even if I don't, no one will believe you."

Loveday backs away as he speaks, while you, Craven, and the possessed Alexander stalk toward him, united as a family. Suddenly a flash of lightning breaks open the sky. A tree branch falls and stabs Loveday through his traitorous heart.

For a moment, the shadows seem to illuminate a familiar, triumphant, dark-haired beauty wielding the branch. But only for a moment. Alexander promptly faints, and you and Lord Craven carry him back to his rooms.

....

Go to page 83.

You deftly duck out of Farouk/Fabien's reach and launch yourself at a nearby abandoned stall. Grabbing the first thing that comes to hand—a heavy earthenware tagine that you can barely lift—you swing round just as a pair of strong hands grabs you firmly by the waist.

Fabien's gray-green eyes glow victoriously . . . then quickly dim as you smash the heavy ceramic over his head. You quickly slip the pistol from his waistband, aim it at the nearest henchman, and shoot. You barely graze the man's shoulder, but it seems enough to spook the band of henchmen. They scatter and run deep into the souk. You turn to face Fabien, but he seems to have melted into the crowd, like a spirit summoned away by a vengeful goddess.

"Dash it!" You pull a dazed Kamal to a seated position. He has been beaten severely about the head by one of the henchmen. "I would have at least liked to catch one of those scoundrels for questioning."

He stares at you in wide-eyed admiration. "Truly, you are an exceptional woman, miss. The Lady Evangeline is lucky to have found such a companion."

Though you are charmed by his reverence for your surprising triumph, you have no time for flattery.

"That's very nice of you to say, Kamal, but we must get back to Lady Evangeline. I'm sure she will want to hear about this. Kamal?"

You look down and realize that your trusted friend has collapsed from his head wound. You sigh. Carrying him back is going to be hard work.

Turn to page 220.

You wrap yourself in a cloak and follow the sound of howling to the edge of an eldritch garden surrounded by an ornate wrought-iron gate currently in a state of romantic disrepair. The howls have ceased. Strangely disappointed, you perch atop a stone structure, only to realize it is a fallen angel—the likeness of Lord Craven's first wife.

You leap to your feet, alarmed. Your erstwhile seat is, in fact, her grave.

"The governess pays her respects," growls a sultry voice. You suppress a shriek. Lord Craven is lounging languidly against a broken pair of angel's wings, his eyes and hair wild, a brandy snifter in one hand. There is no mistaking the look in his eyes—unchecked desire. Your body riots with passion.

"How strange—" You breathe deeply and hope to shake the fear—or is it excitement?—from your tone before continuing. "How strange to be so far from home and alone with naught but forgotten crypts and fallen angels to keep one company."

Lord Craven rises slowly. You drink the sight of him like wine. He stalks toward you, his beautifully muscled frame straining against the pressures of lust. "The only eyes that can perceive any wickedness yet to occur here are long dead, girl."

You fix him with a level, if hungry, gaze. "I am currently faced with a pair that speak quite to the contrary, if I may be so bold."

"You may be much bolder, girl." He places your trembling hand on his manhood, which has grown as stiff as the eldritch garden's wrought-iron gate.

....

Do you give in to your hopeless, wild passion right there in the garden? Turn to page 288.

Or do you run to preserve your purity, if only for a moment more? Turn to page 324.

"Lord Craven is lounging languidly against a broken pair of angel's wings, his eyes and hair wild, a brandy snifter in one hand."

"You, sir, have crossed a line," you say, each word icy enough to cause severe frostbite. "Farewell."

And with that, you turn on your heel. You really do look wonderful turning on your heel.

"You are right. Forgive me," Benedict cries as you charge away, but it is too late. You stride purposefully down the hall and refuse to look back.

He is just a man, just a foolish man . . . so why is it you cannot get him out of your mind?

Lady Evangeline immediately discerns that something is amiss as you stomp to her carriage.

"Are you quite all right, my dear?"

"I am *wonderful*," you snarl. "Your cousin is a fool, but I myself am *splendid*."

"Oh, dear," she sighs. "I take it he overstepped the mark?"

"You could say that."

Lady Evangeline sighs again.

"I do understand your frustration, my dear, but truly he is the kindest of my cousins, once you get past that layer of sardonic brooding."

You glare at her.

"It is a very thick layer at times," she admits. "But before you set my carriage on fire with your anger—and please understand that I have no objection if you do; I could do with a new one. Still, I must ask . . . are you quite sure you wish to continue?"

You turn and stare at her, wide eyed. Well, are you?

. . . .

Do you wish to press on ahead and save Benedict's skin? There is still a mystery to be solved . . . and perhaps you still cannot stop thinking about his manly form and tousled locks. If so, turn to page 222.

Or do you want to be done with all this nonsense and choose a new path for yourself? If so, turn to page 243.

You are torn from your camel and your blindfold is yanked off. Fabien's harsh hands linger tenderly for a telltale moment at the nape of your neck. You brush off a twinge of guilt as you squint in the blindingly bright sunshine. A soft, throaty, seductive voice that you do not recognize accosts your ears.

"So there you are. *La petite anglaise*. My rival." Every syllable of this short speech is laced with bitterest poison.

Your vision settles, and finally you are able to clearly see the woman standing before you. You let out an involuntary gasp. You had expected great beauty, but Delphine's exquisite looks surpass even that. Her dark, silky hair is piled carelessly atop her head in a way that is both effortless and alluring. It contrasts beautifully with her milky skin, still moonglow-pale despite the sun. But it is her face that captivates you most—the delicate features combined with the sharp angles of her cheekbones, and she possesses the most arresting eyes you have ever seen. Queens are called to mind, and goddesses, as well as the snake that provides the sweet relief of death after a doomed journey in an endless desert. In short, Madame St. Croix is breathtaking.

As Fabien holds you aloft like a sacrifice to a false god, Delphine grabs your face and pulls it toward hers, a mask of eerie perfection. She inspects your mere mortal visage, tilting it to and fro, her perfectly oval nails digging half-moons into your cheeks. Her spectacular eyes, catlike in shape and angle, are so dark they look to be almost entirely pupil. If Fabien's eyes are the green of the Nile, hers are the black-red of the Nile turned to blood. She bores these eyes into yours.

"You are pretty in a common way," she sneers. "I am surprised someone so *simple* has gained her favor this time. I was expecting a woman of exceptional beauty." Delphine speaks coolly, but makes no effort to conceal the old wound of her sadness. "*I* was her favorite once, you know."

Joy somehow sings in your heart. Could it be true? Could the lovely and exciting Lady Evangeline think of you as her favorite? More favorite than this strange, terrifying, extraordinary creature holding you hostage by way of her own jealous rage? Before you can ponder this exciting idea further, Delphine continues. "*Mon Dieu*, I can remember the first time we met. She was the bored, much younger wife of an old diplomat. So lovely. Her husband had no interest in the fairer sex. She married him knowing that, by the way, knowing that he would not disturb her. And yet, when it came down to it—"

You hold your tongue, rapt in fascination as Delphine continues her tale.

"I made a mistake. A mistake I was sorry for, one that I would have forgiven her for were the tables turned. I would have forgiven her for *anything*. And yet my pleas, my love, it was not enough. She sided with her husband, the man she married for convenience, over *moi*."

Delphine casts a scrutinizing gaze over you once more, her unearthly eyes shadowed with a raw pain that almost makes you feel sorry for her.

"I have tried so many times across the years to speak with her, but she is cold—cold like all you English. But still, I needed her so that I could be happy again, so we could—*mais non*, so we *can*—complete our life's mission."

You suddenly realize what she is thinking.

"You want to raise the lost Temple of Hathor from the desert!" you exclaim. Delphine's eyes flash black fire.

"Perhaps you are not quite as simple as you look. Yes, *ma petite*, I plan to raise the temple. But for that to happen, the legend states that two lovers must enjoy love's purest joy within its grounds. And there is no one I love apart from Evangeline! And despite her passing interest in you, I know in *le cœur de mon cœur*, there is no one on this mortal plane she loves more than *MOI*!"

To punctuate her near-fatal love for Evangeline, Delphine snaps at the tip of your nose. The bite is gentle enough, and although she does not draw blood or break skin, you feel shaken to your core. Fabien rips you from her grasp—protectively, you think. Despite yourself, you tremble in his strong arms. Delphine throws her gorgeous head back and laughs like a jackal.

"Of course, after all my years of trying to follow her and being blocked by this parry or that feint, all I needed to do was let her follow my bread crumbs. All I needed was to set a trap of irresistible intrigue. I would not need to chase her. She would come to me."

"The turquoise canister!" you gasp. Breaking out of her reverie, Delphine cuts her eyes at you as if remembering you are still present. You detect that she sees Lady Evangeline the way someone near death would see a mirage on the horizon. It is the only thing she *can* see. It is the only thing she *will* see. Perhaps that sight has gotten her through hell.

"All I needed to do to see my love again was to set a simple trap, then take away her latest toy. Because that is all you are—and all you will ever be. It is all anyone can be to her!"

Delphine lunges for you at the same time that Fabien draws you back, and impossibly close to his legendarily muscled body, at the same time that a cut-glass voice trills out across the desert.

"I wouldn't go as far as saying *that*."

Your heart swells. "Evangeline!"

"Evangeline!" Delphine whispers, her eyes wide in savage longing and wonder.

"The very same," drawls Lady Evangeline as she steps out from behind one of the tents that make up Delphine's campsite. You thrill to see that she is now clad in breeches that show off every contour of her shapely form, along with a loose white shirt unbuttoned shockingly low. She flips you a roguish wink.

"How are you faring, my dear?"

"Marvelously!" you say. And you are not lying.

"Splendid," she says. "I would expect nothing less."

Lady Evangeline turns to Delphine, who has remained speechless since her former lover revealed herself. "Hello, Delphine. Hello . . . and goodbye."

Lady Evangeline pulls out her gold pistol and aims it directly at Delphine. Her bright eyes smolder like precious gems pulled from the inferno.

"Ready, aim, fire," Delphine says, a cool smile playing across her lips.

"Don't think I wouldn't," Lady Evangeline snaps.

"I don't doubt it," counters Delphine, pulling open her dress so Evangeline may aim truer. It also has the added side effect of exposing her magnificent bosom. You blush at the sight.

Delphine drinks in the glory of Lady Evangeline, smiling more like a woman in bed with her true love than a woman facing her end. "You could not hurt me any more than you already have. In fact, death will come as a relief."

To your horror, rather than backing down, Lady Evangeline slowly cocks her pistol. "Is that so, darling?"

You can't be certain, but some part of you wonders if some part of Lady Evangeline is enjoying this. Fabien's grip tightens protectively on your shoulders, almost imperceptibly slipping the sleeves of your dress down to expose your shoulders.

Things are getting entirely too hot in this desert.

It is clear that cooler heads, namely yours, will need to prevail. But how exactly do you intend to do that?

....

Do you demand that Delphine and Lady Evangeline work things out sensibly? Right now, before homicide occurs? If so, turn to page 143.

Or do you call out Delphine on her vicious abuse? You have every sympathy for her broken heart, but once you cross the line into kidnapping and nose-biting, there's really no turning back. If so, on to page 262.

"Lady Evangeline pulls out her gold pistol and aims it directly at Delphine. Her bright eyes smolder like precious gems pulled from the inferno."

You rush to the safety of your bedchamber and slam the door, your heart racing and your breath coming in shallow pants.

You can run, but you cannot hide . . . from desire. There is a knock at the door, and as you open it gingerly, every particle of you trembling in fear, Master Craven crashes in, his clothes in tatters, bleeding from his well-muscled chest.

. . . .

Of course you have to tend to his wounds . . . and perhaps a few other things, too. Turn to page 165 and get ready to kiss your purity goodbye!

"We have raised the temple," you say to Lady Evangeline before exploring the soft palace of her mouth with a tender, tantalizing kiss. "But my temperature is rising now. Let us study each other and then study all the temple has to offer, inside and out."

"There are great archaeological discoveries to be made, topographies to explore," she agrees, flushing with desire.

"Oral histories to be given," you say.

"And received." Lady Evangeline arches a mischievous brow.

"Again and again." You are aflame with ideas, plans, and realms of research for this new and fruitful partnership. "Farewell, lady pirates!" you cry to the whooping lot of new friends. "You are fearsome, and admirable, and we shall all do this again sometime!"

Together, you and Lady Evangeline burst into the impossible temple, laughing and tearing at each other all the way. It is surely full of many wonders. You can't get deep inside fast enough. There are so many discoveries to be made, and you plan to make at least ten more tonight.

The End

"We must go, my love!" you cry to the groaning Lord Craven. He rolls off you, throws on a robe, and accompanies you to locate the source of the banging.

Before you find it, however, you hear Master Alexander scream as if pursued by the hounds of hell. You turn to Craven, your eyes wide in horror, and you both race to the child's aid. As you round the corner, you find yourselves faced with something far more frightening than any hellhound.

Alexander is cowering in the corner, clutching a stuffed toy, tears of fright streaming down his young face. In front of him—glowing with the unearthly light of hellfire—is his mother!

The apparition turns to you with dead black eyes, her lovely mouth arrested in a terrifying rictus grin. "You have taken my place!" hisses the ghoul. "But not for long! I shall take you! I shall take you all! Back with me . . . to hell!"

"No, you bloody well won't!" cries a reassuringly broad Yorkshire voice. There, barreling down the hall with a cross around her neck and a bible in her only hand, is Mrs. Butts.

"Out the way, love!" she cries to you. While you and Craven stare, gobsmacked, Mrs. Butts raises the Good Book high above her head. "Don't worry, loves, I've done this before! How do you think I lost my arm and earned these scars?"

The phantom Lady Craven starts floating toward you, uttering strange guttural noises that belong to no human language, death dancing in her eyes.

"Get out, demon!" screams Mrs. Butts as she flicks holy water from a canister hanging at her hip. "The power of Christ—" Suddenly she is silenced, thrown across the room with a wave of the creature's hand.

While Mrs. Butts groans from a corner, the ghost laughs in triumph before turning on Lord Craven. "My love!" she hisses. "My dear husband! You will come with me! You will suffer for all eternity, too!"

You throw yourself in front of him. "Not while I'm here!" You grab Mrs. Butt's bible and cross and thrust them at the ghost of Lady Craven. "You will have to take me! Take me instead and leave this family, for I love them and there is not a thing I would not do to protect them!"

The specter reaches for you, but as she does, her hand starts to melt. "What is this?" she shrieks. "What is happening?!" A beam of white light bursts through her and fills the room, illuminating her many portraits in eerie blue fire before they crumble into dust.

The ghost of Lady Blanche Craven roils and twists in agony. "No! This cannot be!" Nevertheless, the light consumes her, exploding her spectral form into nothing. In her place lies a single red rose.

Alexander runs to you, and you and Lord Craven embrace him tightly, united as one loving family. "You saved us, miss!" he cries.

"I-I don't understand," you whisper into his hair as his father's powerful arms encircle the two of you.

"I do, love," says Mrs. Butts, pulling herself up to seated. "You were willing to sacrifice yourself because you love them. True love can conquer anything, including wicked lost souls from the depths who would destroy us. 'Tis the most powerful thing in th' world."

The sun rises, filling the room with pure, heaven-sent light. It is as if the deadly fever that consumed Hopesend has finally broken, and there is hope for life . . . and perhaps love. You turn to Lord Craven, astounded. His green eyes are clouded with tears and pure passion. He kisses you ferociously, as if you were not only his love but also his salvation.

"Oh, my darling!" he cries. "You are not only my love, but also my salvation. You have rescued me entirely."

"Are you going to be my new mama?" Alexander asks sweetly. Lord Craven looks at you with hope in his eyes.

"Of course, darling. Of course!"

And so begins the start of your new life as lady of the manor. You rechristen it Hopesbeginning.

The End

You raise a hand to Ollie's face, tenderly yet regretfully. He looks down, knowing what you are about to say.

"I'm sorry, Ollie my darling," you whisper. "But our time has passed. I think that in your deepest heart, you know it is true." Ollie looks up at you, tears shining in his eyes.

"And, I daresay, you love another?" He nods toward Mac, who is skulking silently at the other side of the entrance hall, looking like a massive, bekilted oak tree plagued with melancholy. You know not what to say. Ollie smiles wryly.

"He is a lucky man. Have a care, my darling. Be well."

"You, too," you say. He nods, and you see him to the door. He mounts his horse and rides off into the sunset, presumably to be the hero of his own thrilling series of books.

You look after him wistfully. Your chapter with Ollie may be closed, but the story of the rest of your life is only just beginning. You walk back into the house and into the arms of Mac—your hulking, ginger paramour slash fellow orphan educator. He looks at you with love in his eyes.

"Are ye mine then, my love?" he says. "Will ye stay with me . . . for now and for all time?"

....

Well, will you?

If you opt for a tough but meaningful life helping orphans while having thrillingly adventuresome sex with a rugged Scotsman for the rest of your days, turn to page 234.

But if, honestly, a life spent stuck in a crumbling castle, where your closest friend is a dog named Dodger, sounds less than fun and you just want to get out of here, turn to page 20.

You give Cad a piece of your body—by slapping him across the face! He pauses for a moment, then turns to you bearing a viper's smile.

"You like it rough, do you?" he snarls, grabbing your wrists and literally ripping your bodice.

"Get your filthy hands off me!" you snap back. You try to position your knee within manhood-striking distance.

Unfortunately, he notices what you're doing and expertly pins you against a statue of Cupid, with your knees on either side of him, offering you no opportunity to inflict damage.

"Not so fast, sweeting. You won't play that trick on me again."

Desperately, you cast about for an escape route. The hard stone of the statue digs into you, but it is nothing compared to the hard stone of the man in front of you. Cad grabs your face with his free hand and forces you to look at him. He sneers, his cruel eyes flashing triumphant.

"I must say," he crows, "my brother may be a fool, but he is a fool with good taste." His eyes run over you in a way that makes you shiver. You say nothing, staring at him mutinously and then spitting at his hell-born face.

Angered, he pushes your face roughly against the statue.

"Don't make this hard for yourself, sweeting," he hisses in your ear. "I think you'll find that if even my sap of a brother can satisfy you, then I will be more than enough to—"

"Unhand her! NOW," growls a dangerously low voice. You look up in relief.

"Benedict!" you cry.

"*Benedict!*" moans Cad, rolling his eyes. "If you don't mind, this young lady and I are rather occupied. I suggest you take this opportunity to leave us and get off my property for good. Before I call the authorities."

Benedict stalks forward silently, his eyes silvery with rage. Cad gulps despite himself.

"How dare you," Benedict says a little too quietly, his voice the eerie calm before the storm.

"Now see here, Benny," says Cad, releasing his grip enough for you to slip away from him. Cad barely notices as he turns to face his dangerously silent half brother. He reminds you of a cornered snake facing a particularly deadly mongoose. "You are—"

Again he is cut off as Benedict lands a deft punch to his jaw and another to his nose.

"Not the face!" howls Cad, and he launches himself at Benedict. Throwing his sibling against a statue of Cupid with such ferocity it makes you wince, he lands several heavy slugs to Benedict's stomach.

You watch, dazed, as the two brothers—one light, one dark, yet perfectly matched—battle for mastery of the other. You search desperately for some tool with which to help Benedict.

"Always such a stick-in-the-mud, Benny," Cad jeers. "Always so easy to provoke with your foolish notions of honor. And what did it get you? I have your home, I have your title, and now once I have beaten you, I shall have your whore, too! Perhaps you would like to watch?"

If Cad meant to throw Benedict off balance with his taunts, he could not have chosen a worse way to do it. You see a strange light cross Benedict's dark silver eyes that makes you shiver in both fear and desire.

Even Cad seems to sense his mistake. He tries a swinging right hook that Benedict expertly dodges. A fire has been lit under him now, and he comes at Cad with a series of brutal punches that send the rogue collapsing to the ground.

Benedict launches himself on the slumped golden form of his half brother with another volley of blows. As Cad whimpers, you realize with horror that the strange light in Benedict's eyes is in fact a death gleam. It is up to you to intervene—lest this brave, wonderful fool, who has managed to break through the once-impenetrable walls of your heart, does something that he regrets.

"No, Benedict!" you cry. "He's not worth it!" Your voice seems to snap Benedict out of his murder daze, and he stares at you in wonder. You stare back at him, your eyes loving but your expression unflinching.

"Please, my love. Do you wish to hang for fratricide?" Benedict pauses for a moment, then shakes his head and raises himself off the ground. Turning to Cad, he spits on his cringing form.

"You are nothing to me. Nothing at all," he says, his voice cold and impassive. He then turns to you, his eyes ablaze with passion and concern.

"Did he hurt you?" he asks, so tenderly that you feel your throat catch.

"I shall be quite all right, thank you," you say, as you watch relief course over his handsome face. He raises a strong hand to stroke the hair out of your face with a gentleness that takes your breath away.

"Oh, my darling," he says as he leans in to kiss you. You close your eyes, but feel him yanked from you by a certain would-be ravager.

"Oh, no, you don't," snarls Cad as he throws Benedict to the ground and draws out a pistol. "I mean to have my way, and I'm not letting anyone, least of all my pathetic waste of a half brother, stop m—"

For the third time Cad is cut short—this time by you smashing an urn-shaped garden ornament onto his head.

He slumps to the ground, out cold. Benedict stands shakily, his eyes blazing with admiration and desire. You gasp with pleasure as he pulls you into a fiery kiss. Whatever happens between you in the future, you will never forget this moment.

Still, reason must prevail, if only for now, for you have an unconscious fake heir to deal with. Benedict, as if reading your thoughts, pulls away and looks coldly at his brother lying on the ground.

"We should go."

....

Benedict is right. Get out of there and go to page 148.

You down your tea, square your shoulders, and decide that this will not do. Whoever sent this letter clearly meant to scare you, and you will be damned if you let them succeed.

You head to the great hall, where Mrs. Ferguson is attempting to teach the children sword dancing with distinctly mixed results. You ask the kindly housekeeper where you might buy the many supplies that you can't really afford but desperately need.

"Och, the only shop in town is Buchanan's," she says. "They're good folk and will give you a fair price."

And so you find yourself rambling across the rolling green Highlands to find Buchanan's shop. The dramatic scudding clouds and craggy outposts soothe your soul . . . and you begin to wonder what it would be like to live here.

Spotting the village in the distance, you quicken your pace. As desperate as you are for bread and bandages, you are even more eager for answers to the questions that have been plaguing you since the fire.

Buchanan's is surprisingly well stocked for a store in a tiny village. But it is the vision standing behind the counter that truly astounds you. With darkest auburn hair and eyes the color of wild heather, the shopkeeper is so exquisitely lovely that, were the members of the Royal Academy to see her, they would come to serious blows for the priviledge of painting her portrait.

The vision, utterly unselfconscious of her pulchritude, smiles at you with a welcoming visage.

"How can I help ye, hen?" she asks warmly. Finding yourself lost for words, you hand over your list. She gives it a once-over with her magnificent eyes and then calls to the back room, "Gerald! Can I get some help wi' the top shelves?"

As a brawny man with jet-black hair and a heavy beard emerges from the back room, she turns to you.

"I dinnae mean to pry, hen," she says, "but would ye be one o' the Sassenachs that wee Angus has brought up with him from London?"

"I-I am," you say.

"Och, are ye asking after yer old sweetheart, Fiona?" teases the man. He winks at the flame-haired beauty. She laughs and pushes him.

Your heart sinks. "You—you know Captain MacTaggart?"

"Ye could put it that way!" chuckles the man. Fiona laughs and pushes him again.

"What my husband is trying to say is Angus MacTaggart and I were sweethearts when we were wee bairns."

Your heart has now utterly plunged. Yet you must be doing a good job of hiding it, for the gorgeous woman continues unabashed.

"Och, I fancied myself in love with him, I did. But then Mac got into a spot of hot water after he burned down Abercrombie's barn."

"A fire?" you say. *Another fire!*

"Aye. You wouldn't think it now, but he was a wee tearaway when he was young. He would have got in serious trouble with the law, but then Old Abercrombie offered to waive the charges if he joined the army. So off he went, and I was heartbroken."

"Aye. For about two weeks, until I came along." Her husband winks at you.

"Beast! It was at least six!"

"And what about Mac—I mean, Captain MacTaggart? Did he find love again?" You force yourself to ask the most difficult question of all: "Perhaps with a lady named Constantina?"

Fiona frowns. "I have heard of no one by that name," she says. "But I do know that the rapscallion that left Glenblair was not the somber man who returned. He puts on a brave face, but he has been changed by something that happened out there at war. Something he never talks about. Anyway, that'll be three shillings and sixpence."

You pay the Buchanans, thank them for their time, and leave with the supplies. You have much to ponder on.

· ·

Do you head straight home and get to fixing the house, and maybe finding some answers? Turn to page 162.

Or do you take the scenic route, so that you may gather your thoughts about what to do next? Turn to page 31.

You drink deeply his scent and run your tongue over the plush protrusion of his bottom lip. In response, the reverend slips his own tongue into your mouth, the serpent seeking the forbidden apple.

Now, truly, you swoon. He gasps with pleasure and stares intensely into your eyes. When he speaks, he is breathless and raw with power and pleasure. "You have played into my plan beautifully . . . but I didn't want to feel for you the way I do!"

You stare at him in shock. "What . . . plan?" you ask between shivers of pleasure. You grip his fine, white-blond hair in your fingers and twist. He emits a pleased, pained little cry and you guide him down your neck to your breasts. He playfully bites your taut nipples through your gown.

"My real name," he says, between mouthfuls of you, "is Simon Loveday *Craven*."

"What?!" you yelp—in part because *what?!*, and in part because he has slid two holy fingers into your mouth to wet them before dipping them in your holy water again and again and again.

"I am next in line to inherit Hopesend," he reveals as he works you into a fine frenzy. Sweat shimmers on his fair brow, and you pause between his admission and your desire to free his straining member from his all-white ensemble and sink him like a treasure into the sea of your mouth.

"I . . . had hoped . . . ," he gasps, "to convince Lord Craven to give me the home willingly. When he . . . refused . . . I decided to make him . . . appear to be mad. Manvers was all too ready to help me frame Craven for any misdeeds that would make . . . the home . . . easier for me . . . to claim . . ."

You pull away right before he climaxes. His eyes are wild and longing, but you aren't quite in the mood right this second. The naughty vicar has been up to *what*?

"Manvers was easy to convince that a little . . . theater would help do the trick. All he had to do was wear some sort of ghostly garb that would make Craven think his dead wife was watching him from the great beyond."

"You would have had Lord Craven and Master Alexander killed just so you could claim a house?" you ask, bitterness creeping into your tone . . . and parts.

"A mansion and title, yes," Loveday says with a sneer. "I wasn't outright villainous at the first, but when Craven started sleeping with the *help*, as he put it, Manvers had kittens about how it would desecrate the late Lady Craven. He never knew how I had desecrated the late Lady Craven over and over, right in this very spot."

All your blood that has not run entirely cold takes the opportunity to do so now.

"So all of this—us—was part of your plan?" you say acidly.

"Of course not. You were to be a pawn, the pièce de résistance once they found your lifeless body in the eldritch garden."

"You were going to kill me just to stake your claim on a house you do not need, on a title that means nothing, for a fortune that is not truly yours?" You seethe with rage.

"Of course!" He laughs at you and rises to his full, delicate height, so in love with himself and his power that you are by turns aroused and disgusted. "But now you have awakened a passion in me! You give me hope that I could find my place as a Craven in this world, at Hopesend and beyond. You may even help me find redemption after all this is over. Join me, my lady. Join me and revel in taking what you deserve from those who do not."

His silver tongue slips between your lips again. Why do all the good kissers have to be bad guys?

....

Do you run from this sodding crazy fool and his murderous plans? If so, turn to page 74.

Or do you really have what some would call a destructive penchant for bad boys and want to go all-in on this runaway carriage ride to hell? If so, turn to page 146!

"I have never been to Cairo, and I would love to see more of it today," you reply. To your surprise, Evangeline's understanding smile is laced with something that looks almost like regret. But why would she regret the departure of a simple creature such as yourself when she has work to do?

"Quite right, my dear," she says briskly. "Why lock yourself away when there is a world to be explored? Have a wonderful time."

With that she stalks out of the room, head held regally in the posture of an ancient goddess.

"Where do you suggest we go?" asks Kamal, his formerly doleful face lighting with pride for the city of his birth. "I think Cairo market would be most interesting for a new visitor! After that, we could perhaps see the famous Hanging Church?"

"That sounds marvelous." You push the memory of Evangeline's sad eyes far from your mind. "Lead the way!"

Kamal gestures down the nearest corridor. "Farouk, we need you!"

A dark figure looms from the shadows. He nods, his face almost entirely covered by a turban and face wrap, except for a pair of arresting, Nile-green eyes. You shudder, sensing something dangerous beneath the surface, like a crocodile hiding beneath tranquil water. Kamal seems unperturbed and turns to you.

"Farouk will keep us safe on our travels. It is a shame that he was not there last night, for he might have prevented this robbery."

You don't know what to say, so you nod silently, keeping your eyes on the enormous figure now following you. You really do not have a good feeling about this.

. . . .

Do you take this chance to make excuses and return to Lady Evangeline? An afternoon in Cairo market is one thing, but an afternoon in Cairo market being "protected" by Frightful McTerrorface is quite another. If so, go to page 151.

Or do you go to the market as planned? Bodyguards *are* meant to be intimidating. And he might turn out to be useful. If so, go to page 21.

You find Craven pacing in the library, half drunk on brandy and the past.

At the sight of him, you are furious with longing, and just plain furious. Leave it to this man to flee his responsibilities and run from his desires at the very moment that both require him.

"Put the brandy down, man. It is time for action, not self-sorrow."

He laughs unkindly, and drinks deeply while squinting into the gathering moonlight, feeling sorry for himself.

"You know not my sorrow, woman," he growls.

That's it. You've had enough. You slap the brandy from his hand and the smirk from his jaw. He looks at you in shock.

"I do hope your full attention is now on the matter at hand, rather than on your own self-pity," you say coolly.

"Th-thank you," Craven stammers.

"You must be strong now, for your son. But first, you must tell me what the *devil* is going on. We're a team now, damn it. The beast will out, so out it. Now."

Craven looks at you longingly, imploringly, the barest sheen of tears in his eyes. Oh, hell. You kiss him deeply, softly, and lightly trace the line of his gently hardening member with the palm of your hand, just for encouragement.

A confession issues forth from his lush mouth. He speaks like a poet, tearing pages out of his own journals. He speaks like spilling ink.

"Blanche was beautiful, and I loved her, even if I only married her for her money. She only married me for my name. I was a lord with a decrepit family home, and she was a wealthy Swiss chocolatier's daughter raised in England. She had all the trappings of the ton with absolutely no title, and I had all the trappings with none of the wealth. 'We are both outsiders,' she told me, 'but come inside, and we can climb as one.'

"I was young and foolish enough to believe her. I fancied myself a writer in those days, which meant I had to marry for money in order to provide for my family. Can you imagine my mother, the Dowager Dragon as you call her, living out the rest of her days, fed only by the hand of charity?"

You stifle a chortle. Indeed, you cannot. He continues.

"Even though we were happy for a time, that all changed when the twins were born. She was unfaithful far before then, of course, but I never disillusioned myself to think I was her only love. Still, that she felt the need to make her indiscretions so flagrant and cunning struck me as particularly cruel. On our honeymoon, on the shores of Lake Geneva, we struck up friendly conversation with a company of fellow poets. She took a particular liking to the most obnoxious—and published—of them all. She enjoyed telling me of his conquests, in the bedroom and on the page. She enjoyed making me feel inferior.

"When the twins were born, she left me for him, for a time. She could not bear the screaming of the babes, but she could more than bear the endless prattling of the poet. When she finally parted ways from his company and returned to me, her entire manner had changed. Her passions were wilder, her angers more ferocious. She focused fresh waves of hatred on the children, insisting that they needed to be 'dealt with' or 'seen to.' I did not like the way she looked at them, and I tried to be home whenever I could. I tried to make us a family in manner as well as name."

Your eyes widen as Craven muffles a sob in your midsection.

"If I'd been less of a fool, Helena would still be alive. Alexander would be happy, and you—you would not be here."

"You do not wish me here?"

"I wish it more than anything in the world. But I know that if you stay, I will damn you. The way I have damned everyone around me."

He lifts his eyes to hold your gaze and continues, speaking simply. "This is for you, my love," he says and hands you a small, smooth, polished-ash box.

"What is this?" you ask quizzically and take it from him.

"A new beginning," he says, casting his eyes downward. A diamond dewdrop of a tear slides down his plush lashes and shatters on the box.

You remove the lid to find a letter of recommendation on his finest stationery commending your governessing skills as well as full first-class passage to America. Your mind is scrambling to work out what this means when he speaks again.

"Of course, I will give you all the money you need, any amount at all, for whatever it is you choose to do. A woman of your skills and drive will most likely wish to work, even if she does not need to. Hence the recommendation. But if you do not wish to work, and perhaps want only to travel, that is just as well. I can pay to—"

"Pay me to leave you?" you interrupt, your broken heart lodged in your throat.

"No, love, I—" he stammers. "This is not payment. It is the best way I can think of for you to be free."

"What if I do not wish to be free?" You allow your tears to fall like daggers. "Do you not love me?"

"Of course I love you, woman! I love you more than life and breath and reason! I love you more than wind and air and—"

"Then why send me away?" you say, your voice trembling.

"Because I am terrible for you. I am a monster, and you are an angel—" He is unable to finish, interrupted by you snorting and rolling your eyes. "A fallen angel, fine. But still, you are more angel than I."

There's a lot to take in here . . . and a decision to be made.

Do you wish to heal this tortured soul with your love—and some *loving*? Turn to page 231.

Or do you wish to take him up on his kind offer and leave? Turn to page 183.

"Rebecca Caddington. One of my dearest friends. We found ourselves rejected by society and therefore found support and companionship in each other. Along with *the group*, of course," Madam Crosby says, sipping from a glass of fine champagne to punctuate the more elegant of her thoughts.

"The group?" you ask, emboldened by your umpteenth flute of bubbly. You can scarcely believe how finely appointed the rooms of the Rose & the Smoke are, and in your half-waking state, you fancy that the curtains and diaphanous silken decor are in fact bewitching glamours cast on filth and trash by the lovely madam's magical voice.

"The women," Madam Crosby intones, and she beams her quiet smile your way. "The ladies of the *New* New Female Coterie. A group of self-selected castoffs and strangemakers who found their solace— and their mettle tested—with one another. Years ago, Mrs. Caddington was one of our liveliest members. She was one of the sharpest wits I've ever known. She could have done much better than that stuffed shirt she chose after her first husband lost his mind."

The last sentence pulls your focus so tightly that you gasp for breath.

"You mean, after he died?" Lady Evangeline asks.

"Oh, that's right. Men die, don't they?" Madam Crosby signals to a rather handsome manservant for another bottle of champagne.

"Whether he died or not, you said he lost his mind. A most curious sentence," you say.

"It isn't so curious when taken as point of fact," Madam Crosby drawls. You can't place her accent. American? French? Nova Scotian?

"Lady Caddington's first husband

was a renowned theater critic in his day. The flourish and restraint she showed on the stage, he commanded on the page. It's how they met, you know. He had taken her to task on an off night, when she was doing a version of *Othello*. He had written some line about a distracted performance. She consulted us all on what she should do. I initially thought it merely a blow to her vanity, but she turned to me and said, 'The way he phrased it. How he saw it, how he heard. So few have that sense. It is the language of the soul, and he thinks me a novice speaker.' I suppose if one must love a man, one who is able to speak the language of the soul is acceptable. Of course, he wrote only favorable reviews of her from then on. What they say is true of language: If you do not use it, you lose it."

Madam Crosby is a woman who knows when she holds another in her thrall, and she has the presence of mind to pretend ignorance to her considerable power. She also has quite the tolerance for alcohol. Your mind, however, is far adrift in a sea of champagne. You attempt to anchor yourself to the weight of her words.

"So you're saying," you force out between hiccups, "that the mad first husband . . . is still . . . *alive and well*?"

"Alive, certainly. Well . . . ," Madam Crosby downs her sparkling beverage as if it were water. "How well can anyone be when they've spent the better part of their twilight years in Bedlam?"

"Bedlam?" you say, stunned.

"As you know, my dear, Bedlam is the vilest asylum in all of England," Madam Crosby says, regarding you with a gaze of practiced calm, laced with something like primal anger. "Which Mrs. Caddington knew full well when she sent her first husband there to rot."

"Why the devil did she do that?" you say. You reach for a finger sandwich from a tray the handsome manservant produced moments ago. You take a satisfying bite and relish the late-night pairing of watercress and intrigue.

"Why wouldn't she?" counters Madam Crosby. "He could no longer give her good, or even interesting, reviews. He could not feed her ego or pay her bills. He could, however, be secreted away in a living death while she moved on to a wealthy nobleman to solve some of her other problems."

"You can't mean . . . Lord Granville? Benedict's father?" Your eyes widen, and you help yourself to just one more sandwich.

"I can and do," Madam Crosby responds, and her voice is edgier than before. For a moment, you see the whole history of this heartless Mrs. Caddington written on her face. Perhaps they were lovers, perhaps very close friends, but in any case, the lady Madam Crosby so admired had taken a turn for the very dark when she sent her first husband away.

"This means Cad's claim is invalid. Benedict's claim is safe. Cad is still a damnable bastard. I must tell them so at once. Madam Crosby, thank you. Lady Evangeline, please. Let's away back to Kent."

You grab one more watercress sandwich for the road and hurry to leave, but you run smack dab into . . . Benedict!

....

Turn to page 278. Go on now, git!

"You failed!" you hear Manvers cry out, stiffly, to an unknown conversation partner. "The chit should be gone by now! Did you not give her the false diary? Did you not warn her of the sinful beast that she dares to bed, desecrating the memory of my lady?"

"I tried!" cries a familiar voice you cannot yet place. "But the young lady turned out to be made of stronger stuff than either of us realized!"

"No, it is you who has turned out to be weak and incompetent! The girl needs to go or, I swear, I will expose you and ruin you for your sinful exploits with my sweet lady!" The manservant's voice rises and becomes uncharacteristically agitated. "My lady was not made for your base desire! Nor for Lord Craven's! She was pure and true, and you tried to muddy her waters!"

"I muddied nothing! I was naught but her plaything!" cries the second voice. "She used me. She took my joy for vanity! We were all her playthings, until she tired of us! Me. Craven. We were wanted until we were no longer desired."

"Do not speak ill of my lady!"

You cannot take it anymore. You throw open the door of the morning room to see Manvers arguing with none other than . . .

"Reverend Loveday?!" you cry, unable to contain your surprise. The handsome vicar cowers in shame. "What have you done, sir? What have you *done*?"

The vicar drops to his feet. "The late Lady Craven, many times over," he weeps. "I should have married a simple girl. But Lady Craven was so exotic, so fiery, so . . . hungry. I could not stop myself. I am sorry! I am shamed!"

"You ruined my life!" Lord Craven cries, raising his hand as if to strike the Reverend Loveday. He lowers it almost immediately, upon seeing the angrily arched eyebrow you throw his way.

"Please, have mercy on me. Forgive my sins. I am a man, I am but a man!" The vicar claws at your face and pulls it close, then whispers, wild-eyed, "The boy. Manvers has the boy."

You pull your face from the wretched vicar's grasp, spin on your heel, and witness Manvers striking a match on the side of a portrait of the dead Lady Craven. He holds the flame to the small Master Alexander, who is tied to a wooden chair, which is tied to the rest of the wooden furniture in the room.

"Manvers, no!" you yell.

"Miss!" Alexander calls. Your head snaps to him, his little face peering knowingly at you from its roped confines. "*Find your move.*"

You can't know for sure, but it seems that the child flicks his little wide eyes to an area just beneath the portrait of the late Lady Craven. You act on instinct and crash past Lord Craven, the vicar, and the insane Manvers until you face the portrait dead-on.

Find your move. Master Alexander's echoing of your own words echoes in your mind, and suddenly you punch through the portrait's eyes. You are both shocked and unshocked to find your fist tear through the canvas as if it were no more than a spider's web.

Your hand, now busted through the face of the late Lady Craven, feels its way around a small, secret shelf. Your fingers detect the outline of a pocket-sized leather volume, what you guess is the lady's true diary.

As you snatch up the book, the scent of fire and smoke snatches your nose. You spin around to see Manvers setting fire to anything he can reach while training a small golden pistol on your heart. Craven and the vicar desperately attempt to untie Master Alexander.

"You should never have come here, girl," Manvers spits at you. "All of this could have been avoided if not for you. You angered her, you see. You angered her ghost, and so I must take action to protect her."

"Nonsense," you spit back. Acting on instinct, you flip to a random page in the diary. You begin to read with all of the confidence you can muster: "'I despise it here, and I should never have come. Craven is terrible since the baby has been born, so fatherly and kind. It repulses me, how dull he has become.'"

You cringe at the words and the effect they have on Lord Craven. Still, you read on. "'I have taken the vicar to my bed. It thrills me to corrupt a pure man.'" You shudder. The vicar slumps in disgrace and self-loathing. "'Plus,'" you continue, "'his manhood is always as hard as it is for me to pay attention at chapel.'" At these words, the vicar blushes even more deeply.

"What is the use of reading her secret thoughts? These thoughts belong to my lady!" Manvers takes dead aim at you with the pistol.

"'Manvers is worse than the others,'" you continue. "'He is so simple and devoted, I often think of asking him to jump off a cliff to please me.'" As you utter these words, Manvers deflates. "'He is as obsessed with me as a father would be with a child. He disgusts me. I anxiously await the day he dies, so that I may dance on his grave and then forget where he is buried.'"

"Stop your lies! Stop your lies!" Manvers drops the pistol, half begging, half damning you. Though doing so crushes you, and seriously makes you question Craven's prior taste in women, you continue.

"'I'd wager if this secret diary were ever read aloud to him, Manvers would beg for it to stop being read, so ridiculous is his devotion to an entirely false version of myself.'" You close the sinister little tome and throw it aside.

Manvers sinks to the ground. Lord Craven and the vicar have freed the child, at last. It took them long enough. Manvers looks from you, to the portrait, to the men, and then to the child.

"Nothing matters anymore," he sobs. And with the kindling of some hidden spark, all of Hopesend Manor is aflame.

Turn to page 89.

Your eyes come to rest on Fabien's statuesque form as he stokes the flames. His eyes may be the misty green of the Nile, but his skin is the dusky color of the desert sand. In the past, at some of the ton parties you attended while the Dragon's companion, you would wander near groups of married women, free from the constraints of paid companionship. Sometimes you would hear these women speak in hushed and tipsy tones about men with certain body parts like "steel wrapped in silk." You were never entirely sure what they meant, but now you know. Fabien's entire body is a firm girder wrapped in taut, tawny velvet.

The object of your thoughts flashes his eyes up at you. Their Nile green is now flecked with golden fire. "You look at me with the weight of the world," he says, while holding your gaze steady in his own. There is a barely composed thirst in his eyes, which he drops to drink deep of the oasis that is the sight of your body.

You realize that you are parched for him as well. How majestic would it be, you wonder, to feel those hands as big as twin sphinxes, but twice as mysterious, run all over your curves?

You must know. And you must escape. You know exactly what you will do.

"I want you," you say, "to put my blindfold back on."

The massive man's breath catches in his throat. "Am I so displeasing to look upon?"

"You know you are not." Your voice remains even.

"Then why do you wish to lose your sense of sight?" he asks, his eyes now burning brighter than the fire itself.

"I wish to lose all of my senses with you," you say. You feel a deep pull of pleasure in your sex as he shudders with visible delight.

He retrieves the blindfold from his belongings and wraps it delicately over your eyes. As he tightens the fabric, his bare chest brushes against your breasts. Your nipples harden, the apexes of two pleasure pyramids ready to be pillaged by vandals.

His own nipples respond to the response of your nipples, and as your sight darkens, your other sensations come alive.

"Kiss me," you whisper. You sense his plush mouth hovering near yours. You feel the heat from the fire warm your face, and the heat from your own desire warm your sex. "My neck first," you say, just before his lips brush your own. "Make me wait."

The giant man with the sphinx hands sinks into the sand and expels a sigh of total lust and abandon. He kisses your neck as Cleopatra did Antony for the first time: with nothing but total certainty, epic cleverness, and deadly desire.

You feel more womanly than ever before, full and free and wild, yet also wholly in control. "Lower," you whisper into what you think might be his ear. He obliges, and you feel his hands stroke the line of your neck, all the way down into the valley of the pharaohs between your breasts. Your body spasms with delight.

"I have taken orders most of my life," Fabien whispers harshly, but not unkindly, into the shell of your ear. "I will happily continue to take yours, but I beg you, now let me please you with mystery, my lady." He slides his tongue across your collarbone. Caresses the inside of your elbow. Traces the outline of your knee.

"You are the charmer, and I am the snake," he says, before filling your mouth with a kiss that makes you strain against your bindings for more. "But let this snake dance . . . for *you*."

You are heady with not knowing where his charmed-snake tongue will strike next. You kiss, hungrily, deeply, softly, and soon your sex is filled with the charm of Fabien's agile tongue and clever fingers.

"Yes," you cry. "Oh yes!" You think you will wake the spirit of Nefertiti with your pleasure. With only a vague memory of what started you on this delightful excavation of your own desire, you straddle what you soon feel to be Fabien's erect obelisk.

"I have known longing before, but not this kind of desire," you say. "It feels as if we are two halves of a scarab torn asunder, finally rejoining our fates in this desert midnight." You undulate rhythmically atop him, a genie rubbing its own lamp. "Free me from my bindings, and let two become one."

"Yes," he cries. "Oh yes, my queen." He unties your binds, freeing both his hands and yours to grant your wishes deep into each other—and into the night.

Together, you set off on a truly magic carpet ride.

Afterward, basking in the afterglow, you ask to share a cup of wine. He procures two earthenware mugs and pours a bit of wine from a flask into each.

"I feel drunk enough on you, *chérie*," he says with a laugh. You can tell that, for the first time in a long time, he feels genuinely relaxed and happy. You would think the same of yourself, had you not recently been kidnapped and taken into the desert. Still, your heart twinges with a little guilt as you kiss him deeply and, while he is distracted, slip into his wine a drop of the sleeping draught you always carry in case the Dowager Dragon had trouble falling asleep after a long night of hateful and petty gossip.

"A toast to two becoming one," Fabien says, his Nile-green eyes almost smiling.

"To two becoming one," you echo. Fabien drinks deep. He is sleeping like the pharaohs in their tombs when you take the camel meant for you away from him, far into the desert, and deep into the night.

Turn to page 91.

You race after the apparition in double time, hitching up your skirts almost to your thighs, hurrying with ground-eating strides.

You chase the filmy, flimsy thing up the stairs, almost to the entrance of Lord Craven's sleeping chambers, and you think you have it cornered. You reach out a hand to grab the flying raven hair, but the ghost rounds a bend and you trip on the final stair.

You are sent flying, throwing out hands out to break your fall. You slide across the runner, burning yourself along the way. Yet when you rise, you are alone. All that is left of the ghost is the pain in your palms.

What the devil is going on here?

. . . .

If you think this is a bunch of damned nonsense, go to Lord Craven and demand answers. Turn to page 60.

If you suspect that this ghost truly has come to haunt you from beyond the veil, you must seek advice and comfort from Mrs. Butts. Turn to page 312.

You turn slowly to face him. Rafe Caddington. He is beautiful, in the way a tiger is beautiful. Or a snake. Deadly beasts all share a certain elegance. And arrogance. His hand has traveled up the length of your arm and come to rest at the point where your neck meets your collarbone. He circles the edge of your clavicle with his gloved thumb and emits the softest "augh" at the tiny gasp the action elicits from you.

Your eyes narrow, and you manage to slap him full in the face. You can do nothing to cool the burning heat dancing in your lower regions, but that is neither here nor there. Cad touches his cheekbone and looks at you with derisive pleasure rather than anger.

"Is all this inquisition necessary?" Cad asks, his eyes locked on your own in what you wonder is an attempt at mesmerism. "You do realize, good woman, that you are in Manberley and not the castle at Udolpho?"

"As surely as you realize that your claims of being the rightful heir of this place are as dubious as that warm smile you wear, sir." You level your gaze at him, and he laughs at the pleasant rarity of a master being beaten at his own game.

"Wheresoever did my bore of a half brother find you?" He lets his eyes slide down your frame with the lazy, luxuriant hunger of a predator who has thoroughly trapped his prey. Before you can snap back your reply that he did not find you anywhere, Cad continues. "Tell me, are you one of Crosby's girls, brought here on the low?"

You open your mouth to admonish him, but he claps an elegant hand over it to silence you. He uses the other to spin you and pin you tightly against his well-muscled, elegantly dressed body. His mouth is at your ear. His breath is the ocean, your ear the shell. Your bodies roar with the knowledge of each other.

"Be mine," he urges, and your body has half a mind to submit to this wild desire, here and now. But you think of Henrietta's tears and steady yourself. His hand releases its hold upon your mouth but stays to rub your lower lip with his thumb. You shudder in disgust and desire.

"I will never marry you. Swine." You spit this last word into the air.

He tightens his grip around your waist.

"Do not mistake me, sweeting. I want your honor, not your hand. I have no wish to marry. Bother my dear brother Benny for all that, if you have it in you to pine for a stuffed-shirt pauper. Still, a sweet little chit like you could do worse than to be the kept woman of a man like me. Rich. Well-stationed. Legitimate. So hungry and so satisfying in all the ways that matter."

You admit feeling some titillation at Cad's little speech, but the best part has been his provision of time, during which you have repositioned yourself for a little . . . reproach. Your aim is true, and with a sharp movement of your leg, you send the handsome devil careening in pain into the wall. As you do, Lady Evangeline appears in the archway of the curtained alcove.

"Honestly," she says, shaking her head pityingly.

"*Men*," you say and then make haste to join her.

Turn to page 28.

About the Authoresses

Kitty Curran and Larissa Zageris are ardent admirers of trash, brooding men, and genre fiction. They write work that is sharp as a knife and soft as a secret lover's kiss. Kitty also draws. They are co-creators of viral hit *Taylor Swift: Girl Detective* and chroniclers of intrigue in all its forms. They live in Chicago.

Acknowledgments

We are forever indebted to the steadily burning fire that is Maure Luke.

We also share deep gratitude for the Quirk Books team, including the keen eyes and sharp style of designers Andie Reid and Molly Murphy, project editor Jane Morley, proofreader and editorial assistant Rebecca Gyllenhaal, the marketing and PR team, and finally, the fair Blair Thornburgh, our editor.

Larissa would like to especially thank Danielle Zageris, Sharlene Zageris, Janis Zageris, Matthew Thomas Thompson, Joseph White, Ellen Domonkos White, Megan Anstrom, Drew Krehel, Jaime Calder, Charlie Rubin, Katie Tibaldi, Joe Tracz, and James Dolbeare for their support.

Kitty would like to thank Tristan Cooper for love, support, and real-life broodingness, Cassia Curran for being a sister in torrid teenage reading and also literally a sister, James Curran, Margaret Hung, Mo McKibbin, Rachel Price-Cooper, Alli Brookin, Vladimir Skofenko, and Joanne Smith and Rebecca Corbishley for being the subjects of her first romance-novel parody.

Final thanks to you, dear reader, for choosing to indulge yourself with this book.